A COLLECTION OF MONSTERS- 2ND EDITION

A COLLECTION OF MONSTERS- 2ND EDITION

JASON LEACH

CHAPTER 1

A Collection of Monsters
   Jason Leach
With Kevin Mayberry
A Collection of Monsters
by Jason Leach with Kevin Mayberry
Copyright MMXXIII
All rights reserved
No part of this book may be reproduced or transmitted in any form or by any means, electronic or mechanical, including photocopying, recording or by any information storage and retrieval system without the written permission of the author, exept where permitted by law

For Aaron and Sean
For Theresa and Will
The ones we lost along the way

Table of Contents
1. Cellmate
2. (Un)frame
3. Self Help
4. The Mountain
5. Bait
6. Night Train
7. Passenger
8. God Complex
9. Tales from a tavern on a stormy night
10. One more for the road: My true monster story

Cellmate

Prologue

2019, a small town near the Canadian border. It had been an exceptionally brutal winter, with snowfall measured in feet instead of inches more often than not. One neighborhood, in particular, had received the brunt of it. Semi-secluded, with electric lines that had yet to be put underground, those six streets had lost power repeatedly over the season, sometimes for days at a time. It would be safe to say everyone was a little stir crazy. So it was a pleasant shock, with spring still weeks away, when the town awoke to what felt like a morning in mid-June. It had been years since the last Indian summer, and then usually in the autumn months, but the town wasn't looking a gift horse in the mouth. By noon the thermometer had edged into the low eighties and people wasted no time taking advantage. The children were the first out of the house to explore the warmth, dressed in shorts and t-shirts, hastily dug from the depths of their closets, playing tag, tearing down sidewalks on long-neglected bikes and skateboards, slaloming around islands of rapidly melting snow, some almost four feet high. Windows were thrown open, burgers were tossed on grills and it seemed like everyone was outside. Even as the sun began to set, the streets remained full of people. It seemed No one wanted to surrender the day for fear the warmth would leave as quickly as it had arrived. But there was one exception.

A house, halfway down the block on Charleston Avenue, stood in contrast to the celebration surrounding it. Windows shuttered, doors bolted, the only light in the house coming from a window on the second floor. The sole occupant looked out at the people below, a glass of scotch in his hand. His sixty-fourth birthday was less than a month away, but he looked older, especially around the eyes. His clothes were baggy on his frame, as if he had recently lost a lot of weight. The room the man stood in was sparse, to say the least, with only a small wooden desk and a twin bed for furniture. There wasn't so much as a picture on display. The rest of the house looked equally unlived in. The man had rented the place the previous fall, the only rooms that had seen any use were the kitchen, to heat up a can of whatever happened to be on sale that week, and the bathroom for the usual reasons. He'd gone through the rest of the house on the first day but that was to nail the windows shut. There was a long wool coat hanging in the closet, the only item besides food and booze that he'd purchased since moving in. He remembered the first time he slipped that coat on, as he stepped onto the front stoop of the house, ink on his rental agreement still drying. He watched the real estate lady give a brief wave as she pulled out of the driveway. As he stood there, taking in the view, the first snowfall of the season began. Most people in this part of the world would've had a look of concern upon seeing that, steeling themselves for that harbinger of a northeastern winter, but the old man felt a great relief as he watched those flakes drifting out of the gray.

"This is the right spot." he had said to himself. "I've bought myself a little time to think this through." But that was then and this is now and as he stood at the window watching his neighbors enjoying the warm evening, that relief was gone.

He had known something was off this morning as he slept..The sun shining through the window, usually a bit of welcome warmth, felt like it had been focused through a magnifying glass. A bead of sweat ran down one of the deep wrinkles on his forehead. He was dreaming he was back on E block, playing gin rummy with Burns, listening to the inmates bitch about the heat. They were joking around like they always did, passing the time, when he heard a scratching sound. He looked over Burns's shoulder at the door across the hall. STORAGE it said, painted in faded red letters. He felt his hands go numb as his cards tumbled to the table. He stood up. Burns continued to play his hand as he headed toward the door, just a step or two. Burns called over his shoulder, "Hey Zale, better leave well enough alone." He was right, everyone knew not to linger too close to that storage closet. He looked back at Burns, still fiddling with his cards, but now the bottom half of his shirt was soaked in blood. The scratching grew louder. He was about to ask Burns if he heard it too when the door exploded outward, splitting in two from the force of whatever was behind it. He woke with a scream in his mouth, jumping up from the bed. His legs gave way and he fell back, his ass catching the mattress- barely. He sat there, heart thumping in his chest. He wiped the sweat from his face, realizing the heat wasn't just in his dream. He had been on edge the rest of the day, needles of panic working their way up his spine.

He stood at the window now, listening to activity below. The resident old fart, Myrna something or other, was grumbling at the children as they ran past her.
"Enjoy it while you can, there prolly be ten inches of fresh snow on the ground two days from now!"
She's right, the heat won't last, he thought. It was halfway through February. Winter still had quite a few right hooks and uppercuts left in her. It did nothing to ease his panic. Today was his official warning. Spring was almost here, Summer not far behind, and he had to make a choice: continue heading north or take a stand. It was a hell of a choice. He couldn't imagine what he could possibly do to stop what was coming for him, but the thought of heading further north...how far would be far enough? Canada? The North Pole? And what if It found him anyway? It's not like he knew all the rules, even after the decades he'd spent dealing with It. Thinking about this exhausted him. He put it out of his head for the moment. There was something else he had to take care of he'd put off for too long.

He swirled a knuckle of scotch around his glass and tossed it back. He waved and smiled at a mother and her child that had spotted him at the window, but the smile didn't reach his eyes. He was scared. Fuck, let's be honest, he was terrified. The sun sunk a little further and street lights began to flicker on. The old man closed the blinds and sat down at the desk. He poured another belt of scotch and opened the first drawer. Inside was a rather large handgun and a box of bullets. He thought having it with him might be a comfort, at least the illusion of protection, but he knew better. He shut the drawer harder than he needed to and opened the second drawer, taking out a box of fancy stationery his wife had given him for his birthday almost twenty years ago. He'd never had a use for it, but couldn't bring himself to throw away a gift Marta had given him, especially since she had passed. It was one of the few things he grabbed when he left his house last summer. Again, let's be honest, when he fled his house in the middle of the night. The night of the phone call.

"Look at me, the world's oldest runaway." He opened the box of paper, his name- Edward Zale- etched in calligraphy on the top of each page. He was surprised to find tears making their way down his weathered cheeks. Marta had been gone over a decade now, but that fact never failed to catch him off guard. He guessed it always would. Zale wiped his eyes and picked up the pen.

"You got me this stationary half-jokingly, in case I ever wanted to write down my prison stories, but you wouldn't believe one word I'm about to put on this paper."

Zale took a deep breath and began to write.

I once heard writing down a traumatic event can be a form of therapy. Since I could never tell a shrink any of this, I thought I'd give the pen and paper a shot, even though I'm breaking one of the golden rules- No written record of 01. But as I sit here, starting on another bottle of scotch and summer not too far away, I can't help but think it's time the rules changed. There needs to be a record about what happened on E block, about Dennis and about inmate 01, even if no one believes it. I wouldn't blame them. I've tried to make sense of my years there many times, but some things can't be deciphered. Inmate 01 was one of those things. Is one. Only a handful of us were witness to the aftermath of that last day of August, 2017. The same handful give or take that knew about 01 and its secret history on E block. The few of us in on the lie had grown to be good friends. More than that, we were family. We were long timers, twenty years or more on the job. Everyone but Dennis Schuster. He was new, but a hard worker and he grew on us quickly. I trusted him almost immediately, which wasn't something I did easily. If things had gone to plan he never would have known about 01, but one of our inmates threw a wrench in those works when he tried to murder one of us. Dennis had stepped up when the shit hit the fan and he saved the day. He deserved an explanation for what he had seen that day and he got it. He got it. It keeps me up most nights. What if I had just kept my mouth shut. Or lied? Would everything have gone differently on that last day? Honestly, I don't think so. Too much had happened both in the prison and out..too much to just let go. Still, it keeps me up. Dennis and inmate 01.

Introductions

1.

December 2017. It had been snowing for the past three days when Dennis Schuster pulled his ancient Buick into the employee lot of the Newcastle correctional facility. He had a knot in his stomach that had been steadily growing since he woke up this morning. At the sight of the large gray building, partially obscured in the haze of falling snow, that knot grew into a semi-panic. It was expected. He had always had bouts of anxiety before starting a new job, especially one this important. This was the first big step, God help him, to an actual career.

Time to grow up, a voice echoed in his head. Words he would have resisted only a few short years ago. that was before Julia and Little Sean. Dennis looked at the picture he had placed in the corner of the dash. His wife, Julia, still pale, recovering from a harder than usual delivery, Sean's red face peeking out of the blanket he was wrapped in. Hard to believe he was almost a year old now. Hard to believe how difficult it had been to leave them tonight.

He had met Julia in high school, though it felt like he'd always known her. Back in those days, he was considered a bad boy. Fighting, cutting classes to grab a smoke, only a passing familiarity with schoolwork, and even at seventeen, the start of what could become a severe drinking problem. Julia was his opposite in every way. Straight A student, always first to volunteer for after-school activities, and zero tolerance for anyone that would stand in her way. Bad boys were not a part of Julia Fenton's life plan, which was a problem for Dennis, because he had fallen in love with her. He wasn't the sort of person that prescribed to the notion of love at first sight, or at all. He was more than happy to date his way through the senior class then make his way to a community college and do the same. That was until he met Julia.

She was talking to a friend and as she turned in his direction it was as if she were moving in slow motion. It seemed he had hours to study her. Her eyes, every freckle on her nose, her lips slightly parted as she smiled. Her hair, a deep red, was tied in a ponytail and she was pushing some loose strands behind her ear. Just as Dennis never thought about love, he also never would have described an attraction to someone as electric, but that is exactly what it had been, for both of them. When their eyes met they had each stopped in their tracks locked onto each other. The moment seemed to last for hours, then someone pushed past him breaking the connection and when he looked back at the stairs, she was gone. But to his pleasant surprise, she ended up in two of his classes.

After two brutal weeks he worked up the nerve to talk to her, yet another thing he was unaccustomed to. Talking to girls had come so easy until now. He caught up to her after class and asked her to a movie. She had agreed, though to his surprise she had done so reluctantly. He knew she had feelings for him as well, he had caught her looking at him while he was sneaking looks at her. They grabbed some dinner after the movie and things seemed to go well, if a little awkward. As he walked her to the car he planned to ask her out again, but he'd barely opened his mouth before she stopped him. She was both kind and brutal in her rejection.

"Dennis?" Dennis smiled, a dimpled display that had charmed more than his share of girls since he started caring about such things, though he could tell it wasn't working on Julia. It made him want her more.

"Yes?"

"Dennis, I can't do this again. To be honest, I should have just said no to this whole thing." She looked as pained as he felt as he stood there, attempting a smile, but dying inside. "We're just too different. I'm serious about my grades, and you barely show up to class. I didn't even know we were in English together until last week, and you sit two chairs away from me. I'm sorry, but it wouldn't be fair for either of us." She got in her car and drove off, leaving him to process. She was right of course. She was on her way to doing great things and Dennis was on his way to being a sixty-year-old clerk at a gas station.

After their talk, he backed off. He gave her plenty of space in the halls, if they did cross paths he'd give her a slight nod and keep on trucking. Not that it changed the way he felt. He'd had many girlfriends, but none of those girls had stuck in his mind the way Julia had, and the bitch of it was he knew she felt something too. She had made herself clear and he accepted it, but what she had said stuck with him. After much consideration, Dennis decided to do what most people say they will do their entire lives, talking about but never actually get around to doing: he changed. At first, he was doing it for her, but as time passed he began to do it for himself as well, and for the first time in a long while found that he had started liking himself again. He stopped drinking, spent more time in class. He started listening and was surprised that, by doing so, a lot of the work came easily to him. He was never going to be a genius, but in a little over two months he was earning a B average in most of his classes and was staying after school for help with his problem subjects. He was learning and he found, to his surprise, that he liked it.

Three months into his transformation he was walking down the stairs and spied Julia walking up. He realized that he had been so busy lately with studies that he hadn't had time to think about her, and seeing her round the corner of the stairwell made his heart pound. He nodded at her and started to make his way to the other side of the stairs when she blocked him and planted a kiss on his cheek. He was speechless.
"I'm proud of you." she said, standing so amazingly close he could smell the sweet scent of her shampoo. He said nothing, still shocked by the kiss. Julia continued. "And I misjudged you. If you would forgive me for that, I'd like to ask you out." He looked at her slack-jawed. She laughed. "Close your mouth before you catch a fly." Dennis snapped his jaw shut, still incapable of getting out more than a grunt, so he just smiled. This

time it worked. A little. Julia smiled back. "I'll take that as a yes." He nodded vigorously.

They were pretty much inseparable after that. There were bumps in the road, of course, Julia's father being the biggest one. No slightly above average student with zero college prospects was ever going to be good enough for Oliver Fenton's daughter. Dennis never received more than a one pump handshake or a two-word response from the man. At their wedding, Oliver was overheard, more than once and rather loudly, lamenting his daughter's horrific choice for a spouse. Dennis knew he wasn't going to win the man over and he never confronted the man about his behavior because he didn't want to add stress to his and Julia's relationship. He figured the bastard would eventually figure out that all he was doing was alienating the daughter he claimed to love so much. The first step toward that was little Sean. It was all hands on deck when Julia told Oliver she was pregnant four months after the wedding. He went on an epic rant that night. This was the end of her education! The end of any hope of a career! The three of them would end up in a trailer park with Oliver supporting them! The birth of his first grandchild softened him, even more so when he realized that Dennis kept his word and was working whatever hours necessary to keep Julia in school, which she did, baby and all. Dennis figured one day he would get more than mumbling small talk and a weak handshake. Twenty years, tops.

2.

Dennis shook himself out of the memory. It was time for work. He checked his watch- 8:52 P.M., adjusted his badge- Dennis Schuster, Corrections Officer, it read, accompanied by an unflattering photo of him from the shoulders up. He took a deep breath and opened the door. Bracing against the cold, he flipped the hood of his parka into place as he made his way to the first guard tower, mindful of the patches of ice. The last thing he wanted to do on his first night was fall on his ass. The guard in the booth looked bored as Dennis showed him his badge through the window. A loud buzzer went off and the gate began to slide open, daggers of ice falling to the ground as the frozen metal screeched along the track. It seemed to take an eternity. He hurried through as soon as the gate had opened wide enough to admit him and half-jogged past the tower thirty yards towards the only door on this side of the dreary structure. A large sign in bold red letters was painted above it- E BLOCK. Known to most people as death row, E Block was nestled in a small valley with the rest of the prison on a hill overlooking it. A covered staircase connected E Block to the rest of the prison. Dennis could faintly see lights on the hill as he reached the door, two dozen orange eyes peeking through the gloom. Another buzzer went off and the door unlocked. Dennis waved at the tower guard, steadied himself and opened the door.

3.

The change in temperature was almost dizzying, stepping out of the now full on blizzard into what felt like an oven set to broil. the first thing he heard as he shut the door was something of a surprise, given the setting- laughter. Not something he heard much of at the last prison he worked for, at least not of the good-natured variety. And he didn't expect to hear it on death row. The source of the cheer was coming from a large table at the opposite end of the large rectangular room. Five older gentlemen were in the middle of a loud but friendly card game. As he made his way toward them he observed the room. It was basically a wide hallway, on his left just a wall with a fire extinguisher halfway down, on the right five cells, all currently full. At the end of the hall, beyond the last cell, was a storage closet adorned with two very large padlocks. There was an ancient security camera mounted in the far corner of the room, slowly sweeping back and forth down the hall of cells. He smiled as he walked down the corridor, looking at the cinder-block wall to his left, painted light green on top, dark green on the bottom. And the smell of the place... The smell of age, something he had noticed in the previous prison he had worked in and the various elementary schools he had attended growing up. (He was an army brat, so he'd seen his share of new schools.) He wondered for a moment if prisons and elementary schools shared the same paint vendors, and how that was slightly disturbing. The inmates were doing what inmates do, passing the time. A couple of them were watching the guards' poker game, laughing themselves a time or two. One slept, or tried to. One read a Frankenstein's monster of a paperback, cover-less, pages taped and re-taped, clearly an old favorite. A couple of them looked up with mild curiosity as he walked past. In the corner across from the table of guards stood a battered two foot tall Christmas tree, decorated with paper clips and post-it notes and topped with an upside down soda can. As he approached the men at the table he smiled, trying to conceal his nervousness, but assuredly failing. One of the guards left the game and met him halfway. He looked to be in his late fifties, fit with a full head of white hair. He returned Dennis's smile and shook his hand.

"You must be Schuster. I'm Lieutenant Zale. How was the ride in? I heard on the radio that the roads were getting rough."

"It was fine sir. A little ice but nothing too serious."

Zale nodded. "No need for the sir business, Zale will do fine. Come over and meet the other guardians of E Block."

"Yes, si- Zale." Dennis followed Zale to the impromptu poker table. The men turned to greet the newest member of tribe E. To Dennis's relief they all had kind faces, and his relief deepened after only a brief conversation with them. At his previous post, there was always an air of tension. Most of the guards had a very open disdain for the inmates in their charge and didn't care who knew about it. Every other month an inmate was being treated in the infirmary for an assortment of 'accidents'. The vibe was certainly different here, and he welcomed it. Zale made the introductions.

"This portly gentleman to my right is Burns."

"As always, Zale, you may bite me. How are you kid.?"

"To my right is Sharpe, he's the strong silent type." Sharpe threw Dennis a salute. "And finally these two are Casey and Grilles, more commonly known as the Wonder Twins."

Dennis grinned as he shook hands. "The Wonder Twins?"

Zale slapped Casey on the back. "Indeed. During the riot back in '87 these two worked C block. When the shit hit the fan they held the block single-handed."

Casey shook his head. "It was an interesting couple of hours."

Burns snickered. "And believe me, kid, you'll hear the story about a million times before it's over with." Grilles nudged Dennis.

"Burns is just mad cause he spent the entire riot trapped in the bathroom."

"Trapped, hell, I was hiding."

Everyone laughed, Schuster a little more than the rest. His nervousness had abated. The group exchanged war stories for thirty minutes or so and in that time Dennis decided he'd made the right choice coming here. These were good men. During a lull in the conversation, Zale put his hand on his shoulder, guiding him away from the rest of the group. He talked as they walked down the hall.

"I figured I'd hold our monthly meeting on your first day so you could meet everyone, get a general idea of how things work around here. We're usually on two-man shifts, sometimes one-man shifts thanks to budget cuts. You transferred from Hollings?"

"Yes."

"How long were you down there?"

"Ten months."

Zale nodded. "To be honest with you I had some trepidation about bringing in someone from Hollings. I've heard a few tales about guards that don't have the best temperament when it comes to handling the inmates."

Dennis frowned. "Not to speak out of turn, but I've seen that behavior first hand on more than one occasion."

"Needless to say that mentality does not fly here. But I have a knack for reading people, and I don't have that feeling about you."

Dennis straightened up. "Oh, no sir, Zale, not at all."

Zale nodded. "So, almost a year at minimum security. That's a good start, but you're on E Block now. This is a different world. I know it doesn't look like much right now, and to be honest, ninety-percent of the time it's just like this. Calm. Quiet. For most of these men, the appeals have been exhausted and they have come to terms with their fate. They have hobbies. They found Jesus. Both have their soothing effects. But there are those special days when one of these gentlemen wakes up and realizes that his time is coming soon and he has nothing left to lose, so he decides to act out. And those are the days that test us. But this is a good crew. Competent. No bullies or dim wits. And they'll teach you well if you're inclined to learn. Sound good to you?"

Dennis smiled. "Yes it does"

"Good. You won't be down here long. None of us will. In a little over two years the prison's getting an upgrade. That includes a brand new E Block. When that day comes most of us old timers that haven't already retired will be nudged in that direction. Shiny new guards for a shiny new prison. There's no bitterness there. Most of us are ready to hang it up. It's a good job, but it can wear on you." Zale looked distracted for a moment. Schuster was about to ask him what he meant but Zale continued.

"Keep your nose clean, follow the rules and you might end up running the place if that's something you see yourself doing. But until that day, your first shift begins now. I'll be your partner tonight. Walk you through everything. You can hang your coat over there and we'll start on the one never-ending truth of Newcastle Penitentiary -paperwork."

Zale patted Dennis on the back and headed toward the table. Dennis removed his coat, watching as Zale joined the group, joking as he sat down. He had a big grin on his face and it got wider when he realized why- He was actually happy to be at his job.

4.

Two hours later a mountain of papers had been signed in triplicate and filed away. Only Zale and Dennis were left at the table, playing cards. The inmates were mostly quiet, except for one singing an old Billy Joel song slightly out of tune. Zale took another card and growled, adjusting the cards in his hand as if that might improve what he had been dealt.

"Damn. You're gonna clean up if you ever come by Casey's on poker night."

"I'm usually not this good."

Zale snorted. "I've heard that one before. Usually on days I go home with empty pockets."

The door at the end of the hall opposite the exit clanged open, making Dennis jump. Zale perked up. "Ah, chow time. I see you brought your dinner but just so you know they always toss a couple of trays on for us. Charlie C! How goes it?"

A man walked in pushing a cart full of food trays. He was in his late thirties but looked allot older. He was dangerously thin, wearing a look of befuddlement that seemed carved on. He peered around as if surprised to see people in the room.

"Oh, I'm OK. Still alive, so that's something I guess."

Dennis gave a salute. "Hi, I'm Schuster."

Charlie nodded vaguely and went back to his cart.

Zale laughed and lowered his voice. "Don't mind Charlie, He's harmless enough, just not operating on all cylinders. He's the closest thing we have to a mascot around here. Been a Trustee for what seems like forever. He enjoyed a variety of drugs before he found his way inside..and quite a few after, I would imagine, but that's D Block's concern. We have our own borders to deal with"

Dennis gestured at the inmates. "So, what's the deal?"

Zale smiled. "I was wondering when you were going to ask." He walked away from the cells, Dennis following behind. Zale nodded at the first cell, speaking in a low voice. "The man Charlie is sliding a tray to right now is Abe Benedict, armed robbery gone wrong. He probably wouldn't have ended up on death row for it but the clerk he shot was a seventeen-year-old girl, high school valedictorian and runner-up for Miss Teen Azalea. He's lucky the town didn't rip him apart with their bare hands. Next is Dooley. Long history of violence there. Stabbed a man to death in a bar fight then killed the guy that tried to break it up. He was a real instigator when he first joined us. Ranting and raving at all hours, throwing food and whatever bodily excretions he could produce at us when we'd walk past. He spent the better part of his first two years gagged and tucked in a straight jacket. He's mellowed out quite a bit. Then we have Jerry Rampling. Pretty cut and dry for old Jerry. Killed his parents for the insurance money. Since he's sitting in that cell you can correctly assume his plan had some holes in it. Next to him is Steven Yost. That son of a bitch decided just raping young women wasn't enough, so he started strangling them as well. He killed five before he was caught. I try not to think about what they've done, to make it personal, it would be impossible to do this job if you did, but he is one sadistic son of a bitch and when he meets the needle I will not shed a tear."

Zale pointed to the man in the cell closest to the guard table, right next to the storage closet. He wasn't standing at the cell door waiting for his food like the rest. He sat on his bunk staring at the wall.

"And last but certainly not least, our longest resident, Raymond Monroe. The only guy in here that makes Yost look appealing. One afternoon Ray was puttering around down in his basement when he apparently decided that it was a perfect day to kill his wife and their two-year-old daughter."

Dennis thought of little Sean and felt a stab of anger.

"It only gets worse from there. Two weeks pass, people start asking about the family, Ray tells everyone they are out of town visiting her mother. Perfectly feasible, until a couple neighbor kids playing in the woods behind Ray's house find three foul smelling garbage bags."

"Christ...three?"

"Yeah, he cut them up so it would be easier to bury them but, according to the detectives that interrogated him, he forgot to dig the holes. Between you and me I think that would be a detail I'd remember. Anyway, He's been here for almost ten years. These days he rarely does more than sit in his bunk and stare at the wall. His lawyer had a couple of shrinks in here last week to do another psych Eval, I assume they're gearing up for a final appeal. I think he's full of shit, but like I said, it's best not to dwell on the crimes, working with them as close as we do every day.

Know what they're capable of, but separate it. We aren't judge or jury, we're just the guys that keep them safe and alive until they're led out the door."

Dennis nodded. "Understood."

Just then a small commotion erupted at the first cell. Benedict, killer of homecoming queens, had refused his meal and was yelling at Charlie, who had the look of an animal that was rapidly sinking in quicksand.

"You can shove that tray up your ass Charlie! We had meatloaf two days ago and three days before that! I want something else or I'm going on a hunger strike!"

Charlie tried to placate him to no avail. "I can talk to the cooks, but the prison got a big surplus of meatloaf so we probably got a couple more weeks of it. You sure you don't want it? Benedict looked at him like he was a cat that had just gained the ability to speak.

"I believe I told you where to place that tray. And if those twats in the kitchen send me this garbage again they can have a couple meatloaf enemas as well!"

Zale sighed. "You can count on Benedict to bitch about the food at least once a week."

"You want me to talk to him?"

"I got it, you'll have plenty of opportunities to deal with Benny's fickle palate."

Zale made his way down to the argument. Dennis watched the exchange for a moment but found his attention being drawn to the storage room. He'd look away, only to find himself staring again. There was nothing conspicuous about it. The double padlocks seemed like overkill, but other than that it was just a wooden door covered in a million dings, smudges and scratches like every other surface in this place. Still, looking at it set him on edge. Bad vibes, his uncle would have said. The door gave him the same feeling in his stomach you get when the phone starts ringing at four in the morning, because when has *that* ever been good news? He took a couple of steps toward the closet without realizing it. He was also unaware that Raymond had stopped staring at the wall across from

his bunk and was now staring at him. Dennis was wholly focused on the door now as he took another unconscious step forward. A dull itch was slowly working its way out from the base of his skull. He scratched at it, to no avail. The itch was inside. Raymond slipped off of his cot and slowly moved toward his cell door, not taking his eyes off Dennis. Dennis didn't notice. He was now close enough to reach out and touch the door if he wanted to. That's when Raymond spoke, almost in his ear.
"You can feel it, can't you?"
Dennis jumped back, startled. "Excuse me?"
Raymond nodded as if Dennis had answered his question. "Everyone can."
Dennis was red-faced from having an inmate get the jump on him like that. Raymond could have easily grabbed him, then Christ knows what could have happened. He was glad Zale was otherwise preoccupied. That was the last thing he needed his commanding officer to see, especially on his first day. He looked at Raymond, and his first thought upon seeing the inmate up close was that, if he was trying to get a stay of execution by faking crazy, he had gone above and beyond. Raymond was pale, which was normal for someone that only saw a few hours of sunlight a week, but his eyes ...
Dennis had a friend, Thomas Ajai, that had served two tours in Afghanistan. They had all gone out for beers when Thomas had gotten back, he and the guys they had hung out with in high school. After they had knocked back a few, one of the guys asked Thomas if he had killed anyone during his tour. Thomas hadn't answered, he just drank his beer, but he had the same look in his eyes Raymond did right now. Three weeks later Thomas had killed himself. Dennis tried to sound nonplussed when he responded. "Feel what, exactly?"
Raymond ignored him, looking past Dennis's shoulder as he continued to speak.
"It's not as bad in the winter. I don't know why, maybe it hibernates or something, but the summer is bad. Not just for the prisoners, I hear the guards whisper about it sometimes when they think we're asleep. They

act like everything's fine, but I see it on their faces, the way they look at that door sometimes when they walk past. The way you look right now. They know something's wrong, but hey, they get to go home, don't they? Spend the weekend playing with the kids and washing their cars and having a beer or ten. They get *distance*. I'm not so lucky, I've been trapped with it twenty-three hours a day for almost ten years. Right next to it. Zale's wrong, I don't want another appeal, I just want out, and if it's with a needle in my arm so be it. I don't know how much more I can take. The thoughts ... it almost never stops now." Raymond pointed at the supply closet. "It's trying to drive me crazy. And it's working."

Dennis looks at the supply closet door, then back to Ray. The feeling of wrongness was creeping back, but he shook it off. He stepped over to the door. Over the years the prison had settled and the door was separated from the jamb enough to peer inside. It was dark, but the light coming from under the door let Dennis see the contents of the room clearly enough. There were a few shelves littered with cleaning supplies, rolls of paper towels and urinal cakes. several other boxes were piled against the back wall, but there was no one in the room, this he was sure of. He walked back to Raymond.

"Mr. Monroe, there isn't anyone on the other side of that wall."

Raymond snickered. "No? So why are two of the world's largest padlocks hanging off of that door? To protect the toilet paper? You could ask Zale, but I doubt he'd tell you anything, being the new guy. But he knows, you can be sure of that. They all do."

Raymond shuffled back to his cot and sat down, his eyes returning to the storeroom wall. Dennis stood outside his cell for a moment, looking at him. He went back to the table and Zale met him there, curious about what had transpired.

"Everything OK, Schuster?"

"Oh, yes, it's fine."

"Was he actually talking?"

"He was, but he sure as hell wasn't making any sense. He said there was someone in the supply closet threatening him. I think you're right, he's looking for an insanity defense."

Zale laughed. "I've been here just about twenty-five years, can't say I recall ever seeing any strangers milling about in there."

Zale patted Dennis on the arm and headed back to the table. What should have diffused Dennis's odd feelings about the storage room only intensified them. Dennis hardly knew Zale and what he did know he liked, but he had the distinct impression that he had just been lied to. When Zale joked about that room, the laughter didn't reach his eyes. Dennis decided to let it go, no need to rock the boat on the first day, but there was something there. Just looking at that room told him that. He'd never admit it but Raymond had a point. Who puts deadbolts that big on a room where you store urinal cakes? He would find his moment to discuss it with Zale. He was sure he'd get a straight answer.

Acclimation

1.

The next few months were uneventful. Christmas trees gave way to heart-shaped boxes of chocolate, then to shamrocks and pots of gold. Spring seemed to arrive in the blink of an eye. (Though on E Block time always seemed to pass slower, as any inmate could attest.) Life for Dennis was going well, both in and out of Newcastle. He thought that he was a good fit on E Block. He got along with the other officers and had built a tentative respect with the inmates. He would pass a quick word with them as he began his shifts, with the exception of Raymond. He had kept his distance from him since their conversation on his first day, though as far as anyone could tell that was the last time he'd spoken. Dennis spent most of his off hours moving his family into their new home, something closer (but not too close) to the prison. The move happened not a moment too soon. Little Sean had skipped the crawling phase almost entirely and had gone right to walking. The one bedroom apartment that had seemed so perfect a year ago, had become more than a little claustrophobic, especially with a one-year-old ball of energy slaloming between their feet. Now Sean had a yard to play in, which he did at every opportunity, coming inside under the most vocal of protests. Everything was just about perfect. Except the door. The damn storage room door. After a day of unpacking at the new house, Dennis was sitting outside having a couple beers, something he did more and more now that the days were warmer. Sean was playing in the sandbox, pushing his dump truck back and forth.

That kid's going to need two baths and a shower to get all the sand off him, he thought with a grin. Julia stepped out of the house behind Dennis and wrapped her arms around him. He put his arms over hers. Julia kissed him right below his ear, which never failed to get his utmost attention.

"You two OK out here? I'm going to try to get in some studying."
"Absolutely. I'm going to sit here a while, see just how dirty one toddler can get."
Julia laughed. "The answer is more than you could imagine." She walked over to Sean and gave him a kiss on the forehead. He looked up at her and smiled, a handful of sand in each hand. Dennis watched them with a love he never would have thought possible. Julia headed inside, pausing to give him a kiss of his own, decidedly more adult. Dennis smiled as he watched her go, hips swinging ever so slightly He grabbed another beer from the small cooler next to his chair. Three left from the six-pack.

Let this be the last one tonight, he thought. Sean had added another vehicle to the sandbox, a bulldozer. Dennis watched him, smiling, but before too long his mind wandered back to the door, something he thought about more often than he cared to admit. The look on Raymond's face, his certainty that someone in the storage room was driving him insane and the look on Zale's face when he mentioned it. That last one especially. Raymond might be crazy and his paranoia might have rubbed off on Dennis a little, but Zale? He just didn't seem the type to suffer any bullshit, including stories of secret inmates hiding in the walls, but the look on his face when he told him what Raymond had said. And seriously, what the hell was up with the padlocks? The whole thing was kind of hard to just put out of his head especially when he had to walk past that door every day and watch Raymond sit on his cot and stare at the wall. He had tried on more than one occasion to bring it up with the guys but didn't know how to start that particular conversation. Zale and a few other guards had gone in the room from time to time for supplies, Dennis had positioned himself to get a good look inside while the door was open and of course it was just a room. No boogeyman hideaway, no imp sitting on the shelf beside the mop handles whispering to Raymond through the wall, but there was something odd. Before anyone opened the storage room door they would make a call on their private cell. Every time, and always out of Dennis's earshot. Once when he was working with Burns, he decided to try and glean a little information. He made himself busy at the other end of the hall and waited until Burns made the call. Dennis then nonchalantly (he hoped) made his way toward him, hoping to eavesdrop on the conversation. But that proved futile as the call was just as hurriedly ended, but he thought he heard Zale on the other end of the line right before Burns hung up. Now, why in the hell would a guard call in a visit to a storage room to a superior officer who happened to be on his day off? A double padlocked storage room...

The sun had dipped below the roof, casting a shadow across the back yard. Dennis shook off thoughts of the storage room. He finished his beer in a gulp and eyed the cooler. He shook that idea as well. Instead, he watched Sean as he played in the sand and tried not to think about the door. He mostly succeeded.

By the first week of April, the door and what might be lurking behind it would be the last thing on Dennis's mind. One night he went to check on Little Sean and found he had a cough and a slight fever. By four in the morning, the fever had jumped to 105 and the cough had turned into gasps for breath. Dennis and Julia rushed him to the hospital. After what seemed like a million tests, the doctors discovered that he had a lung infection. The kid ended up staying in the hospital for two weeks. Dennis and Julia split their time between their jobs and sitting by Sean's hospital bed. A couple of the nurses brought a small table in for Julia so she had somewhere to study, not that she was able to do much of that. They were both out of their minds with worry. In those nerve-wracking two weeks, they may have gotten ten hours of sleep between them. When they were finally able to take him home they were barely able to let him out of their sight. They looked at each other in a panic whenever he issued the slightest cough. Julia rubbed eyes that were glassy with tears and exhaustion.

"If this kid ever gets sick like that again I'm going to lose my mind."

"You're going to have to get in line."

"Should we let him sleep with us? Just in case?"

"Yes, until he's eighteen." Julia laughed.

"That could prove a little awkward. Let's say sixteen, seventeen tops." "Agreed."

2.

Spring was unseasonably cool, not that anyone complained. E Block was infamous for its shoddy air conditioning and it got hot fast in that old building. Around the middle of May the guards got together for their monthly staff meeting, where Burns read a notice from the warden announcing a small round of budget cuts, which meant each guard would be working a couple of their night shifts solo. A couple of the guards grumbled uninterested acknowledgment at this news but Zale looked concerned, bordering on panic. Burns, who happened to be standing next to Dennis, gave him a nudge as he laughed to himself, unaware of Zale's worried looks.

"Oh boy, Gillies on a night shift alone. Who the hell is gonna keep him awake?" Casey chimed in. "He can always let Benedict out to play a couple of hands with him. I'm sure he'd like the company." Gillies turned in fake indignation.

"You guys are a riot. You should take that act on the road. And never come back." He walked off down the hall. Everyone got a laugh out of it but Zale. He looked a little worried as he took Casey aside and whispered something in his ear that wiped the humor off his face pretty quick. Casey shot a quick look at Dennis, then just as quickly looked away. Zale patted Casey on the back then made his way down the hall. He called back over his shoulder as he opened the door.

"Okay, guys, good meeting, see you all together next month." As the door slammed shut. Casey signaled to Dennis. "Hey kid, let me talk to you for a sec."

"What's up?"

"Zale wanted me to hang out with you on your first solo night." Dennis looked at Casey to make sure he wasn't joking.

"Wouldn't be my first solo night if you're there with me Casey."

"I know kid, sorry. Orders from the big guy."

"Maybe I should talk to him, see if I did something wrong-"

"Nah, nah, nothing's wrong, nights out here alone can be a little weird sometimes, Zale thought it wouldn't hurt to have a-"

"Chaperone?"

"A *friend*. You're a good officer and one of the best recruits we've ever had here. Trust me, this has nothing to do with your abilities." Casey punched his arm then made his way to the exit. Dennis thought of giving Zale a call, talking this through, but he had a feeling that if he did, that call would go unanswered. He was pissed. He was new here, but he was far from a rookie. He'd had his share of night shifts at the old prison, and that place was a nightmare. And he was good at his job, he knew that, so if it wasn't him.. Dennis looked over at the storage room. It was the first time he'd given it a thought in weeks. Maybe they don't want me alone with that? Either way, he planned to have a long discussion with Zale about it. Soon.

3.

Three days later Dennis and Casey sat at the table at the end of E Block, working on their millionth hand of blackjack. Earlier that day the thermometer had edged passed ninety for the first time that year and even now, at a little passed four in the morning they spent more time wiping sweat out of their eyes than flipping cards. They had run out of anything interesting to say to each other a few hours back. Dennis checked at the clock-again- and discovered it was only two minutes later than the last time he looked. Casey caught him staring at the clock and smiled. "These night shifts can drag out, huh kid. Believe me I know." He let out a huge yawn and pushed away from the table, rubbing his eyes.

"Jesus kid, I gotta take a walk, stretch my legs. My wife would give me hell if she knew I'd been sitting on my ass for three hours straight. She says sitting is the new smoking." Dennis smiled.

"So I've heard. Take a break, I think I can hold down the fort." They both looked around at the sleeping inmates. Casey grinned, gave a little salute, then headed for the exit. Dennis decided to stretch his legs as well. He walked down the hall, cocking his head left then right, trying to pop his neck. Now that he was the only one on the block that was still awake he became aware of just how quiet it was. He didn't think a prison could be this silent. It unnerved him. Dennis turned back toward the table when he heard the laugh. It stopped him cold, heart pounding in his chest. The laugh had come from behind the storage room door, of course, and he recognized it in an instant.

Jesus Christ, that sounded just like Sean. He looked at the inmates. They were all still asleep. Casey hadn't made it back inside yet. Dennis stepped up to the door and pressed his ear to it. "Sean?" It was impossible, he knew that, but that was Sean, he would have sworn on his life. He was about to call his name again when the feeling came over him again. That sense of *wrong*, that itch at the base of his skull that he couldn't scratch. He tried to pull back but he couldn't. Suddenly his head was full of images, unspooling faster and faster. Casey walked back in from his stroll, wiping his forehead. "Jeez, it might be hotter out there than it is in h-" He saw Dennis pressed against the door and his stomach dropped into his shoes. "Oh shit." He whisper yelled down the hall. "Hey Schuster? everything alright?" Dennis couldn't hear him. He was lost in a memory. In it, Dennis and his wife were on the couch watching a movie, a usual Friday night after little Sean was finally put to bed. He leaned in to kiss Julia, lingering for a moment, breathing her in. She smiled and slid closer to him, laying her head on his shoulder. He pushed her hair behind her ear then reached for the popcorn. As he did the memory became something else. He heard a sound from the kitchen, like someone dragging their feet across the tile. He saw a shadow fall across the living room floor, thin and elongated. He reached in the bowl but instead of popcorn what he pulled out was a very large knife. He sat there staring at it, moving it back and forth, catching the light on the blade. He looked over at Julia. She was engrossed in the film. He smiled and slowly moved the knife upward until it caught her attention. She looked at the knife and then at Dennis, curious. No fear, just curiosity. He continued to smile as he drove the knife into Julia's chest. The curiosity turned to shock as he pushed the knife deeper. She gasped for air as a dark red blob blossomed across the front of her shirt. She tried to pull away but Dennis held her close. She cried out but all she could manage was a weak gurgling noise. Her lips were spattered with blood. Dennis pushed the knife in until he hit her spine, twisting it, watching the color drain from her face. He smiled as he watched her claw at the hilt of the knife. He smiled as he looked in her eyes as she tried to comprehend how this happened, how he could have done this to her. Julia's breathing became a shallow rasp. As her head fell back against the couch he gave her a long kiss. Just then he heard a laugh. Little Sean in his room, awake, probably wanting some water. Dennis yanked the knife out of Julia's chest, wiping it on her shirt. He made his way down the hall. "Hang on buddy, I'm coming. I'm coming" He started humming as he pushed his son's door open with the blade of the knife. Little Sean was standing in his crib, both hands raised. Dennis tightened his grip on the knife. Casey made it down the length of the block, calling out to Dennis several times, but all he got in return was that blank stare. He reached Dennis and put his hand on his shoulder just as the Dennis in the memory was bringing the knife down into Julia's heart. He recoiled from Casey for a moment, then clung to him, not responding as Casey called to him over and over in a loud whisper, trying not to wake the inmates. Casey looked in his eyes. Dennis was a million miles away, the blank stare replaced with pure terror. He was making a mewling sound, and it was getting louder. Casey shot a quick look at the prisoners. Still sleeping, for a wonder. But they wouldn't be for long if Dennis really lost it. As he struggled to get through to Dennis, Casey thought about slapping him in the face to jar him back but didn't want to make even more noise than they already were. Then he remembered something he had seen once at a hypnotist show in Vegas. He had taken the wife for a week of gambling and endless buffets. In one of the side rooms there was a magician, the Great Renaldo, or some such shit. Casey had just grabbed another huge plate of crab legs from the hotplate and poked his head in to see who the mild applause had been for. There was a man on stage in a tux, hair greased back to his skull, twirling a wand. Next to him was an overweight man in a blue flowered shirt tucked into khaki shorts, topped off with a fanny pack. The apotheosis of all tourists. Casey would have bet all the cash in his wallet he was also sporting a money belt. Khaki Shorts was currently walking around the stage clucking like a chicken while Renaldo twirled the wand and looked as amazed as the audience was supposed to. After a painfully long moment, Renaldo reached out and gave the human chicken a tug on his earlobe. The clucking stopped immediately and Khaki Shorts looked around as if he was waking from a dream. Another smattering of applause ensued. All of this flashed through Casey's mind in an instant. *Well, if it worked for the Great Renaldo...* Casey let go of Dennis's hands, instead, he grabbed his ear and pinched the hell out of it. The pain was sharp and it snapped Dennis out of his stupor just as fast as it had for the tourist, but Dennis didn't look confused. He remembered exactly what had happened. Casey took a step back, readying himself in case he flipped out again. "Kid, are you alright?" Dennis looked miserable. "Oh my God, Casey... What the hell happened.."

"Hey, don't worry about it right now, come on." Casey took him by the shoulders and led him to the table. "Here, have a seat." Casey gave him a bottle of water and he downed it in three gulps.

"I don't know what ... you guys were right to partner me up. I obviously can't do this. I'll let Zale know I'm quitting first thing in the morning and-"

"What are you talking about? You want to quit over this? Kid, everyone conks out for a minute or two on the night shift. And with a little one at home, I'm sure you don't get many full nights of sleep anyway, am I right? Hell, I was asleep for most of my walk."

"Casey, I wasn't asleep, I don't know what that was... I was with my family. Oh God, I was with them and I ki-" Casey took his shoulders again and gave him a little shake.

"Kid, it's all good. It was sleep deprivation. It can make you think weird things, okay? No harm, no foul. Our guests didn't see anything, and I'm not putting it in my report, so why don't we just pretend this didn't happen?" Casey was trying to give him an out, and under his casual smile, he looked desperate for him to take it. Dennis decided to go with it.

"Alright, Casey, if you think it's best." Casey smiled.

"I do. We have enough paperwork around here, do we not?" Casey laughed, but there was fear in his eyes. For Dennis a little, but also for something else. Dennis looked at the storage room. What happened hadn't been caused by sleep deprivation or a nightmare. The entire incident was fading fast like a dream when the lights came on, most of it anyway. Casey patted him on the back and smiled. "You know what? We only have a couple of hours to go, why don't you take off, I got this covered.""Casey, I don't want to leave, especially after this-"

"It's fine, I'm a night owl anyway. Go home, get some sleep. Tomorrow is another day, and other such hippy bullshit." Dennis smiled, and that seemed to put Casey at ease. a little.

"Okay, I guess I'm heading out."

"Good. Everything will be fine in the morning kid, you'll see." Dennis had his doubts but he decided to leave it for now. He gathered his things and said his goodbyes. As he walked down the hall he took a quick look at the storage room and Raymond's cell, right into Raymond's open eyes. Dennis froze in his steps again as Raymond stared back at him with a mixture of pity and contempt. He turned over in his cot and faced the wall. Dennis got moving again before Casey noticed anything was wrong.

4.

He drove home ten miles under the speed limit, not trusting his shaking hands to go any faster. He pulled into the driveway, killing the lights before they flashed into the bedroom. He made his way to the door and as he reached the porch the automatic light popped on. He was met with his reflection in the storm door and it took all he had not to scream. He was covered in blood. Julia's blood, the knife he had used to kill her in his hand. He looked down at himself in a panic, to find nothing. He stumbled back, wiping the cold sweat from his face. "Jesus Christ. What the hell is happening to me?" Dennis tried to put the key in the door. On the fourth attempt, he made it. Dennis burst through the front door and made a beeline for Sean's bedroom. He found him asleep on his stomach as he usually was, hands curled underneath him. A half-full sippy cup of water sat nearby. He must have gotten thirsty, he thought with a shudder. He shook his head.

That's it, he thought, *I'm done. I can't deal with whatever this is. I won't quit but I'll put in for a transfer. C Block isn't that bad. Whatever keeps me away from that fucking room.* Dennis kissed the baby on the forehead and made his way to his room. He was usually quiet to avoid waking Julia when he came home from a night shift, but he had hardly gotten his shoes off before he leaped in the bed and pulled her to him. She was startled, then pleased, then startled again.

"Baby, are you OK? Did something happen tonight?"
"No, no, it was ... " he was about to say dead, but that conjured an image of the knife, "uneventful. I just missed you."
She smiled. "I missed you too." She pulled him to her and they slept that way the rest of the night, never not touching.

5.

In the light of morning, as he held Sean on his lap and Julia sitting across from them, thoughts of transferring faded. He knew what had happened wasn't a dream. It was that room, of that he was sure, but he wasn't going to let it run his life. But he was going to make damn sure to stay as far from it as he could. And he was pretty sure that he wouldn't have trouble getting the guys to take any solo night shifts he had coming up. Hell, any solo shifts at all. He felt better thinking it out. He had a plan for his life now. Whatever mysteries were waiting behind that door could stay there.

Confrontation

1.

Raymond Monroe had always known there was something wrong with him. Even as a child, he was aware many of his thoughts and fantasies could never be shared with anyone lest he would be shunned, or worse, sent away. So as the years went by he learned how to suppress them to an extent, and to mimic the people around him in order to appear as a 'regular' guy. He feigned interest in the same things his friends, and later on girlfriends, were interested in. He laughed when they laughed, comforted them when they they were sad. He learned to get along. But the only thing that ever held any real interest for him was the thought of killing someone. It didn't matter who, or how old they were, or if they were a man or woman. He wanted to know what it felt like to end someone's life.

He finally got the opportunity his second year at college, during Christmas break. He came stumbling out of a bar he frequented near closing time. As he turned to take his usual shortcut to the dorms through the alley, he saw a homeless man sitting against the wall, wrapped in a filthy blanket. It was damn cold out and no one else was on the streets. The man looked up as Raymond walked toward him, lifting his hand to him.

"Change, sir?" Raymond stood over the man, staring at him. Through him. The smell of him overwhelming, his eyes hopeful as he held his hand out, counting on some Christmas spirit to land him a few quarters. Suddenly every urge and fantasy Raymond had kept contained for almost two decades burst to the surface. Before he was really sure what he was doing, he grabbed the man by the back of his head, covering his mouth and nose with his own filthy scarf. The man, who was on the back end of his sixties and hadn't eaten in three days, didn't put up much of a fight. Raymond watched him fade away. He thought it would excite him or bring him some great insight into himself, but instead he felt nothing, which in itself was a strange new thing. After all these years the compulsion to kill was gone. He backed up and looked around for possible witnesses. When he was satisfied he was still alone he continued home, tossing the scarf in a dumpster and wiping his hand on his jeans without stopping. As he neared the other end of the alley he turned, giving the dead man one last look.

This must be how everyone else feels all the time, he thought as he walked away. Four years passed before he killed again.

2.

He had been married to Kathy for a little over three months when she received the call her grandmother had died. He held her as she cried, told her all the things she needed to hear, then two hours later saw her onto a plane to her parents house. The thought of killing someone was the furthest thing from his mind that night. One moment he was driving home from the airport, then it seemed an instant he was two towns over, parked by the side of the road talking to a prostitute that was leaning through his passenger window. Not realizing the horrible mistake she was making, she hopped in the car and he had driven them down a dirt road and before the car had come to a complete stop he was on her. The killing of the prostitute was the polar opposite of the old man in the alley. This woman hadn't been slowly starving to death, and she had spent more than a few years on the streets dealing with variations of men like Raymond. The ride over already had her alarm bells ringing. He hadn't said a word since she stepped in the car, just looked straight ahead and muttered under his breath. She was about to tell him to pull over and let her out when he turned onto the dirt road. By then it was already too late. He was locked in. She fought back with everything she had but In the end, he took her. When he finally finished, he stumbled from the car shaking and exhausted. He caught a glimpse of himself in the car window, and his stomach did a flip. His face and neck were bloody and covered with scratches.

"Oh no...I'm going to have to call in sick, can't let anyone see me like this." Kathy would be gone for another four days, which he hoped would be enough time for the cuts to heal, they. They were shallow scratches. Another thought shot through his mind- *My skin is under her nails*. His stomach did another flip. He pulled her body from the passenger seat and let her slump to the ground. He grabbed a bottle of water from the back seat and poured it on her hands, washing away whatever blood he could see. He decided at that moment that this was his last kill. It was too risky. He enjoyed the feeling of actually not *feeling*, but he enjoyed his freedom more. He meant what he said, but he had made this decision right after a kill. It's very easy to pass on a meal when you've just finished eating and nine and a half years later Raymond was convicted of murdering his wife and child and four days after that began his first of many nights on E Block. It wasn't as bad as he had thought it would be. There was no privacy, which bothered him, but there was only one other inmate at the time and the guards were decent. And he loved the order of things. Breakfast at 9:00, lunch at 12:30 an hour in the yard at 3:00 (He could have done with less, he'd never been much of an out-doors type anyway), dinner at 6:00, lights out at 10:00. He liked routine, always had. It wasn't the worst place to wait for his final punishment.

3.

Things went smoothly for Raymond for half a year. Then the inmate in his present cell, Norm Keener, lost his final appeal. In the following month he was executed and four new inmates were relocated to E-block as a result of overcrowding. On the day the new boarders were due one of the guards, Gilles, tapped on Raymond's cell. "Rise and shine Ray, it's moving day."

"Moving? Where to?"

"The senior inmate gets the cell next to storage. Standard procedure," Gilles said, but wouldn't look Raymond in the eyes. He was clearly lying but Raymond had no clue why. He would find out soon enough. Immediately upon moving in the new cell he felt a jump in his anxiety. He had never in his life remembered any of his dreams, good or bad, but after moving into the last cell he would wake almost every night from nightmares of some unseen thing dragging him into the earth, certain that he had screamed aloud in his cell. Then the prison experienced its first heat wave of the year, and Raymond experienced his first hallucinations. As he sat on his bunk listening to the idiot next to him berate the guards and mash his dinner between the bars, he was suddenly inundated with the most vivid images of cruelty and horror. That wasn't entirely out of the ordinary, he'd had dark thoughts since puberty, but never with such clarity. It was as if he was seeing these things happen right in front of him. Before long, Raymond began to realize these new and improved thoughts weren't originating from him, but being pushed into his mind and whatever was doing it was coming from the storage room. As the months passed Raymond accepted these strange occurrences as a part of his incarceration. It was ingrained in him to hide who he was from the world, especially thoughts like this, so he kept it to himself. He was able to ignore all but the most powerful of the visions, which usually knocked him off his feet and left him with a migraine.

As the years passed, Raymond discovered those big ones almost always hit in the summer months. The summers were the worst, when the constant sense of dread was coupled with the painful visions. And it all seemed to emanate from the storage room. Raymond adapted, it's what he did. Then last year, something new. The visions increased in frequency, and the subject matter became very specific. The only vision he had now was the day he killed his wife and daughter.

The vision always picked up about twenty minutes before the actual murders. He was in his basement, puttering around with some woodworking project. The fluorescent light above him was buzzing louder than usual and had begun to flicker. Raymond got on his knees and looked under his workbench for the box of bulbs. As he rooted for the box his eyes fell on the tattered brown rug that covered the concrete floor. He traced his finger along the cloth. He never realized before just how much that rug looked like the filthy blanket the bum had been draped in. He could swear he smelled him just then, that stench. He could see the dirt under his fingernails as he held his hand out to him.

"Change?", the bum had asked. Yes, there had definitely been a change that night. Raymond clenched two handfuls of the rug in his fists without realizing it. He had no idea how long he was on the floor staring into space before his wife called to him. She had made sandwiches, if he wanted one. At the sound of her voice, the urges he had tamped down for so long came back stronger than they had ever been. He stood and walked over to the safe in the far wall and opened it, taking the gun from inside. He started to sweat as he checked to see if it was loaded. The voice in his head was in a panic. If he did this they would catch him for sure. Even if the husband *didn't* do it, he's the first person they suspect. If he did this, there was no going back. None of the arguments mattered, nothing could stop what was coming now. In his mind they were already dead. He tucked the gun in the back of his pants. The light above him flickered and buzzed. Raymond rubbed his eyes, heart pounding.

"Kathy? Could you come down here? Bring Nicole." He watched them walk down the stairs, his wife curious. As he held out his hands for the two of them to join him. Raymond pushed a stray strand of his wife's hair behind her ear.

I need to make it quick, he thought, *they shouldn't suffer*. He leaned down and kissed the top of his daughter's head. He stood up, perfectly straight. He pulled the gun from his waistband and shot his wife just above her left eyebrow. Before his daughter could make a sound he turned the gun on her. He stood over them for a long time, watching their blood pool together as it soaked into that brown rug. Then he walked to the wall where his tools hung on pegs, nice and neat. Everything in it's place. He grabbed his hacksaw. The radio played as he cut up his family and placed them in garbage bags. He had no emotion at all, no fear or sadness. He was numb. He hummed along to a few of the songs as he worked. He couldn't remember, did he turn it on before he called them downstairs or had Kathy done it while she was doing laundry? The clothes were folded in the basket, still warm from the dryer. Kathy was still warm as he started using the saw on her.

That same memory, Twice a day, then four times, then ten. Each time it happened it felt like a tank was trundling over his head, at the same time paralyzing him, so all he could do was lay there, screaming inside. For months it continued like that, and Raymond had given up on trying to push it back. In the last few weeks, parts of the memory began to distort. At the point where he pulled the gun on his family everything shifted and, for a moment, his wife and child disappeared. He was on a couch with a woman, a red head, and it wasn't a gun in his hand but a knife. He didn't know how he knew, but he was certain the woman was the new guard's wife. Then he was back on the blood soaked basement floor, saw in hand, only now he wasn't alone. There was someone crouching in the shadows under the stairs. A tall, thin figure he could only catch glimpses of in his peripheral, watching him. He could sense that It was enjoying what he was doing, that It was smiling in the dark. A week before Christmas, the previous year, Raymond's lawyer had indeed filed an appeal due to diminished capacity on behalf of his client, a document Judge Brewer threw out with a thin smile on his face. (The fact that Brewer had twin grandsons the same age as Raymond's daughter when she was murdered may have had some sway in his decision). His lawyer vowed to keep fighting. Everyone assumed Raymond's silent treatment was just part of the plot to bolster the belief that he was, in fact, going crazy, but Raymond was incapable of subterfuge. In fact, by the first official day of spring 2018, Raymond was well on his way to losing his mind. The conversation he had with Dennis on his first day was the end of his coherent interaction. By the middle of June it took all he had in him just to remain focused on eating a few bites of dinner or going to the bathroom without wetting the front of his pants. Then two nights ago, Raymond was laying on the cot when he felt a huge one coming on. He braced himself, waiting for the pain. But instead of agony, a wave of calm washed over him. For the first time in years his thoughts were completely his own. He laid in his bunk, weeping to himself, shocked by the emotion he felt. Then he heard a whisper, weak and rasping, like a dying child's last breath. It was coming from the storage room, of course. He couldn't make out what was being said so he crept to the wall and pressed his ear against the cold cement. He stood that way for a while, nodding occasionally, tears still streaming down his face. Then he got back in his bunk, knowing he would have his first good night's sleep in over a decade. And knowing he had work to do. July 5th will be the new Independence day, he thought as he drifted off. E Block's secret prisoner had broken him. Now it was time to put him to use.

4.

Dennis didn't sense anything amiss as he parked his car in the prison lot and hopped out, a smile on his face. Gone were the parka and gloves, replaced with sunglasses and a short sleeved version of his uniform. He was a polar contrast to the ball of nerves he was as he made his way up that icy sidewalk just eight months ago. Since the incident with Casey, Dennis had given the storage room a wide berth. Even at a distance, he felt that deep itch at the base of his skull a time or two, and when he did he'd excuse himself and take a walk outside. He had gotten a hold of how to handle whatever was happening on E Block, or he thought he did.. He just had a three day vacation, enjoying the Fourth of July at the lake with Julia and not-so-little Sean. Any negative thoughts had been wiped away sitting with Julia and Sean on the pier, watching Sean's face as the fireworks erupted over the water. He let that moment linger as he strolled up to the guard shack, giving the officer on duty a wave. Mark, his uniform soaked in sweat, halfheartedly waved back. There were two fans running in the shack, neither making much of a dent in the heat. "All quiet today, Mark?"

"No troubles except for it being hot as hell. They said it might hit triple digits before the day's over." Dennis cringed. That was the last thing he wanted to hear, working in a hundred and twenty-year-old prison with a notoriously unreliable air conditioner.

"Let's hope we get another afternoon shower. That seemed to cool things down a bit yesterday." Mark looked at the cloudless sky and grunted.

"I'm not holding my breath. Hey, when you get in there tell Burns to answer his walkie when I call in, will ya?"

Dennis smiled. "I will, but you know he doesn't like to be disturbed when he's in the can."

"Yeah, I've heard it about a thousand times, but still, relay the message."

"Will do." Dennis was still smiling as he walked up the path to the main building, but the smile faded as he reached the door. He could hear muffled yelling. The inmates. He fumbled the key into the lock trying to get the door as quickly as possible. He finally got the lock to turn and burst into an asylum. The light was dim, as several of the overhead lights had been broken. The inmates of E Block were at their cell doors, panicked, yelling and clanging on the bars. Dennis saw two very distressing things: Raymond's cell, open and empty, and Burns lying on the floor in front of the table clutching his stomach.

Dennis grabbed his radio as he sprinted down the hall. "Officer down! Repeat we have an officer down and an inmate out of his cell on E Block Repeat, E Block! Raymond Monroe is out of his cell!" Mark radioed back immediately.

"Copy, S.W.A.T. and paramedics are en route." Dennis reached Burns and snatched a couple of towels from the table and tried to staunch the flow of blood coming from what looked like three stab wounds in Burns's stomach. As he pressed the towels over the wounds the prison alarms began braying. Time seemed to have slowed to a crawl and sped up at the same time. The inmates were still yelling. Sweat was dripping into his eyes as he hunched over Burns, who was still breathing, however shallow. Red flowers were blooming across the towels Dennis had pressed to Burns's stomach, and blood was starting to pool on the floor around his midsection.

"You're gonna be okay Burns, paramedics are on the way, hold on!"

Burns turned his head at the sound of Dennis's voice. He lifted a shaky hand and pointed at the storage closet.

"Schuster, you gotta stop him. Stop him before he lets that thing out."

Dennis stared at Burns, confused.

"Raymond is still in here?"

"Yes, in the storage room. Stop him Dennis!"

"Burns, I can't let go of this-" Burns swatted Dennis's hand off his stomach, holding the towels in place himself. He was panting now, obviously in great pain, but Dennis saw fear more than anything else. Not for himself, but for whatever was happening in the storage room.

"I got this, just stop that asshole before he sets It free."

Sets *what* free? Dennis wanted to ask, but the intensity in Burns's eyes told him this was not the time. Dennis turned to the storage room door. It was ajar, the two padlocks laying on the floor nearby. The light wasn't on, but Dennis could hear Raymond inside, breathing heavily as he tossed boxes around. He pushed the door open, letting in a widening strip of light. He eased forward, expecting Raymond to charge at him at any moment, but he needn't have worried. As the light from the hall filled the storeroom, he could see Raymond facing the back wall, the shiv he'd used on Burns still in his hand. He was frantically throwing boxes of supplies right and left, revealing what appeared to be a smaller door hidden in the back of the room.

"What the hell?" Dennis said under his breath as he pulled the nightstick from his belt.

"Raymond!" Dennis couldn't disguise his shock as Raymond spun around. He looked like he had lost thirty pounds since he had seen him the night before. His eyes were sunken and darting around as if he were trying to look everywhere at once. He held the shiv out in front of him. Dennis took another step into the room.

"Why don't you drop that." Raymond looked down at the weapon as if he hadn't realized it was in his hand.

"No. I can't. I'm sorry about Burns, but I had to. I can't stand this anymore. It said the thoughts would stop if I let It out. And that's what I'm going to do." Before Dennis could respond Raymond charged him, swinging the homemade knife wildly as he ran. Dennis brought his arm up to defend himself. He felt a flash of heat as the shiv carved a five-inch gash into his arm. The second swing buried it in his forearm to the bone. Dennis struck Raymond with the club several times but it was as if he were hitting him with a bag of cotton. Dennis dropped the club and went for the shiv, knocking it from Raymond's hand, where it skittered into the corridor. Dennis heard S.W.A.T. charging into E Block. Still on the floor struggling with Raymond, he yelled for assistance.

"Hey, I'm in here! In the storage-" Raymond slammed his forehead into Dennis's nose. He saw stars as Raymond kicked the supply closet door shut and jammed a wedge into the door jam. Dennis tried to get to his feet, but Raymond was on him again, slamming him down on his back in front of the door, choking him. Dennis could hear S.W.A.T. outside the door now, slamming against it, but it didn't budge. Dennis tried to pry Raymond's hands off his throat, to no avail. He looked up into his face and saw no expression. His eyes were as blank as the day Raymond told him about the monster in the closet. Dennis began to feel light-headed, his vision beginning to ebb away at the corners, as if he were being drug backward into a tunnel. A thought drifted across his mind.

I think I'm dying. When the image of Julia and Little Sean floated through the murkiness, *No, not dying,* he thought. *Not like this.* Dennis managed to raise his leg up enough to kick Raymond in the groin, knocking him off balance. Raymond lost his grip around Dennis's throat and he was able to gasp in a few precious mouthfuls of air. Raymond came at him again, but he wasn't letting him get a second chance. Dennis shot his foot out, catching Raymond in the stomach, then climbed over him, swinging repeatedly at Raymond's face. He landed one or two good blows, knocking him into semi-unconsciousness. As Raymond fell over the door burst open and S.W.A.T. charged in. They drug Raymond into the hall and cuffed him, but the fight was out of him. A paramedic helped Dennis to his feet, examining the damage to his arm.

"I'm fine," he said, his voice raspy as a result of Raymond trying to squeeze the life from him.

"What about Burns?"

"Stabilized. We need to get him to the hospital, but he won't let us take him out until he talks to you." Confused, Dennis followed the paramedic into the hall, pushing the storage room door closed behind him. Burns was on a gurney, his midsection properly bandaged, an IV in his arm. When he saw Dennis he pushed the oxygen mask away from his mouth. He took Dennis's hand.

"Thanks, son, you saved my ass."

"I don't know about that."

"Bullshit! You did, and I won't forget it. I'll have them put you in for a commendation." He shifted his eyes to the closest paramedic, then back to Dennis.

"Move a little closer, it hurts to talk." The paramedic checked his pulse.

"We need to get you out of here." Burns grabbed Dennis's arm.

"One second, doc." He pulled Dennis in close.

"Raymond didn't open the door, did he? The *other* door?"

"No." Burns eased up a little, relief washed over his face.

"Thank Christ. I don't know how I could live with myself if It got out on my watch. Not that I'd live very long if It did." The paramedic was getting angry now.

"This man has several stab wounds to the stomach, we have to get him to the hospital. Now!" Dennis stepped back, roughly a thousand questions in his head. The paramedic put the oxygen back on Burns's face, but he swatted it away once more.

"Cover it back up, kid! And don't look inside!" They wheeled him down the hall. One of the S.W.A.T. guys walked over to Dennis.

"What the hell is he talking about?" Dennis shrugged.

"Beats me. They must have him on some pretty good drugs." The S.W.A.T. guy let out a nervous laugh and headed out the same direction they took Raymond.

5.

One last paramedic stayed and finished cleaning up Dennis's arm and applied a few butterfly stitches to staunch the bleeding. She gave him a once over and shook her head.

"You really need to come to the hospital. you're going to need several actual stitches in that arm, and your nose is probably broken as well."

"I can't right now, I'm the only one here watching the inmates. As soon as my relief shows up I'll head there."

"Make sure you do." She put a bandage on his arm that spotted with blood immediately. As she was finishing she received a call about a five car pile up. She hurriedly packed her gear and made her way out. as the metal door closed behind her, E Block was enveloped in a surreal silence. Dennis had never heard E Block this quiet. He felt a wave of dizziness overcome him and he barely made it to the one chair not overturned during this afternoon's madness before he collapsed. He raised his hands in front of his eyes. They were shaking, caked in dried blood. Now that the adrenalin was beginning to fade he could feel each cut and puncture on his arm, like little pockets of fire. They pulsed with his heartbeat. He closed his eyes, taking a couple of deep breaths. Dooley was still at his cell door, staring at the mess.

"Hey, you OK boss?" Dennis opened his eyes, sitting up straighter.

"I'm fine Dooley." He realized he did feel a little better. A little. Dooley smiled.

"Good, good. So you think they will deliver dinner on time?" Dennis was about to tell him where he could stick his dinner request, when he had a thought. He didn't know if Charlie C would be around with what passes for food at the prison, but it wouldn't be long before this place was crawling with investigators, and he told Burns he'd cover that door back up. He stood on legs that felt like they were made of sand and walked across the hall into the site of his epic battle. The room looked like a bomb had gone off in it. Dennis waded through the spilled supplies and got his first good look at the secret door. It was small, maybe five feet tall and made of steel. It reminded him of a door in a submarine, complete with a locking wheel in the center. It looked like it had been last opened around the time the pyramids were built. It was covered in dust and cobwebs. There was a sliding latch, roughly ten inches by four inches, set near the top. He tapped the door with his knuckle. It issued a dull thud. steel. Thick steel by the feel of it. As he examined the door more closely he saw it was covered in etchings, symbols that could have been hieroglyphics and what looked like words, though none from any language he had ever come across. He ran his finger across one of the symbols then jerked his hand back. The symbol had quickly become too hot to touch. It felt like someone had laid a torch against the other side of the door. He looked at his fingers expecting a blister, but there wasn't so much as a red mark. Maybe it was just static electricity, he thought to himself, convincing no one. As he stood there, this close to the door he suddenly realized that he was terrified. He was on the brink of running. It was that feeling of wrongness again, now a hundredfold. He had felt it during his fight with Raymond, but he had chalked that up to adrenaline. The image he had tried so hard to forget forced its way into his head. Plunging the knife into his wife as she sat on the couch watching television, her eyes wide and full of disbelief.

"No!" Dennis covered his eyes with his hands. He had broken out in a cold sweat. He tried to shake it off.

"I have to get this door covered and get the hell out of here." But he didn't move.. Instead, he reached out and slid open the latch, revealing thick, yellowed glass. He stood there for a moment. trying to stay calm and failing. Burns had told him not to look inside, but after the day he had, he thought he'd earned a peek at whatever the hell was behind this door. He knelt, putting his face as close as he could to the door without actually touching it. He took the penlight from his belt, marveling that it had survived the battle, and shone it through the glass. The view was distorted but he could make out a small room, maybe only four feet on every side. The walls were also steel, also covered in the same strange etchings. At first, the room appeared empty, until Dennis shone the light across the floor and let out an involuntary yelp, stepping back from the door. There was someone in there.

"That can't be." He eased back to the door and peered in again. There was a figure sitting cross-legged, leaning back against the far wall. The person was incredibly tall, way too tall to stand up in the room he was housed in. His face was obscured, but the weak light revealed a very long, thin torso clad in a black, silken material that was rotting right off of his body. His impossibly long arms were at his sides, elbows coming close to touching the floor. Hands so pale they were almost transparent rested on his knees. Around the figure's wrists were a pair of ancient shackles that reminded Dennis of the kind he'd seen in the old westerns he and his dad watched on channel five when he was a kid. The shackles and the chain connecting them were rusted and frail looking. The figure was so still it could have been a sculpture, except for the fingers. It was drumming fingers that had to be seven inches long over and over on his knees. Slowly. . . as if patiently waiting. Over and over.

Dennis watched this with a growing terror. That itch at the base of his skull had spread, he felt as if his head was stuffed with gauze. His bruised throat and multiple stab wounds were forgotten. He was paralyzed. He tried to talk, but all that came out was a weak croak. Waves of violence and despair washed over him. Later, when he thought about that moment, he was glad correctional officers didn't carry firearms because he was sure he would have taken his out and shot himself in the head with no hesitation. He finally shook himself out of his stupor.

"What the fuck is going o-"

As soon as Dennis began to speak the figure on the floor moved. It was on its feet, moving faster than Dennis could register. It slammed its body into the door, causing flecks of rust to fall from the frame. Dennis screamed, pinwheeling backward, landing in a pile of scattered supplies, his hands raised in front of him. He looked at the door. It was hunched just on the other side. Dennis could hear it breathing. He looked up at the small window and saw the thing had pressed the bottom of its face against the yellowed glass. It was smiling. Thin black lips spread back to reveal a mouthful of gray teeth, a smile that seemed to span the length of the window. Then It was gone, one last muffled scrape against the door, as if the thing inside was running its fingers along the steel. Dennis scrambled to his feet, slamming the latch back across the window, mercifully concealing the horror on the other side. Then he stumbled out of the room and into the nearest chair, shaking and terrified.

6.

Five hours after Raymond's escape E Block looked as it always had, except for the newly empty cell. Investigators had spent over an hour taking photographs and interviewing the inmates. After they'd gone, Charlie C and another custodian came in with a mop bucket and a cart carrying the much delayed and clamored for dinner trays. While Charlie handed out the food, the custodian, Stern, Dennis thought his name was, unceremoniously mopped up Burns's blood. When they were done they asked Dennis to unlock the storage closet so they could straighten up in there.
"That's alright guys, I took care of it. The storage room is clear." Charlie shrugged.
"Hey, thanks, man. Less work for us." He turned to his helper.
"Let's head back to the kitchen." Dennis let out a sigh as the door at the end of the hall slammed shut. The storage room was far from clear. After he'd found the strength to stand up again, Dennis lingered in the storage room just long enough to cover the submarine door with boxes. At the hospital, he replayed the events over and over again as the E.R. doctor put, what turned out to be, twelve stitches in his arm. Another investigator, who was there waiting to talk with Burns, found him and asked a few more questions while the doctor sewed him up. After he was stitched and re-bandaged, the investigator walked him to his car.
"We have all we need I think, you head home, take a day or two off." Dennis smiled.

"Yes sir, I plan on doing just that." And he did, but not just yet. He started the car and called home. He had called Julia on his way to the hospital to let her know what had happened before she found out on the internet. She tried to sound calm, but he could hear the worry in her voice.

"Are you OK?"

"Honey I'm fine, just a couple scratches. Burns got the worst of it by far."

"When are you coming home?"

"I'll be there as soon as I can, OK? I just have one more interview." What he didn't tell her was he was going to be the one asking the questions during this one. He had arrived back at the prison an hour ago, fascinating the relief guard they had sent over from C Block with an abbreviated version of the story he had told the investigators.

"That's fuckin insane, man! I wish I'd have been on over here, I'd have shown that prick the inside of his fuckin' skull." Dennis smiled weakly. This idiot wouldn't last five minutes on E Block.

"Hey, I know you have to be tired, you can head out if you want. I have to talk to Zale anyway."

"Oh man, really? That works for me, Bud I'm gone." Dennis was more than happy to see him leave. He picked up a chair and walked it down to the exit. He had no intention of sitting near that storage room. As he walked he checked the inmates. All asleep. Good, he didn't want an audience. He and Zale were going to have a conversation, and Dennis was going to get some answers. As he sat there, alternating his gaze from the storage room to the outside door, he replayed the events of the day in his head for the hundredth time. What came back to him over and over were faces. Burns, pained and afraid; Raymond, crazed and desperate; and the thin gray nightmare grinning at him from behind the window. He looked at the exit, mentally commanding Zale to hurry the fuck up when he heard a noise from the end of the hall. Dennis was on his feet in an instant, nightstick in hand. He looked towards the inmates, but they hadn't moved. Dennis inched down the corridor. He tried to swallow

but his saliva had dried up. He had only taken a few steps when there was a loud clang behind him. He let out a weak shout, spinning around to see Zale. He closed the outside door, looking as surprised as Dennis.
"Jesus, you look like hell. What are you still doing here?"
"I wanted to talk. Have you heard anything about Burns?"
"Let's go sit. Grab your chair."
Zale and Dennis headed to the table, Dennis more and more tense as they neared the storage room.
"Burns is out of surgery. They let me back to see him for a minute."
They sat down at the table. Zale wiped the sweat off his forehead,
"He's gonna be OK. Won't be eating anything spicy for the rest of his life. He lost a few feet of intestine."
"Christ."
"And he won't be coming back here. Especially if his wife has anything to say about it. He was retiring in four months anyway, so I'd say it's a done deal. To be honest I don't think he wants to come back. He was scared. The kind of fear that makes doing this job impossible."
Dennis stood up and walked down the hall a few feet, giving the storage room a wary look. "I know how he feels."
"You might have been scared, but you did a great job today. Saved Burns's life. He wanted me to thank you again. There's something else you should know, Kid. Raymond is dead."
Dennis sat back down, shocked. "What?"
"He collapsed while they were taking him to isolation. Massive stroke, they said. Died instantly."
Dennis let out a disgusted laugh, shaking his head. "A stroke. Well, I guess that's that."
"What's wrong?"
Dennis raised his voice, then immediately lowered it again. He respected his boss, but he was furious. "Seriously? What's wrong? How about the fact that there's a person sitting in a hidden cell behind the supply closet. That's a good start. And that I lied to two state investigators in my official report about it, which means that I'm now a co-conspirator

in whatever the hell is going on here. Which is what exactly, Zale? Who is that back there? Is this some Guantanamo thing? Are you torturing him?"

Zale looked at Dennis and sighed. It was his turn to stand up. He walked down the hall, looking in the cells. They were all still asleep.

"It seemed the excitement of the day had taken its toll on our inmates. Let's go outside, get some air. It smells like bleach in here."

They step into the mini courtyard where most of the guards still went to smoke, even though it's prohibited these days. It was still damn hot even at this hour, and Dennis immediately began to sweat.

Zale leans up against the wall. He looked both nervous and weary. "Okay. Are we torturing someone in there? No. Yes... shit, I don't know. I don't think so. Is it cruel and unusual, dumping... someone in a cell without the benefit of a trial and with no chance of ever being released? Yes of course, but then again, the *prisone*r is cruel and unusual. You've been here long enough to know something on E Block's not quite right, and I'm guessing you got a good look at him,*It*...today. Maybe that's part of the reason you didn't report us. You know that this-" Zale pointed in the direction of the storage room. "-isn't normal. So maybe we're torturing It, but It's torturing us too. What happened here today, Raymond getting out and stabbing Burns, that was its doing. No one could prove it, but I know it killed Raymond."

"How is that possible?"

Zale sighed, running his hands over his face."Not now."

"What?"

"I said not now. This is a long story and one I never thought I'd have to tell again. Go home, hug your wife. Let her process that-" Zale pointed at Dennis's arm.

"-take the next two days off and we will have this conversation Friday evening, away from here. Over drinks. Lots and lots of drinks. OK?"

Dennis bowed his head, deflated."I guess I don't have a choice, do I?"

"I'm not screwing with you Kid, I'll tell you everything, though once I do you're gonna wish you could scoop it right back out of your head."

7.

Twenty minutes later he was pulling into his driveway. His arm was singing again, but he figured he should get home before he took the Percocet they had given him at the hospital. Julia had the front door open before he reached the first step. She stopped, shocked at what she saw- eyes already turning black from the broken nose, along with other small cuts and scrapes on his face, his left arm bandaged elbow to wrist, with tiny specks of blood dappled across the front of his shirt. He had expected her to be angry after his drastic downplay of his injuries, but as she stood there shaking, back lit from the glow of the living room lamps, she looked furious.

"A couple of scratches?"

"Baby, it's not that bad-"

"Not that bad! Your arm, your *face-*"

He stepped closer and saw her eyes. It wasn't fury. She was barely holding herself together. It was that moment, looking into her eyes, that he thought about just how close he came to never coming home again. He stumbled up the last stair into her arms, then the tears fell down her face and she let out a choked sob that almost made Dennis join in the waterworks. He grabbed her, pulling her as close as he could, feeling fresh pain in his arm and not caring, she was holding him just as tight. He took her in the house, swatting the door closed. And then they were kissing, gentle at first then harder, the two of them clawing at each others clothes. They started for the bedroom, but only got as far as the couch. In a moment he was inside her, hearing her moans in his ear, both of them trying to find a way to get closer. His pain forgotten, he only wanted to be kissing her, holding her. When they were done they fell back, exhausted and happy. The pain returned but he didn't care. They had slept there most of the night, Julia snuggled on top of him, neither one of them had mentioned what had happened at the prison, Dennis figured what had happened between them was all the discussion they needed.

Spinning Yarns

1. Friday night. They were at a bar was called Reggie's, named after the owner, a hole the wall that sat just off highway five. Years ago the bar was the place to be on a Friday night, but after the double whammy of the textile factory closing its door and the expressway coming through the best Reggie could hope for on weekends were his regulars and the occasional lost driver, hunting directions and maybe a beer or two. It was, however, the perfect setting for Zale to tell his story: privacy accompanied by large amounts of alcohol. They sat in the back booth on seats with the stuffing slowly escaping from a dozen different places and a table covered in the carved initials and witticisms of twenty five years worth of drunken patrons. Dennis still had his arm bandaged, and both of his eyes had blackened, but he still looked a hell of a lot better than the last time he and Zale had spoken. Dennis was thinking about that night as the waitress brought them a second pitcher of watered-down beer. Zale had demolished the first one and was pouring a mug from the second as he looked into the impatient face seated across from him. He sighed.
"I'm not stalling, I just don't know exactly how to start."
Dennis poured himself a glass of the questionable beer. "Why don't you just begin at the beginning."
Zale laughed at that. "The beginning...yeah. that might be a longer story than you think. Let me..."
Zale finished off the mug. Dennis, to his credit, sat patiently. Zale wiped his mouth with the back of his hand and sighed. "What I'm about to tell you was for the most part told to me by my boss back in nineteen eighty-four, which was told to him by his boss, so on and so forth. That's a biggie, nothing written down, nothing documented pertaining to inmate 01. In that respect, We treat 01 just like the storytellers that passed down their histories around the campfire for generations. I know a lot of stories can become soft around the edges when they're passed that way, with bits and pieces dropped in or taken away to suit the latest teller. But the history of inmate 01 has never been embellished, as if it would

need embellishment. You don't forget these stories. Not one detail. Even when you want to." Dennis looked confused. "Zale, what-"
"Just.. be quiet, will ya? I'm telling it, just, let me get to it my way."
Dennis sat in silence, and Zale told the story of inmate 01
"Newcastle penitentiary opened in 1895. It's the second oldest prison in the Midwest. Back then E-Block was the whole shebang. Everything else was added on over the next century. The place was touted as the strongest prison ever built, to incarcerate society's most violent criminals, but it started with a couple of horse thieves. Two brothers, Castillo and Estavo Jimenez. They had rustled cattle from Mexico to the Dakotas before they were finally caught, and after a fair and partial trial, they were set to be hung. The two men were despondent, but not for themselves. They were heartbroken for each other. They had each plead guilty as the sole perpetrator, trying to spare his brother the noose. According to anyone that knew them, they were as close as any two brothers could be. You might think there's no point to me telling you that, but It comes into play. Castillo was in the late Raymond Monroe's cell, his brother in Yost's. Sometime around the third day of their incarceration, the prison had some visitors." 2. 1895. It was a beautiful Spring morning the day 01 arrived. The Jimenez brothers had been brought in the night before, but they hadn't had much to say. They were on their bunks, unconsciously sitting in the same fashion, back against the wall with their right leg pulled up to their chests. E Block was barely recognizable in its inaugural state. The block wall that the inmates face across the hall from their cells is now broken every few feet by a series of small barred windows, and shafts of light cut through the dust that covered the plank floor. There was farmland surrounding the prison, and with the iron door at the end of the hall propped open, the sound of horses and the occasional yell of "yah" or "get movin!" could be heard in the distance. A single guard, Seth Tolliver, sat at a table very similar to the one that occupied that same corner now. He was whittling a piece of wood, stopping every few minutes to eyeball his burgeoning master-

piece. Where the storage room was now there is a rickety row of shelves containing half a bottle of whiskey and a dented bucket.

As Tolliver began to carve again he heard horses, what sounded to be at least a dozen of them, moving in fast. He pushed back from the table and walked to the nearest window. Two wagons were tearing down the dirt road at a full run, one was a average coach, but the one following behind it was a beast. The top half was draped in a large piece of ragged canvas, ropes crisscrossing underneath, holding it in place. It was being pulled by eight rather large horses, all of which looked on the verge of collapse. There were three other men riding horses as an escort around the larger wagon, all of them armed. The two carriages roared into the courtyard, one of the men jumping from the smaller coach before it had stopped, also armed.

Tolliver dropped his chunk of wood and took a step back, panicked. He looked at the brothers still sitting silently in their cells and whispered to himself, "Dear Lord, it's a jailbreak."

His hand went to his nightstick, then dropped it. All that would do would get him killed quicker. The first man out of the carriage was clearly the leader of this strange group. He yelled something to the men Tolliver couldn't hear while pointing at the larger wagon. The men nodded and began untying the canvas, revealing several large pieces of flat steel stored in racks along the wagon's sides, and in the center what appeared to be a coffin, though one larger than Tolliver had ever seen. The men began removing the plates. The leader of this calamity then headed inside. Tolliver jumped back from the door, straightening his uniform. His thoughts on the men being jail-breakers had now drifted to some sort of inspectors, though no one had sent word of such. As the man in charge strode through the iron door, the guard put out his hand and was about to introduce himself when the men from the wagon marched inside, straining under the weight of the steel plates they were carrying. As they passed, Tolliver could see etchings carved into the metal, some of them looked kinda like the hieroglyphics he had seen in an exhibit about mummies at the state fair a year ago. Two other men followed behind, lugging in a rather large welding device. Bringing up the rear was a priest. Tolliver thought the horses looked bad but this man looked ready to fall into his grave. He was thin and pale, cheeks splotchy with dark red blemishes. Tolliver would have guessed it had been at least three weeks since he had eaten. When he entered the building he immediately slumped into the nearest chair, grabbing a kerchief from his robe with shaking hands, wiping his forehead.

The leader of the group grabbed the hand Tolliver had forgotten he had offered and gave it a quick shake. He then flipped out his badge.

"Good afternoon, sir, Theodore Valentine, secret service. Your Warden is expecting me. We have a lot to do and its best we have it done as quickly as possible."

The nervous guard blinked, looking around at the suddenly crowded prison. "Is this an inspection?"

"No, not an inspection. Is Warden Bertram here? In our last correspondence he told me he would be ready to receive us on the fourteenth, which is today."

"Yes, sir, the Warden is here, but it's not Bertram. Warden Bertram's wife caught ill a week before they were to arrive. A fever of some sort. She passed. Warden James is his replacement."

Valentine closed his eyes. His jaw worked as he took in the information. He shook it off, forcing a smile.

"That is going to make matters more difficult, but what's done is done. Please bring the Warden here at once, tell him it's of the utmost importance."

"Yes sir, I'll be right back." He ran out the door as the men began welding the first two walls of what was to be inmates 01's cell. The resident horse thieves had moved to the doors of their cells, finally finding something to momentarily break them out of their funk. The priest leaned back against the chair, gaunt and silent.

Valentine patted the priest's shoulder and looked out one of the small windows in time to see Tolliver disappear into a modest building up the hill from the prison. He was only gone a few moments when he popped back out, this time with a portly gentleman in tow. Valentine could hear the man's booming voice even over the welding. He sighed as he handed the priest a glass of water.

"And now I have to explain this impossible situation to yet another blowhard that is not capable of understanding. I'll try not to hold that against him, half the time I can't believe what has transpired over the past few months." The priest nodded over his glass of water.

As they neared the door, Warden James brushed Tolliver aside and blustered into the room, red-faced from the walk down the hill and his growing anger.

"You there! Valentine, is it? What is the meaning of this? What are these men doing to my prison?"

Valentine sighed again, then put on what he hoped was a winning smile. "Good afternoon, Warden, as I'm sure your man told you, I'm agent Valentine of the secret service-"

"Yes, he told me, what I want to know is just what in heaven's name these men doing?"

"Some of these gentlemen are from the Pinkerton agency, the rest are men hired to assist us. They are constructing a cell. A special cell for a special prisoner. I do apologize, Warden Bertram had been apprised of all of this, but I am not surprised he didn't inform you, what with the events concerning his wife. I would have been aware of these developments sooner, but we have been out of communication for the past month, so I will fill you in now. The United States government has arranged for the incarceration of a very dangerous prisoner."

The warden looked past Valentine at the workers, who were now sliding the submarine door into place. "Dangerous prisoner? This is highly irregular, Agent. I received a telegraph from the director just three days ago and there wasn't so much as a peep about any construction or prisoners, dangerous or otherwise, being incarcerated in my prison."

"And there wouldn't be, sir. Very few people know about this and for good reason. I was to be the liaison between Washington and Warden Bertram, but as I said we were unable to receive correspondence."

The warden eyed the construction, then brought his attention back to Valentine, shaking his head.
"You are not making any sense to me."
Valentine clenched his fists behind his back. "Sir, if you will?" Valentine gestured toward the door. The two of them walked out into the brightness of the day. Valentine turned to the warden. "Warden, this penitentiary was never supposed to be just a penitentiary. To clarify, it was constructed to house one specific prisoner. We have a unique problem on our hands, Warden. For two and a half years the Pinkertons and Scotland Yard tracked this criminal through Europe and Asia and across the Atlantic into South America. A year ago our government was informed of the fugitive crossing into the United States and surrounding territories, and the secret service became involved. It was made clear to us that bringing the fugitive back to Europe would be an impossibility, so thirteen months ago construction began on this prison as we continued to track..him and were finally able to apprehend him in the Ozark mountains two months ago. We have been en route to you since then."
"The Ozarks? That's only a month's travel at most. Even by stagecoach-"
"That is all part of the dilemma concerning this particular prisoner, Warden. He had to be brought in on certain roads and during specific times of the day. To the only safe geographic location in the northern hemisphere that has a hope of containing him."
The warden became a darker shade of red. "This is pure nonsense! Who is this prisoner?"
"He doesn't have a name, only a number. 01."
"No name? Can he not tell you? Is he mute?"
Valentine grimaced. "If only he were."
"Could no information on this man be found at his trial?"
Valentine rubbed his hand across his forehead. "Warden, there was no trial. Scores of people, both agents and civilians alike have been killed in pursuit of this fugitive, and even after his capture, the deaths did not cease. We began our journey here with twenty men. Only seven of us survived the trek. He killed the rest, including my partner and one of

our priests. None of us would have made it if not for him.' Valentine gestured to the priest, slowly nursing his glass of water. "I don't think the poor man has slept two hours in the last thirty days."

"He killed your men after he was apprehended? He attempted escape?" Valentine ran his hand through his hair, a look of weariness coming over him. "What I tell you now will sound like the ravings of a loon, but it is the truth and nothing but. After all the years and lives lost in the pursuit of this murderer, we finally had the upper hand. We were so close! Our bloodhounds cornered 01 in a large deadfall. We could hear them ahead, barking their victory. Then we heard the animal's screams. The bastard killed them all. As we charged the clearing we found their bodies, one tossed into the crook of a tree, neck broken, others torn in half. He turned as we neared and there we got our first good look at him. At *It*. It's a sight I will never forget. It was if the creature had been drawn in charcoal, only existing in shades of gray and black. It was near eight feet tall and very slight, arms and legs out of proportion, like stretched taffy. Its skin was hanging from it in folds. And it's eyes... Or I should say lack of. No eyes, no sockets, just more folds of skin where they should have been, Its head sloping back from the brow-line. Not that it seemed incapacitated without them, It's tracked our slightest movements easily. It did not move to confront us, just stood there and smiled at us. That repugnant, endless smile. I almost shot it right then, it took all my fortitude not to. It turned toward the man who was unfortunate enough to be nearest to it. The man, Laurence I want to say his name was, let out a scream. He stumbled around a moment before tripping over a fallen tree. He fell to his knees, digging the palms of his hands into his eyes, screaming for his mother. Later that evening he told us that he felt he was going mad, that all he was able to see was a memory of when he was twelve, coming home from a day of hunting squirrel and discovering that his father had hung himself in the cellar. The image replayed over and over in his mind, his father's face blue and swollen, his body slowly rocking back and forth like wash on the line. We pulled Laurence away, all the while that thing was standing by the deadfall, smiling, as if was he that had caught us. I raised my rifle to shoot the abomination right through the center of that sick grin, but the priest stopped me. He was still fresh then, as we all were. He walked towards the thing, reading from an ancient leather book, speaking under his breath. The sight of the rifle hadn't affected the creature at all but the priest's words certainly did. The grin faded and was replaced by a look of surprised obedience. Its shoulders slumped and it dropped to its knees. The priest stepped closer, taking a pair of shackles from his robe. They were covered in the symbols that are on the cage my men are constructing. The priest tossed shackles to the creature, still speaking softly but rapidly. Without raising its head It snatched them out of the air, quick as lightning, tightening them down on its wrists. The second priest produced a hood and pulled it over its head. After that, we circled it at a distance and led it to the sarcophagus. It stepped inside obedient as a pup and laid down. We bolted it in and as far as we know it hasn't moved a muscle since, but as we found out it doesn't need to move to hurt us. It has other skills. As we headed west we learned the boundaries of those skills. If you walked too close to the wagon it was lashed to, you would have dark, murderous thoughts, or terrible memories would resurface, like Laurence of his mother. They would get in your head and claw around in there until you backed away. It affected some men more than others, but everyone felt it to some extent. One of the men, barely sixteen, fell asleep on watch that first night. We woke the next morning to find him dead, throat slit by his own hand. We counted ourselves lucky he didn't take us all with him. I experienced it myself the following evening, during the night watch. I felt a hot pressure on the back of my neck, then my head was filled with the vilest images, acts of murder and degradation. That's when I knew for sure. That thing had killed the boy as surely as if it had slit his throat with its own hand. After that, we kept further out. Ten feet seemed to be his.. communication range I suppose you would call it. I can see the confusion on your face, warden. This is madness, I confess, but true. Every word. There are things in the world that we cannot make sense of, and this is one such thing. But it doesn't change the fact that it must be dealt with. Locked away, and never let out." The warden looked concerned, even frightened, but his fear was directed at Agent Valentine. He was sure the man had lost his mind. He cleared his throat. "Agent Valentine, I understand your anger at the loss of your men, but to suggest they were murdered by..by a person's thoughts? I'm sorry, but I find that hard to swallow. And calling a man with physical deformities a thing, a creature, jailing him without a trial, placing him here for the rest of his life, with no record of his incarceration.. as two Christian men, I believe we can come to some-"

Valentine raised his hand. "It is not anger that drives me, and I am not a religious man."

"But you said the priest's prayers kept you going."

"The priests saved us all, but I am quite sure the incantations spoken to that thing would never be sanctioned by the Catholic church. If he lives he may be excommunicated for this, but he kept 01 subdued and us alive. You still don't understand, but you will."

The men working on the cell turned off the welders. The thick, symbol covered sheets had been sealed to the frame, some of the seams still glowing a deep orange. One of the men nodded at Valentine.

Valentine nodded back. "It looks like we are ready. Gentlemen?"

The two men in suits that were hovering behind Valentine exited the prison along with the welders. The priest made his way to his feet, though for a moment it was debatable that he would remain there. He pulled the leather book from his robes and followed the men outside. Valentine turned to the exasperated warden, gently guiding him out of the doorway.

"They are about to bring him in. We should head down. And Warden, be prepared. When it passes, you will not feel yourself."

Valentine lead the warden down to the table. The warden stood on his toes and peered out the window as the remaining travel party surrounded the wagon. All the steel plates had been removed for the construction of the cell, leaving only the skeletal frame of the cab and what the men called the sarcophagus. They slowly pulled the large box off the wagon, setting it upright. the priest made his way to his feet and stood just outside the door, reading from his book in a low voice as the men drew their weapons, standing in a wide circle. one unarmed man slowly unlocked several bolts keeping the lid secure. as he unlocked the last bolt the lid slid down, exposing a small bit of the interior. the unarmed man leaped away, terrified, as the lid slid over into the grass with a deep thud. The priest spoke louder as the men moved forward, huddled around the box for a moment, then they were on the move. The fugitive was as Valentine described him. They were surrounding a figure that was easily two feet taller than the tallest man there. His head was hooded, hands and feet shackled. As they moved closer to the door the Warden caught glimpses of the prisoner's body. The same hieroglyphic type etchings that covered the recently constructed cell walls also adorned the chains. The prisoner was wearing the same black silk clothing Dennis would see through the submarine door over a hundred years later, but now they were in much better condition. the priest followed behind the men, reading from the ancient book in a language the warden had never heard before. He held the text in a grip so tight his knuckles had turned white, and he was reading at a speed that was impossible to separate individual words. As the procession passed the cells the Jimenez brothers backed to the walls of their cells and Tolliver almost fell over as he made space for their passage. The only two men actually touching the prisoner were the two men in suits, and as they neared the warden could see their sleeves had been pulled up slightly, and the same symbols on the cell walls and the shackles were carved into the man's arms. he could also see a few carved into their necks right above their collars.

The Warden thought *They must be covered in them.*

As they lead the prisoner past the warden, the figure turned its shrouded head in his direction. The Warden immediately began to shake. "Lord Jesus." His stomach roiled. It felt as if time were slowing as a dull, hot itch bloomed at the base of his skull. He heard laughter. He looked around, thinking it might have been Valentine, but he stood silent, his eyes never leaving the prisoner. The itch intensified, and the warden felt his bowels loosen. Cold sweat began to drip into his eyes. He suddenly had a very vivid image in his head. He was ascending the stairs at his home. He was carrying a wooden boat, one he had carved for his son when he was a child. He raised his head and there was his son as he was twenty years ago, still in short pants. He was sitting on the top step, hands outstretched to his papa. The boy smiled as his father approached, not knowing what papa had planned for him. James smiled back as he reached out and touched the boy's cheek. Suddenly he grabbed his son under both arms and yanked him up over the Bannister. He started crying as the Warden shook him, laughing in his face. He held the boy even higher, then hurled him off the landing. The boy screamed as he fell, then silence as his head made contact with the floor with a wet thud-

Warden James let out a cry and took an involuntary step back. Without taking his eyes from the procession, Valentine grabbed his arm, pulling him close.

"Hold steady sir, hold steady. I want you to understand why we are doing this today. I want you to remember. The thoughts will pass once it's inside. but I need you to remember. To keep this fear with you."

The warden was shaking profusely, on the verge of tears.

"My son... I was killing him... and I wanted to do it.. I was enjoying it-"

"That thing wants to kill, revels in it and would happily use you to do it. It put the images in your mind. That discomfort at the base of your skull, that itch, did you feel it?" "Y-yes." "That is the warning sign. Tell your men, if that feeling comes over any of you remove yourself from the vicinity of that cell as quickly as possible."

The cattle stealing brothers were praying almost as fast as the priest rattled off his incantations. They finally reached the submarine door and shoved the new prisoner inside, careful not to enter the room themselves. As soon as the door slammed closed the feeling of dread that had stolen over the room eased, but not entirely. The warden was able to breathe again. Valentine let go of his arm and he was able to steady himself. The priest was a different story. He had dropped the book and slumped against one of the men, his nose bleeding. They retrieved the tome and escorted him outside. Valentine shook his head, morose.

"He is finally free of his duties concerning that beast, but I fear too much damage has been done to the priest. I don't think he will survive the trip home. But he will be remembered. All of them will. I'll make sure of it."

The men exited, closing the door behind them, leaving the Warden with Valentine and the horse thieves. And prisoner 01.

The Warden took a kerchief from his pocket and wiped the sweat from his face.

"Why did you let the priest stop you?"

"Pardon?"

"At the deadfall, you were going to shoot.. if you felt even half the despair and disgust I just felt..I would have shot. Nothing could have stopped me."

Valentine shook his head. "It only makes things worse. Apparently the blood is poison. To touch just a drop leaves can kill you, but not before sending you into a mindless rage, inflicting harm upon yourself or others. Even the smell of that things blood can drive you mad. No, this is the only solution."

"It's not human."

"No."

"Then What?"

"We have no idea. The priests say that its been here a long time, visiting misery and Havoc on untold numbers. All we know for certain is that it is the most dangerous thing anyone has ever come across, and it can never be allowed to leave that cell."

    3. Zale stopped talking. Dennis sat, staring at him, a look of both exasperation and alarm on his face. He took a large sip from his mug and spoke. "Zale, you're telling me that...whatever that is has been sitting on E Block over a hundred years?"

Zale finished off his beer. "That's what I'm telling you."

"It's not possible."

"I know it's not, but it's the truth, son. Every word. Look, I felt the same way you did when I found out. After my first year on E Block the crew decided I was ready to hear the truth. But I had known something was wrong down there way before that, just like you did. I've seen you staring at that door, even when you don't realize you're staring. For us, It's just something we all had to get used to. You learn to ignore it, as much as you can. Or you transfer to a different part of the prison. It's happened before. No judgment if you do. This is above and beyond the normal scope of the job."

Dennis sat silent for a moment. "I thought about it. Transferring. I decided against it."

Zale smiled. "I'm glad you did." "So what happened then?" Zale deliberated another drink, but decided against it. "With 01 safely incarcerated, the prison began to get back to normal. The warden was still in shock at what had happened, but he was in agreement with Valentine- It could never be freed. Agent Valentine and the warden retired to his office, where he was given the rules. 4. The warden was seated behind the large, ornate desk in his office, pouring a glass of whiskey with a shaky hand. Valentine produced a flask and took a few long sips himself. He sat down opposite the warden, looking in his eyes.

"What I'm about to tell you is very important. To ensure prisoner 01 stays put, you must follow these instructions to the letter."

The warden polished off the whiskey. The hand that poured the second glass was slightly less shaky.

"Yes, of course."

"First, no one in the employ of this facility is to speak to anyone about prisoner 01. not with their wife, not with a friend after a few drinks too many at the local pub. If they do let it be known they will be facing repercussions from the United States secret service."

The Warden shuddered. He couldn't imagine whispering a word of this to anyone, especially his wife.

"Two, that cell is never to be opened for any reason."
"What about food and water?"

"It hasn't eaten a thing in the month since it's capture. It feeds I'm sure... just not on the same things we do. If it does eventually starve to death, count yourself lucky. Three, there are to be no written records in regard to the prisoner. Any pertinent information will be verbal. If you need to contact me about our friend, send a telegraph consisting of one word- Goliath. I'll be on the first train out. The same protocol holds for new guards as older guards retire or pass on. Any doubts a new guard may have about the veracity of your story can be quashed with one look through the glass and five minutes at that proximity."

The Warden poured another shot. "Yes, I believe it would."

"The most important thing. The symbols carved on Its cell and It's restraints weaken it, but I am certain it will never stop trying to escape. And to drive you all mad in the process. Keep your distance. You know what it can do now. What it can put in your mind."

The Warden closed his eyes. "All too well sir."

Valentine stood. "Then that is everything, Warden. I'm sorry to place this upon your shoulders and walk away, but I must. There is important business I must attend to, most having to do with cleaning up this creature's path of destruction. I will send a priest to read from the book once a month, to make sure all is as it should be."

Valentine handed Warden a slip of paper. "My home address in Boston. For any correspondence you feel compelled to send."

The warden, who looked like he aged twenty years in the last hour stood and shook Valentine's hand. "Thank you, sir. We have... much to acclimate to." Valentine felt a wave of pity for the man. He didn't envy his position.

"Good day sir. And good luck."

5. Reggie's was now empty except for the table in the corner. Three empty pitchers stand on the table, but the two men sitting across from each other were sober as judges. Zale leaned back in his chair, appraising Dennis.

"That's all of it, as it was told to me...Christ, thirty years ago now. Time does escape us. So, any questions?"

Dennis laughed loudly at that. "Oh, one or two. I'll start with an easy one. Why do you keep the work table right across from the storage room, knowing what it does to you, being that close?" Zale snorted. "It was down at the other end of the hall for years, then one day the safety inspector dropped by and declared it a hazard. Impeding the fire exits and whatnot. So we moved it back. It's not like we could argue the point." "Who all knows about this?"

"Just the boys on E block. The guards I mean, not the inmates, though being that close to it they have to know *something*."

Dennis straightened. "Raymond sure did."

Zale flinched at that. "I know it was a special hell, leaving him next to that nightmare all those years. But what choice did I have? The place was full. I couldn't very well ask for a prisoner transfer because he was living too close to the God damn boogeyman."

"So the Warden is no longer in the loop?"

"No. They were at first, but then it was decided that information would be given on a case by case basis. By that I mean if the new Warden was deemed an incompetent asshole or not. The last one with knowledge of 01 died six months after I started at the prison. Cedric Ham. A good man. His replacement was a sniveling prick my C.O. never trusted. Neither did the rest of us. From then on 01 has been strictly E Block business. And it's worked out fine. It's not like we need to include It in the budget.

"What about the secret service? Have they ever been in contact? Maybe they can safely take it away from here now?"

"The prison never heard a word from the secret service after Valentine left. Nor did a priest ever show up to read the good word to our friend. One of the guards back in the nineties, Fuller, I think, had a nephew in the secret service, he asked him if he could find out anything he could about an Agent Valentine. As it turned out, Valentine never made it back to D.C. after his conversation with Warden James. He died when his coach lost a wheel and flipped over about two hundred miles from here."

"Jesus.."

"So no report was ever filed. As far as Washington is concerned this thing doesn't exist. 01 is our problem exclusively."

"Did It ever eat?"

"Never. As I was told Warden James thought for sure It would be howling for food and water by the end of the first week, but there wasn't a peep from the other side of that door. After a week and a half, he thought it must be dead or dying. By week three he was sure of it. How could it possibly be alive? Even monsters have to drink. So he opened the slit in the top of the door and had a peek inside."

Dennis asked the question he already knew the answer to.

"What did he see?"

"The same sight I've seen myself the two times I was brave enough to look inside. The only thing anyone has ever seen. 01, sitting on the floor, tapping those long fingers on its knees."

Dennis sat back in his chair, letting out a breath he didn't know he had been holding.

"So It's never moved? "

Zale shook his head. "Not that I've been aware of. Why, did you see something?" The image of 01 standing at the door grinning floated through his head. "Nope, just curious." Dennis didn't know why he lied, maybe he just wasn't ready to spill that horrifying can of beans yet. He pressed on. "Has it ever talked? Tried to communicate with anyone?"

Zale signaled the waitress for a final round. "I'm assuming you mean besides the lovely images it puts in our heads every chance it gets? And...My apologies for not telling you from the start, but we had to be sure about you, kid. We tried to keep you at a distance, maneuvered you away when you seemed to be getting a little wonky." Dennis nodded. "It's OK, I get it. At least now I know why I was given a chaperone on the night shift." Zale smiled. "Anyway, It only spoke out loud once that anyone knew of, but that was more than enough."

"Who did it talk to?"

A black cloud passed over Zale's face. "My C.O. Todd Jeffries. He was the resident expert on 01. This back in '88. I wasn't considered a rookie anymore, but I still had a lot to learn. Jeffries didn't have a family and his only real friends were his fellow guards. He was fascinated by 01 and over the years It became his pet project. He always said he wanted to learn everything he could about it, know your enemy and all that. If you ask me he was just obsessed. He spent hours at the library, researching books on folklore and myths, looking for the smallest scrap of information, but he never found anything. I guess we weren't the only ones that didn't want to document that bastard. He'd even drop by on his days off, play a couple of hands with whoever was on shift, always with one eye in 01's direction. At that time the storage room hadn't been built yet. There was this beat-up oak bookcase covering 01's door, and Jeffries would leave a tape recorder running on one of the shelves whenever he went home. Hoping to catch it talking to itself, I suppose. He had hours and hours of tape, but we never heard anything on them but static and the occasional guard or inmate talking in the background. Except once. Jeffries called us all over to his house one Saturday morning. He had a bottle of whiskey set out, and when we passed on it he laughed."

"You might change your minds after you hear this. This was recorded last Thursday, around three fifty A.M."

Childers perked up, surprised. "Hey, I was on last Thursday night." Jeffries nodded at that and started the tape. It started the same as any of the other tapes we had heard bits and pieces from over the past few months. There was the unmistakable sound of one of the inmates snoring, the steady fwap of cards being flipped over at the table, a game of solitaire no doubt. Then it started. We could hear wet, gurgling breaths. It sounded like the person was standing very close to the recorder. The breathing got faster and faster before it cut off. There was nothing for a moment and then a huge crash and what sounded like a gunshot. We all jumped, and I think burns might have actually started for a weapon he wasn't wearing. Then there was the laugh. It was something you'd expect to hear in the basement of an asylum. This shrieking cackle that seemed like it would go on forever. It sent chills through all of us. When it finally died away it was if it had never happened. The inmate was still snoring, Childers was still flipping cards. The Childers standing there listening with us had gone white as a sheet. He opened his mouth to say something when the Childers on the tape beat him to it. Every hour guards working shifts alone called in their condition on walkies. Tape Childers was doing that right now.

"Childers calling in 0400 hours. Everything is quiet and clear." After a moment the fwap of the cards began again. Childers was beside himself. "What the fuck, guys! That didn't happen! That can't be right. That can't be right.."

Zale grinned to himself. "Childers took Jeffries up on that drink after all. Actually, I think it ended up being four. Childers never listened to those tapes again after that, and it was almost two years before he'd take another night shift. I opted out on the tapes as well. That laugh was it for me. Jeffries, of course, doubled down, even though he said listening to them too long gave him migraines. I guess it shouldn't have surprised us when he came in one July afternoon and informed us that he was going to cut the shit and try communicating with It. We laughed at that until we realized he was serious. We tried to talk him out of it, but he wouldn't be swayed. He was an intelligent man and a curious one. He had to know what it was and he wanted our help. We reluctantly agreed. I can't really give you a good reason why we went along with it, except maybe deep down we were just as curious as he was. There were only two inmates housed on E Block the Saturday He talked to 01, and I'm sure they thought we had lost our minds. the C.O. had moved the bookshelf away from that little door and had pressed his ear against it. His tape recorder was on the floor, the microphone facing the door. Me, Buck Childers and Hugh Larson, who had come in on his day off to assist in the madness, were all at the opposite end of the hall, ready to grab the C.O. in case things went off the rails. We all had in those bright orange earplugs, which must have confused the prisoners even more, but I remember they never asked one question that day. Maybe it was the looks on our faces, or maybe they knew more about the resident at the end of the hall than we thought they did. Jeffries was talking softly into the door, we heard nothing with the plugs in, just saw his mouth moving. that went on for a couple of minutes or so then suddenly he stood up. His eyes got big and they were darting back and forth. He still had his ear to the door. I started toward him but he signaled to me that he was fine but the look on his face said differently. It was a mix of confusion and fear and he was getting paler by the minute. He seemed to stand there for hours, even though by my watch the whole thing had lasted less than three minutes. Suddenly Jeffries let out a yell and pushed away from the door. He was stumbling around in a circle, like someone trying to find a light switch in an unfamiliar room. We ran down the hall and grabbed him, took him outside. Buck stayed behind to watch the prisoners. As soon as we got him out the door he pushed us aside and threw up. He was able to stand on his own, though he was shaky. I asked him what It had said to him and Jeffries just stared at us. He looked as if he has aged twenty years since he had walked down that hall.

"At first.. it was nothing, then I could hear whispers. It was reciting a bunch of numbers. Just repeating them over and over."

Burns looked almost as scared as Jeffries. "What, like coordinates? Christ, are more of these things coming?"

"No.. I don't know. I don't think that was it. Then it rattled off a bunch of names. Betty Gafney was one, Gary Potts, no one I know, just names. I can't remember all of them. Then...then It started showing me things. Not the shit we usually get from It when we happen to get too close, this was... I asked It where it came from. And It showed me.. oh, Jesus. It was so much. So much-"

Jeffries leaned over and threw up again. We helped him over to the bench and sat with him. but it was like he didn't see us. He started into the parking lot.

"It was too much. My God."

Childers put a hand on his shoulder. "Boss, are you OK?"

"Yes... I'm fine, it... it was a lot to take in." He stood up. "I'm going to stay out here a bit, get some air. You all head back in.

I stood with him. "Sure boss, that sounds like a good idea. Take your time."

"I'll be in shortly." Twenty minutes later he came back in mostly himself again. He finished out his shift and gave us all a wave as he left, but It was almost a week before he came back."

Dennis was amazed. "Had it done to him what it did to Raymond?"

Zale shook his head. "It never broke him mentally, but I guess it tried. Maybe it came close. From the day he came back he never said another word about what had happened or about 01 at all. He was finished. No more tape recordings, no more research. He had us pack it all up and toss it in the trash. He wouldn't even go down to that end of the hall unless he absolutely had to. He also decided the bookcase wasn't enough of a buffer between us and that little door anymore. He was the one that built the storage room in front of 01's cell. Paid for it out of his own pocket, though I and the other guards handled the construction. Jeffries couldn't get that close. He told us the room was to keep a nosy Warden or inspectors from finding out about our secret border, but we knew different. He couldn't bear to look at it anymore."

Two months after Jeffries conversation with 01 things were back to normal. The storage room was finished and Jeffries was acting like himself again. Joking with the guys, telling his bullshit stories... We were at the table, having our monthly meeting. Jeffries was in a chair halfway down the hall, reading the paper. Childers said something that cracked us all up, Jeffries was about to comment, then he froze. The color ran out of his face. He dropped the paper as if it suddenly caught fire and skittered to his feet, knocking over his chair. Everyone in the room was on their feet in an instant, even the inmates. Burns hurried to Jeffries, ready to catch him if he collapsed, which looked very possible. "Boss, are you O.K.?" Jeffries was looking down the hall at the storage room. "I'm fine." He looked around, more through us than at us. "I think I'm heading home early." Without another word he grabbed his briefcase and headed out the door. We stared after him, baffled but none of us were brave enough to speak up. After he'd gone I picked up the paper.

He'd been reading the article about a factory explosion in Brockton. I don't remember what they made there, but one of the byproducts was apparently very flammable. Through some bit of carelessness a section of the factory exploded, killing five people. I read the entire article, still not understanding what could have caused such a reaction in Jeffries until Childers, who had been reading over my shoulder let out a yelp. "Holy Christ!" Childers was pointing at the bottom of the page, almost jumping up and down. "The names! The fucking names!" I skipped to the end, reading the names of the people murdered in the accident. This time it was like a kick in the stomach. I didn't recognize the first three, but the last two... Betty Gafney. Gary Potts."

Dennis sat up in his chair, shocked. "The names 01 gave Jeffries? Jesus Christ, Zale. Are you telling me on top of everything else this thing is psychic?"

"Son, I don't what It is. But those were the names It gave him. And I bet my life that the numbers It repeated to him were the date of the accident. It didn't matter. Jeffries quit that day. He never set foot in the prison again. He also cut himself off from everyone on E block. After three months of unreturned calls, I decided to pay him a visit at his house. It took him a long time to get to the door and when he finally opened it I couldn't believe what I was seeing. last time I saw him he was a healthy man. A few pounds overweight, but still able to run circles around most guys half his age. The person that opened the door was a skeleton draped in yellow skin. My jaw dropped. I couldn't even speak. Jeffries managed a grin. When he spoke it sounded like his throat was full of glass. "Jesus, that's one hell of a poker face you got there. I knew it was bad. Been avoiding the mirror. Come inside, I can't stand for very long. Hell, I can't do much of anything for very long." We went inside and Jeffries hobbled to his easy chair and collapsed into it. I couldn't stop staring at him."Jeffries, what happened?"

"Lung cancer. Something felt wrong inside ever since the day I... talked to It. I went to the doc a week after I quit. He gave me the news, told me it was treatable, that we caught it early. Three weeks later I go in for a check-up, the doctor comes in the room, and his face looked like yours when I opened the door. He tells me the cancer has spread. I say spread to where? He tells me it's everywhere, that he's never seen Cancer spread that fast. He gave me some powerful pain pills and sent me home. Now I'm just waiting it out." "Why didn't you tell us?" "So you guys could what? Come over here and watch my body eat itself alive? That's not me." "I'm so sorry." "It's fine, I'm ready to go. If the pain gets to be too much I've got enough pills to send myself off. Just do me a favor. Don't come back here. And don't tell the guys. They'll find out soon enough." So I left him and I kept my mouth shut about his illness. A week later he was dead." Dennis looked horrified. "Do you think 01 did that to him?"

"I know it did. They said it was if he had been exposed to massive amounts of radiation. He had been exposed to something, we just couldn't tell them what. Our dirty little secret. Raymond told you it was talking to him. I didn't pay that any attention because I just assumed he'd overheard us one night and decided to use it to his advantage. I should have been more alert. What happened to him and Burns is on me. Because in all the years we've had 01 in our charge I've learned one thing for certain. It's evil. The purest evil you could ever come across, and I've worked on death row for twenty-two years. 01 eventually takes its toll on everyone. The brothers I mentioned, the horse thieves? It only took two days living next to that thing to drive them both insane. One beat his head on the bars until his skull fractured. The other bit open his own wrists. After tearing his veins open with his teeth he crawled to the door of his cell, reaching out towards his brother. I hope it was to say some sort of goodbye and not to try and do the same thing to him. Then there was the summer of '33. According to the inmates that witnessed the event, Two guards, men that had been friends since childhood, were playing a game of cards when they both became convinced that the other was cheating. They were found dead the next morning. They had fought until they tore pieces off each other. The turnover rate for guards is twice as high on E block. There were other instances of short tempers and harsh words over the years, but most times it was diffused by the simple knowledge of why it was happening. Illnesses are higher on average. Those are blamed on the building, old and full of asbestos, but we know different." Zale took a large gulp of beer and slammed the mug down, wiping at his eyes.

"Christ, I hate it so. That fucking..ghoul. just sitting there, day after day, patiently waiting for someone to open the door. I've prayed many times that one day I'll slide that window open and find that thing dead. Finally dead. But that doesn't seem very likely, and times running out."

"What do you mean?"

"I mentioned it on your first night, but I didn't let on just how serious it was. In less than two years the prison is getting an overhaul. That's new mattresses and a paint job for the buildings up on the hill, but it's also a brand new death row." Zale finished off his beer. "E block is getting demolished."

Dennis's eyes widened. "Oh my God.."

Zale grunted. "Exactly. And when they knock down E block, 01 pops out of its cell and Christ knows what happens then. We can't let that play out. As soon as we got the news of the demolition we started going through our options. There's really just one."

"And what's that?" Zale looked hard at Dennis. "I'm putting a lot of trust in you tonight. You now know things some people that worked E Block never knew. But you came through for Burns, and everyone liked you right from the start, which is unusual. What we have planned... if we get caught we'll definitely lose our pensions, maybe serve some jail time. So never a word, not even to the wife, OK?."

"Nothing that was said here tonight will ever be repeated. Especially not to Julia. She'd commit me." Zale let out a small laugh.

"Okay, two weeks before the overhaul, the inmates are being relocated. The entire prison will be cleared out. The Sunday before they come to knock her down, we're going to do a little demolition of our own. Casey has an old Tomcat. We're going to bring it out here and dig a hole under the new foundation lines, cut that son of a bitch's cell right

out of the wall and drop the whole thing inside. Then we're going to cover it in concrete. That thing might never die, but it's not getting out, and it's not going to fuck with anyone else's head."
"Zale, not to be a buzz-kill, but won't the construction crew notice the big hole in the side of the building? What if they decide to investigate?"
"I'm sure they would if there was anything left to see."
Dennis looked worried. "What does that mean?"
"It means we're going to burn E Block to the ground."
"Jesus, Zale."
"It's the only way. It's separated from the rest of the prison, so we shouldn't have to worry about it spreading. The building's over a hundred years old, the wood's so dry it's mostly kindling at this point anyway. It'll be ashes by the time the fire trucks show up from Langdon, and they'll be more concerned with the rest of the prison. With any luck, the whole thing will be written off as a prank that went a little too far. The police aren't going to waste too much time investigating the destruction of a building that was getting knocked down anyway. At least that's what we are hoping for. We talked it out and decided this was the only way to keep 01 contained. And we can retire knowing nobody else ever has to worry about that nightmare again."
Dennis took one last sip of his beer. "Your secret is safe with me. And I know I'm not one of you old-timers, but when you do this, when you bury it, I'd like to help. For what It did to Burns. And to Raymond, as weird as that sounds."
Zale shook his head. "No, it's not weird. Nobody deserves that. We'll do it for Burns, for Raymond, for Jeffries and the countless others that thing has ruined over the years. Now I think we better hit the road, Reggie's been giving us the stink eye for a half hour now." They walked to their cars. Zale gave a nod as he drove out of the parking lot. Dennis watched his taillights drive up the ramp and disappear from view. He thought of the brothers, lying dead side by side in their cells, the guards that had torn themselves to pieces over a card game. But the one that would haunt him was Warden James and his vision of killing his child.

He thought again of his own nightmare, walking towards Little Sean's room, knife in hand. He closed his eyes. "You don't get to do this to anyone else. We're going to put you in the ground." But even then, in the back of his mind, there was doubt.

Calm Before The Storm

1. Another year. It was both uneventful and unremarkable, but when you are working on death row uneventful is not necessarily a bad thing. Not to say it didn't have its ups and downs. A couple of weeks after the ball dropped in time square Gilles went in for a biopsy. He was rightfully on edge until the diagnosis came back benign. The guys on E Block threw him a 'We're glad you're not going to die' party, complete with ice cream and chocolate cake. Gilles was genuinely touched. He hadn't admitted, even to himself, just how scared he had been waiting for that phone call. He tearfully thanked all the guards and by the end of the night, even the inmates were given a piece of cake.

Dennis took his family on vacation to Julia's cousin's in California and little Sean saw the ocean for the first time. They took about a thousand pictures as he ran in and out of the waves, squealing with delight.

A month later Dennis and Julia had an argument that bloomed into a fight that put Dennis on the couch for almost a week with nary a word said between them. It was the worst fight of their marriage and like most, it started with something small and kept alive by pure stubbornness. Dennis was starting to think it could be the beginning of the end of them, as unthinkable as that was. Then a huge summer storm blew through, knocking out the power. Little Sean wouldn't go back to sleep unless all three of them were in the same bed. After he dozed off a heated yet whispered argument ensued for the better part of an hour that ended in tears and apologies on both sides. The war was over.

Zale threw a huge cookout and everyone not on duty was there, families in tow. Everyone fell in love with little Sean, and he reveled in the attention. Julia ended up being the life of the party as she regaled everyone with tales of an angsty teen Dennis. He suffered the embarrassment. She was a damn good storyteller. On the prison side of things, it was business as usual. An inmate on C block sharpened his toothbrush to a point and cut one of his wrists. As soon as he saw the first drop of blood hit the floor he lost it, screaming at the top of his lungs that he was dying. Three stitches later he was fine, and now enjoying monthly conversations with the prison psychiatrist. Another inmate lost an eye in a brawl down in the rec room, retaliation for a stolen Twinkie.

On E Block, orders had been officially passed down- on midnight, December fifteenth Abraham Benedict was sentenced to death in the gas chamber. For his part the usually boisterous man took the news in stride. The appeals had run out, he had been expecting it. In not so official circles, the Guards solidified there strategy to rid themselves of 01, with Dennis now on board. They felt good about their plans, even more so with the inclusion of Dennis. The thought of finally being rid of that demon was more than they had hoped for and it looked like it might actually be a possibility. But at the end of the hall, behind the metal door covered in symbols that originated from another world, 01 sat and waited. If it had ever heard the song it would have told them that life is what happens when you're making other plans. And death. 01 tapped its long fingers on its knees and smiled in the dark. It had plans of its own.

She

1.

She was born over five thousand years ago in the mountains of what is now Afghanistan. She was the youngest of four daughters and even as a child her mother knew she was different. She had the sight, a gift that had skipped several generations but had returned stronger than ever in her. Even as a small child her visions were powerful, as were her nightmares. Almost every night she would dream of a world inhabited by monsters so horrid she couldn't bring herself to describe them and strange symbols scrawled in blood on walls of stone. She tried to ignore the dreams as much as a child could, trying instead to focus on preventing the tragedies she saw in her head.

When she was four she saw her father and his friends attacked by a wild animal while out on a hunt. She begged her father not go hunting with his friends the following morning, but he had never had time for such things as the sight and dismissed her with a laugh, kissing her on the top of the head and telling her not to trust in such foolishness. The hunting party went into the woods at dawn. She stood at the edge of the forest and watched her father and his friends walk into the brush. He turned once and waved to her as he vanished from view. She never saw him again.

Mother was afraid to let others in the clan know of her daughter's visions. She had been told the stories of what could happen to women with the sight, banishment or even death, but the girl would not be silenced. When she was seven she saved several fishermen from a flash flood at the foot of the mountains. Two years later she freed the livestock from their pen before a lightning strike that would have killed them all. In little ways, she helped the clan thrive over the years, and they loved her, even regarded her as a totem, but there was a disaster on the horizon that no vision could protect them from. A drought swept through the foothills and the surrounding plains and her visions could show her no safe place to escape to. The reverence the clan felt for the girl evaporated with the river. Crops died, followed by the livestock. By the second rain-less year, the whispering began. It could be the girls' visions that had angered the Gods, causing them all to be punished. Maybe it was time to return to the old ways. Maybe it was time for a sacrifice.

Mother heard the whispers and knew that her biggest fears were coming to pass. Her oldest daughters had taken mates and moved on years before, and now it was just the two of them. *Easier for just the two of us to run*, she thought as she knelt by her daughter and shook her by the shoulders. The girl, now twelve, woke with a start. Mother pushed her hair from her brow. "We have to go child." The girl sat up, confused. "Go where?"

"I told you that there may come a day the gift that brought you so much love may turn on you. That day has come, child. If we do not leave tonight you may not live to see the sunrise."

Frightened and confused, the girl packed her few belongings, tears in her eyes as they left in the cover of night. As they moved through the fields The girl looked back at the only place she had ever called home. She could see the light of the fires leading into the village, then it was gone, enveloped in the darkness.

2.

They wandered aimlessly at first, staying away from traveled roads. Mother taught her how to track and hunt, and they rarely went a day without full bellies, and the girl's visions kept them safe from potential dangers that may have crossed their path. Mother kept them on the move for fear of settling long enough for her daughter's gift being discovered. Their time on the road was long and over the years the girl had become a beautiful woman, far from the hills where she had spent the best part of her life. And then another tragedy no vision couldn't prevent. Mother fell ill. It began with a cough that turned to fever and after a few weeks she had lost any craving for food or drink. Before long they were only able to travel one or two hours a day before her mother was spent. Mothers illness worsened until she was unable to move from her bed. In the end she couldn't speak. She sat by her mothers side, her tears falling on the thin hide blanket they had slept in. Her mother looked up at her through the delirium, smiling as she touched her daughters face. She closed her eyes and she was gone. She buried her mother in a nearby field, cutting through the snow and hard pack with a sharp piece of shale, hands bloody as she lowered her into the ground. The thought of traveling the world without her mother filled her with sadness and despair. She wandered the roads, lost, using her skills to keep her alive and fed, barely, drifting wherever her instinct took her, unaware that she was being followed.

3.

He had been tailing her for weeks now, ever since he witnessed what had happened with the boy. He had been at a small trading post, haggling with a merchant over a hunk of meat when he saw her. She had his complete attention even before she did the impossible. She was tall and slim, jet black hair pulled back in a loose ponytail with a strip of animal hide. Her large brown eyes were wary and alert and more than a little sad. She was about to pass by when she stopped mid-stride, staring unblinking into the distance. He watched this with growing interest. The merchant noticed her strange behavior and was about to ask her if she was alright but the man silenced him. Just then she turned and sprinted back the way she came, the man following but keeping his distance. There was a boy of about three strolling in the middle of the dirt path, his mother picking flowers a few feet away. She sprinted for the boy, grabbing him into her arms and diving into the high grass on the side of the road. A instant later an ox being led up the road by an old man broke free of its restraints and charged up the path, right where the boy had been standing. The man ducked into a small crowd of onlookers, processing what he had just seen. She saved the boy before there was anything to save him from. He could hardly contain his excitement. He had seen something similar years before in a village far to the south. He had been mesmerized by an old man that would stare into nothing just like the woman did before telling you things about your past he could not possibly know. He had thought about that old man often as he traveled, what he could do with a gift like that. And now this woman... his mind flooded with possibilities. It would take some time but he wouldn't let this opportunity slip away. She had the sight and he planned on using it to his advantage.

So he followed her, observing. Learning. She was alone and lonely, he surmised by the way she looked at families that passed her by on the road, she had lost someone recently. the. She was wary of men traveling alone, as she should be. He wondered how long she had been alone on the road, it seemed like a long time, and she was wise to its trappings. He would have to take this slow. He set up his camp a respectful distance from hers, but close enough that he heard her shrieks in the middle of the night and the weeping that sometimes followed. Bad dreams. Very bad, from the sound of it. After a month he figured he had gathered enough information and decided to befriend the woman, using his own special gift-charm. He approached her camp, hands slightly raised. She was on her feet in an instant, taking a defensive posture. He said in his best befuddled voice, "I am sorry, it is just that I have not eaten in three days and the smell of the rabbit was too much to ignore. May I trade you some flint for a small piece of meat? If I am disturbing you I will be on my way." She softened when he mentioned the food. She broke a quarter off the animal and handed it to the man. "Here, I have gone hungry and I would not wish it on anyone. No trade, it is yours."

"Thank you so much. You have saved me." they were fast friends after that. As they walked together he took a calculated risk and told her of his family and how they had died in a fire (a lie, he never knew his family) and how he had terrible nightmares as a child (also a lie). She responded immediately to his tales of loss and they became fast Friends. As they traveled she taught him to hunt, a skill he had never learned and only feigned interest at learning. After a few months on the road together their friendship turned into more. One Spring night as they laid naked under the stars she told him that she loved him and he said the same(not a lie, at least not completely) She felt happiness again as she gazed at the night sky or walked the long roads, no longer alone. But there was a small voice in her head telling her happiness was fleeting and this would end in blood. When the voice came to her in the dark she would push it down, holding him tighter as the clouds wove their way through the night sky.

4.

Some time they had professed their love to each other, she confessed to him what he had already known, and he sat in manufactured wonder as she told him of her power and listened with genuine apprehension as she told him of escaping her village in the middle of the night before they could sacrifice her to the old Gods.

This presented a problem for him. His grand plan was to set her up as the shaman, reaping the fortunes her celestial protection would offer. And now to discover her visions had almost cost her her life. She would never agree to his plan. But he had always been a quick thinker and in a flash of inspiration made a slight alteration to the plan that would make it safe enough for her and doubly beneficial for him. Fall eased into particularly brutal winter. One night, as the wind whipped snow and ice against the lean-to they had built and the chill persisted no matter how many pelts they covered themselves in, he told her of the great idea that had just come to him- to find a prosperous village and there present himself as a shaman, offering visions she would relay to him. She was trepidatious to say the least. He argued, gently, that by doing this they could finally leave the road and find a permanent home and eventually start a family. It was the thought of a family that allowed him to wear her down. With the small voice still protesting, she agreed to his suggestion. The following year they came upon the perfect place.

5.

The village lay in the shadow of a large mountain range. There were several well-constructed huts set back from the river, children running and laughing through fields being prepared for sowing. She fell in love with it immediately. It reminded her of her home and she felt a calm here she didn't even know she had been missing. Her mate took her hand and led her through the curious villagers. They reached the elders and he bowed deeply. She followed suit. He clapped his hands behind his back and addressed the leader of the clan. "It is fortuitous that we have come to your village when we did. Fortunate for us to have the pleasure to meet such a powerful and worldly people. And for you, because I too am very powerful. A shaman known along the western borders and beyond." There were some awed murmurs. Many had heard of shamans but had never actually seen one. He smiled at her, then turned to the clan leader and said something that dashed any sense of calm away in an instant. "If you allow me and my mate seven days here in your village, I will prove my worth to you. In that time we will break bread with you, sleep in your bed, enjoy your company. If in seven days, I have not had a vision that will benefit your people, then you may do with us as you will. She looked around, trying to hide her panic. Many of the men in the clan, including the leader, were eyeing her. She knew how she looked, had faced her share of eager men on the road, but this she never expected... to be put in that kind of danger by her own mate.. He looked her, smile still on his face, as if he didn't know in a week's time he could be killed and she would be raped. Sometimes months would pass before she had a vision and she had told him this. Still, he smiled. The clan's leader stood and looked out at his people. He then turned and nodded back to them and nodded. "I accepted your bargain, Shaman." A cheer went up from the village and in no time a celebration had begun in honor of the new mystic.

6.

Later that night they lay in their temporary bed of straw in a hut given to them by a farmer hoping that letting a Shaman sleep in his home would give him good luck. She stared at the wall for a long time until be could no longer be silent. She turned to him for the first time in anger. "Why?" Why would you promise such things to them?"

He continued to look at the ceiling, seemingly unaware of her ire. "I have a version of the sight myself and it told me the leader of this village would never have agreed to let us stay without an exchange. Everything will be fine."

"How can it be? I told you that I can not force the visions, they come to me when they choose."

"You also told me that you have never truly tried. I think that if you tried hard enough you will be able. And what better place to try than in this luxury. And if by the sixth day no visions come... we leave. We wait for nightfall and run awa-"

In her mind she was suddenly back in her village, her mother frantically gathering their few belongings as they prepared to run. Years on the road.

"No!" She sat up, now full of rage. He backed up, a little afraid. "My days of running are over. I will find a way."

He smiled again, touching her hair. "I knew that you would. It is what you do my love. You save people." He turned over and went to sleep. She stared at the back of his head, anger boiling. Yes, she saved people. This time the people she had to save were the two of them. She stayed up for a long time, staring into the dark, scared, angry but mostly sad because today she learned that she couldn't trust the man she had chosen to be with.

The next morning she began in earnest attempting something she had never done and was almost sure was impossible. She sat in the shadow of the mountains. She cleared her mind and waited. For two days she sat there, listening to the river, to the birds signaling each other, praying to her Gods for even the smallest vision. Nothing came.

By the fifth night, her panic had increased to the point where she could no longer concentrate. That small voice in the back of her mind began to scream for her to run, and she contemplated it for a moment before shaking it off. She had been on borrowed time for years. No matter what happened, she would face it. After all, there were much worse places to die. With that she laid down, resigned. As she closed her eyes and drifted off she saw the river that flowed past this village. Children splashed at the shore, chasing each other as their mothers smiled at their antics. Several people were filling basins, further down others were bathing. As one of the women scooped water in the basin it turned black. Suddenly Large tendrils of dark liquid began to snake through the water until the entire river was black as ink. The clay basins began to break open, the black water smoking as it hit the sand. The children playing in the water began to fall onto the shore, their skin dissolving. Their mothers ran to the river to help them, but all that remained were bones lodged in the rocks. She bolted up from her bed, shaking the images from her mind. She was both horrified and relieved as she woke her mate. She had finally had a vision.

7.

Early the next morning the elders of the village were summoned. The 'shaman' strutted for his audience, a look of severity on his face. He threw open his arms. "My new friends, I have received a vision. There is a danger to the entire tribe, young and old, powerful and weak! The river has been poisoned. To drink from it will bring sickness and eventually death." A murmur drifted through the elders. The woman looked at her mate, confused. She had told him of the children and black water but mentioned nothing of poison. An older man stood. "I drank from the river this morning and I am not sick, and as most can see I am also not dead." There was laughter from the villagers. The prospective shaman ignored the snickering. The leader of the tribe raised a hand, silencing the crowd. "How do we prove what you say is true? The shaman nodded. " The proof will reveal itself this very night. I am sorry to say but anyone that drank from the river this morning will be sick by nightfall. More murmurs, louder this time. The shaman raised his hands. "Do not fear, you may get sick, but you will not die. I sense that the poison that is corrupting the river is not yet strong enough to kill. But by tomorrow.. we must act fast. With your permission I will lead a party to find the source of this corruption!' There was talk among the elders, mostly doubtful, but after the conference, the leader nodded. "You may take five men to search for this poison. Pray that you find it." They left immediately, striking a path upriver. She watched her mate disappear into the woods, a nervous rumble in her stomach. What was he playing at? As the day progressed no one went near the water and just as he had predicted, as the sun began it's decent a few people began to fall ill. Fear began to sweep through the village. What would they drink? Or give to the livestock? There was no other source for miles. She tried to calm them, but the unease grew with their thirst. Her mother's voice was in her head from so long ago, telling her it was time to leave, that the village had turned. Then, laughter coming from the woods. Her mate and the other villagers burst through the trees, smiling. One of the men that had traveled with the shaman clapped him on the back. "He was right!

A bison had been killed a few miles upstream and had fallen in the river. It was rotting. It would have killed many. He saved us."

The leader stood and faced his people. "It seems we have a true mystic among us! Let us welcome him and his mate into our tribe! Tonight, a celebration!" The shaman and his mate were hugged and praised, and the party in their honor went late into the night.

When they finally lay down the new shaman drifted off almost immediately. She watched him for a long time before nudging him awake. He looked her with one cocked eye, not a hundred percent sure where he was. "What happened?"

"I want to know why you told them it was poison."

"What?"

"You told the village the river was poisoned. I never said that. How did you know?"

"I suppose that I just interpreted it that way. The black water sounded like poison to me." He closed his eyes.

"You seemed convinced. Like you knew for certain. You led the men like you knew just where to go."

He opened his eyes, sighing. " I took precautions."

"Precautions?"

"As we made our way here we passed a freshly killed bison. On our first night here, after everyone went to sleep I went back to that spot. It was very ripe by then. I pushed it into the river. And I'm glad I did. If not you would have had nothing to tell them and then where would we be."

She sat on the edge of the bed, stupefied. "You- you were willing to poison these people, to kill them-"

"It was not going to kill them. Because you saw it coming, as I knew you would."

"Gods...and if I did not see it? Then what?"

"Then I would have had a vision of my own. But because of your gift, I was able to tell them the exact day the sickness would come. It was the detail that helped convince them."

"I can not believe that you are so-"

"I am done talking about this. I am done talking tonight. And before you speak to me that way again remember where you are and who brought you here. Unless you would like to give up this bed for a muddy field by the side of the road."

He turned over, leaving her to stare at his back. Her eyes filled with tears and she angrily wiped them away. She was done running and she was done crying.

She was trapped here. She could spoil the ruse by ignoring any visions she may have, but that would put the people of the village in danger, people that she had already begun to love. No, she would stay and play her part. She would be happy despite

8.

Over the following year, she had made a nice life for herself in the village. For the first time in a long time, she felt a part of something. She had two visions during that first year, both involving dangerous storms. Her nightmares of creatures and strange symbols continued, leading to her mate's decision to sleep in a separate hut. It suited her fine. They had become more and more distant. He drank until dawn with the leader of the village most nights and had taken a girl from the village as his second. That suited her as well. Let him climb on top of her in the middle of the night, panting and smelling of fermented fruit. She still very much wanted a child of her own but had come to realize that it may never happen. Instead of lamenting this, she adopted the children of the village, teaching them the ways of her old tribe. They took to her quickly and she found that teaching came easy to her. One afternoon, as she showed her small class how weave baskets she felt a wave of nausea. She sat down on a rock, head spinning. One of her students asked her if she was alright but she didn't hear him. She was witnessing the end of the world. In her vision, the village was going about its normal routine. It was colder, early fall. She looked down and was shocked to see that she was quite pregnant. She touched her stomach, marveling at the tightness of it. She barely had time to enjoy this amazing development when she heard the sound of horses, dozens of them, rapidly approaching. They were charging across the river, their riders carrying spears. She watched as they rode through the village, killing every man, taking the women and children. They set fire to the huts as they rode out. There was no one left standing as they headed back across the river, and as she watched this one of the riders veered toward her, trampling her before rejoining his men. The feel of the hooves coming down on her stomach broke her trance. She stared around at the children as if she had never seen them before. She clutched her now flat belly. "I have to talk to the shaman, children, we will learn more tomorrow." She left the confused children and sprinted to her mate's hut. She snatched open the door and as she began to tell him what she had seen, she heard yelling. And hoof beats. The shaman sat up, alarmed.

"What is it?"

She looked back the way she had come. On the other side of the river the horsemen from her vision came riding in. She felt the strength run out of her legs. "No...it was to be months from now.. " The shaman burst through the door, going pale as he watched the riders growing closer.

"By the Gods. Run. Run!" He shoved her out of the way and ran for the woods, not waiting to see if she followed. She stumbled after him, in shock as the horses moved closer. She made it to the woods just before a horseman tore down the path. She hid behind a fallen log and was happy to see some of the others had made it as well, but there were so few of them. She couldn't see what was happening from where she was hiding, but she didn't need to. The vision was still very clear. *Why would it show me what I had no chance of preventing?* The attack was over in minutes. When the sound of the retreating horses had faded to nothing, people began to walk out of the woods. It was different than her vision. First, there were bodies, but thankfully very few. Women and children were gone, but again not all of them like her vision. Some of the women that had managed to hide were weeping as they called for their sons and daughters. She wept as well, for the first time furious at her visions. The leader appeared, covered in blood, most of it not his own. Unlike her mate, he had fought during the raid. He caught sight of his shaman and he ran at him. The shaman stood petrified as the leader grabbed him by the throat and lifted him off the ground. "What do you have to say about this mystic! You live in luxury in my village and in return you repay that debt by warning us of the coming danger! Where was our warning? One of my mates was taken! Maybe I should take one of yours now, and put your head on a pike as a warning to others that fail me!" The shaman was sputtering, trying to speak. The leader dropped him on the ground. Clutching his throat, he wheezed out a reply. "I beg you, please spare my life. The vision did come, but it was delayed... the horsemen must have a shaman of their own. It clouded my visions but now I am aware of him and I can rebuke his magics. I can find their village and we can get your mate and everyone else back safe."

She stood a few feet away, marveling at the lies he spun, how easy they fell from his mouth. *Did I fall into his trap as we traveled the road? Lulled by his words? Was I that foolish?* With growing anger, she thought she may have been. The leader, still furious, weighed his options. With a grunt of disgust, he stepped back from the shaman. "You have until nightfall to show me a way to my people. If you fail me again I take your head." The leader stormed off, the rest of the village began helping the wounded and burying the dead. The shaman went to his hut. She followed. As soon as she stepped inside he grabbed her, slapping her across the face and throwing her to the floor. "What are you trying to do, get us both killed!" He hissed as he stood over her, fists clenched. She was on her feet in an instant, the image of her swollen belly flashing through her mind. She swung at him, barely missing as he dodged, falling back against the wall. She leaped at him and felt a grim satisfaction as he recoiled in fear. "You will not touch me ever again. Or you will get no more help from me." He laughed with false bravado. "Help? Like today? You have ruined us here. I'm leaving. If we can make it back to the trees we will have a-"

"I told you before I am done running. But please, go. They will kill you before you made it a thousand feet."

"Then what is it you suggest we do, great mystic!"

"I suggest we find the horsemen."

You told me many times that you cannot make the visions come-"

"No vision. We track them. It rained the past four days. There were twelve of them on horseback. They left a trail an infant could follow, something our leader should have seen but his reliance on you and his rage has dulled his instincts. We go now with a pair of scouts, find their village. Then we can plan from there."

He looked at her as if he had never really seen her before. "Yes, that may work. I will inform the elders."

"There is something else you should tell them. The vision I had was not about the raid today.

"Then when was it?"

"They come back in a few months. They burn the village down. No one lives the next time."

"How do you know when they come back?"

"Because in my vision I am about to give birth."

He looked at her surprised, then nodded. "If we find them today then we will not have to worry about that happening." He looked quickly at her belly then left the hut. She watched him for a moment then began to tremble, falling to her bed, weeping. She was not done crying yet, it seemed

9.

An hour later she and the shaman were moving through the woods, escorted by three soldiers, though she was not sure if they were there to protect them or detain them. Probably both. Even when the horseman had attempted to cover their tracks, she could follow the path with ease. Out on the hunt like this reminded her of her mother and their time on the road, learning her valuable skills. She smiled at the memories of her mother, but it also hurt so much. She brought the small party to the horsemen s village a little after dawn. *Now I see why the rid-*

ers were so careless in covering their retreat. The village was enormous, horses and men outnumbering their own three to one. Several of the men were training in combat with a variety of weapons. Attacking these people would be suicide, they were far too strong. She looked around at the men that had escorted them here and saw the same look on all their faces. They made their way back. The scouts filled the elders in on what they had seen. The leader sat in his chair, defeated. His anger diffused.

"You are absolved, shaman. If you had warned us of the attack and we had dealt real damage to them, the retaliation would have wiped us out entirely. Maybe that is why the vision came so late."

Maybe it was, she thought. *Maybe I was shown the second raid as a warning not to attack.*

The leader shook his head. "We have lost many today, living and dead. It is best we forget and try to rebuild with what we have left."

Suddenly the shaman stood. "If I may... I know a direct attack is not possible, but we might be able to win despite our numbers. To save the women and the children."

The leader laughed. "How? You saw it with your own eyes. They are superior."

"Let me consult the Gods, I may find a way." The shaman left the group. She watched him go, wondering what new danger he was dropping them into now.

Late that night there was a knock at her door. Before she could answer her mate walked in. She looked at him, on the defensive. He smiled at her, something he hadn't done in a long time. Like he had during their time on the road. "I would like to ask you a few questions. Is that alright?" She said nothing. He took it as consent. "Everything you have seen in your visions has come true, yes? Has proven real?"

She nodded, still wary. "Yes."

"Yes." He sat next to her, closer than he had been in some months, his smile even wider this time. It was disturbing. "I know you hate to think about them, but your nightmares... Could the nightmares might also be visions. Could the monsters be real as well?"

She had often asked herself the same thing after she had one of the nightmares.they seemed so real, the smells, the feel of it. She would on occasion wake with scratches or bruises, injuries she had assumed she inflicted on herself in the throes of the horrors she was seeing in her mind. But the dirt.. Sometimes, not always but sometimes after a particularly bad dream, when she sat in her bed shaking and drenched in sweat she would look down to find her hands and feet peppered with a damp, black soil. The same soil covering the mountains in the colorless graveyard world she visited so often. She closed her eyes shaking the memory with an effort.. "I do not want to believe it. But yes. They may be. Why do you ask me this?"

He stood and started pacing, then physically stopped himself. He sat down again, taking her hand. "Because, if the demons in your dreams are real, we may be able to bring one of them here to save us." She snatched her hand out of his, recoiling. She involuntarily shuddered at the thought of it. She looked at him in disbelief. "Over the past year, I have come to think of you as extremely reckless and even possibly a fool. But I was wrong. You are not a fool. You are mad. *Nothing* could ever make me bring one of those things to this place. To the people I love. And even if I were insane enough to do such thing how would it be possible?"

"Please just- just listen to me." No screaming. No anger, just the smooth talker she had met those years ago. "You told me every time you dream of the monsters you also see symbols, drawn in blood?"

"Yes, but-"

"These symbols are something I have thought about often. It reminded me of stories I have been told of the old magics. And if that is true then the symbols could be the way to summon them."

She shook her head, horrified. "You have no idea what you are saying. These things... Nothing I have told you can truly describe them. Nothing I could say could let you know how it feels to be near them, to smell them, the dread they emit from their hides . And you want to bring them here."

"I have felt fear, several times. Right here in this village. You said no more running, that these people are your family. I too want to stay, watch our child grow up." He touched her belly. She recoiled slightly at this. He continued. "But if what you told me in your vision is true, we all die. Is that what you want? To watch everything you love destroyed? Or taken as slaves or worse? The leader has made his decree. The clan will not run. So our choices here are few. In the old magics, the symbols could summon a beast and they could also control it. We can bring one of the beasts here, have it kill the others before they kill us all, then send it back where it came from. We would be free. For all you know, you have been dreaming of the monsters all these years for this very reason." He got on his knees in front of her. "All I want you to do is think about it. Think of these children and our child. If you decide to help me, let me know." He kissed her hand and stood, leaving the hut.

She sat on the edge of her bed for some time, mind reeling. She never thought anyone would ask such a thing of her, and she never thought in a thousand lifetimes that she would consider it. Her mother told her the stories of the old clans and the witches that protected them. Her family was descendants of one such clan, her visions a gift passed down in their blood. In the stories, the witches were able to control creatures they summoned out of the dark. Her vision had shown her death, but no solution. Now she had been given a possibility. Her entire life she had shied away from the horrors in those dreams. Now if she decided to do this she would have to immerse herself in the dreams, to try and remember every detail. What frightened her the most was that deep down she thought her mate might be right. As much as the thought scared her, it excited her too. The next time I dream, I will see if I can remember. A test. She laid down and after an hour of tossing and turning she fell asleep. She didn't have to wait long to begin her test, two nights later she had a nightmare.

10.

For the first time in her life, she didn't shy from the images that had terrified her for so many years. She was back in a world that felt wrong in every way, where even the sky was difficult to look at. As she concentrated on her surroundings she realized with revulsion that she was actually looking through the eyes of one of the countless creatures that swam around her in the thick, steamy water. She looked down at arms now twice the length of her own, pale and wrinkled. She was filled with a horror that bordered on madness but she stayed in the moment. She could feel them in her(It's) mind as well, a thousand pieces of conversation, none of it decipherable, but she felt that if she tried, she could communicate, not that she had any intention of doing that. Instead, she stretched out her new long arms and with a little effort, she moved the body she was inhabiting to the edge of the bubbling pool. There was an altar sitting amid piles of bones. Several small six-legged animals had been sliced open, their blood used to scrawl several symbols on the stone. Looking at them she was surprised at how familiar they were to her, and that with a minimal effort she could suss their meaning. *The monster I am traveling in knows what they mean, so I do too. This may not take as long as I had once feared*, she thought as she began to memorize as many symbols as she could. Suddenly a slight itch bloomed at the base of her skull and began to grow. She heard a buzzing in her head and she involuntarily pulled back. Suddenly she was awake, trembling. She shook off her disorientation quickly wrote down as many symbols and definitions as she could remember. When she was done she sat back, looking them over. There were many, but it was like a puzzle with several key pieces missing. She would have to endure many more dreams, but now she knew that as deceiving as her mate could be, he was right about this. When she had all the symbols she could bring the beast here, and she could control it.

The next morning she showed her mate. He was elated. "This is just from one night?"

"Yes. But this is only a small part of-"

"But you can do it. And you know what they mean! This is wondrous. It means we will have a power no one can match. We can destroy the other clan with ease."

"And save our people."

"Yes, above everything. Save our people." A year ago she would have believed that. Not because he would have meant it, but because she had still been blinded to his ways. No more. She was here for her clan and for the baby growing inside her.

11.

Over the next few months, she continued as she always had in the village. She taught the children, fished in the river and helped with planting crops and the rebuilding of storm-damaged huts, as much as her expanding belly would let her. At night she pored over the symbols, and two or three nights a month she had the dreams. She had gotten quite adept at navigating the borrowed body and had intuited that the sensation at the base of her skull was a warning. They were aware of her now and were cutting the connection sooner and sooner, but as far she could tell she was in no danger. By the end of summer, the symbols covered two walls of her hut. She knew she had the symbols that could bring the creature here and send it back, but she still missing the keywords that would keep It under control while It was in this world. As summer turned to fall the old worries began to creep back. There were still symbols to collect and the dreams had, for the first time in her life, ceased. It had been almost a month and a half since her last, and she was anxious. *I would never have imagined I would feel anything but joy that those dreams had stopped*, she thought and then, *maybe They stopped them. The monsters. They found a way to keep me out.* She thought of telling her mate but swatted that away. He would just take what she had and present it to the elders, hoping for the best, and it just was not enough. She sat in front of her wall of alien language, running her hand over the swirls and lines. She read over the incantations that would bring the creature here. It was very similar to the one that would send it back. Just the rearrangement of a few lines and swirls. Going on instinct she changed the verbiage, for lack of a better word, on one incantation and stood back. She read the last two altered words aloud and felt a jolt pass through her. For a split second, she was back in the pool. She sat on the bed, heart pounding. The mingled fear and excitement was back. *I can send my mind, my* spirit, *to the pool just like in my dreams.* But even with that short blip to the pool, she knew it wasn't anything like visiting that world in a dream. It was real and escape might not be as easy as just waking up. But there was no choice. The raiders would be back in a week, maybe two, to finish her clan for good. To kill her child. She stood at the wall and took a deep breath. She read the incantation in full. Everything was different. For the first time in all her visits here she could feel the heat of the water she floated in and it was almost unbearable. And the itch at the top of her spine began immediately, the buzzing so loud it felt like her head was full of wasps. She cried out with a voice that had rarely if ever been used, a dry twisted croak. She and tried to maneuver to the edge of the pool, but the pain and confusion were so intense she could barely control the beast she was inhabiting. With all her will she moved toward the familiar altar. As she moved she noticed something very alarming. The creatures that had been pressed against her at every turn since her first visit here were gone. She looked around and noticed that they had backed away, forming a circle around her. They followed her with their eyeless faces, mouths unhinged and drooling. She slowly continued toward the altar, the circle moving with her. There were three more symbols to memorize, she could see them down in the corner of the altar, still too far to see clearly. The circle was tightening now, she could hear the wet sound of their breathing as they moved in. She decided it was now or never. She leaped into the air, surprising many of the creatures as she sailed over their heads. Her borrowed vessel landed with a thud on the altar. She could hear the others moving towards her, gnashing their teeth. She reached the symbols she was looking for and as she did she felt the first of those long fingers grabbing at her. She struggled to read the lines as the hands pulled her away. She felt the cuts opening on this body as if it were her own as they scratched and bit at her. Now she began to struggle inside as well as the consciousness she was sharing awoke and turned Its fury on her for the first time. It showed her images, letting her know that if she stayed in the body she would be eaten alive, and the creature she was invading would welcome if it meant It would be rid of her. She read the last symbol, using the monster she was inside to help her remember. As she read she felt the first bites, chunks of flesh being torn from her. She cried out as she experienced the enjoyment the monster felt at her agony. She closed her eyes, ready to leave this place of nightmares for the last time. The creatures had swarmed her now, bloody pieces of her(It) dropping onto the altar as they bit into her. As she sunk into the pain she tried to remember the words that would send her back. With the last of her strength, she thought at the beast, *I will not come back..I swear it. I swear.* She uttered the incantation with that alien voice and was gone. In an instant she was in her bed, Soaked through and covered in a hundred cuts, skin blistered and steaming form the pool. She writhed in pain, falling to the floor, unable to cry out. She felt herself fading away and with the last of her strength drew the symbols on the dirt floor. She passed out and knew nothing for the next three days.

12.

She opened her eyes, disoriented. She was in her bed. She tried to move but it felt like every muscle in her body was being stung or- She remembered the attack and froze. Her first thought was the baby. She clutched her belly and felt some relief. The child was safe. She appraised herself. The cuts(bites) were healing nicely, the redness from the boiling water almost gone, but mentally she was drained. And she realized something else. She was terrified. After experiencing what those creatures truly were, she decided that she couldn't bring one of Them into her world. Not for a second. There would have to be another option. Some battles could not be won and maybe they were not meant to rescue the ones they had lost. She called out and her favorite pupil, a girl of 13, appeared at the door. The girl rushed in to help. "I was so worried. I am glad you are finally awake!" They embraced and the child helped her stagger to her feet. "Call for the shaman, child, I must talk with him."

"I will but he is with the elders." Her legs gave out upon hearing that. She scanned the floor, looking for marks. *Did I write the last ones down?*

Please, please say I did not. She headed for the door, the child supporting most of her weight at first. "Do you know why he is with the elders?" She asked but she feared she already knew the answer. "The shaman says he has the final symbols. We can go into battle and bring my mother back!" She smiled at the girl, trying to conceal her fear. She made her way across the village and found her mate laughing loudly as he stood among the elders, the celebrations already begun despite the early hour. He saw her and clapped his hands together, spilling some of his wine in the process. "You are awake! We were wondering when the poison from the thorns would pass from your blood. I told them you had taken quite a fall into the brambles while we were collecting firewood." She sent the girl on her way, standing on her own now. "Yes, I fell much better. May I speak with you?"

"You may." They walked down to the river. As they made their way she saw a group of men making a replica of the altar from her dreams. *Of course it is exact*, she thought, *I gave them every detail. What have I done?* She sat on a stump, legs still shaky. She looked up at him. "You gave them the symbols."

"That was our plan, was it not?"

"It was. But that last time I went to the that place it was not a dream. I used the symbols to send my self and I saw them, truly saw them. Felt Their desires and thoughts and rage without the veil of the dream to protect me." She pulled up her sleeve, revealing several cuts. "Until I felt the joy they took in doing this to me and one of their own. Imagine what They would do if we brought one of Them here." He began to pace, the old petulance back as he turned on her. "If you had decided this then why did you write down the last symbols?" "Out of habit, I suppose. If you were not aware, I almost died for them. I do not remember writing them down."

"I was aware. And I thought that if you *did* die it would not be for nothing because you had finished the puzzle. So I took them to the elders and tonight we have our revenge." "You are not listening to me, these things are-"

"I do not care!" he screamed, fists clenched. He looked around to see if he had been heard, but the river had muffled his outburst. He lowered his voice, but the anger was still there. "I told the elders I would find a way to fix this and I found it. And when I summon that powerful force here and use it to destroy their enemies and save their people it will be me they all look to as a leader. As *the* leader."

A horrifying revelation came over her. She felt the sting of embarrassment. *He has played me again. And I fell for it without even a struggle.* She looked at him, full of rage. "This is the real reason you came to me that night. You wanted this from the beginning, so you could take control of the clan." Then, an unimaginable thought crossed her mind. "You have no intention of sending It back, do you?"

He looked at her as if she had lost her mind. "Why would I arm myself with the strength of the Gods and then just throw it away?" She spat out a bitter laugh, holding her head in her hands. "I should not be surprised by your behavior. Disgusted, yes, but not surprised. I will not let you do this."

He smiled at her, though it looked more like an animal baring its teeth. How would you stop me? Because... I am having a vision of my own now. Yes, a terrible vision. The child my mate is carrying is not mine, but the child of one of the horsemen that took our people. She has been in secret counsel with them all along. That is how they knew where to find us. Now, what do you think would happen to you and your baby if I gave the elders such a revelation."

"It is your baby too." His smile faded at that. He turned from her."Go lie down. You look pale. And when you wake the village will have a new leader." As he moved to leave she grabbed a hunk of driftwood from the river bank with the intention of bashing in his skull, but as she began her charge at him a sharp pain shot through her abdomen. She dropped the wood, and stood still, holding her belly. It was still days from her time but women had given birth early, she had seen it in her old village. Usually, the child did not live. She made her way to her hut, unable to control her tears. She laid down and slept deeply for several hours.

13.

She awoke to the sound of cheers. Groggy, she made her way out of the hut into the darkness. The elders, surrounded by the rest of the village, were watching the shaman as he stood on the now completed altar. He was in the middle of a speech, and oh how he loved the sound of his own voice. He pranced back and forth in front of the altar, soaking in the praise. "And so tonight we will take back what belongs to us! And the men responsible will be punished a thousandfold!"

More cheers, even the leader himself looked enthralled. *He has them all believing his lies*, she thought. *They are half ready to take him as their new leader right now.* Again, she was not surprised. She had been taken by his words once upon a time. He stopped the pacing then and became somber. He looked out at the crowd. "But as we know, this is the old magics. Blood magic. *Death* magic. And that requires a sacrifice." She took a step back, teeth bared. Her mother flashed through her mind, telling her the villagers had turned, that they wanted blood. *You bastard*, she thought, *Come for me and my child and we will see who spills their blood tonight.* But it wasn't her the shaman wanted, it was far worse. He gestured and one of her students, the little girl that had helped her earlier today was brought to the altar. The shaman raised his hands. "This girl has offered her blood to save her mother and all the mothers that were taken!" More cheers. One look at the girl was enough to know she did not offer herself freely. She was in clearly petrified. Her tears began to fall again. *He chose her because of me. Because I made the mistake of telling him what she meant to me. He is as much a monster as the thing he intends to bring here.* She looked at the crowd, at the hunger on their faces. It had been many years since the old magics had been practiced, but the lust was always there, under the surface. If she tried to stop this she would be torn to pieces along with the girl, and if it were her alone she would still make the attempt, but the baby, the baby... The crowd had begun to chant as the child was laid on the altar. She looked at their excited, anxious faces and felt hatred for these people she wouldn't have thought possible. The shaman revealed a large blade to the awe of the villagers. She had seen enough. She said a prayer for her student and did something she vowed she would never do again. She ran. There was a cave some miles from the village, she had discovered it months ago while out tracking elk. She made her way there now, stumbling through the dark as she moved further from her home. Even a half a mile away she heard the screams of the child as they took her life and then the low rumble of the clan chanting, the old ways following her on the wind. She stumbled again, this time falling down and as she did another sharp pain shoot through her. She touched her stomach, fearful. She stood and continued. The pains now coming closer and closer. Far behind her, she heard something that could only have been the sounds of slaughter. Dozens of people screaming. He did it. He brought that thing into the world and It killed them all. *I guess things didn't go as planned.* She walked for hours, slow and careful. The pain was almost unbearable. It was still dark as she reached the cave. She laid down on the cold stone, gritting her teeth through the agony. It was time. She cried out, pulling her legs up. though she had been very young she had sat with her sister during her time, and she knew what was coming, but her sister had all the women of the tribe with her. She was alone. *It cannot be helped*, she thought and readied herself. The pain was enormous, worse even than the creatures tearing at her flesh, but it was mercifully quick and as she heard a little cry the pain was forgotten. She took the girl, small but seemingly healthy to her breast, cutting the umbilical cord with a piece of shale. As she held her child she felt another pain go through her. She felt scared and elated when she realized what was happening. As the eastern sky began to brighten she finally fell asleep, her twin daughters in her arms. As the exhaustion took her she heard a sound, a light buzzing. Bees in the cave, she would smoke them out in the morning, but the sound grew louder. Then a sensation she had never had, at least not in this world. She felt the gnawing itch at the base of her skull. She was up in an instant, setting the babies aside and limping toward the mouth of the cave. There was light in the sky, but not enough to see the beast until was too late and it was very close now. She thought of the symbols and to her horror, she realized that the incantations were jumbled in her head and she could not grasp what many of them meant anymore. *I think It took the knowledge from me in the pool*, she thought, *I can not send It back, but I may be able to ward us from It.* She looked around for anything she could scrawl the symbols with, the only thing that would spare her and her children from certain death. Then she smiled as the answer came to her. *It is blood magic after all*. She reached between her legs, using her blood of her children's birth to draw the warding symbols at the entrance of the cave. Not death magic this time but *life* magic. She put the same symbols on her children's foreheads and her own bare chest. As she did the itch died away. Moments later she heard a skitter of rocks and turned. It had arrived. It stared at her, grinning. She looked at the beast, unable to move. She saw several healing bite marks across Its hide and with horror realized this was the vessel she had used to attain the symbols, the very symbols that brought It here. And It knew she was the reason. In the end she did not open the door that brought it here, but she had stolen the key. It took a step inside the cave, then another. She moved in front of her sleeping babies, defiant. She would die fighting for their lives. The thing from her nightmares tried to take another step and It stopped. it was as if it had hit a wall. It stretched Its arms out, running Its elongated fingers along a barrier she couldn't see. Without a sound, it turned and walked back down the path into the rising sun. She crept after It, not wanting to let It out of her sight. It didn't stop, just slowly walked back toward the direction of her village or what was left of it, never turning around or deviating from Its course. She watched It until It was out of sight and then for another half an hour, in case It decided to try again. She jumped up when she heard her babies begin to cry, taking them in her arms and as she fed them collapsed into a deep sleep.

14.

She didn't leave the cave for three days, out of exhaustion and a good deal out of fear. There was a small pool of water that she drank from and some moss that she had fashioned into a slightly less uncomfortable bed, but the stress of childbirth and almost ninety hours without food had made her weak. She bit open a small hole in her wrist and reapplied the warding symbols to herself and the children. She did the same at the mouth of the cave. After seeing to the wound she ventured out, scanning the underbrush for any sign of the beast. No monsters lurking out there that she could see, but many rabbits hopping through the brush. Her stomach rumbled at the sight of them. She set a few traps and then went about making a fire. Before long, not one but two of her traps had sprung. She would eat like a queen tonight. She gutted the animals and as they cooked she used their blood to re-cover the cave mouth in symbols. Better safe than sorry. She ate an entire rabbit and most of the second, then fed the babies. She heard a third trap go over but the sun was setting by then and she would not venture from the cave at night. She sat with her back against the rocks, watching the babies coo at each other. she was, for the first time in a long time, content.

15.

She kept busy during her weeks at the cave. She hunted until the rabbits caught wise to her and moved their grazing area, but by then she had a good portion of smoked meat laid by. She began to supplement the meat with edible plants she found nearby to make it last. And without being totally aware of what she was doing, she had begun to trace the warding symbols everywhere. In the dirt, carved on the rocks, the cave walls were covered in them. She felt safe when she looked at them.

The weather began to turn. She knew she should move on, find better shelter and a reliable food source, but the thought of leaving the safety of the cave filled her with dread. She surveyed her meager food supply and the blankets she had crafted from the rabbit hides, contemplating the odds of surviving winter on the side of the mountain when she heard voices echoing in the valley. It sounded like at least twenty people. It was the horsemen, she was sure of it, come to finish what the beast could not. She hurriedly extinguished the fire and hid in the back of the cave. Then she heard a child laughing, then another. She poked her head around the cave wall and her panic evaporated. They were strangers, but there was not a horse among them, only a very sad looking yak. They were coming from the opposite end of the valley. There were about thirty of them, mostly women and small children, running and laughing, enjoying the last of the warm days, at least for a while. She didn't realize she was crying until she felt the tears streaming down her face. She didn't know how lonely she had become all those days in the cave until she saw people. She made her way to them, babies in her arms. They looked tired from their journey but happy. Friendly. They cautiously watched her approach. She pulled some of her remaining rabbit meat from her satchel and offered it to them. They devoured it with grateful looks on their faces. One of the older women smiled at her. "Thank you, child. It has been a long time since we had meat. Our men went out on a hunt weeks passed and they were not seen again. we were forced to move on." She nodded. "I am very sorry. The valley can be...dangerous."

She told them of her father who had met a similar fate. They became friends as they shared stories and food on the cold hard pack. One of the little boys pointed to the symbols that covered her body. "What are those?" She smiled at him. "They are my protection." She turned to the adults. "If you are to continue on your path there are some things I should tell you, and show you."

That night the travelers stayed in the cave. It was so strange, for the first time the place she had lived so long tonight felt small and alive. The babies seemed to welcome the calamity and the attention they received from the other little ones. As the fire died down she gathered her new friends close and told them her story from the beginning. The children(and most of the adults) listened wide-eyed as she told them of her visions, her travels on the road with her mother, and the dreams. She was completely honest in her involvement in bringing the creature to this world. Many of them moved closer to the fire as she told this part of the tale. She looked around and saw fear on their faces but no judgment or doubt, and for that she was grateful. By morning all of them were adorned in the symbols. One of the few men left in this band of travelers addressed her. He had caught her eye the night before. She did not mind that he looked at her the same way. "We are on our way to the sea, where we were told enough food could be pulled from the waves to feed our clan for a hundred lifetimes." She nodded. "It is true. My mother and I saw it for ourselves on our travels."

"We would like you to come with us when we leave here." There were many nods in agreement at this, which brought her tears close. "But our path will take us close to your village. Can you go back?" She smiled. "With all of you at my side I can. We can leave at first light. Better we passed that place with the sun still in the sky.

"We are in agreement. First light then."

She barely slept that night. Not long ago she was afraid to venture past the entrance of the cave after dark, now she could not wait to have this place behind her.

16.

They were on the path before the sun had cleared the trees, marching at a brisk pace. As they neared her village she began to slow. She felt as if a weight had been placed on her chest. as they reached the path that led into the village, she stopped. She looked the huts barely visible through the brush. "I can not." The man nodded. "I understand. maybe we can find a way past through the hills-"

"No. I can not just pass by. No matter what they did in the end, these people were my family. I have to see."

He took her hand. "I will come with you." She nodded, welcoming the company.

The rest of the group rested in the shade trees, drawing the symbols they had been taught in the dirt as the two of them made their way to the village.

From a distance, it looked as it always had, but as she moved closer she saw the first of the bodies. They were scattered everywhere, picked clean by animals in the weeks since. Most of them looked to have been fighting each other. She saw her mate, or what was left of him. He was separated from the rest. It looked as if he had clawed out his own eyes. She felt nothing but pity at the sight of him. None had survived the wrath of the beast it seemed, except her. As she reached the altar the let out a choked cry. It was her student, her favorite, so smart and eager to learn, so helpful. She laid on the altar, cut from throat to waist, her insides splayed on the stone. She had not decayed and the animals had not touched her. She stood in front of the girl, moving her hair from her face. She looked at the man, who was in shock at the sights around him. "I have to bury her. I can not leave her like this. Will you help me?" He looked as if he might run screaming at any moment, and she would not blame him. But he nodded, wiping sweat from his face. "Yes, I will. By the river? Would she have liked that?"

"Yes, she would have."

They wrapped the girl in the pelts from nearby huts and took her to the river. They buried her there and stood together, praying to the Gods for her safe journey. She had rarely experienced such genuine kindness and she fell in love with him a little that day as he stood with her looking out at a river neither of them would see again. There were supplies she could have taken from the village, but she wanted nothing from here. They continued on their way, later that day passing near the horsemen camp. She barked out a bitter laugh. Apparently, the creature had accomplished Its mission after all. There were horses, or pieces of them leading into the large village. She didn't need to see more. They moved on.

17.

A year later a group of tired, happy people stood on the shore of a sea larger than they could have ever conceived of. She stood looking out at the vastness of it, her girls sitting at her feet, her new mate's hand in her own. It was a far cry from the village she had been born in or the one she had almost died in, but that was part of the beauty. The newness of it all. She looked at her group, each of them had changed along the way, far from the timid people she met at the cave. She passed on the skills of the hunt her mother had taught her to her new family and to the people they encountered along the way, as she taught anyone willing to listen about the beast and the symbols that would protect them from it. Though she didn't know it, she had planted many seeds on her journey, ones that would grow for millennia. The people took her words with them, sharing the knowledge she had given them with others. The word would spread. She looked down at her arm, the warding symbols now carved into her flesh, as it was with everyone in the tribe. When her children were old enough she would teach them of the beast and the witches of the old clan she had descended from. She could already tell the sight was strong in them. They could communicate with each other for hours without so much as a gesture. They will learn and one day they will teach their own children. But for now, she would sit in the sand and feel the warm wind on her face, looking out at the endless sky. She was finally home.

Warden Moss

1.

Your average radio station has a broadcast transmission of about 50 miles. But during certain atmospheric conditions that range can extend much further. 01 was a transmitter with a radius the guards on E Block had thought they had mapped out over the years. They kept the cell closest to 01 empty as often as they could and watched themselves and the other guards when they were in what they had deemed the 'danger zone'. But they would have been horrified to discover was there were conditions that allowed 01 transmit it's dark thoughts much further, into especially susceptible people. The first time 01 became aware It could do this was some thirty years after Its incarceration, the end result becoming one of the most shocking deaths in the prisons history, the suicide of Warden Moss in the fall of 1928. Even with prohibition in full swing, Thurgood Moss was a full-blown alcoholic, though a functioning one. He was what nowadays be called a wet brain. He would never be able to keep his job today, but in '28 most people just looked the other way when it came to hidden bottles of hooch or nips from a flask hidden in a suit pocket. But not everyone was on board with the new Warden's condition. The guards of E Block didn't trust a secret as big as 01 with a lush, so Moss became the first Warden kept out of the loop on all things pertaining to the occupant of the sixth cell.

For 01, Moss represented It's first real possibility of escape. As It sat in Its dark cell, legs crossed, fingers strumming, It sensed something new, far out of its usual reach. A mind, slowly unraveling. Not a fellow prisoner though, no, this was someone of importance. And they were hiding something.. 01 sent out Its tendrils and the link between them solidified. It saw a man seated at a desk in a poorly lit office. His skin was sallow and yellowed, bags under his eyes, and he was in bad need of a haircut(and a bath, to be honest). There was a flask in his hand. He took a swig, the latest of thousands. 01 slipped further into his mind, chipping away at the wall Moss put up to hide the shame that had set him on this path of self-annihilation. It was buried deep, but 01 was persistent.

2.

Warden Moss began drinking to forget an incident that happened when he was seventeen. His first job had been with the long-defunct P and W railroad, loading grain into train cars. The grain was poured into the cars through a large conveyor. On one particularly cold North Dakota morning a seventeen-year-old Moss, unrecognizable from the thin husk that would one day sit hunched in the Warden's office with a death grip on his flask, made his way to the loading platform. A month from his first shave and three from his first drink, there was a smile on his face that proclaimed he had his entire life in front of him, and his future whatever he chose to make it. All of that would change in the next ten minutes. The young Moss hopped on the platform, the near freezing temperatures barely an inconvenience, nodding to his fellow workers as he clocked in, making small talk as he walked to his station. He was preparing to pour the first car of grain when he saw the man. There were plenty of his type, desperate men looking for work that took to the rails for free transit from one potential job prospect to the other. It would only get worse when the bottom fell out of the stock market years later. This particular fellow was doubly unlucky. Sometime last night he had decided to use the grain car as shelter from the near-zero temperatures but had broken his ankle in the jump down. It was bent at an odd angle and swollen against his tattered pant leg. As their eyes met the man actually looked relieved. The railroad didn't look kindly on transients riding the rails, but Moss supposed any punishment they would dole out would be better than another freezing night in that condition. Moss opened his mouth to call out for his boss, then stopped. He looked back down at the man, shivering and in agony, suit coat patched and re-patched, skin leathered from miles and miles on the road. He was suddenly filled with hatred at this living reminder of just how unfair the world could be. The man made him think of his father, a drunk shiftless bastard that was quick to use his fists. For all he knew his pop had run out on their family using these very rails. Not that he was missed. The man looked up at Moss confused, then slightly hopeful. *He thinks I might help him get away*, Moss thought, and this made him hate the stranger even more. Moss looked around at the other workers, already pouring grain. He looked at the man one last time, then he moved the conveyor into place over the car. The man realized what Moss was going to do and he let out a raspy yell. It was lost in the sound of the machinery. Moss flipped the switch. Grain began to pour into the car, hitting the man square in the chest. He tried to stand, fell, tried again. The grain was up to his shins as he finally made it to his feet, propped against the wall, trying to scream for help over the sound of the conveyors. Moss moved the chute and the stream of grain hit the man in the face. He fell backward into the car. The grain was almost deep enough to cover his prone body. He was flailing around like he was attempting to swim. Moss giggled at the sight of him trying to regain his feet. His laughter caught in his throat when he saw his boss heading down the planks toward him. He glanced at the man, still visible and calling out in a hoarse yell. The boss was within ten feet of spotting the man for himself when one of the other higher-ups waved him back. As the boss moved away

Moss remembered to breathe and turned his attention back to the man. He was flagging now, clawing at the wall for purchase and finding none. the grain had reached his shoulders and he had stopped screaming. Moss guessed he was conserving his energy. Whenever the man tried to move Moss would swing the chute so that it stayed in his face. Moss was very calm as he watched the man's struggles became weaker as the grain covered him. The last Moss saw of the man before he disappeared was his eyes. They were bulging and full of grain dust. He seemed to be looking right at Moss, though it was doubtful he could see anything at that point. Moments later he was gone, swallowed by the grain. Moss continued to fill the car, heart pounding. When the car was full he closed the chute. He looked around at the other workers. It was business as usual. He just killed a man in front of twenty people and no one had a clue it had happened. He pushed the chute down the line and began filling the next car. His mind was racing, his body felt like he was holding an electric wire. He was scared and excited and horrified at the same time. That night he began the lifelong process of trying to convince himself that the man in the train car never happened, that everything was fine, that *he* was fine. He was, for the most part, unsuccessful

3.

A week after Moss killed the man in the train car he had the first dream. He had been waiting for someone to contact the railway, authorities from San Francisco to show up and ask a few questions about the body that had assuredly been discovered by then, but no one ever did. He guessed they had written it off as another hobo in the wrong place at the wrong time. But it was only the beginning for Moss. His guilt and denial had manifested into horrific nightmares that plagued him for weeks. In the worst of them, he was heading down old Ferris road sometime after dark. The road was dirt, with trees and thick overgrowth hugging both sides. Before long he heard a second set of footsteps steadily gaining ground behind him, but he was too afraid to turn around and see who it was. As he walked, the trees along the side of the road began to push in until he was waking on barely more than a footpath. The path turned a corner into a wall of impassable vines and thorns. He stopped short. It was then in the dream when the person following him would place a hand on his shoulder. He turned around and there was the hobo from the train car, dead eyes caked over with dust. The man would open his mouth and grain, moldering and black, poured from his lips. Moss would call out, struggling but unable to move as he watched the grain bury his feet, showing no signs of stopping. He could hear the man speaking through the eruption of grain. The man pulled Moss closer so he could hear. The grain was up to Moss's waist now. "Last stop, San Francisco. All passengers must have a ticket." The man then opened his mouth wider and the putrid grain roared out of him. As the grain began to pour down his own throat Moss would wake screaming, gasping for breath. It wasn't too long before the troubled young man found a way to dull the nightmares and the memory, a way many had before and after him. He started with drinking the bottles of hooch his uncle had stashed in the cellar until he was found out and given a beating for it. He moved on, spending his paychecks at a speakeasy two towns over. Before a year had passed he was fired from the railway. His Uncle, concerned about the road the boy was taking, cashed in a favor with an old friend and got him a job at the prison. Moss spent a couple decades bouncing from one prison to another, moving up the ladder until he ended up at Newcastle, new Warden and unknowing captor over a creature from a different universe.

4. The following weeks became a silent torture for Warden Moss. 01 spent its days pushing the memory of the man in the train car into the Warden's mind. It started slow but before long it seemed like his every waking thought was punctuated by the eyes of the nameless man staring up at him as he drowned in the bottom of a rail car. 01's plan was to continue the bombardment until the Warden was broken. Then it would direct Moss to make his way to E-Block and release it, killing anyone that tried to stop him. In Its anticipation of escape, 01 had made an error. Moss didn't need to be pushed to the edge, he was already on the verge of a mental breakdown, had been for a very long time. The guilt

of what he had done had gutted him, and the thought of suicide was so ingrained in him to contemplate ending his life was a normal part of his day. Moss also became aware that the memories he was experiencing weren't just memories. It was like someone was sitting him in down at a picture show and forcing him to watch the murder over and over. And the memory was different. In this altered version someone was watching him as he killed the drifter, a tall, thin figure standing in the shadows of the depot. Smiling. It was worst during the day, but it even when he had made it home, sitting at the table plowing through another bottle of whatever was cheapest, it would slip through. Those dead eyes. He didn't know what was happening to him but he knew he could take no more. It took less than a month of 01's torment before Warden Moss made a decision. On his last day at the prison he walked into the office, nodded at his secretary Miss Bradford as he always did, then retreated to his office. He stood on the other side of the door for moment before reaching behind him and sliding the lock. No need for Miss Bradford to be the first to find the mess he was about to make. He set his briefcase on the desk and clicked it open. There were only two items inside, an envelope with a single word, Confession, written across the front, and a 38 revolver. Moss eyed the drawer that held his flask and ignored the urge to snatch it up. He would do this one last thing sober. He took the envelope out and set it on the desk, far enough away to be spared the brunt of the blood spatter, at least he hoped. He lifted the gun to the side of his head just as 01 settled in for another day of torture. It reached out for the Wardens mind and Instead of the mounting agony It usually felt, this morning there was only relief and It knew what was about to happen. 01 stood up in Its small room, feeling an emotion It hadn't felt in so long It had almost forgotten: confusion. How was this hairless ape able to trick him, when freedom was so close. 01 stood facing in the direction of the warden, large fingers clenched into fists and dug deeper into his mind. It could see the Warden at his desk, gun pressed to his temple and he was smiling. The confusion turned to rage. 01's fists clenched so tight the bones began to and pop and then break. Sims, the inmate residing in Raymond's future cell let out a moan and bolted upright in his cot. The guard on duty happened to be walking by and stopped, startled. Sims was shaking violently.

"Hey, Sims? You alright?

Sims grunted. Blood started to drip from his right ear as he stood and yelled out the last words of his life.

"I'll shoot her through the door!" He mumbled something the guard couldn't understand and then, "Put the fucking gun down!"

The voice didn't sound anything like Sims. It didn't sound exactly human. The guard fell back against the wall as a wave of fury passed through him. He had an uncontrollable urge to make his way up to the warden's office, kick open the door and drive his thumbs into the warden's eyes. He looked to the shelves placed in front of the little door at the end of the hall. He jumped to his feet and got as far from that door as possible. He had been trained well. Sims, unfortunately, didn't have that option. At this point he bit his tongue in half and fell to the floor, convulsing so hard that he broke three ribs. He died a few minutes later. While this was happening warden Moss was in the middle of a struggle. He had made his peace and had tensed his finger on the trigger when his hand froze. He tried to move but it was no use. His hand started to move away from his head, aimed now at the door. "What is happening?" He heard a sound in his head, like pieces of metal screeching off each other, and in the midst of that a voice. *I'll shoot her through the door. Then you'll be in here with me all of the time. I will make that time last forever! Put the fucking gun down!"* Moss tried to move the gun away from the door with all his might. It would not budge. Tears fell from his eyes as he strained. "You're the one that's been doing this to me! Who are you? How are you doing this!" No answer. There was a knock at the door. Miss. Bradford, concerned about the screaming, no doubt. He called out in a calming voice, "I'm fine Mrs. Bradford, please step away from the door." He watched his thumb cock the revolver. *Last chance Warden.* As he stood there unsure what to do, the letter caught his eye, the word neatly written on the envelope. His Ma had taught him to write cursive. He remembered sitting next to her, the glow of the gas lamp flickering as she wrote in those big loops and swirls. He had thought it was beautiful and he had always tried to duplicate it, never quite getting it but enjoying the lessons. It was one of his last good memories, and in the end, it gave him the strength he needed. He grabbed the letter off the desk, holding it to his chest and in the same beat swung the gun under his chin. "I'm sorry. I'm very sorry," He said to no one. To everyone. In his mind he saw the man at the bottom of the train car, staring up at him with hopeful eyes. He pulled the trigger.

The connection between 01 and the Warden was cut immediately and 01's rage faded just as fast. The Warden was dead and the chance for escape died with him, but there would be another. 01 had nothing but time. It sat back down, legs crossed, back to the wall. And waited.

Charlie C

1.

There were few things the guards at Newcastle penitentiary could be certain of, but there was one they agreed on wholeheartedly- Charlie C, perpetually stoned custodian, server of ten thousand prison meals, was the least threatening presence in the prison. Born Charles Carlin, his mother had started calling him Charlie C before they even left the hospital. Charlie was a good kid if not necessarily the brightest, and would have possibly made a decent life for himself, until his older brother introduced him to crystal meth at the age of fifteen. Things went off the rails after that.

By seventeen he had racked up five arrests, by nineteen that number was in the double digits. Before long even Charlie lost count. Not that he cared. By that point, the meth had him completely. He spent his days begging on corners and parking lots and his nights breaking into houses and cars, stopping only long enough to take the spoils to his dealer.

His parents had kicked him out of the house a few months prior for stealing the rent money(for the third time) and was living in an abandoned house with two other addicts in similar situations. As they sat on the living room floor amongst the rat shit and peeling paint, debating how they were going to get their next score, Justin, one of Charlie's 'roommates' had a moment of clarity. He recalled something he had stolen from the floorboard of a station wagon he boosted the night before. He reached behind the dilapidated couch and pulled out a sawed-off shotgun.

Charlie C's eyes widened. "Holy shit dude, where'd you get that?"

"Took it from some bitch after I beat his ass."

Charlie was doubtful of this but decided not to rock the boat. "What are you going to do with it?"

Justin sat back, attempting to think. He had declared himself the leader of this group on more than one occasion, but this was the first time he had to make an actual decision. He looked out the window and inspiration struck. He sat up, a grin on his face.

"The Quick Mart."

Barry, the third member of the trio, stopped picking at a scab on his forearm long enough to contribute to the conversation. "What about it?"

"Do you know how much money those fuckers make in a day? Thousands, bro. Thousands. If we hit them at the right time we'd have enough cash to stay lit for weeks, and that time is right now. Which one of you is gonna do it?"

Barry snorted. "Why don't *you* do it?"

Justin gave Barry his best attempt at a withering stare. "Cause I got us the gun. And I came up with the plan."

Justin said, "Well that don't mean-"

Charlie C stood up. "I'll do it." Of the three of them, he had gone the longest without getting high, and his skin was crawling off his bones. If there were thousands of dollars just waiting for them at the Quick Mart, he was going to collect it. Justin grinned and slapped Charlie on the back. "Well look at the big balls on you! Here you go, boss." Justin handed the sawed-off to Charlie. He grabbed the shotgun with a nod and stuffed the butt of it into his armpit, concealed by his coat, then hurried out the door. He walked with determination, visions of all the crank he would be able to buy dancing in his head.

2.

He was halfway across the Quick Mart parking lot before the realization of what he was about to do set in. He had done a lot of stupid things in the past five years, but armed robbery would be taking things to a whole new level. (Technically unarmed, the shotgun wasn't loaded but Charlie C didn't know that, and wouldn't have known how to check anyway) He began to walk slower and slower until he was all but shuffling as he activated the sensor sending the quick mart's doors sliding open.

The clerk, one Franklin Tran, was busy reading the last few pages of his novel and barely acknowledged Charlie as he walked in. If he had he would have dropped the book and scrambled for his phone. Charlie C looked like a nine one one call ready to happen half the time as it was, but today he was all but screaming impending felony. His hair was unwashed and sticking up in every direction, his eyes were darting back and forth, a look of sheer panic on his face. Charlie C was not cut out for this particular line of work. He wandered the store, randomly picking up items to take to the front, looking in the clerk's direction every six or seven seconds. The fact that Franklin hardly seemed aware that he was in the store didn't ease his mind.

Charlie made his way to the counter with the collection of items he acquired zigzagging through the aisles- A Babe Ruth, two pine tree air fresheners, a can of fix a flat and a pack of coffee filters. It wasn't until Franklin started ringing up the items that he got his first real look at Charlie. He froze mid-scan, the two of them staring at each other. Charlie C chose his moment. He yanked open his jacket and pulled at the sawed-off, but had somehow managed to tangle it in the ripped lining of his coat. Upon seeing this Franklin Tran began fumbling for his boss's large automatic that he kept on the shelf under the register. They both got their guns free at the same time, swung them at each other and pulled the triggers without meaning to. They both stared slack-jawed as the shotgun issued nothing but a dry click and the automatic did nothing at all. (Franklin forgot to check the safety) To anyone watching it would have been humorous, but the comedy ended abruptly as Charlie C grabbed the sawed-offs barrel with both hands and turned the shotgun into a club, driving it down into Franklin Tran's face. The sound of the stock hitting his skull was a deep thud and the force of the hit cracked his spine like arthritic knuckles. Franklin fell back against the wall and onto the floor behind the register. Charlie C ran behind the counter and after several attempts got the register open, where he liberated a whopping sixty-seven dollars. He would have gotten two hundred more if he had lifted the bill drawer but he glanced over at Franklin and forgot all about the money. He was seated on the floor, his hands splayed out beside him. One of his eyes was full of blood, the other seemed to be staring intently at the ceiling. In the middle of his forehead was a two-inch divot, also filled with blood. One of his legs was twitching as if half of him had decided to scoot backward through the wall.

Charlie C, a small wad of fives and tens in his hand, knelt next to Franklin. "Dude, I'm sorry, I was just trying to knock you out, I guess I swung too hard."

Franklin Tran didn't answer. Charlie stood up, crammed the money in his pocket and ran from the store.

    3.

The time between Charlie's exit from the Quick Mart until his arrest might have been the quickest in Blume county history. As he sprinted out the door he almost knocked down an elderly woman and her daughter, Joyce Kilner, who had gone to school with Charlie(they dropped out in the same year). Joyce yelled an obscenity or two over her shoulder at him as she continued Inside. She walked to the counter and called for the clerk. No answer. Her mother nudged her arm and pointed at the shotgun, which Charlie had left laying on the counter. This alerted Joyce that there may be trouble in the Quick Mart. Moments later they found Franklin and called the police. Ten minutes after that the Quick Mart was teeming with police and paramedics. As Franklin was being loaded into the back of an ambulance, two detectives were questioning the looky-lews in the parking lot. They struck pay dirt immediately.

"Yeah, I saw a real skinny guy run out of the store and acrost the lot. He went in that house over there."

The detectives looked at a row of abandoned houses fifty yards from the store and then at each other. Joyce Kilner, who had been standing nearby watching Tran's ambulance tear out of the parking lot, sirens blaring, threw in her two cents. "His name's Charlie Carlin. Everyone calls him Charlie C. I went to school with him for a while." One of the uniformed officers, a rookie, looked at the detectives, incredulous. "It can't be that easy, can it?"

One of the detectives grinned. "Almost never. But sometimes the stars align. Let's go."

The three of them jumped a decrepit fence and made their way across the field. As they neared the house they spread out, the rookie heading for the front. The senior detective took the door the witness said the suspect ran through. As he reached for the knob he saw that the door wasn't completely closed. He shook his head and eased the door open. He stepped into a kitchen that's primary use as of late seemed to be a toilet, and immediately heard arguing. He followed the voices into a living room that smelled of sweat and meth and a dozen other foul odors, where he found Charlie C and his friends arguing over the amount of money he had brought back from the robbery. As the detective watched in amazement Charlie C stood up, throwing his share of the cash on the stained carpet.

"That was everything in the register! If you think you can do better then you rob the fucking store next time. See how many thousands of dollars you get!"

The detective cleared his throat. The three of them turned in unison. The detective wished he'd had a camera. "Just so you know, if you gentlemen decide to rob the Quick Mart again you're going to need another weapon. Fuck hat here left the shotgun behind."

The three men stood speechless as the other officers burst in and cuffed them. And that was how Charlie C was halfway to a jail cell before Franklin Tran was wheeled into the first of his three surgeries.

4.

Franklin had a long and painful year of recovery. He basically had to learn to both talk and walk again. He was able to make it into the courtroom on his own steam with the aid of a walker and though he couldn't remember anything a week before or after the altercation with Charlie C, the video camera in the Quick Mart told the story in living color. The Prosecution wheeled in the largest television he could find and Charlie winced as they replayed the moment he brought the shotgun down on Tran's face over and over. Then in close up. Then in slo-mo close-up. He looked around the courtroom at a collection of angry and disgusted faces. Tran's sister, Lilith, was crying and Franklin tried to console her. Half the jury was in tears as they watched Jerry struggle to hold his sister's hand. He didn't succeed. Suddenly it seemed very hot in the courtroom. Charlie tugged at his suit collar, trying to let in a little air. He'd already sweated through his T-shirt. Christ, he needed a hit! Just a small one. A small one would do just fine.

The jury was out for thirty minutes and the verdict was a surprise to no one. The judge gave Charlie C the harshest possible sentence and a little less than two weeks later he found himself sitting on a bunk in Newcastle federal penitentiary.

The first days were the hardest for Charlie. He had no relationship with any of his family unless fistfights with his step-dad counted as a relationship. None of his people had come to court to support him, and he wasn't expecting a visit from them any time soon. All of that suited him fine. He had told them what he thought of them when they kicked him out for borrowing the rent, but after ten days with no money in his prison account and no meth to smoke, he was about to lose his mind.

With no other option, he shuffled up to the line of payphones outside the prison lunchroom. He called home collect. The phone rang twice and then it picked up. "Hello?" It was his mom. He was surprised at how much emotion he felt at the sound of her voice. Charlie was about to speak when an automated voice cut him off.

"You are receiving a collect call from an inmate at Newcastle penitentiary. To accept-" She had hung up there, and he wanted to hate her for that, but he understood, and at that moment he was too busy missing her to hate her. By the start of his third week in prison he was at the end of his rope. He couldn't eat. his muscles ached constantly, and he spent his nights clenching his jaw until it spasmed. He had decided that morning that he would suck the dick of the first person that gave him even a tenth of a bag of crystal. It turned out he wouldn't have to go that far just yet.

One of the big players in the prison, an Aryan by name of Joe Priestly, had been watching Charlie, waiting until his desperation was at its peak before he struck. Joe sauntered over to Charlie C, who was sitting at a table in the break room, making fists so tight he was leaving red crescent marks in his palms. Joe sat down next to him with a smile on his face

"You don't look so good, sport. Having some trouble?"

Charlie involuntarily clenched his jaw. "Yes. Troubles."

"What are you on? Or what were you on? Meth?"

"Yeah... you don't.. You don't have any do you?'

"Sorry, sport, meth has been hard to come by as of late. The big mover around here is heroin. You ever done H?"

"No."

"Believe me, it can take the edge off." Joe laughed. "Yes sir, it will cure what ails you. Would you like a little? To take that edge off?"

Charlie C almost started crying. "Yes, please. Please. I'll do anything."

Joe smiled again and patted Charlie on the back. "That's what I like to hear."

Joe took a small baggie from the waistband of his pants. He slipped it to Charlie, who had to refrain from snatching it out of his hand.

Joe said, "Take that to your cell, snort a little-" Joe grabbed Charlies C's arm. "-Very little, a pinky nail or two. That shit is potent. I don't need you dying on me before you return the favor, understand?"

Charlie nodded so hard his head looked like it was about to detach. "Yes, sir. And thank you again, thank you." Charlie hurried back to his cell, baggie in his clenched fist. If any guard had come upon him on his way there, he would have certainly been searched, but Charlie's small bit of good luck continued. He entered the cell and sat on the edge of his cot, fumbling the baggie open. He took out a pinch, (just a pinch, he didn't want to upset his new-found friend by overdosing), looked around to make sure he wasn't being watched, then snorted. The effect was immediate and as different from a meth high as you could get. The jitters were gone, like nothing but a bad dream. The baggie tumbled out of his hand and landed on the floor. Time seemed to slow down. He could never remember feeling so relaxed. "Jesus," he attempted to say, but all that came out was a low moan.

Now I know why everyone in here wants this stuff, he thought, as he slowly tilted over onto his yellowed mattress. A skinny kid no older than he was appeared in the doorway. His head was shaved and he had a red swastika tattooed on the side of his face. Even in his current state, Charlie sussed out this was one of Aryan Joe's boys. The kid flashed Charlie a huge grin, but the missing teeth took a lot of the charm out of it. "Good, ain't it? Joe always has the best shit. He sent me to check on you, good thing he did. You should probably be more careful with this." The kid walked into the cell and picked up the baggie. Charlie tried to apologize but all that came out was a grunt and some drool. The kid made the baggie disappear. "I'll hold on to this for you. Come talk to Joe when you can stand up, amigo. He has a job for you." The kid strolled out of the cell. Charlie wanted to follow him, ask him about this job, but all he could muster was another grunt and then the heroin took him.

5.

For the next six hours, he was dead to the world. He awoke with no clue how long he'd been out, but felt like days. He stumbled out into the main room. Joe and his minions were posted at a table near the stairs. He made his way to them and plopped into an empty seat. Joe laughed. "You look a bit more relaxed. I take it that did you right?"

Charlie, still dazed, nodded. "Yes sir, I really needed it."

"I bet, three weeks in here without so much as a swig of NyQuil." Joe leaned in, his elbows on his knees. "I can take care of you, make sure you always have what you need. If you're a team player. You a team player, Charlie?"

"Yes, sir, whatever you need."

"That's good to hear. See, me and my boys are in the import business." The minions chuckled at this. Not to be rude, Charlie C barked out a weak laugh. Joe continued. "Business has been good, until lately. The new trustee has a bias against members of the Aryan nation. That's OK, we more than anyone understand not everyone in this world can play nice together. But this gentleman is fucking with my business, and that is not OK. We could kill this individual, but then what? Risk getting a new trustee that might be just as obstinate, and an investigation into the murder that would affect our business even more? No, I have a better plan. You"

Charlie looked up, surprised. "Me?"

"Yes, indeed. I leave the current trustee right where he is while I prep you. Over the next few months, you're going to be the model inmate, Charlie. I'm gonna give you enough H to keep you mellow, free of charge in return you follow my rules, stay in line. Show everyone around here your value. Meanwhile, we make sure anyone else that could possibly take the trustee job gets dirty. Altercations, drugs discovered during surprise inspection you get the gist. Either way, in six months the current trustee will have an accident and there will only one clear choice as a replacement." Joe poked Charlie in his scrawny chest. "The best part is, you aren't affiliated with any group, so no eyes will be on us. What do you say, Charlie? You want to go into business?"

Charlie C looked in Joe's eyes. He was scared, and even with the promise of drugs he wanted no part of this, but he suddenly had a very rare burst of intuition. If he said no to this man, within the next day his body would be found in the showers, or maybe crammed under the very stairwell he was sitting next to. Either way, he would be dead, sooner than later.

Charlie forced a smile. "Yes sir, that sounds good to me."

Joe's grin widened. "Well, that is good news, Charlie. for both of us. Of course... people have seen us talking here today. And although we have months to go before your promotion, I don't think it would be a good idea if anyone remembered us sitting down here being all chummy. Now, if they remembered us beating the living shit out of you, that's a different story."

Charlie's eyes widened. "But.. but I said that I'd do it."

"I know, sport, and I appreciate that. This is just business. We have to put on a good show. Don't worry, the boys won't hurt anything vital, and we'll bring you some medication later. How's that?"

Charlie's fright abated a bit at the thought of more drugs. He nodded and Joe smiled that wide smile again. It was beginning to make Charlie C nervous.

"Alright", Joe said as he leaned back in his seat, "It's a done deal. This will be the last time we talk, Charlie boy. Remember that. Now run along." Charlie nodded again and stood up. He expected to be jumped, but no one moved. He thought maybe they had changed their minds when he felt the first kick. He let out a surprised yelp and fell to the floor where he was hit with a barrage of fists and feet. The beating seemed to last for thirty minutes, even though the guards had broken it up before it started. He was wheeled to the infirmary, shaking and tearful. There didn't seem to be a place on his body that wasn't in some degree of agony. He guessed not everyone at the table had gotten the memo that they were supposed to go easy. Charlie C ended the night with broken ribs, a dislocated shoulder, and a missing tooth, but he was feeling no pain. The morphine drip he was connected to saw to that.

A week later Charlie was back in Gen pop, bruised but no worse for wear except for his ribs, which would bother him the rest of his life. Joe's plan had worked out exactly as he had laid it out, with one glaring exception- Joe was killed three months after Charlie's beating. He had been found in the showers, castrated and missing his eyes. Joe's successor saw no reason to deviate from the agenda and by the end of the year, Charlie

C became a Newcastle federal penitentiary trustee. The gig turned out great for Charlie. He had extra privileges, free run of most the prison, and he was paid in heroin for his part in the smuggling operation. Three years into his stint as a trustee there was a huge gang dispute that left most of the Aryan's leadership dead or transferred, leaving Charlie C more or less forgotten and that was fine with him. By then everyone knew that Charlie was the one to go-to for all things extracurricular and the guards that smuggled the shit in were more than happy to continue getting their share. For the first time in his life, Charlie played it smart. He kept a low profile, never altered the arrangement. And though he kept himself stoned, he never overdid it. Just enough to keep life bearable. Most of the guards either liked him, were on his payroll or didn't pay him any attention at all, which suited him fine. But Charlie C's fate had been sealed from the moment he stepped off the bus into that prison courtyard almost a decade ago, shackled and wide-eyed, ten hours into withdrawal. He had been marked. 01 was planning another escape and Charlie was the key.

Cruel Summer

1.

June

Sunlight was creeping through the holes in the blinds. He turned over and put his face into the couch cushion trying to delay the inevitable but it was too late, he was up. He turned back over, draping his arm over his eyes. The past few weeks had been laced in a heavy fog, and that was how he planned on keeping things for as long as he could. He grabbed for his phone on the coffee table, snagging it on the third try. He winced as he opened his eyes to check the time. Twelve thirty. When had he gone to sleep? He didn't know or care. He remembered working his way through a bottle of cheap vodka that tasted like battery acid. After that, nothing, which was the point. All he wanted was to be blackout drunk and the cheap stuff got him there fast enough. He tossed the phone at the table and looked around the living room. Fuck, he thought, that explains the brightness. Sometime during the night he had ripped the curtains down and done a number on the blinds to boot. There was also a new hole in the wall. Good thing we moved out of the apartment, he thought as he laid there, looking at the light through his eyelids. The downstairs neighbor would have called the cops for sure. His new neighbors might have called if he had been loud enough. He didn't remember talking to any police last night, but they had been out for a visit twenty-one days ago. Thirty-one days, eleven hours, to be exact. He let out a small moan. "No", he said to himself, fists clenched, "I'm not going to do that." he turned back to the couch cushion, pulling his legs up. Not going to think about that. Cant. I just woke up, please, just a few minutes where I don't remember. But he remembered. No amount of alcohol seemed to be able to erase the memories, only dull them. The conversation with the police is seared into his soul forever it seems. A conversation that played on an endless loop in his head. unless he was asleep, or blackout drunk. Raymond would relate if he were still alive. He shuffled off the couch and into the kitchen, still drunk but not drunk enough. He began the hunt for an unopened bottle. He was starting to freak out a little. In his head, the scene had reset.

1.

He was in his favorite chair when they knocked on the door. Daddy's chair, Julia called it. They stayed with him for almost an hour after, but it was the first five minutes that was stuck on repeat forever in his head, The officer wants to know if they can come in, have a seat. He leads them in, the officers sit on the couch,, he sits in his chair, daddy's chair. He asks the officers what this is about, thinking it must have something to do with the prison. But the officer confuses him by asking him if he owned a blue Pontiac. Asking him about Julia and Little Sean. Panic bloomed, lighting a trail through his entire body. He tried to stand up but couldn't. He told the cop he wanted to know what this was about, and his voice sounded so strange to him, weak and shaky. There was a drunk driver that had veered into the wrong lane on the interstate. He had been going at least eighty miles an hour when he collided with them. Little Sean was pronounced dead at the scene. Julia died en route to the hospital. Julia and little Sean. It was some obscene mistake. How can you die before you've barely learned your first words? She had worn her blue dress that last day, the one that always drove him crazy. He had made some comment about removing it when she got home. instead, a paramedic had cut it off of her as they sped to the hospital, not that it mattered because she was dead on arrival. Dennis was frantic now, searching the cabinets. *I know I have one more fucking bottle in here, I know it*! Then he spied it, on the floor beside the washing machine, still in the discrete plain wrapper the liquor store had placed it in. He didn't give a shit about discretion. He snatched the bottle off the floor. The funeral was a surreal nightmare, with what seemed like hundreds of people shaking his hand, whispering condolences, letting him know if there was anything they can do to just ask. What could anyone possibly do? His two reasons for existence were laying in caskets on the back wall. He held it together until he saw Megan, Julia's mother. She saw Dennis and shambled toward him, her face twisted with grief. She clutched him like a drowning woman reaching for a life preserver. Oliver Fenton was a few feet behind her, his face a mixture of sorrow and vindication. Dennis had been drinking a lot since the accident, still nowhere near the levels he would reach in the weeks ahead, but Julia's father had gotten the jump on him. He brushed his wife out of the way and stood nose to nose with Dennis. His eyes were bloodshot and he reeked of booze. "I knew it. I fucking knew it. I told her so many times to get away from you. I said you would be the end of her. I just didn't think it would be literally." He laughed, a jagged sound that cut through the room. Julia's mother tried to restrain him but he snatched his hand away. "You had her fooled. You had them all fooled, but not me, you cocksucker! And now my grandson is gone, my little girl is gone because she had the misfortune of marrying you!" He lunged at Dennis, but by then several other family members had reached the fracas and grabbed Oliver, gently escorting him outside. As they led him out he continued to scream over his shoulder at Dennis, calling him a murderer. Julia's mother had fallen to her knees, sobbing. He thought he should go to her, but he couldn't. He felt like he was on the edge of a cliff and the rocks were sliding out from under his feet. He made his way through the mourners, trying hard not to break into a run. He found the nearest open door and hurried inside, shutting it behind him. He was drenched in sweat, heart thudding in his chest. He reached in his suit pocket and with shaky hands pulled out a small flask. He looked down at it, holding in a death grip. "No, not now. She wouldn't like that. I'll hold it together for you and little Sean." He managed to keep the flask in his pocket until he arrived home. The first thing he saw when he turned on the light in the living room was one of Sean's toys. The race car, one of his favorites. And there next to the door were Julia's sandals, where she always kicked them off after stepping inside. The two of them were everywhere in this house. He slid down the door, looking at their things. His eyes filled with tears and he screamed. No words, just a guttural howl of denial. He jumped up from the floor, grabbing everything he could find that belonged to them. He placed it all in Sean's room and shut the door. He went into his and Julia's room and grabbed a pillow and a blanket, leaving as fast as he could. He sat on the couch and spun the lid off the flask. He took four large swigs, fire burning a path to his empty stomach. He sat there for an hour, staring at the blank television screen. He'd never heard the house so quiet. Even when they were out for an hour or two and he was home alone there had been an energy here, now... this wasn't his home anymore. This was a tomb.

3.

Now, a month and a half later he was sitting in the same spot, though he looked ten years older. In his head, the cops were knocking on the door. Dennis spun the cap off the bottle and knocked back half of it. His head was getting cloudy, the memory losing some of its edges. He pin-balled off the walls of the small hallway and plopped onto the stool in the kitchen nook. I have to call in another liqueur order before I get too fucked up, he thought. This is the last bottle. If I let it run out... He slurred his way through the conversation with the liqueur store, then stumbled over to the couch. he drank himself into a blackout. Sometime the next day(or the day after, time sort of melted together when you were on the couch) he awoke to someone knocking on the front door. Angry neighbors with threats of the police, no doubt. He found he didn't care much either way. He swung open the door and was surprised to find Zale. He looked strange in civilian clothes, younger somehow. He smiled and Dennis thought, *His old captain, Jeffries, was right, his poker face left much to be desired.* "Zale, how the hell are you?" "Fine. Mind if I come in?" "Of course." Dennis lead Zale inside, moving some fast food wrappers and empty bottles to give him a place to sit. Dennis didn't try to hide the current bottle, but he decided to curb the drinking until the visit was over. He attempted a smile. "So what can I do for you?" "I was concerned. I just wanted to see how you were holding up." "Well as you can see, not too great." Zale nodded. "No, I didn't expect you would be. I went to the funeral. I arrived just as Julia's father- well when that whole thing began. I lost track of you after that." "Yeah, that was something. Leave it to Oliver to make it all about him." He laughed. It sounded like a scream. The cop that never really left his head popped up with his questions. *Do you own a blue Pontiac?* Dennis clenched his fists. *No. Please.* "I know you mean well, Zale and I do appreciate you coming by, but I have to-" "I know what you have to do." Zale gestured at the bottles littering the room. "I did my share of it after Marta passed. But..you told me once you had a problem with the drink when you were younger. Don't let it get the upper hand now. With some people that can happen easily. I'm not going to stand here and pretend to understand your pain, son. Losing a child, I can't even imagine, but Julia... I knew her a little, talked to her on a few occasions, and she never missed an opportunity to tell me how proud she was of you, how much she loved you. I think you know it would break her heart if you got lost in this." he picked up one of the empty bottles, Dennis cringed. "This dulls the pain temporarily but it also extends it. Grieve, son, but don't get lost." Dennis wiped tears from his face. He nodded, not trusting his voice at the moment. Zale stood. "I'll get out of your hair, I just wanted to let you know you got people here for you when you're ready. And your job. It's waiting for you." Zale turned to leave when Dennis said, "I keep asking myself, could 01... could It have been responsible for this somehow? Because if It was then this whole thing is on me-" "Kid, don't do that-" "But I lied! That day, when Raymond got out, I told you that I looked in and it was just sitting there. It was... at first. But then it jumped up, it was at the window. Smiling at me. What if it marked me, what if-" "Enough!" Dennis shrank back in his chair. Zale knelt down in front of him. "I'm sorry son, but.. Don't get me wrong, we both know that thing is a nightmare come to life, that it plays with peoples minds, but this kind of thing.. is far beyond Its scope. This wasn't on you, Dennis" "Then what? What did this?" Zale sighed. "Sometimes life is just cruel, son. Life is just cruel." Dennis crumpled at that, weeping soundlessly. Zale caught him and held him until he was able to stand on his own again.

01

1.

01 had been called by many names since it's arrival in our world, most more imaginative than a number. Not that any of them mattered. Where It came from there were no names. It had lived Its life under a sky of twisting purple and green clouds, the color of faded bruises. 01's world was volatile, permeated with volcanoes in almost constant eruption. Huge pools of thick brine were pocketed along the super heated ridges, bringing the pools to near-boiling temperatures. 01 and thousands of its brothers and sisters nested in these pools.

They had no language we would be able to comprehend, communicating through thought and touch. Images and emotions from a hundred different siblings flashed through 01's mind, where they would be added by it's own and then passed along the endless chain. In its impossibly long life it had only known contentment and a oneness, until the other. As It slithered through the salty water, entwined with Its siblings, It felt something brand new. A thrumming went down Its spine, a low vibrational hum that made Its flesh twitch and spasm. New thoughts began to fill Its mind, alien and violating. The other-mind was primitive but powerful, its consciousness easily taking over Its own. For the first time in Its long memory, it felt fear. The other-mind wanted to see the altar and 01 was incapable of stopping it. It swam through the water, disgusted and shocked at how powerless It was against the thoughts of the other. 01 took it's captor to the foot of the altar. The other-mind was studying the glyphs, pulling their meanings from 01's memories. Furious, 01 tried in vain to contact Its siblings, but It could only hear the other, a female, as she recited the glyphs over and over in its mind. With a burst of intuition, it switched tactics. Instead of pushing back against the other-mind it attempted to enter it. Suddenly the connection was broken and It could hear Its siblings again. It was shocked to discover They had no knowledge of the invader. Worry rippled through the shared consciousness as 01 shared with them what occurred. In an instant, a consensus was reached. What happened once could happen again, and who could say there wouldn't be more of them next time? They swirled together in the pool, sharing ideas and strategies in the blink of an eye. They emerged with a defense. It would take time to perfect, but that was fine. They were very patient.

Over the following weeks, the attacks continued, always against 01. Each time it came without warning and each time the focus was on the glyphs adorning the altar. But now 01's brothers and sisters were aware the moment their connection was broken. They would immediately begin attacking the invader, forcing it out. They had become successful at repelling the attacks, each time learning a little more about their opponent and evolving their tactics. As they moved through the salty water they synced their minds closer than ever before. Soon they were moving like a school of fish, each move perfectly mimicked by the rest. Their minds were as one, Their usual form of conversation gone, now focusing as a group on one image repeated over and over, until it was the only thing pounding through Their minds, a chant recited by a thousand voices in perfect harmony. They had never been as close as They were then, moving and thinking as one organism. They continued this way for days and when the other-mind attacked They were ready. This time They all felt the low hum in their spines that signaled the return of the invader, but it had no chance against their combined will. Without pause, They expelled the invader. A surge of emotion raced through Them. They had won! Victory only strengthened their resolve. They continued the chant, enjoying the power of Their enhanced union, a deafening chorus to those attuned.

The invader tried repeatedly over the following weeks to reenter 01's mind, but the attempts were easily thwarted. The new super consciousness they had created was more powerful than anything they had experienced before, almost like a drug. What They didn't realize was that staying at this peak of mental perfection was draining them physically, which allowed an intrusion far worse than the ones before it. Before, when the other attacked it was still an outsider, a puppeteer pulling strings. This time It had taken over completely. There were no separation. 01 felt the familiar thrum down Its spine and then it was shoved to the back of Its own mind. It saw Itself floundering toward the altar. It cried out and was relieved to find Its siblings could still hear him. They could communicate without the other-mind hearing. They had made contingencies in case the other ever made its way back inside and it was time to implement them. They signaled Their agreement as They closed the circle around their hijacked brother. The other must have sensed danger because in a flash 01 felt Itself leap through the air, landing on the altar, scattering the bones that littered the carved stone. It tried to take back control, to no avail. It yelled out to its siblings, *Now!* and 01 felt a deep satisfaction as the invader felt the force of their retribution. The other-mind cried out as Its siblings began to tear Its body to shreds. As the onslaught continued the other-mind began to lose control and 01 was able to communicate with it. It sent images to the other-mind, showing with pleasure how much worse if would become if she stayed, but still she persisted, as It's black blood poured out faster and faster upon the altar. They were both beginning to fade when It heard the other-mind speak to him.

I will not come back..I swear it. I swear.

Then it was gone, leaving It alone. 01 fell over onto the altar, severely injured. The attack ended in an instant, It's sibling gently cradling its bloody figure and slipping back into the pool, taking It to the depths, where It could heal. 01 lay in the murky water, cocooned in a shell of its brothers and sisters, and though in great pain it was at peace. The other-mind and its own were linked on the deepest level. It said it would not be back and it couldn't have lied. 01 was free of her.

For days 01 laid in the deep water. It healed quickly, but the wounds were deep and It was still weak as It lay surrounded by Its siblings. Even in Its weakened state, It was content, the crisis over. What It didn't know, because the other-mind was also unaware, was that an altar was being constructed in another world, a duplicate of their own and the blood its siblings had spilled across the stones formed a connection from one world to the other. There was no warning when 01 was taken. One moment It was in the warmth of the pool and the next It found Itself lying on the altar. No, the altar was familiar but everything else was different. 01 experienced a cold It had never conceived of. It was wracked with shivers as the winds blasted through the valley across Its skin, the still healing bites and scratches especially sensitive to the bitter cold. It saw without seeing the sky it had lived under Its entire life was gone, replaced with a sheet black as pitch with needles of flickering light blanketed across its face. 01 reached out for the minds of Its brothers and sisters and instead found two dozen frightened primitives. It tried to stand but couldn't. 01 searched the thoughts of the frightened animals surrounding the altar and began to understand what had happened. 01 was laying in the blood of one of the primitives, killed by one of its own. Blood magic. They had taken a virgin, always a virgin, the purist sacrifice. They dipped their hands in her spilled blood and wrote the glyphs on the stone and uttered words they didn't comprehend and tore It from It's home. And for what? Revenge and power. It stood before them, furious, their thoughts permeating its mind. These sad things, afraid but thinking the glyphs they had stolen gave them control. They would suffer for that mistake. It stepped from the altar, the water from the home It was taken from still dripping from Its body. The men and women backed away slowly, except for one. He walked forward, arms raised. He turned and smiled at the group, telling them not to fear, but oh how he trembled. He then turned to 01. "Creature of the infinite darkness, I have summoned you to destroy our enemies and release our people! With these ancient words I command you!" The shaman read from a parchment containing a series of glyphs. 01 smiled and took another step forward. The man faltered, panic shooting across his face. He read the words again, louder. 01 stopped smiling. The man felt a spark of relief that was extinguished a moment later when 01 closed the distance between them in an instant, lifting him in the air and snapping his spine before tossing him to the ground. It faced the others as they stood, frozen in terror. 01 bit into one of the mostly healed cuts on Its arm, breaking it open. It swung Its arm outward, It's blood spraying across the faces of a handful of villagers. It was only a few drops, but it was enough. It watched as they turned on each other.

In the aftermath 01 stood close to one of the large bonfires flanking the altar. Men, women, and children were strewn across the ground, all dead. 01 took a few of them but most were killed by their own friends and loved ones. 01 looked at the slaughter, thinking it might sate his rage. It hadn't worked. The woman, the one it wanted, the one responsible, wasn't here. It sensed movement and swung its head. It was the shaman. He was crawling across the blood-soaked ground, dragging his useless legs behind him. He began to cry as the shadow of 01 fell over him. He grunted as he clutched at the grass, only succeeding in moving in a half circle. 01 took some enjoyment in watching this. After a while It reached down and flipped the shaman over, pulling him close. He sobbed, spittle and snot spread across his face. He had wet himself, either from fear or the paralyses. 01 sent thoughts into his mind, blasting through the fear. *The woman that caused this. Where is she?* The shaman looked around wildly. "She-She was in bed! she was ill! Please-" 01 searched his mind and found her dwelling. It dropped him and reached the hut in three strides, tearing the roof from it. It was empty. It concentrated on her, the invader. The other-mind. After a moment it found her. She was on the move but she wasn't far. It would take her slow for what she had done. It moved out of the village, stopping just once more. The shaman was on his back now, tears streaming down his dirty face. 01 knelt beside him. It took one of Its impossibly long fingers and touched the tip to the open wound on Its arm. It then ran the bloody finger across the shaman's lips. *A gift for you.* It grinned as the shamans eyes began to bulge. It watched for a moment as the shaman writhed in the dirt, gouging the flesh from his face. It then headed west into the valley, the shaman's screams trailing after It.

Between the still healing injuries and the biting cold of the wind tearing through the valley the going was slow, but with every step, It could feel the woman stronger in Its mind. Not in control this time, no, all It could feel now was fear, but not directed towards 01. She was about to birth and she was focused completely on that. That was fine with 01, she would be caught off guard, something she would regret for the rest of her short life. It would make her watch as It dealt with her spawn, then take Its time with her. It reached the cave as the sky to the east began to turn a dull purple. It knew she had birthed and made no attempt to be quiet as It moved through the loose rocks leading to the cave mouth. She was weak and trapped. Her fear, which had abated after the birth of the child, suddenly spiked. It smiled. She had finally felt Its thoughts and It delighted as the terror that flooded through her. Then something unexpected. She was suddenly gone from Its thoughts. It was impossible. It moved a little faster, still no sense of her in Its mind but as It reached the cave mouth It could smell her cowering inside. She had backed against the stone, holding not one baby but two. It felt the despair wash over her. She knew what was to come. The children began to cry in unison, perhaps on some level, they knew as well

It took a step, then another. Then It was stopped. It realized what happened at once. It could feel the glyphs now, painted on the walls of the cave and on the woman herself. She was protected and there was nothing it could do to break that barrier. 01 turned to leave, resigned. It moved down the hill and back toward the destroyed village. The sun had risen on this late fall day and 01 responded to the marginal heat, but it was a far cry from the pools of Its home. It wandered without destination, happening across the rival tribe that had been the catalyst for its kidnapping. It took them all with ease, stripping the animal hides from their corpses and covering Itself. The furs gave some comfort from the cold as It moved through this strange world. It walked day and night, killing anyone unfortunate enough to cross paths with It. Though It could live and breath on land, it had spent most of its life in the water and It preferred it. It was cold and weak from Its injuries. It needed to heal. After weeks on the move through this frozen graveyard, It smelled something on the wind that caused It to scramble to a halt, nostrils flaring. It was hints of sulfur, a smell from home. The smell of the pools. 01 ran toward the source of the odor which lead to another valley, but this one... They weren't as large as the pools of its home, but these hot springs would serve 01 perfectly. It tore the foul-smelling pelts from Its back and leaped into the deepest spring. It was beginning to think this world was only a series of tortures, but now a reprieve. It could finally rest. It nestled under an outcropping of rock some twenty feet beneath the surface and slept.

2.

The springs were wondrous, but they lacked the healing nutrients of Its dark pools. So when 01 finally emerged from the spring, rested and back to a semblance of normal, some twelve years had passed. 01 resumed Its journey, falling into a pattern. It roamed, happening across primitives, setting them against each other or killing them Itself depending on Its mood. On occasion, It would find someone alone in the world and spend time driving them insane. Those were the most enjoyable, though none of it seemed enough retribution for being brought to this pit. When It grew bored of the massacre It would find another hot spring and slumber. Its anger only grew as the years passed, forever cut off from Its siblings. It slept for longer and longer periods, with no real reason to wake. sometimes decades would pass before it would resurface to exact more revenge. In the years that followed it moved across the middle east and into Europe, and as the time passed It began to see changes. Huts were replaced by structures of wood and stone. The land was being cultivated on a larger scale and more people were staying in one place longer. Villages were replaced with towns. And here were so many of them now! The primitives certainly loved to procreate. Though It supposed they weren't really primitives anymore. Each time It emerged It found something new to marvel upon. after one very long hibernation, It stood on the top of a mountain and saw an amazing sight- It was a moonless night, yet there were lights scattered across the valleys beneath him. Fire, but they had mastered it somehow. Lights on poles following streets, not dirt paths but streets laid in cobblestone. The population had exploded during Its last slumber, and so had their ingenuity. 01 slipped through the shadows of one new metropolis, watching the people as they rode by in carriages pulled by teams of animals. 01 was furious at the progress. These creatures had torn It form Its world, never able to return and then they just forgot. No. And no. And no. They would not forget. It smiled as It stood in an alley, the modern men and women passing by unaware. They may be more intelligent, living in buildings of steel, but some things don't change. They had fears. And secrets. It could feel them drifting through the air, waiting to be exploited. 01 was going to find a town to play with, setting people against each other and in some circumstances escalated nations to go to war. It would watch as these cities burned to the ground. It was brought here to destroy, was it not? It wasn't going to disappoint.

3.

As 01 killed its way across continents, both marveling and recoiling at their advancements, there was one development being used in an attempt to stop It- communication.

It had been thousands of years since 01 had left the women and her mewling infants in that cave and It had, for the most part, forgotten her, extending the blame for Its situation to every living person. But she had never forgotten 01, and millennia later her warnings were still being passed on. She also had ancestors spread across all of Africa and Europe, most of them possessing some level of the sight. They set out by ship to every corner of the world, the symbols of protection she had once written in blood now tattooed on their skin, telling the old stories and and the new, recounted by survivors of a shadow man, a creature that could enter your mind, an instigator of bloodshed and death. If the stories were met with disbelief, as they were more and more as the years progressed, the symbols would be carved without the townsfolk's knowledge. On cornerstones, behind signposts, on the rooves of houses. If they wouldn't protect themselves, the messengers would do it for them. They warded hundreds of towns as they moved tirelessly across the civilized world. Before long 01 began discovering townships that were impossible to enter. They weren't visible, but 01 knew it was the glyphs that were hindering It. It was never angry when It was repelled from a hive of primitives. The glyphs were holy and could not be disobeyed. But it carried a deep sorrow that the only reminders of Its home were the very things that kept it from Its vengeance. It was of little consequence. The world was a large place and there were many places left to exact revenge.

With the advent of the telegraph, there came the means to shift from defence to mounting a coordinated attack. In 1850 a small army of men and women decided it was time to act. The members of this hunter cabal were the strongest in the sight, and they had learned to manipulate the symbols, altering some of the incantations, turning one into a locator and others into weapons. They expected to have the beast killed or at the very least captured in a years time. It ended up being almost three years before their first confrontation 01 should have known it was walking into an ambush, but It had been the predator for so long it had no reference for being the prey. Lions that spent lifetimes devouring antelope never expect the antelope to form gangs and strike back.

01 had been on an unsuccessful search for a place to bring to ruin. Though It had come across several individuals unlucky enough to meet

it on the road, It had been denied its taste for mass destruction. After being repelled from the fifth town in as many weeks 01 had decided to sleep, waking again when these people were long dead and their grand children's grandchildren were old and frail. Maybe the glyphs would be forgotten by then, and the destruction of these parasites could resume in earnest

It was sniffing out a resting place when It discovered the hamlet, nestled on the edge of a huge forest. un-warded and full of life. Full of *thoughts*. It smiled wide. It had been so long since It had gotten to play, really play. It would take Its time with them. It waited until nightfall and moved in, using the shadows, unaware of the people flanking It on rooftops and slinking up from behind. They may have succeeded in capturing It right then if not for one careless hunter. The symbols were basic designs but had to be drawn exactly to be effective. One of the hunters had carved the warding symbol on his arm, but had missed a vital piece, one little squiggle on the bottom right of the glyph, and as a result was only partially warded. It was enough for 01. It picked up on the hunters thoughts as he was about to strike. 01 spun in an instant and locked eyes with the hapless attacker, tearing Its way into his mind. The man screamed, falling to his knees. As the others moved in, 01 sprung. It moved up the side of the wall onto the roof faster than any of them could track. A priest came put of the shadows, opening a leather book full of symbols that would soon be read by another holy man in a prison halfway around the world. As he began to read, 01 felt the left side of its body seize. 01 fell to the roof, grasping at loose shingles with its one functioning hand. It was slowly sliding off the side of the building. With a thought, It set the hunter at the priest, driving his knife into his throat. As the priest slid down the wall 01 felt Its strength return. The others charged at the rogue hunter before he could kill again. 01 took the opportunity to escape, leaping rooftops and sprinting into the darkness of the forest. *The woman,* It thought as It ran through the trees. It was in disbelief, but It saw everything in the hunter's mind. *They learned all this from the woman. From stories passed through her descendants.* 01

climbed high in the bow of a large spruce tree. *They won't forget the glyphs. And there will be more. Many more. I should have found a way to kill her.*

01 was right. Within minutes they were headed right for the tree It was hiding in. They could track It now.

4.

The chase that began in the little hamlet would eventually lead hunters and prey to the Americas. Even with the ability to locate It, the hunt lasted over a year, as the group chasing 01 had to rest the horses and themselves, while 01 moved almost non stop. The day It was captured was at the end of a brutal winter, and 01 was weaker than It had ever been. It had gained a little strength from eating the hearts of the dogs they had sent after It, but it wasn't enough. The men broke through the trees, cornering It at the deadfall. One of them, a younger one, moved forward. 01 smiled. They never learned it seemed. This one hadn't carved the glyphs on his body, only marked them with ash, and his sweat had washed most of it away. 01 sent a burst of thought at him and the boy collapsed. Then came another priest, and in seconds 01 was on Its knees, clasping shackles on Its own wrists. Soon after It was placed in Its freshly constructed cell but It wasn't worried. It had no intention of remaining there. Their biggest mistake was leaving It in a place surrounded by people. It had spent most of recorded history learning their weaknesses. It was only a matter of time before opportunity would present itself.

The first, Warden Moss was a failure but lessons were learned. Then came Charlie C. To 01 Charlie was a beacon. Ten-fold as as controllable as Moss and he didn't need to be broken, there was nothing left in Charlie C to break. But the failure of Warden Moss was always in the back of Its mind, so It didn't put all Its eggs on one basket. 01's strongest connection was with Charlie, but It had established varying degrees of contact with over thirty inmates in all four Blocks of the prison, people that had spent a large part of their lives using drugs or alcohol or both, heroin being the most effective in dulling their mental defenses. There were many moving parts, with many players. And when Dennis joined the guards on E-Block, the final piece had been placed. It was time put Its plan in motion.

5.

A month before the riot, Charlie woke to the sound of the morning alarm as he always did. He reported to the kitchen where he worked food prep(and stowed the drugs that had been smuggled in for sale later in the day.) After breakfast he made his way to the library where the day's books and magazines were ready and waiting for delivery.

He moved through the prison, dropping off reading material and assorted illegal contraband. During lunch, he worked in the shop. He had requested that detail specifically. It took him back to his childhood, the only part of his life that was ever good. He remembered it clearly, being five years old and hanging out in his father's makeshift workshop in the corner of the garage, the smell of sawdust, hammers clanging, the occasional curse word.

For the past two years, he had been carving a wooden horse, and it had come together better than he could have ever hoped. He kept it in a box on the far shelf and everyone knew to leave it alone. He took it down now, thinking that today he would work on the mane, which had been giving him a bit of trouble. In another couple of months, carving would be finished and he could start the staining process. He had been thinking to himself that maybe he could send it to someone. His Dad had died of a heart attack during his third year inside, but maybe he could give it to his Ma. If she saw that he didn't always destroy everything he touched, that he could create something beautiful, she might not hate him anymore. As he looked the horse over this fantasy played in his mind before being abruptly replaced. Now there was a voice speaking in his head, so quiet it could have been his own thoughts- *Go to the bucket of wood scraps and get the strongest pieces. You need to make shivs. Thirty of them.* Charlie brushed the horse aside without a second glance. He walked to the large bucket at the end of the table and began to sort through it, finding twenty that he thought would make good shivs. He started sharpening the wood with only cursory looks at the guard. No one was paying him any attention, as usual. After the pieces were sharpened he grabbed the electrical tape and wound makeshift handles, so whoever these were meant for didn't get any splinters when they used them. Another voice in his head, his true voice, was ringing an alarm. *What am I doing? This is dangerous. If they catch me-* The other voice superseded his own, soothing, quiet. *They won't catch you, the guards never watch you. They like you.* This calmed him. He finished the shivs and put them in a box, laying his horse on top of them. He headed out the door and by the time he made it to the kitchen he had forgotten that he had even made them. The dinner shift was deliveries. That was fine with him, he liked delivery. He liked to walk, and most of the other inmates were nice, even the ones he didn't pass drugs to. The next day was the same as the one before. Kitchen. Books. Shop. This time he even got to work on the horse's mane a bit, after finishing the last ten shivs. An hour later everything was back on the shelf and he was off to the kitchen, his extracurricular activities forgotten again. Soon, the voice said in the back of his mind and he nodded. "Yes," he said, not realizing that he had spoken aloud or who he was talking to. Soon.

The Great Escape

1.

August On Dennis Schuster's first day back on E block, it was 87 degrees before the sun had even poked over the horizon. When Dennis drove through the first set of gates three hours later the thermometer pegged the temp outside at a hundred and two. The air shimmered off the asphalt of the prison parking lot as Dennis pulled into the nearest empty spot. The A/C in the car was on max but the sun-baked him through his driver window. *Hard to believe the day I started all this was under a foot of snow. Seems like forever.*

It had taken him several minutes to work up the nerve to step out of his house this morning. When he heard the front door shut behind him the anxiety gripped him like a vice, shutting him down. He stumbled back onto the porch steps, gasping for air. He wiped tears off his face for the millionth time and stood up, charging toward the car. The first thing he saw as he shut the door was the picture of Julia and Sean taped to the dash. He slammed his eyes shut, trying not to scream out. He reached out, blindly shoving the picture into the glove box. He sat for a moment, deliberating on just going back inside and drinking this ridiculous idea away. After a long pause, he wiped the sweat from his face and turned the ignition.

He closed the car door and began the walk to E block. This was probably a huge mistake, He thought to himself. I'll just stay as long as I can. They can't force me to stay here and if they try I'll just quit. He had done this to himself and now he had to at least make an effort.

2.

Yesterday, a week after Zale's visit, he had awoken in a war zone. The house had already been in drastic need of a cleaning, but he had taken things to a whole new level. Holes in the walls, fridge left open for God knows how long, He had apparently attempted to cook something and then forgotten about it. Luckily he had the presence of mind to extinguish the fire, though not before blackening the ceiling above the stove. The worst part was little Sean's room. He hadn't set foot in there in weeks, couldn't bring himself to, but that had apparently changed last night. When he finally regained consciousness he found himself on the floor next to Sean's bed, dried vomit on the floor, the toy box he had made for him last year overturned, the side kicked in. He looked around at the destruction and began to sob, low primal sounds that he barely recognized as his own voice. Twenty minutes later he pulled himself to his feet, righting the toy box and putting the assorted trucks and army men back inside. He cleaned the vomit off of Sean's floor and moved to the kitchen. With a twinge of remorse, he poured the two remaining bottles of vodka down the sink. He then took a long-overdue shower. While he stood in the steaming water the memories started over again. The police were knocking at the door. He didn't fight them this time. It was a nightmare, but it was a nightmare that would never end if he didn't face it. After his shower, he called Zale. He answered on the first ring. "Kid, you OK?" Dennis almost started crying again at the concern in his voice.

"Yeah, I'm alright," he said in a cracking voice, "I was calling to see if you could get me on the schedule for tomorrow."

"You know I think we can find something for you. How does eight sound?"

"Sounds good to me. I'll see you in the morning." He hung up and slid down the wall, the tears, never too far away, back again. But for the first time in weeks, he felt a glimmer of hope. There might be a way out of this. But now, 30 hours from his last drink, he was sure he had made a big mistake, but he wasn't leaving. At least not yet. One step at a time. One step at a time.

3.

In the hidden cell at the end of the hall, 01 began to feel excitement. It was the hottest day of the past five years and It was reveling in the strength It absorbed from that heat. There was an energy in the air. This was the day. It thought briefly of Raymond, the ape that used to live in the empty cell. It was a fluke that he had come so close to opening the door. 01 had been playing with him for years, but even with the close proximity, It hadn't progressed very far. Raymond had never been one for drugs or alcohol in his life before incarceration, and that coupled with his particular psychosis hindered 01's access. Some were just harder to corrupt than others. But even the strongest would fall being that close and given enough time, and there was all the time in the world on E block. The wall in Raymond's mind finally began to crack and he fell fast. 01 tossed Raymond at the door expecting him to fail and he did. But that incident allowed 01 to delve deeper into Dennis's mind, and the plan changed. Charlie would stay in the main prison, keeping them busy. Dennis was the star now, and he was back. 01 shifted in Its cell. It was almost time to begin.

4.

It took all Dennis had in him not to turn and run the minute he opened the door to E block. The woefully outdated air conditioner mounted at the end of the hall, not quiet to begin with, had started the morning by making some new noises. Instead of the usual rattle thump, it now sounded like someone was trying to beat it to death from the inside. The inmates looked like someone had doused them with a fire hose. Most were down to their skivvies and their usual jovial moods were nowhere to be seen. Gilles had taken his uniform shirt off and tossed it over the back of the chair. He was at the table, his T-shirt soaked through, fanning himself as he halfheartedly shuffled the cards. Someone from maintenance had brought in a huge industrial fan constructed sometime before world war two, but all it was doing was blowing the hot air around. Gilles popped out his chair the moment he saw Dennis, a huge grin on his face. He looked like he had been running a marathon rather than sitting at a table playing solitaire. Gilles grabbed his hand. "Christ, I'm glad to see you. One more hour in here and there wouldn't have been anything left of me." Dennis forced a grin. "They told me it was bad, but.."

"Yeah, supposedly there's a repair crew on the way but I wouldn't hold my breath."

Dennis nodded. "Where's Casey? I thought he was on with me today."

"He is. Got caught behind a huge pileup on the Fort Meyer bridge. Could be a couple of hours before he shows up. Are you OK? No offense, but you look like you're about to make a break for the door." *If you only knew*, Dennis thought. He shook his head. "No, I just.. Nothing. It's just nerves. Been a while." Gilles looked at Dennis appraisingly. "Yeah. I, uh.." He looked unbelievably uncomfortable. "Look, kid, you sure you got this? If you need some more time-" Dennis almost jumped at the offer, then he took a hard look at Gilles. He was pushing sixty, a hundred and thirty pounds on a good day and looked on the verge of dehydration. Dennis smiled and patted him on the shoulder. "You've had enough time in the hot box. Get out of here, I have it covered."

"You sure?"

"Absolutely."

A look of pure relief came over Gilles's face. "Alright kid, I'm outta here.

I'm gonna drink half of Lake Michigan and go to sleep for about twelve hours."

Dennis sat down at the table as he walked out, his smile fading as soon as the door clanged shut. He looked at the inmates, his misery reflected in their faces. *It's going to be a long fucking day*.

5.

Charlie woke with the alarm, making his way to the kitchen for breakfast detail. Halfway through food prep, the voice returned. It's time. retrieve the stakes. Charlie was about to argue with the voice that he couldn't just leave in the middle of breakfast but he had the feeling that it would be a really bad idea to contradict what the voice told him to do. Charlie C went to the guard running breakfast detail. "Boss, I gotta leave."

"Why? What's wrong?"

I got some kinda stomach thing. It started this morning I thought it was gone but.."

"Alright, head to the infirmary." The guard didn't give him a second look as he headed out the door in the opposite direction of the infirmary. Charlie swung by the library and grabbed his magazine cart. He tossed a large stack of periodicals on top and made his way to the exit. The guard tipped him a salute as he passed by. Five minutes later Charlie wheeled his cart into the wood shop. Officer Miller, an overweight asshole close to retirement, gave him a look. This could be a problem. Miller didn't especially like him, but he had an idea. "It's a little early for horsey carving isn't it Charlie?" Miller happened to be one of the five guards in the prison that looked the other way when the drugs and other contraband was brought in. Correction, Looked the other way for a price. Charlie moved in close and whispered. "I think I dropped a delivery yesterday when I was in here. A sixteenth of meth." Miller laughed. "Woo boy, and you think that it's still here, with all the junkie pieces of shit coming in and out those doors? Good luck with that Charlie. Go ahead, have a look." Miller laughed again as he settled back down with his fuck book. Charlie headed to the back and grabbed his box down.

He began quickly slipping the shivs into the middles of each magazine. Miller continued reading his opus. When Charlie was done he put the magazines on the bottom shelf, where they would be better concealed. He pushed his cart back to Miller. "I guess it wasn't here after all."

"No shit. Hey, let me know when you tell your boys you lost their meth. I haven't seen a good as whipping in a long time." Miller laughed slapping Charlie on the back as he pushed his arsenal out the door. Charlie hoped whoever got the shivs would put one of them in Millers eye.

6.

Dennis mopped sweat from his forehead as he sifted through forms and requests and several dozen other collections of mundane prison bullshit. A small headache formed almost immediately. He found himself looking at the clock every few minutes, and every minute that clicked by seemed to last ten. He looked at the pile of paperwork, which seemed to grow every time he looked away. He wiped the sweat out of his eyes yet again, growing angrier. He was hot, he was anxious and he needed a God damn drink. The inmates snapped at each other as they tossed and turned in their bunks, more than ready to share their shitty mood. Yost flopped over on his side then stood and made his way to the cell door, giving Dennis a sour look. If he had a tin cup, Dennis was sure he would have started running it across the bars. "Hey, Schuster! What's going on with the A/C?" Dennis unclenched his fists with some effort and tried to sound calm. "A maintenance crew is on the way, Yost, just calm down. They'll fix it soon as they can."
"Can't we just turn it off? Its blowing mostly hot air and that sound is driving me out of my fucking mind."
Dennis sighed. "We can't turn it off from here."
"Well I hope they fix this soon, this is torture!"
Benedict decided to chime in. "I bet some of those girls you raped and killed would say this is a dry run for you. You know, for when you get to hell."
Yost smashed his face against the bars to get a better view of his detrac-

tor. "Shut the fuck up, Benedict! Like you're any better than me!"
"Hey, at least I didn't-"
Dennis slammed his fists down on the table and shrieked, "All of you shut up! It's bad enough in here without this bullshit!"
The inmates quieted at once, taken aback. There was something in his voice. That wasn't just anger. They had seen and heard it all in here over the years. That was the sound of someone about to crack. Jerry ventured to his cell door. "You OK boss? You seem a little agitated. Want to talk?"
Dennis barked out an angry laugh. "Think I'll pass on therapy with the guy that killed his fucking mother."
Jerry blinked and backed away. Dennis Felt like an ass. That was not how things went down at this prison. He was about to apologize when a burst of static erupted from the walkie, making Dennis jump.
"Schuster? Report."
Dennis winced at the shrill sounding voice. The hourly safety check. Christ, have I only been here an hour? His headache worsened. He snatched the walkie from his belt before it could go off again.
"This is Schuster, everything is clear. Does anyone have an ETA on Casey or the repair crew? I could use a break and we're roasting down here."
The walkie squelched again, sending a spike through his forehead.
"Casey's still trapped in Fort Meyer. Could be another hour or more before he gets back. I've got calls into the rest of your crew but so far I haven't heard zip. You might have to go solo. That OK?"
Dennis's hand tightened on the walkie. "I guess it has to be, doesn't it?" "More bad news, the AC guy is also delayed. Apparently, there was a problem at the hospital. Coolant tanks ruptured or something. So I don't expect him anytime soon. Patients before prisoners, you know? Don't worry buddy, you'll have my voice to guide you through."
The voice let out a piercing laugh, sending another spike of pain behind his eyes. Dennis used every ounce of self-control he had not to throw the walkie on the floor and stomp it to dust.
"Roger that," Dennis managed through gritted teeth.

"Alright, buddy. Think cool thought down there, I'll talk to you in an hour."

Dennis hurriedly turned the volume down on the walkie before he had to hear the asshole laugh at his own joke again. He paced the hall, wincing the closer he got to the combined noise pollution of the fan and air conditioner. He looked at the door. What would they do if I just left? He wished he had at least brought a flask, then he could have snuck off to the bathroom- No. Fuck no. He wouldn't start that habit. It was just a couple more hours. He could do that. he grabbed his water bottle off the desk and drained the now warm liquid in two swallows. He sat back down and thought of Julia.

7.

While Dennis was on the walkie wishing he could strangle the voice on the other end, Charlie was making his way through the different blocks of the prison, making his special deliveries. He was questioned only once, and he shrugged it off, telling the curious guard they had decided to change things up a little. The guard shook his head. "Sounds about right, changing deliveries and not telling the guards on duty."

"Yeah, I'm sorry about that, I'm just following orders boss."

"Go ahead Charlie, not gonna hold you up for their mistake." So Charlie went, spending the next hour handing out deadly weapons. He passed each one through the bars with a nod. He whispered to each of them, "Today is the day." They nodded back, having received their instructions. When he was done Charlie was given one last order. He didn't want any part of it, it was so much worse than making the shivs, but there was no choice. He wheeled his cart to the control room door. He waved and Dave buzzed him in. There were only two men inside, Dave and the the tower guard, who had stopped by for a quick chat. The two were old friends, and Charlie had seen them in here like this on several occasions. The tower guard, Charlie thought his name was Steve maybe, had one of the only firearms in the prison, a high powered rifle that was currently laying against the wall by the tower guards feet. He shouldn't have had it inside, but everyone was still in their cells, except for a couple of harmless trustees. "Charlie, what can I do you for?"

"Just here to see if either of you would like some breakfast."

"That sounds good to me, I could go for some eggs."

"Not a problem." He looked to maybe-Steve. The tower guard shook his head. "No thanks, I'm about to head up to the crow's nest." Charlie eyed the rifle and for the first time in years thought of Franklin Tran. *That was the first time I held a gun. This will be the last I guess.* Neither guard was paying Charlie much attention, which was going to be helpful for this next part. Charlie took a couple of steps back so he was behind the officers and then yelled out, pointing at the rec room floor below. "Oh my God, what are they doing to him?" Both men jumped to the window, looking down at the floor. Charlie grabbed the rifle and pointed at Dave and maybe-Steve. Suddenly he was back in that shitty convenience store, holding the sawed-off shotgun. This one was heavier, much heavier. And it wasn't empty this time. Maybe-Steve Dave were still looking down at the floor. "What the hell are you talking about Charlie.." He turned and his voice faded away like someone had turned down his volume. Possibly-Steve took a step forward, hands raised. "Charlie, I don't know what's going on here, but we can still fix this. You-" Charlie shot him in the face. He didn't want to but the little voice in his head was no longer that little. It was commanding now. There was no resisting. Dave screamed out as bits of brain and blood dripped onto one of the consoles. Charlie turned the rifle on Dave. "I'm really sorry about this." Charlie saw Franklin Tran's face and he closed his eyes, pulling the trigger again. With both men on the floor, he dropped the rifle and moved to a console covered in a sea of buttons and switches. The walkie on Dave's belt crackled. A voice came over the static. "Lewis to command, you guys hearing gunfire?" Charlie ignored the walkie and moved his hand over to the four lettered switches on the right-hand side of the panel. He flipped each one, A, B, C, D. With that every cell in the four blocks of the prison opened. Several inmates popped their heads out, confused. Others took advantage of the new open door policy and went for a stroll. Thirty of the inmates sat on their beds, awaiting instruction. 01 stood up in Its cell, grinning Its jack o lantern grin. *Now*, It thought at Its flock, *kill*. Charlie looked up from the console as if waking from a dream. He looked at the ceiling. "Kill who?" 01 cocked Its head for a moment, then answered. *Anyone. Everyone.* Charlie nodded, picking up the rifle. Below him, thirty men walked from their open cells, shivs in their hands. The riot had officially begun.

8.

Dennis sat at the desk, plowing through the paperwork. He looked at the clock, grabbed the next report, filled it out. Sweat dripped off his face onto the forms, smudging the ink as he wrote. He didn't notice. He fell into a pattern. fill out a form, check the clock. fill out a form, check the clock. He was averaging three minutes a page. He thought he could beat that time. He filled out a form, looked at the clock. Christ, he wanted a drink. Suddenly he heard someone talking, seemingly from inside his own head. *Now, kill*. A pause, then, *Anyone. Everyone.* He stood up, looking down the hall. It wasn't the inmates, they had laid back down, too hot to cause trouble. *That voice...* He had never heard it before but it seemed very familiar. He looked at the storage room door, the first time he had paid it any attention since he'd arrived. he took a step toward it when a very loud alarm began to blare, competing with the broken air conditioner. Dennis grabbed the walkie. "Hey, this is Schuster, what the hell is going on?" The voice on the walkie was no longer in a laughing mood. "We are in lockdown, repeat, we are in lockdown, reports of gunshots in C-block, inmates are out of their cells on all blocks. Stay put, we may have a riot on our hands." The walkie abruptly cut off. Dennis headed to the door at the end of the hall. Gunshots? How the hell did they get a gun into the prison? He locked the door, the alarm braying. He cringed, hands against his ears. *Why did I come back here? How did I think I would ever be ready for this again?* He passed by the prisoners, now awake and hanging off of their cell doors. He sat back down at the table, ignoring their questions. He was edging into a panic. *Can't leave now, no matter who comes to relieve me. God damn riot, of all days. This can't be happening.* The inmates were yelling but they were mostly drowned out by the cacophony of sounds. The heat seemed to intensify. Dennis tried to go back to the paperwork, anything to dull the anxiety, but he could barely get past the first line. Suddenly a vivid image of Julia and little Sean popped into his head. They were all in the back yard, he and Julia holding hands while Sean played with his trucks in the sand. It was cloudy, and getting worse. A thunderstorm on the way for sure, how Sean hated those. As lightning began to flash in the distance, Dennis saw something strange going on with the tree in the corner of the yard. The trunk seemed to be moving. Then those long, pale fingers slid across the bark, turning it black. Half hidden in the leaves Dennis caught sight of that smile, teeth gnashing, drool pouring from the sides of Its mouth. At the table Dennis clutched his pen, almost snapping it in two. He groaned, his heart slamming in his chest. The alarm abruptly shut off but Dennis didn't notice. The back yard disappeared and another scene replaced it. The two cops at the door, hats in hand, grave looks on their faces. Dennis shook his head. "No. No, I can't. Please." In his head, the cops sat with him on the couch, but it was different this time, worse than before. So much worse. As the officers sat down with him this time they pulled out a folder and tossed it on the coffee table. "We have some bad news we're afraid", the one cop said, his boredom evident on his face. "We need you to look at these photos, let us know if you recognize anyone. Or what's left of them." The other cop snorted laughter at that. Dennis looked at the folder with disbelief. The last thing he would ever do was open that folder, but he saw his hand reaching for it. A couple of the inmates were looking at Dennis with mounting concern. He was sitting completely still, mumbling something under his breath. Then he jerked back, looking straight ahead. "No. Please, no." In his head, the cop took out his notepad and flipped it open. "Wife's name is, excuse me, *was* Julia?" The other cop snickered again. The first cop continued. "And Sean, little Sean, correct. I got to tell you, Denny, I've been a cop twenty years, ten of those highway patrol and I've never seen a mess like this." Dennis caught movement out of the corner of his eye. Someone was moving around just behind the swinging doors. Someone or something. "It was her head." Dennis looked back at the officer. "What? What did you say?"

"I said when I got to the scene something was laying about forty feet from the car. I thought maybe it was the kid's ball at first. Turns out it was her head." Tears streamed down Dennis's face. He shook his head back and forth. The officer grabbed the folder out of his hands. "Hey you don't need to take my word for it, all the proof you need is right here." As he opened the folder and Dennis snapped out of his trance. He pushed back from the table, almost tipping it over. Papers went see-sawing to the floor. He grabbed the sides of his head. "No, I can't! I fucking can't!" All the inmates were up now, either at the doors or back against the wall. The cop in his head turned to Dennis, a sadistic grin on his face. "Where you going, I didn't even show you what happened to the brat." Dennis screamed at the top of his lungs, punching himself in the sides of his head. He fell to his knees. The inmates looked at each other, more than a little afraid. Then the images were gone and Dennis sat on the floor, weeping, trying to catch his breath. The heat was bad enough, and screaming like that had made him a bit dizzy. He crawled to the chair and plopped into the seat, eyes stinging with sweat. he didn't bother to wipe it away. Jerry ventured a foot or so from his cell door. "Schuster? You, ah, you OK?" Dennis looked in their direction. He would have killed every one of them for one fucking drink. "I'm fine Jerry, just the heat. Why don't you-"

There was a huge thud from behind the storage room door as if someone had charged it with a battering ram. Dennis was on his feet again in an instant, nightstick in hand. Jerry jumped back. "What the hell, Schuster?" Dennis looked at Jerry and others. "You didn't hear that? Any of you?"

Benedict said, "I didn't hear nothing but you screaming, boss man. Maybe you should call for some assistance, you know?"

Dennis ignored him and slowly made his way to the door. he took out his flashlight and had a look inside. All was as it should have been. He put the light away and started to turn back when he heard the same sound he heard the first time he encountered 01. The sound of those long fingers sliding across the door. Dennis felt the bottom drop out of his stomach. "Please, Christ no. No! Don't do this, I beg you." Benedict had his face crammed in the bars, trying to see down the hall. "Who is he talking too?" Yost was pale and shivered despite the heat in the room. "You know who he's talking to." Dennis wandered away from the door, mumbling. He bumped into the table, Not seeming to notice. "No more.. I can't handle anymore." Then there was a voice, the same one that he heard earlier. That wet gurgling rasp, but Soothing, now. No, Dennis, no more. come here now, I have something to tell you.

Yost was the only one that can see Dennis clearly and the view terrified him. Dennis had stopped screaming and was facing the supply closet, slumped and slack-jawed. His mouth twitched every few seconds as if he's trying to speak. His hands open and close rapidly.

"Oh shit, Hey Schuster! Dennis!" Jerry piped up. "What the hell is he doing now?"

"Nothing. That's what scares me.

Dennis didn't hear any of this. The sound of the broken air conditioner slowed then faded away. It was completely quiet inside Dennis's head for the first time in months. He stared at the door, hearing nothing but raspy breath on the other side. And then the voice again, like dead leaves crushed under your feet. Listening to the voice gave him a headache, but what it had to say... "Dennis. If you let me out of here, I will bring back the boy." Dennis clutched his face, tracing bloody tracks in his cheeks. If it had promised to bring them both back he wouldn't have believed, it would have been too good to be true but Sean, Little Sean... maybe It could. For all he knew that thing was immortal. And Little Sean, had barely a life at all before it was snuffed out. It wasn't fair. He deserved more than that. Dennis snapped out of his daze. He looked over at Yost, then back at the door. "OK. OK, I'll do it." Without hesitating, Dennis walked to the door and began unlocking the padlocks. Yost tightened the grip on his bars. "Hey, Schuster! Hey, you shouldn't do that!" Jerry now has his face mashed into the bars. "Yost, what's wrong with him?"

"He's opening the God damn storage room." Benedict chimed in. "Hey if you're in the mood to open doors, Schuster, I'm right here."
"Shut the fuck up Benedict! Schuster, please listen to me! Don't open that door!"

Dennis ignored all of them, tossing the padlocks to the floor. He opened the door and walked in, clicking on the overhead light. The bulb flashed brightly for a moment then went out. Dennis barely noticed. He reached the back wall and began tossing boxes left and right until the small submarine door is in view again. As he kicked the last of the boxes out of the way, he had none of the fear he had the first time he saw that small door. He placed his hands on the door, sliding them down to the latch. Dust and flakes of rust floated to the floor. Dennis tries to move it, but it wouldn't budge.

Yost called out again, but he got no response. He sat down, his back against the bars, panicked. "Something really bad is gonna happen." He got no argument.

Dennis yanked on the wheel, straining until his eyes bulged, but it wouldn't move. Suddenly he heard a laugh, the same one he had heard during his first night shift. Little Sean. He was in there! He yelled out and grabbed his nightstick, jamming it in the wheel for leverage. He put his foot on the wall and pulled back with all his might, screaming out as he did. Finally, it began to turn. His stomach rolled over. "Sean! I'm coming to get you, son! It's OK! I'm going to fix it!

Yost stood up and screamed one last time toward the door. "Schuster!! Whatever the fuck you are doing in there stop now! I'm begging you!"

Dennis gave one more yank on the nightstick. It broke in half but as it did the wheel spun over. the door cracked opened for the first time in over a hundred years. A stench roiled out from the crack in the door that made Dennis retch. A moment later those impossible fingers snaked out of the room and grasped the door, shoving it open. Dennis looked up at the grin, now with no glass between them and he knew. He wasn't going to get his boy back, of course he wasn't. His boy was dead and he would soon be joining him. Tears spilled down his face as 01 put one of its gnarled fingers under Dennis's chin, lifting his head. it caressed his cheek, sending convulsions through him. He retched again. 01 leaned down, its mouth beside Dennis's ear. Then It spoke aloud. "Thank you."

Yost stood at the door, more concerned by the silence coming out of the room than he was with the noise. Then he heard a scream that was cut off abruptly. Yost backed up and sat on his cot. He started to pray without realizing it.

9.

Two hours after the riot began it was over. Twelve guards and over fifty inmates, including Charlie C, were killed. The siege surely would have lasted longer but halfway through the ordeal a majority of the armed instigators dropped their weapons and surrendered, looking confused at what was going on around them. A headcount was taken, with E Block being the last building secured since it was separate from the main facility. After several attempts were made to contact E Block went unanswered, the SWAT team was ordered down the hill to investigate. Inside, E Block was silent with the exception of the hum and clank of the dying air conditioner. Then there was pounding on the outside door. There was a burst of static as Dennis's walkie, now laying next to Jerry's cell, went off. It was Zale's voice on the other end. "Schuster, you read me? Get to the door if you can, kid, no one can seem to find the God damn keys to this ancient door. Schuster you in there? Dennis?" Then more pounding. Several muffled voices can be heard outside, then silence. The next moment the door burst off its hinges. The SWAT team charged the room, expecting just about anything but what they actually saw. They all stood silent. Zale pushed his way past the team. "Can someone tell me what the hell is hap-" Zale stood with SWAT, just as dumbfounded. Then he saw the open storage room door at the end of the hall and his stomach shot to the floor. he started down the hall on legs that felt like paper. The SWAT leader called out to him but he didn't hear him. He made it closer to the door, heart thudding in his chest, trying not to look in any of the cells as he passed. He knew what he was going to see in the storage room before he got there but it still put him on his knees. The little door was open, the stench of its former captor lingering in the air. Tears mixed with the sweat on his face. "Dear God, Dennis, what did you do? What did you do?" The team leader joined Zale at the end of the hall. After a quick look in the room, he grabbed his walkie. "Someone needs to get the warden down the hill, right fucking now. Tell him we have multiple escapees from E block, and at least one hostage."

10.

An hour later Zale and the warden were seated in his office. It wasn't as hot in here as it was on E block, but it was close. Zale was half slumped in his chair, pale and motionless. He looked like he had aged ten years since he had sat down. The video they were watching had just ended. The Warden sat in silence for a moment then he leaned back in his chair which elicited a protesting creak and wiped the sweat off his face with an already soaked handkerchief. He jabbed a finger at the screen. "Play that again please."

Zale closed his eyes then pushed play on the remote. The screen showed the grainy, black and white footage from the old camera in E Block that swung slowly back and forth own the hall. The video began with the camera passing the inmates, all of them smashed against the bars and wordlessly yelling. It reached Dennis as he was opening the storage closet. The camera swings back just as he begins to hurl boxes away from the back. Zale doesn't want to see any of this but he does. He watches, hands clutched on the arms of his chair, unable to turn away. He thought about their conversation at Reggie's, about Dennis's first day. How cold it had been that night! Back then Zale thought they had their 01 problem figured out, but one thing he never took into account was that 01 might have plans of its own. Zale flinched. The worst part of the video was coming up. As the camera made its way back down the hall Dennis can be seen slowly backing out of the storage room, hands raised. Then he is violently snatched back into the room by an unseen force. Zale closed his eyes. *Christ Dennis, why? Why would you do it?* Just as the camera began its journey back down the hall a figure can be seen stepping out of the shadows of the room, incredibly tall, wearing all black. His face was obscured by the door jam. The camera moved across the inmates, who are all now clearly terrified, shrinking back from the cell doors, pounding on the walls. As the camera passes Benedict he falls to his knees, grabbing at his eyes. He looks like he is trying to pull them out. As the camera makes its final pass it reveals that every cell is now empty, as is the door to the storage room.

The warden waved his hand at the Zale. "That's enough, don't you think?" He wiped face again then looked at Zale. "That USB holds two weeks of camera memory. I watched it back to the beginning. Only one person went into the storage room. Gilles, I think it was. He grabbed some napkins off the shelf the locked it back up. No one else went near it. So, while also trying to suss out why thirty of our most docile inmates suddenly took it upon themselves to tear this prison to the ground, I have the even more urgent question of just who the fuck was lurking in your storage closet and how they could have possibly gotten in there in the first place. Do you have any ideas to share?" Zale thought about it. If there was any way telling the warden about 01 could help them find Dennis, he would have done so in a heartbeat, but he knew all that would accomplish would be getting him committed. He shook his head. "No sir I don't." *But you're going to have to go back a hell of a lot further than two weeks to get any answers.* The warden slammed his hand on the desk. "Were you also unaware of the secret room hidden behind the boxes of toilet paper?" Zale cleared his throat. "I was aware of the door but never had any reason to investigate it." The warden laughed at that, shaking his head. "Jesus Christ. Well, there certainly is a reason to investigate now. What about the rest of your buddies down the hill? Did they ever express in curiosity in the hobbit hole hidden in the storage room?"

"Not to my knowledge."

The warden sat back and took a long look at Zale. "You know this is the end for you here, don't you? You and everyone on your crew. I expect resignations from you all effective today."

"Yes sir, I think that's for the best." Zale turned to leave, then paused. "I couldn't help but notice in the official statement as well as in the A.P.B. there was no mention of the...the person in the storage room."

The Warden snorted. "What would you have had me say, Lt.? That a giant being held against his will on death row crawled out of a supply closet, tucked four inmates and a guard under his arm and vanished into smoke? That would go over well on the six 'o clock news. And assure a trial you and your boys. SWAT knows about the little room but I explained to them that part of the prison is very old, for all we know they were torturing inmates in there once upon a time. They agreed to be discreet about the situation. They don't think it has anything to do with the disappearances." The Warden stood up. "This prison has had enough bad publicity. Higher than average homicide rates. Higher than average suicide rates. And the stories we've all heard and choose to ignore. That the prison is haunted or cursed or possessed."

Right on all counts. Or you were. This prison isn't haunted anymore, Zale thought. The thought of 01 free in the world popped in his head and for the hundredth time since he walked into E Block this afternoon and his stomach dropped. The Warden continued. "Utter nonsense of course. But if this video ever made it out...We don't need to muddy the waters. We've sent out an ABP and we made our statement. During the riot, four very dangerous men escaped death row with a hostage. I have every confidence that they will be found and I'm sure when they're captured they will be happy to put the experience behind them, without mention of the mystery man, given the right incentives. And in a few months E Block will be knocked down and that little room will be a memory, and hopefully all the talk of goblins and spirits with it. I think you can agree with that right, Zale?"

Zale looked up from his daze. "Yes, sir."

"Good, now I believe we both have some calls to make." Zale made his way out of the warden's office. The Warden pulled the USB from the television, gave it a look and dropped it into his cup of coffee. A few drops splashed onto the desk as it sank to the bottom of the mug.

Epilogue

Sometime before dawn. The sky outside the window was just beginning to brighten along the horizon. Zale still sat at the desk, the now empty bottle of scotch set on a stack of papers covered top to bottom in his slanted handwriting. He looked around the room as if waking from a dream. He pushed back from the desk, wincing. His hand was cramped and his spine felt like a cylinder of broken glass. One of the many joys of being old. He stretched, joints popping and cracking as he did. He hobbled to the window and looked out at the advancing light. *Christ, I wrote the night away,* he thought as he opened and closed his writing hand. He looked down and saw a touch of frost in the corners of the window. *I guess Indian summer is officially over.* He wasn't particularly upset by the news. Zale looked back at the desk and the story he had written. A confession of sorts. Not quite done though. There were still a few important things to get to, and how he dreaded it. After all that came before, What he still had to tell was worse. Much worse. He sat back down at the desk. *One last story. I better hurry before I lose my nerve.* He picked up the pen and finished it.

Dennis and the escaped inmates of E Block were never found. The manhunt lasted two months and the FBI had joined in before it was all said and done, but in the end, they didn't have so much as a single valid lead. No surprise to the few of us that knew the truth. The public backlash was huge of course, what with four murderers on the loose, and the Warden felt pressure from every direction.

He threw Dennis under the bus, a move that surprised none that knew him. He called a press conference, the revised official statement being that for the inmates to have escaped so efficiently they must have had inside help. Cue the scapegoat. Dennis, already mentally unbalanced after a car accident earlier that summer resulted in the death of his wife and son, had snapped. Not a hostage at all, Dennis had, in fact, freed the inmates and loaded them into one of the prisons transport vans during the riot and vanished. He may have even instigated the riot as cover. The best evidence had the crew headed to Mexico, as two of the inmates were reportedly seen together near the border. This was complete bullshit. Gloria Dunham, the eyewitness that reported seeing the inmates had been dismissed as a notorious frequenter of tip-lines. In the past year alone she had called her local police with the whereabouts of no fewer than thirteen felons. (All discounted) Secondly, there was no way Dennis could have stolen one of the transport vans because the prison only had two transports and they were both still in the prison garage. It didn't matter. The public was far less concerned with the escaped killers now that they were off terrorizing the people of Mexico, and if they did have Dennis held hostage, no one was beating down the door to get him back. He had no family and any sympathy for him had been on the decline ever since his father in law had trashed him in an interview for the local station, blaming him for the death of his daughter and grandson. Of course, none of us E Block guards were around by then. I called the boys soon as left the Wardens office and told them the news. By the end of the day, we were officially retirees.

During that first month we had our share of reporters asking about Dennis and the jailbreak. We all responded with a smile and a 'no comment.' I never slept more than a couple hours a night after the riot, and what sleep I did get was nothing but bad dreams. Most of the time I sat in my old easy chair, drinking coffee and thinking. About 01, where It might be and what It might be doing. And about Dennis. After the first month with no trace of them, I began hoping that he was dead, as horrible as that sounds. Because the alternative... I hadn't talked with my men, correction, my former men since our last day. After all that had happened, I figured we needed time to separate from it all. A couple of days after the warden dumped the whole mess on Dennis's doorstep on live T.V. I got a call from Burns' wife. He had survived Raymond's attack but it turned out it was just borrowed time. Sometime the night before last he'd suffered a massive heart attack and passed away. She was wracked with guilt because since the accident they hadn't slept in the same room. He had become an insomniac(I could relate) and he had taken to laying on the couch downstairs so he could watch Netflix without keeping her up. "He loved the documentaries." She told me through sobs. I tried to console her, but I think she mostly just wanted to talk to someone about it with so I shut my mouth and listened. "I've always been such a heavy sleeper, but I thought I would hear him if he needed me. I guess I was wrong. And he looked so... so scared when I found him. Terrified, really. He knew the end was coming and he had to face it alone." She began crying again but I was stuck on what she had said. Easily terrified wasn't a phrase I would use to describe Burns. Even facing death as he did earlier that very year he was mostly just pissed off about it. The only thing I had ever seen him afraid of, the only thing he was afraid of the day he was stabbed was 01. And it got me thinking, just what did Burns face alone in that living room that could have scared him that bad? Scared him to death. After we hung up I called the other guys to commiserate. I got in touch with everyone but Sharpe. He was the bachelor of the crew and a loner in his off time. I figured he was just off having a beer. But after several more calls the next day I began to worry. I was thinking of Jeffries and the cancer that ate him alive. I decided to pay Sharpe a visit.

 The next morning I was sitting in his driveway. It was unseasonably hot for October and I sat with the door open but I was having trouble making myself get out of the car. What was I going to see when he opened the door? A frail bag of bones? Or something worse. Leprosy maybe, or a plague. It turned out to be neither, but it was no less disturbing. The front step was littered with a week's worth of unread newspapers. A quick check in the mailbox showed me the same. Sharpe could have been out enjoying his retirement, the papers and and mail meant nothing, but then there was the front door. No correctional officer, former or otherwise is going to leave the house for a week and forget to shut the damn door. After calling out his name a few times I decided to go in and have a look. Everything looked in order until I reached the living room. There was an overturned wine glass on the rug, laying in the center of a red stain that was never coming out. There was a paperback book in a chair nearby, torn in half. There were a few drops of wine on the pages. Or I thought it was wine on first inspection. But the more I looked at it the more I was sure it was blood. The queasiness in my stomach that had never really left me since the day of the riot came back triple. I called the police, knowing what I was going to hear. A grown man was allowed to disappear if he wanted to. I called anyway, made the report for all the good it did. The next day his car was found in a rest stop a State over, keys still in the ignition. Foul play was suspected but there were no leads to follow. I could have told them I suspected an immortal demon that had recently escaped death row might be responsible, but they probably would have doubted my story. My doubts, on the other hand, were fading fast. A heart attack is one thing. Add a missing person in the span of two weeks, both of them former guards on E block... that's something else. When I heard about the car accident three days later, I was certain. We were being hunted. Casey went out to grab a gallon of milk for his wife. On the way back from the store he lost control of his car and crashed into a ravine. No rain, no visual impediments. He just drove off a cliff. An eye witness, a hiker out with her dog, said it looked like there may have been another person in the car when he went over but no evidence was found to corroborate that. I have a couple of buddies on the force and they showed me photos of the crash. Casey had been almost decapitated, which my cop friend admitted was pretty severe for the short distance the car had rolled, but stranger things had happened. This I could vouch for. What really confused him was the driver's side door. "When a car rolls down a hill, doors and windows are smashed inward, from hitting rocks or tree stumps, what have you. this door looks like it was kicked open from the inside. Which is impossible. Casey was deceased before the car reached the bottom of the ravine and even if he did survive, no human can kick a car door so hard it folds in half." I went home, feeling a terror I had never felt in my adult life.

We were being picked off one by one and no one would ever believe it. Later that night I called Gilles and suggested that we should meet and talk through any options we might have. "You think that's smart boss? I mean if we're in one place won't that just make it easier for It to get us?"

"I told you, Gilles, you don't have to call me boss anymore, and I think we'll be OK if we meet in a public place." I didn't mention that if that thing wanted us, it wouldn't matter where we were or who was with us.

"That's true. We could meet at Reggie's."

I winced at the suggestion. The last time I was there I was telling Dennis that monsters were real and he was now the caretaker of one. Christ, that seemed so long ago. I agreed to meet him there at noon the following day, but plans changed. Around ten in the morning, I got another call. It was a house fire. The place had burned to the ground before the fire department made it to the scene. Gilles was found inside, so was his wife and their youngest, Emily, who had come home from college on a visit.

After the fire I thought hard about leaving, but where would I go? Me and Marta had spent most of our lives here. Now that she was gone the house was all I had left that was ours. I probably would have stayed right there until my own 'accident', but sometime near the end of October, I received a phone call. The weather had finally changed, and a freezing wind was battering the house. It was late, around three in the morning. I had a thin blanket wrapped around my legs, the only part of me that ever really gets cold. Most of the lights in the house were on, and my gun was in my lap. I had just started to doze off when the cell phone vibrated across the coffee table. I jumped up, twisted in the blanket, knocking the gun to the floor. I was lucky I didn't hit the floor myself. Brilliant, I thought as I snatched up the gun, maybe I can shoot off a fucking toe next time. I picked up the phone and turned it around. Unknown number. I'd gotten about a million of those, most of the time it was someone trying to sell me a timeshare or life insurance, but I was pretty sure all the little insurance salesmen were sleeping at this hour.

My heart started thudding so hard in my chest I could hear it. I hit the answer button but I didn't speak. At first, there was nothing on the line, then I heard sobbing, hoarse and choked. It was Dennis. I don't know how I knew from just that sound but I did. My grip tightened on the phone. I tried to speak but all that came out was a dry croak. I did better on the second attempt. "Dennis? Dennis, do you know where you are, son? If you can tell me where you are I can get someone-"

"Please." He sounded like an old man, broken and lost. I could hear something else in the background, a soft chuckle. The sound of it sent tremors of revulsion through me. I sank back into my chair without noticing. I tried to speak but my words had gone again. All I could get out was a whisper. "Dennis, I want to help you, son, if you ca-"

Dennis ignored me. He knew as well as I did there was no help to give. As he talked I could hear the fear, the pain, in every word.

"I'm- supposed to give you a message. Can you hear me?"

"Yes, I can hear you."

"What is happening is- your fault. You, your friends and all the ones before you. But they're the fortunate ones. You are going to be kept for a long time. You are going to suffer. You.." Suddenly there was a commotion on the other side of the phone. Then Dennis was back and it sounded like he was running. He panted into the phone as he screamed. "Zale! Don't let It take you! It's Hell here! It's Hell! It's-" Then the sound of the phone skittering across the floor. There was a pause, then the phone was picked up and I could hear breathing, slow and measured. Then one whispered grunt, barely decipherable. "Soon."

We were fools to ever think we could rid ourselves of 01. I think now that we were never in control of anything, not Its jailers, but a nuisance to be waited out. Dennis had asked me when I visited him the summer his family was killed if I thought 01 could have had something to do with it. I laughed it off at the time, but the thought bothered me enough to do some checking. The man that hit Julia and Sean was a delivery driver. His route never took him anywhere near the prison, but I dug a little deeper. I had a friend at the the prison run his name and it turned out the driver had a brother in D block. Visited him twice a month. It couldn't just be coincidence but the thing is, the visitor center was as far as you could get from E block, which opened up some truly frightening connotations. If that driver was manipulated by 01, then whatever we thought we knew about 01 and Its sphere of influence was out the window. If It could reach that far, then its conceivable It could have been involved in the riot. Not that it matters now. Any chance we had of containing It, however slim, is long gone. I wish there was something I could do, someone to tell, but 01 was our responsibility. I'm the last link in the chain now and I pray that after I'm gone It will fade away, back to whatever hell it came from. Whatever happens, I won't be around to see it. Dennis was right, I can't let that thing take me, to be tortured and tormented for the rest of my life. Dennis is most assuredly dead and that thing is hunting for me now, I know it. No, I've decided this Winter will be my last. When the snow starts to melt and the days arch longer, I'll go downstairs and get in the bathtub, put my gun under my chin and finish the business 01 started. It will be a while before anyone finds me, but the mess will be contained. It's the least I can do. Until then I'll keep watch, and I'll remember. Rest in peace Dennis, wherever you may be.

She sat on a plateau as her great-grandchildren, three girls and two boys, played in a field of flowers below. She smiled as she watched them chase each other through the tall grass, then a memory surfaced. She was at the mouth of the cave, her cave, nervous as she looked down at the people that would become her new family. Then for the first time in many years, she thought of the creature she helped bring to this world. She touched the symbol carved into her chest, now faded and hidden in her wrinkled skin. She chuckled as she touched the scar. Time was a bastard. So much had happened they had reached the ocean. She and her family had made a good life for themselves on that shore. They spent their days fishing and tending the crops. The years were bountiful but in the back of her mind, she felt her happiness was temporary. She was always waiting for punishment, retribution for her part in bringing the beast and four years af-

ter settling on the beach, judgment was passed. One of her daughters had slipped away and went climbing on the rock face at the southern end of the shore. She had always been the more adventurous of the two girls, always the first in the ocean for a swim or into the fields to explore. They found her lying at the foot of the rocks, blood pooled in the sand around her head. She was broken by her child's death but not surprised. Retribution had come.

    Two winters came and went before she was any semblance of her former self. She had lost one of her own and prayed that was enough to pay for her sin. Things returned to normal and time slowly slipped by. Now her daughter was thirteen and as strong in the sight like her mother, maybe more so. She had become fiercely protective of her only child, never wanting her to stray very far. Her daughter obliged. She taught her daughter as she had been taught, of the hunt and of the old magics. One night she woke with a scream caught in her throat. She hadn't had nightmares about that other world since her last visit to the pool. This was different, but more vision than dream, and it would not be denied. She was to leave her beach and once again travel the roads she thought she had left behind. The beast was out there and people had to be warned and warded. She couldn't know it but her vision occurred at the same moment 01 was crawling out of Its hot spring, rested and recuperated.

    She left the village the next morning, her husband and daughter beside her. they refused to hear any argument that involved them being left behind. They headed north, exploring, educating and protecting. She wasn't on the road long before she heard her first tale of the beast. An old merchant recounted a tale of a small village on the edge of the desert where he would trade. The last time he passed through the entire village was gone. Shredded tents and bleached bones strewn in the sand were the only reminders anyone had ever been there. He leaned in and in hushed tones said, "The worst part was it looked to me like they had done it to each other. The bodies still intact seemed to have died at their neighbor's throats." She told of the destruction of her village and the creature responsible that pursued her to the cave. She no longer told people her part in the creatures summoning in order to protect her family from the wrath of those she told.

Many would take their anger at the creature out on her family and not think twice about it. She shared the warding symbols with the man, who carved them into his arm before the sunrise.

Three years pass and her daughter, now a beautiful woman, had found herself in love with a young man. She came to her mother with the news. They wanted to return to the beach. She understood. The beach was the only home her daughter had known and it was natural she would want to start her own family there. She searched her own heart and found it was at peace. She had done enough. It was time to go home.

Soon after returning to the beach her daughter gave birth to a girl of her own, whom she named after her sister. A year later she welcomed her grandson. Both of the children showed signs of the sight. They would be taught. In the days before her grandson's tenth birthday, her husband cut his hand while making the child a skiff. It became infected and within weeks he had died. She buried him in the hills they spent so many evenings strolling through, the one true love of her life. There would be no one after him. She did not feel his death was punishment. That bill had been paid in blood years before. This was simply life, as bitter sometimes as it was sweet. She focused on the future. Her grandson was stronger in the sight than even she had been, and he helped her remember the symbols she had so long forgotten. The two of them would sit by the fire late in the night, writing the symbols and their meanings down on parchment, but kept the operation a secret unless anyone was foolish enough to read the wrong words and find themselves in that world of terrors. They were dangerous to have but she felt they would be very important for the children yet to come. Now as she sat on that hill overlooking her village, children laughing below, thinking of the creature that strangely was responsible for this life. She came here more and more often, watching the sunset as she did with her man so many times before. She let out a heavy sigh. Her time was close, she had felt it for a while now, and though it made her sad, the tears were not because she was almost finished in this world but because she wanted to see what her grandchildren would become. She didn't want to miss a moment with them. The sun was almost touching the sea now. She looked out across *the waves, eyes misty. I've taught them all I could. They will be safe. But you.. She scrawled the warding symbol in the dirt with one arthritic finger, the last of thousands. What are you doing out there, right now? Sleeping? Feeding? How many sit in the dark, scared to sleep because if they close their eyes they might see your face? Or hear those long fingers scraping along the wall, the last sound they may ever hear? If I could I would comfort them, tell them that I been in your thoughts, almost drowned in them. It was a vile place, but informative. She remembered the altar, reading the symbols over and over, seeing the bones of the six-legged things the beasts had used as food or sacrifice or both. But, there were other bones as well, long and thin, bones that only could have come from the beasts siblings. They are powerful and they are terrifying, but they do die. You will outlive me and by a long stretch, I have no doubts, but you will not live forever. She laid back, a smile on her face as the sun dipped under the horizon. She closed her eyes and thought of her family as the first stars appeared above her.*

(Un)frame

1.

Elizabeth was halfway home after a three day marathon of paperwork, arguments with backers, and a modicum of actual progress on the project. She was exhausted, and her last instruction before she left work was to not to be disturbed for at least 8 hours, so she was more than a little irritated when the phone rang and she saw that it was Stan, one of her partners calling. She picked up, trying not to sound as angry as she was, Stan could be a drama queen sometimes. "Somebody better be dying, Stan. Like on the floor in a puddle of blood dying."

"Its Jerry, Liz, uh, you need to get back to the office." She felt a jab of concern. "Oh, Christ, is somebody actually dying?" "No, nothing like that but-" "Jerry, listen to me. I haven't had a day off and two and a half weeks, I haven't slept more than 2 hours since I don't even remember. What could possibly be so important I cant get a few hours sleep?" "Uh.. I don't really don't think we should talk about it on the phone." This cut through the exhaustion and the irritation.. Jerry was a lot of things, but he was most definitely NOT a drama queen. If he didn't want to mention it over the phone, it was important. "All right I'm turning around, I'll be there in 10." When she arrived back of the office Jerry and Stan we're standing in a line, looking like they had just got caught looking at their dad's Playboys. "Guys? What happened?"

"It's about (Un)frame."

Elizabeth's concern quickly dissolved into anger. "(Un)frame? I thought something was wrong with the AI. You dragged me back for this low tier money grab?"

Elizabeth, along with Stan and Jerry, had spent the last four years working on a cutting edge AI. It was one of the most intelligent they had ever seen, and they were within months of unveiling it, if they could keep the investors at bay for a little longer. The (un)frame project, in which AI took any image and expanded it, was just a gimmick for the masses. People seem to enjoy crap like that, and Elizabeth was fine with it. It would keep her company's name in the public eye, earn them some cash, but it certainly wasn't something that she was concerned with.

"Boss, I know you're drained, God knows we all are, but you have to see this." Jerry and Stan led her over to his computer terminal. He swiped The mouse and the monitor came back to life. A cheery graphic popped up on the screen- Welcome to (Un)frame! Jerry clicked an image from the files.

"This is from one of my family vacations about thirty years ago. This is the only picture from that trip to survive a fire at my folks house. That's me and my brother standing by our old station wagon. It's a fairly close up shot, not much for the AI to work with, but that was the point. I wanted to see what it could do with limited information. This is what it gave us. I expanded the image a dozen times now. We got the same results every time. The exact same expanded image. And.... it didn't extrapolate some random nonsense, it somehow created that exact day. I don't know how but it did."

Elizabeth let out an aggravated snort of laughter. "Jerry, you know that's not possible."

"I know it isn't possible, but.. here It is. Look at the expanded part of the picture. There, on top of the station wagon, that big container my dad strapped to the roof where he stored our luggage. We called it the big mac. And there by the back of the car, the cactus. A few minutes after this picture was taken my brother tripped and fell face first into that cactus. We spent two hours in some Podunk Arizona emergency room while they pulled a hundred prickles out of him. And the store, Barney's souvenirs. With the faded red door. And that little statue on the stairs, the donkey wearing a sombrero. I remember begging my parents to buy it for me. Boss, i cant explain it."

Elizabeth was more amused than angry now. The two of them looked genuinely frightened. "Guys, there's nothing to explain. This doesn't mean anything, its just really good AI for Christ's sake, it extrapolated what little it could from the location, found some pictures of this gift shop online and gave you a approximation. A really good approximation, from the look on your faces."

Stan shook his head "This computer is never connected to the internet, it's fir design only. We did do a search on the place, it isn't there anymore, it's a gas station now. But even the pictures we did find from this time frame don't show this angle of the parking lot. This was just the AI, Liz." She pointed to a figure in the background of the picture. They were wearing a large black floppy hat and a black Trench coat. Only the lower after the face was visible, and it was distorted and blurred.

"And what about this twelve fingered nightmare lurking around in the back, was he on the family vacation as well?"

"That's just a random artifact. But this sure as hell isn't. Check the reflection in the back window." Elizabeth looked closer and saw a man's face slightly obscured by a camera. Jerry tapped the monitor. "That's my dad." He took out his phone and showed them a picture of his dad, older but clearly the same man. "How in the hell did this thing know he was taking the picture?" Elizabeth shook her head. "Jerry, I-" Jerry held up his hand. "Hold on. Stan, show her the Christmas picture."

Stan reluctantly pulled a picture out of his wallet. It was him and his sister sitting in front of a Christmas tree. The top half of the tree was not in the pic.

"I was about seven or eight when dad took this. On the top of this tree is an ornament my sister made in the first grade, a coat hanger bent into a star and wrapped in tin foil. My mom put that thing on top of the tree for a decade. She has the only pictures of it, and they're not online. She wouldn't know how to upload picture if someone held a gun to her head. We ran this one a few times as well. Same results." Stan placed the picture on the scanner and initiated (Un)frame. the picture popped up on the Monitor and begin to expand. Sure enough as the picture expanded, it revealed the tree with a giant aluminum star perched crookedly at the top.

"Now, look at this." He expanded the picture further to reveal a slight woman in a red bathrobe sitting on the couch smiling as she watched the children unwrap their presents. "That's my mom, who forbid anybody from taking a picture of her in that ratty bathrobe. But here it is, complete with the little yellow flowers on the pockets. And behind her, that God awful wallpaper with the dancing gnomes. I always hated that wallpaper." Elizabeth took a step back, appraising them both. "So.. what are you telling me here? That you think this thing can what? See backward in time? That's crazy."

Jerry shrugged and pointed to the laptop. "I would have said the same thing until I saw those."

Stan pointed at her. "You do it. I mean, if you think this is some sort of elaborate prank, that we'd call you back here knowing you hadn't slept in 72 hours-"

"I didn't say that." She looked down at the computer. She felt a flutter go through her. There was something, as if she was being drawn toward it. "I believe you, of course. But..I guess I should see for myself, right?" She walked across the hall to her office and took a picture off of her desk. She started to walk out, stopped and grabbed a small red vase off of a shelf as well. She headed back to the guys and held out the two items. "This is a picture of me and my grandma." it was a picture of a 10-year-old Elizabeth sitting on a couch next to an older woman. "You see that little table next to the couch? This vase used to set on that table. But when I was nine I was chasing my brother through the house. I knocked that vase on the floor, smashed into a hundred pieces. See?" She passed the vase to them. It had been broken and clumsily repaired. "I'd Never seen my grandma so upset. It turned out my grandpa had sent her that vase while he was stationed in Korea during the war. The vase made it back, he never did. So obviously it meant a lot to her. After I found that out and I spent half the night gluing the thing back together. When she saw it the next morning we both sat and cried for about ten minutes. It was a bonding experience for the both of us. After that incident the vase set on a shelf above the couch. And as far as I know the only person that had a picture of it was her, and she's been gone for years. So let's see what happens gentlemen." Elizabeth placed the picture on the scanner and pushed the button. It appeared on the laptop. She sat down, and that strange sensation came over her again. She hit the enter key and the picture began to expand. A moment later Elizabeth inhaled sharply. The photo revealed the shelf above the couch, and the cracked red vase set in the middle. Elizabeth sat back in the chair, staring at the screen. She ran her hands through her hair. "Holy shit."

Stan gave her a look. "So we are all agreement that this thing can somehow see backward in time?" Elizabeth nodded. "Yeah, I'm in agreement. Its not just the vase. You see this cut on the couch?" there was a small slash in the front of the cloth couch that had been stitched together. "Grandma said that it happened during one of their moves. I had completely forgotten about it. How the hell..?" Her eyes moved back to the vase sitting on the shelf in the picture. Suddenly that tingling in her stomach was much stronger. An urge over took her. She started typing into the prompt. Stan looked concerned. "What are you doing, Liz?"

"I'm not exactly sure, I just have this feeling..." Elizabeth typed the sentence, *The vase was never broken*. Jerry read what she had typed and rubbed his jaw nervously. "Boss, I don't know why, but I think that's a really bad idea." Elizabeth reread what she had typed. Her finger hovered over the enter key for a moment, then she pushed it. As soon as her finger left the button an intense pain shot up her spine into her skull. She screamed as she fell back in the chair, vision blurring, ears ringing. Stan and Jerry rushed to her. They turned her over on her back. They were talking to her, but she couldn't understand them. Another jolt of pain shot through the back of her skull, not as a bad as the first, but enough. She grabbed her head. Jerry and Stan got her to the little couch in the corner of the office. Her brain felt like it was being split in half. Suddenly she had two very specific memories. One was of her chasing her brother around her Grandma's living room, they were laughing. She almost had him when she slipped on the hardwood floor, her elbow knocking the vase over. Her Grandma's face, so angry. But then another memory pushed its way in. She was still playing tag, but this time her brother ran left instead of right, taking the chase outside. The vase remained untouched. She was shaken out of her new memories by Stan, who was very near panic. "Elizabeth! Can you hear me, are you okay?" The ringing in her ears began to subside and she was able to nod slowly. "I'm OK." She held her head as she sat up. "My head.. i feel like..It's like someone deleted a file and, but they didn't do it correctly, and both files are occupying the same space." Stan looked at her strange. "What the hell are you talking about?" Jerry let out a yell. "Oh my God!" He pointed at the computer. In the picture the vase had moved from the Shelf to the table. Elizabeth looked at the picture, then looked over at the actual vase. she let out a small scream. It was no longer broken.

The three of them stared In disbelief, none of them able to speak. Jerry picked up the vase, holding it as if he were handling a brick of plutonium. "Not a scratch on it." he said. "How is this possible?"

Elizabeth shook her head. "I have no idea, but.. I knew it would work." Stan looked like he was 10 seconds from running out the door and never returning. "Put it back Liz. Reverse it. Please." Jerry nodded in agreement. "Yeah, boss, you have to", he said, his voice cracking. "This is...not natural." Elizabeth sat up, still woozy, the pain in her head now a dull ache. She made her way to the computer on shaky legs. She moved the curser over the undo button. She looked at the vase and clicked the mouse. her vision doubled and her headache was gone in an instant. She heard a loud crack as the vase split back into glued pieces In Jerry's hand. He let out a Yelp and quickly set the vase on the table, wiping his hands on his shirt. The picture changed as well, the vase back on the shelf. Stan wiped sweat from his forehead. "Jesus Christ."

Elizabeth turned to face the guys. "Do either of you have the slightest clue how this could have happened? I'm open to any suggestions, no matter how crazy." Stan laughed. "This thing can not only show you the past, but lets you change it. Einstein or Stephen Hawking may have had some theories, other than that your guess is as good as mine."

She ran her fingers across the keyboard. "Anybody curious to see what else it can do?"

They looked at her in disbelief. Stan said, "Absolutely not! This thing just tossed the laws of physics into the trash! You want to tinker around with it?"

"Stan, we have inadvertently invented some weird variant of time travel. this is the most incredible discovery in human history. I know it's not what we were trying for, but here we are. We can't just walk away from it. For instance..there's something everyone is curious about." Elizabeth started typing and the printer whirred to life, shooting out a piece of paper. She took it and flipped it onto the scanner. The picture appeared on the screen. Jerry stared at it, mouth open. Stan looked at the screen, a half grin on his face. "You got to be fucking kidding me."

Elizabeth looked back at the laptop, which showed John and Jackie Kennedy in the back of the convertible in the middle of Dealey plaza. "I'm not going to tamper with anything back there, but don't you want to know what really happened? People have been speculating about it for decades. Don't you want to know for an absolute fact who was in that book depository? Come on guys, this is the biggest conspiracy theory ever. Let's answer the question once and for all." Before they could utter another word of protest, she hit the button and the (un)frame began. The picture expanded. No one was talking now, they were crowded around the screen, eyes wide and intent as the picture opened out into the plaza. People were pointing and smiling and taking pictures of their own on ancient cameras. Some were frozen in mid applause. Little children were jumping up and down, laughing and pointing, unaware of the horror that would unspool mere seconds from now. Jerry gave Elizabeth a tap on the shoulder. "Please tell me you're recording this." "Of course I am." Elizabeth expanded the photo wider and to the left, opening up a view that couldn't possibly have been seen by the original photographer. She then began to zoom in across the plaza and up the side of The Book Depository. Elizabeth's eyes went wide and she froze. Stan looked at the screen slack jawed while Jerry pushed the hair back from his forehead. He said in a shaky voice, "If you were looking for a Pulitzer Prize winning photo, we just found it." She had stopped at the sixth floor and there he was. Oswald was just inside The window, in the process of aiming the rifle at the street below. "Holy shit, guys." she said. Stan could finally speak again. "I guess that mystery is solved. it was him all along." There were so many conspiracy theories sometimes I actually doubted it, but its him. That weasily little face of his.

Elizabeth felt that flutter again. that pull. She said to herself, "I can fix it." She started typing again. Stan immediately became apprehensive. "Liz, what are you doing?"

She didn't hear him. She typed the prompt, *Lee Harvey Oswald was apprehended by police 3 hours before he could assassinate John F Kennedy*

Stan said, "Christ, Liz, you told me you weren't going to screw around with anything back there and instead you escalate to thwarting an assassination of john Kennedy? You can't, Liz. You just can't."

Jerry stood next to him. "I agree, this is nuts. Look what happened to you last time. I thought you were having a stroke or an aneurysm or something."

"It wasn't that bad. It actually started easing up a bit at the end. My mind was just having trouble accepting the reality of two events occurring at the same time." Jerry chuckled. Stan didn't. "Oh, is that all? Whatever it was it knocked you on your ass, Liz. What do you think will happen to your mind, to all our minds, if you push that button?"

"I've been thinking about that. I was effected, but you two didn't experience any effects at all. Because you didn't directly experience the event. It was my memory. You weren't there. And none of us were there when Kennedy was assassinated. Hell we weren't even born yet. Its just information we received in high school. A memory of a memory. You might feel a little lightheaded, but nothing like what hit me. Trust me, Stan, it won't be the same."

"And you want to test this on a hunch?"

Elizabeth shook her head. "Its more than a hunch. I can't explain it, but the first time I hit that button, it's like I was connected. Like I was supposed to use it.. I was right about the vase. And I'm right about this"

She pushed the button and found out just how wrong she was. Elizabeth and Stan felt a bloom of nausea, but that was their only side effect. Jerry was a different story. He let out a scream, clutching the sides of his head. Blood sprayed from his nose. Stan caught him as he started to convulse. He braced him so he couldn't hurt himself. He looked back at Elizabeth. "Turn it back! Liz! Hit the button!" She moved her hand over the button, but didn't push it. She kept her eye on Jerry. "Hold on, he's coming out of it."

"What the hell is wrong with you, just push the-"

"No! He'll be fine, just wait a minute!" the convulsions ceased. Jerry sat up with some help from Stan. He looked like he had just been told something terrible. He scrambled for his phone. "Please, no." Stan helped him to his feet. He was swaying slightly. His nose was still bleeding and one of his eyes was bloodshot. Stan put a hand on his shoulder. "Jerry, are you OK?" Jerry brushed him aside. He fumbled his phone out of his pocket and slowly made his way out into the hall. Stan started to follow when Elizabeth called him back. "Leave him alone for a few minutes, he'll be OK." "Did he look like he was OK! I hate to shit on your mystical connection to the machine, but Jerry's reaction didn't seem very fucking mild to me!" Elizabeth ran her hands through her hair. "I know. I don't understand why it hit him so hard." "We don't understand any of this!" "Just calm down, please. Take a breath. And while we wait-" Elizabeth grabbed Stan's phone off the table and waved it. "Aren't you curious what's going on in the new world?" Stan looked at her with disbelief. "You don't give a damn about him, do you? You're so wrapped up in this-" "Of course I care! Jerry is one of my oldest friends. But he clearly wants to be alone. Give him a minute to process what happened." She tossed him his phone. "Don't you want to know what happened?" "Why don't we already know? Isn't that how it worked for you? Memory overlapping memories?" Elizabeth shrugged. "Maybe it happened so long ago it takes a while to catch up." Stan shook his head. "Jerry sure seemed to know something." "There's an easy way to find out." She pointed at his phone. Stan looked out the door Jerry walked out of, then to Elizabeth. "Fuck." He sat on the couch and started searching. After a minute he shook his head. "Well, you did it. He didn't die, at least not in sixty three. John F Kennedy served two successful terms, campaigned for his brother's unsuccessful presidential bid. Robert wasn't assassinated either, but he was a senator for twenty four years... John moved to the family compound shortly after his presidency, and resided there until he died in ninety two." Elizabeth shook her head. "Son of a bitch. I remember that, do you?" Stan nodded, looking a bit queasy. " The funeral was on TV for two days. This is a really weird feeling.. After Kennedy came Nixon, who also served two terms, no resignation. Apparently Watergate never happened." Elizabeth smiled. "Or he just didn't get caught this time." "After Nixon came...Bradford? Who the hell is Bradford?" Elizabeth shrugged. "No clue."

"After Bradford was Stephens, then McCain... Jesus Liz, you changed the entire political landscape. God knows what else is going on, let me check the news.." Elizabeth went to the window and opened it. "Looks the same to me." Stan laughed. "I don't think we can just pop our head out the window and assume everything is as it was." Elizabeth gestured outside. "I'll tell you what's happening. The usual wars, the usual riots, the usual global warming that no one's doing anything about. All the same. Always the same." "Same or not, you have to reverse this" "Why the hell would I do that?" Stan said, "Because we don't know this world. We don't know what's going on behind the scenes. For all you know we could be on the brink of a nuclear war." "The same could be said about the timeline where Kennedy died." Stan looked very uneasy. "Liz.. saving Kennedy caused thousands of changes over the past sixty years. I'm not just talking about world events. I mean in our own lives. Some people I knew, from my past, aren't there anymore. Can't You feel it?" She nodded. Memories were starting to overlap faster now. There was something else, she couldn't remember what yet, but it was bad. Stan glanced down at his phone and lost his thought. "What the hell?" Elizabeth looked worried. "Stan, what is it?" Stan was furiously scrolling through his phone. "They're talking about the white house, but they're saying it's in Tennessee." "It is in Tennessee." Startled, they both turned to see Jerry standing in the doorway. "It was relocated in 2005, after four dirty bombs were detonated in Washington D.C. It left a hundred and thirty square miles of uninhabitable land. Almost a million people died." As if it had flipped a switch, Stan and Elizabeth both began to remember everything. The news reports, drone camera footage of thousands of bodies burning in the streets, too Radioactive to be retrieved, half the city turned to Rubble. A Memorial was constructed in Virginia, the closest point to ground zero while still staying in the safe zone. Liz sat down in the nearest chair. Stan looked sick. Jerry walked in the room and flopped onto the couch. "My dad lived just outside of Washington D.C. When you pushed that button I felt it, what you said. Like I had two memories of the same time. I got this flash of my Mom, years ago, calling me, telling me that he died. I knew it was true, that it had happened. I tried to call him anyway, but his number wasn't in my phone anymore. Then more memories kept coming. We couldn't bury him. Nobody could get into The Hot Zone. Ma died a few months later." Elizabeth put her hand over her mouth, horrified. "Jerry, I am so sorry, I never would have.. if I had any idea this could have happened.. I'll change it back, Jerry, right now. She hurried to the computer, putting her hand on Stan's arm as she went by. She hit the button. There was that double vision again, then silence. Stan and Elizabeth looked at Jerry as he grabbed his phone and scrolled through the numbers. He let out a relieved sob as he put the phone to his ear. "Dad? Are you okay? No, I'm fine, I was... I was just checking on you. Hey I'll call you back in a minute." He hung up the phone and stood here with the tears rolling down his face. Stan walked over and gave him a hug. Elizabeth kept her distance. She didn't think Jerry would want her near him at this moment. Maybe not for a long while. Jerry wiped his eyes and looked at his partners with exhaustion. He didn't seem to have recovered as quickly as Elizabeth. "Guys I think I'm going to head home. It's been a hell of a day." Stan nodded in agreement. "I'm right behind you buddy, but first-" He grabbed the laptop that contained (un)frame and unplugged it. He took it to the safe and placed it inside. Elizabeth watched this with a twinge of anger. It was smart to secure the laptop, but the safe couldn't be opened without at least two of them present. That kept the laptop away from thieves, and her. She put on a smile. "You two are going to have to race me for the parking lot. I'm the one who tried to leave here two hours ago, remember?" Jerry looked stunned. "Two hours? My god it feels like, I don't know.." Stan clapped him on the shoulder. "Sixty years?" Jerry let out a weak laugh. "Yeah, something like that. As they made their way to the door, Elizabeth grabbed the USB they recorded the JFK footage on and slipped it in her pocket. An hour later she was showered and on her second glass of wine. She was exhausted, but there was no way she was sleeping after what had happened. She had connected the USB to her flat screen and was sitting on the rug in front of the couch pouring through every frame. She didn't really know why she was doing it or even what she was looking for, but she kept at it for over an hour, until she saw someone familiar. She stopped cold, almost knocking her wine glass off the coffee table "You've got to be kidding me." it was black coat man, the AI artifact from Jerry's picture, complete with floppy hat and seven fingered hand. He standing between two old ladies, both of them with their freshly done hairdos wrapped in kerchiefs. One of them had a tiny American flag and was in mid-wave, the other had her hands clasped to her chest, a huge smile on her face. The artifact was staring at the Cadillac Kennedy was riding in. His face was still blurry but she could see a look of sadness on its face. She zoomed in. It was identical to the one in the other image. She turned off the USB. *I've seen a hundreds of artifacts and none of them have been identical. Not that anything about any of this makes any sense but...* She felt a knot in her stomach at the sight of that thing. She turned the USB back on, this time flipping to Stan's Christmas picture. She magnified the image and it didn't take much searching before the knot in her stomach grew. There was a small bit of hallway revealed on the right side of Stan's picture. At the end of the hallway was a table, half visible. Someone was sitting at the other side of the table, their shadow cast on the wall. It looked like the brim of a floppy hat.

2.

When Elizabeth arrived at work the next morning, the guys were already there. They were sitting at the conference table, the laptop between them. Jerry was still pale and not quite recovered from yesterday. She set her coat on one of the chairs. "What's going on guys?" Stan said "I guess you haven't watched the news this morning." He turned on the television. A reporter was in mid conversation "-With no one claiming responsibility. Once again over ten thousand people died yesterday evening, the cause still unknown. The death toll is expected to rise as reports continue to cone in." Stan talked over the reporter. "Ten thousand people dead. Another twenty thousand hospitalized with symptoms including severe seizures, bloody noses. The majority of the deaths were people over sixty, the highest concentration around the Dallas-Fort Worth area. They think it might be some kind of terrorist attack. You want to take a guess when this happened? Reports started coming in around 15 minutes after you saved Kennedy." Liz covered her mouth in shock. "I don't know what to say, I had no idea something like that could happen."

"That's the point. None of us had any idea what could happen, that's why I pleaded with you to leave it alone." He pointed at the television. "If this didn't clue you in, I'm going to say it right out loud. This is the most dangerous thing that's ever been created."

Liz shook her head "No, this is going to save us. Sure, in the wrong hands-"

"Wrong hands!" I'm assuming in this scenario we're the right hands and we killed 10,000 people last night! Someone could type one sentence into that thing and undo the Goddamn universe. This thing needs to be destroyed."

"Destroyed? Are you out of your mind? Listen, I would never give this to the public, but if we could sell it to the government-"

"Christ Liz, you think the government would be any more suitable to have this? We'd be just as dead just as fast.. no, it needs to go."

"There's no way in hell I'm going to toss an opportunity like this out the window, Stan. They would pay millions for this, tens of millions."

Jerry slammed his hand on the desk. "No!" with some effort, he made it to his feet, holding on to the chair for support. "There's no way we can let that thing out of this room, Elizabeth. And since half the tech inside it is mine, I think I got a say in it."

Stan stood up. "If you don't destroy it, I'll go to the backers. They're already on the verge of shutting us down. If they get even a hint of derision in the ranks, they'll pull out. I don't want to do it but I will if it comes to it."

"You.. son of a bitch, you'd throw away everything we built?"

"To get rid of that thing? In a heartbeat."

Elizabeth looked at them both. There was no give in either of them. She was furious. "I'll get rid of it! I'll throw a fucking fortune in the toilet! Are you both happy?"

Jerry shook his head. "I don't think I'm going to be happy for a long time. I'm going home, I still don't feel a hundred percent. Or even sixty percent. I'll see you tomorrow." Jerry shuffled out the door. Stan stood at the table, looking at her. She let out an angry laugh. "Are you seriously going stand here and watch me do it? Is your trust in me that far gone?" Stan put his head down, a guilty look on his face. "Of course not, I-"

"I'll start the file purge, it's going to take about an hour, is that OK with you?" Stan stood indecisive for a moment, then nodded his head. "I'm sorry Liz, I wish you could see things our way on this. I'll be at my desk. I got a lot of work to do." Elizabeth sat down at her desk, seething. How dare they do this to her. She brought them in on this project! This was her baby, and now they want her to abort it. Fucking bastards. She pushed back from her desk. Across the hall, Stan was on the phone with one of the backers. Stan the voice box, the smooth talker. She could cheerfully smash his head in right now. He let out one of his fake, ass kissing laughs. She closed her door and turned the TV up to drown him out. A reporter was on the scene in Dallas, the site of most of the deaths. *The old people that died around Dallas. Once upon a time they were young people, and I'm guessing they were either at Dealey Plaza or they were watching it go down on TV. That's why it hit them so hard.* Elizabeth felt a wave of guilt. *I never would have done it if I had known..* she started the laptop and searched the menu. She was about to start purging the files when something caught her attention. They were interviewing survivors. Many complained of experiencing varying levels of pain and the nosebleeds, but not one of them had mentioned anything about confusion or false memories. She touched the laptop and a certainty came over her. *There's a Zone around the machine*, she thought. *A bubble. if you're in the bubble, you remember both timelines, outside, you experience the pain, but no new memories.* She looked at the laptop. A message on the screen asked her if she was sure she wanted to purge the files. She took a look over her shoulder at Stan, then clicked no. She remembered a story Stan told her one night. It was about 6 months before the two of them met. He was sitting in his shitty little apartment, no job, no prospects. He flipped a coin. Heads he would stick around a little longer, Tails he would pack everything in and head back east, try his luck there. It landed on heads and the rest was history. She pulled her phone out of her pocket. *History..* if she could remove Stan from the equation, Jerry would never stand against her. If she had never hired him, she wouldn't constantly have him telling her what she should do, constantly vying for leadership of her company.. Jerry's gone home, which means he's out of the bubble. He won't remember what's about to happen. Without another thought she plugged the phone into the laptop and scrolled through her photos until she found what she was looking for. It was a picture of the three of them the day they signed the lease on this building. It was only a couple of years ago but I felt like a hundred. She pressed a button and the picture appeared on the laptop. She felt brief concern for Jerry, he took a hard hit yesterday, but she dismissed it. *I've known Stan years longer, if anybody's going to get the worst of it, it's going to be me*

Across the hall, Stan was still on the phone. He was in the middle of a joke when he glanced across the hall and saw the picture of the three of them in the (un)frame program. "What the hell?" He hung up without another word and started across the hall. Elizabeth heard his footsteps and leapt from her chair, locking her door. Stan grabbed the door knob, violently shaking it. "What are you doing Liz!" Elizabeth was back at her desk. "Sorry, but you didn't leave me any choice." Stan slammed his shoulder into the door as Elizabeth typed, *Stan flipped the coin and it landed on tails.* Stan raced back to his office and grabbed his chair. He charged across the hall. She watched as he lifted the chair above his head, screaming. He was about to bring it down on her window when she slammed her hand down on the enter key. Pain tore up her spine, branching out through her body. Her back arched and her jaw slammed shut as she fell back onto the floor. Blood poured out of her nose and her hands clenched and unclenched, her vision gone. After a couple minutes the pain subsided some and her vision begin to clear. She tried to stand but her legs wouldn't work. She looked at the window where

Stan had been standing. It was still intact and Stan was nowhere to be seen. She looked over at the picture and now it was just her and Jerry. She crawled to the couch and laid down, putting a pillow over her eyes. She was awoke 20 minutes later to the sound of her cell phone ringing. She reached out for a non-existent nightstand before remembering that she was at work. She sat up, still woozy, random jolts of pain thundering through her head. As she looked around for her phone, she noticed the changes. The furniture was cheaper, mismatched and hand me down. Her desk was smaller . And the place in general was just a lot messier. Fast food cups and old hamburger wrappers were strewn about. *Stan was such a neat freak, I didn't realize how much he cleaned up around here.* She looked down at her outfit. She was never a fashion icon but she had a little style. These clothes were on par with the furniture. Memories were starting to overlap. *It's just been Jerry and me, splitting everything. There's a lot more cash floating around when you're only paying a third.* She made it to her feet and walked to the mirror, shocked to find she looked about twenty pounds heavier than she did a half hour ago. Jerry's burger runs hadn't been balanced against Stan's pleas for salads at least twice a week. *Doesn't matter. It can all be fixed. And I still have the machine.* Her cell phone rang again. it was an unfamiliar number but she answered anyway. Hello? "Yes I'm calling from Mercy General, on behalf of a Jerry Singleton. He has you listed as his emergency contact." "Yes, what happened?" She had a feeling she already knew. "It appears Mr. Singleton may have suffered a small stroke." Elizabeth closed her eyes. "Oh my God, I'll be right there."

3.

Forty minutes later Elizabeth entered Jerry's Hospital room. He was in bed attached to a hundred different wires. There was a patch over his left eye. She knocked on the door and he looked at her, confused at first, then recognition kicked in. He half smiled and said with a shaky voice, "Boss, how are you doing?" Elizabeth laughed. "How am I? I'm fine, I'm more concerned with how you are, buddy." Jerry shrugged, or tried to. "I'm OK. They said it was a stroke, but-" He leaned closer to her with some effort. "It felt just like what happened yesterday, only a little worse." He lowered his voice. "Hey, you didn't use the, uh, program, did you?" Elizabeth managed to look almost insulted. "After what happened yesterday, of course not." Jerry patted her arm. "I'm sorry, I shouldn't even of asked." She smiled. It's okay Jerry. We don't really know anything about the program, maybe it was an aftershock or something." "Yeah, that's probably it." "Hey, do you need anything? Some real food, maybe?" Jerry smiled. "No, I'm okay. Actually I'm kind of beat, I think I'll just try and get some sleep. Thanks for coming in. I'm sure I'll be getting out of here soon." Elizabeth gave his hand a squeeze. "Okay, you get some sleep. If you need anything, just give me a call." "Will do boss." Jerry turned over on his side. Liz watched him for a moment, then stepped out of his room and leaned against the wall. She rubbed her eyes. "I'm Sorry Jerry, but it had to be done."

4.

That night she sat in the office, going over all the records. She was going back and forth between the computer and their files, becoming more and more frantic. She didn't want to face it, but there was no getting around it. It looked like their progress had gone from being two months from launch to almost a year. Half of their backers were gone, their accounts almost drained. She swiped her hands across the desk, hurling magazines and files across the room. Papers see sawed to the floor. Elizabeth let out a scream. She got on her knees, scooping up papers, then stopped. She tossed the papers back on the floor and laid down. Fucking Stan, the tamer of investors. *I had to get rid of him. he would have taken it all away.* But now.. All that work.. evaporated. She wiped the tears out of her eyes and sat up. She eyed the corner of one of the magazines hiding under a pile of papers. She pulled it out and looked at the cover. Quantum Tech top 10 up-and-comers. The face on the cover was very familiar to her. William Chen had twice beat her to some very deep pocket investors and one very large grant. She tossed the magazine back on the floor. That grant would have been all she needed to finish her work. No more begging investors, no more working until the middle of the night. No more God damn struggling. And now it starts all over again. She got to her feet, kicking papers out of her way as she made her way out the door.

5.

The next month was a difficult one. Elizabeth spent every day and most nights at the office, talking to the remaining investors and working on the project. Jerry ended up being in the hospital for 8 days and even when he returned to work he wasn't himself. He'd suffered some permanent damage, though he wouldn't tell her how bad it was. She finally had to politely send him home, as he was hindering more than helping. And to be honest, she had enough on her plate, she didn't need the constant reminder of what she had done to him. thirty days in this new world and all she had managed to do his barely break even. She glanced at her desk drawer, where she had stowed the machine. She didn't want it in her sight. She tried for three days to get a meeting with anyone of importance in the military to talk about (Un)frame, but the only person she was able to reach was a local FBI field agent, and when she told him about the machine he informed her it was a federal offense to prank call a government agency. She couldn't sell it, and she was afraid to use it. One more prompt might be the nail in Jerry's coffin, and she wouldn't be far behind. She was still getting tinges of pain weeks later. Her concerns were pushed aside the following night. It was almost four in the morning and she was on a phone call with an investor in Germany. Five minutes in and she knew he was calling to pull his backing. She didn't have the strength to argue with him or the balls to plead for a project that had nothing to show, except the one thing she couldn't show. Instead she just hung up. *I'll have to close the office now. Work from home. Or this might be over.* She laid her head on her desk and had a good 20 minute cry. She composed herself and walked over to Jerry's desk, opening the bottom drawer. He always kept a bottle of something in there, for cold nights. *This is as cold as it fucking gets*, she thought as she grabbed the whiskey and sat on the couch. She inspected the bottle. It was the good stuff, hadn't even been opened. She was going to remedy that. She spun the lid off the bottle and took two giant swigs. She immediately felt a little better. She continued. By the time the sun was on its way up the bottle was all but gone. Elizabeth sat slumped on the couch, staring at the wall. She looked around the office with dismay. It wasn't great, but she loved it anyway. She stumbled over her to her desk, pulling open the drawer and yanking the laptop out. She held it above her head, rage in her eyes, ready to rid herself of this curse. Then she set it back down, almost dropping it in her inebriated state. She stared at the laptop. OK.. *so I shut it all down and slink back to some office job, everything I worked for the past 5 years goes up and smoke, or.. maybe I do this one last time. I die, or I fix it all. I don't care which at this point.*

She touched the laptop, almost caressing it. "Help me.. tell me what to do." She waited for that spark. Nothing happened. She grabbed the laptop, cradling it like a child. "Please!" suddenly she had a flash. A memory of the night she trashed the office. Of the quantum tech magazine. She set the laptop down and began searching. She found it half buried in a trash can. She picked it up and looked at the cover, featuring the one and only William Chen. She tore the cover off and took it the scanner. The laptop whirred to life as the picture popped up on the screen. She sat at the desk, trying to think through the haze of the whiskey. She typed a prompt, then read it. Then Reread it. One sentence, but there was no coming back from it. *William Chen never existed*. She hesitated. She was responsible for those people in Dallas, but it was an accident. This ... she would be deliberately erasing someone from the world. She moved her hand away, then that feeling came over her again, that connection with the machine. She didn't want to admit it, but she'd missed that connection. *It's not murder, not really. It will be like he just.. never was.* That decided it. She pushed the button. The world went dark.

6.

The sun had risen far enough that it shone in her face through a crack in the window. She squinted her eyes, trying to focus. Everything was red. She wiped the blood out of her eyes as best as she could, and tried to turn over. Her left arm wouldn't work. Her head throbbed with every beat of her heart. She grabbed for the desk chair but it wasn't there. Neither was the desk. She tried to get up again and made slightly better progress. Her left arm was starting to tingle with pins and needles. She could move her fingers slightly. She looked around the office and saw that it wasn't her office anymore. From the dust on the floor it looked like it had been that way for a long time. There was a box of yellowed papers in the corner, and two half covered mannequins propped up near the window. All of her things were gone, including the laptop. Adrenaline shot through her and her head pounded in agony. She used the wall to get to her feet looking around the deserted room. *Jesus Christ, no. What have I done? What the fuck have I done?* She tried to scream, but nothing came out but a dry hiss. There was a ringing that she had first mistaken for her ears, but it was a phone. She stumbled around until she found the source, a black purse she had apparently passed out on. She picked it up and took out a phone she didn't recognize. The caller was named Nicki. New memories began to overlap. She knew Nicki, it was her assistant. "My assistant?" She answered the phone. "Hello?" "Oh my God, Mrs. Foster are you OK? I've been trying to reach you for hours." "I'm fine, Nicki, I just had.. a bit of a rough night. How is everything where you are." Elizabeth made her way across the room to a broken mirror and took a look. The weight she gained was gone and then some. Her blood covered clothes probably retailed for around two thousand dollars. *Fuck me.. fashion icon.* "We are set here, ma'am. The Germans will be here in forty minutes. Everything's in place." "The Germans.." more memories flooded in. She staggered, then stood up straight, smiling. *My God, I didn't lose anything. I gained everything. And in forty minutes a group of German gentleman are going to be in my offices downtown to sign papers For seven figure merger.* Her work was done. It was time to reap the benefits. She closed her eyes, tears mixed with blood fell down her cheeks. She turned her attention back to the phone. "Nikki I'm going to need a ride, I'll send you a pin. I also need a change of clothes, I have two dresses in my office have them downstairs and ready when I walk in." "Yes ma'am, an Uber will be there in five." Elizabeth walked upstairs just the Uber pulled up. It was just then she realized she wasn't dunk anymore. *Different timeline.* She'd never get used to that. Hopefully she wouldn't have to. She hopped in the car and rattled off an address that popped in her head as she was saying it. The address turned out to be the heart of tech in the city, a place she had dreamed of setting up shop but could never afford in a million years. Yet here she was. She made it. Just then a pain shot through the right side of her head. Her left arm began to tingle again. She flexed her hand several times. The Uber pulled up at a large office building and a skinny blonde woman, Nicki, ran out the doors with an arm full of clothes. Elizabeth got out of the car and Nikki is skidded to a halt. "Oh my god, Ms. Foster what happened?" Elizabeth looked down at her blood covered shirt. "It's nothing, just a minor accident. What's the ETA on the investors?" "Twenty minutes and counting." "Great, get upstairs make any final preparations I'll be there soon as I change." She cleaned herself up as best as she could and picked one of the dresses at random. She stood in front of the mirror, appraising what she saw. Her eyes were bloodshot but there's nothing she could do about that. She put on some makeup and did what she could with her hair. This wasn't a beauty contest. She didn't have to put on a dog and pony show. For the first time in her life she was excited to talk to investors because she had set the terms. A sharp pain blossomed behind her eye. The vision in her left eye was greatly reduced. She ignored it. *One thing at a time. First get the deal settled. Next stop a neurologist to fix everything I've done to myself over the past month.* She walked into the lobby confident and happy, making her way up the stairs. Her confidence faltered at the top once she saw Nicki on the phone, sobbing. She went to her, stomach suddenly in knots. "What's happened?" Nikki hung up the phone "it's Jerry, ma'am. His neighbors heard him collapse this morning. They took him to the hospital, but it was too late. He died." Elizabeth's head began to thud again. She asked a question she already knew the answer to. "When did this happen?" "Early this morning, around six." Right around the time she had erased Chen. She felt like she was going to throw up. *My final sacrifice. Poor Jerry.* She shook it off. "We can't concern ourselves with that now. The investors are here. This is our moment And we're going to take it. Its what Jerry would have wanted. We'll mourn later." Nicki looked shocked as Elizabeth brushed past her. The investors had began entering the conference room. She walked towards them, passing two doors on the way. Her own, Elizabeth foster, President, and across the hall Jerald Singleton, Vice President. She read that last without blinking an eye as she put on a smile and greeted the investors.

7.

A few hours later Elizabeth sat alone in her office, an unopened bottle of champagne tn her desk. There was to be a party after the merger, but nobody was in a celebratory mood after they found out about Jerry. She told everyone they could go home early if they wanted. They all did. Jerry was always the popular one, no matter what timeline. She grabbed the champagne and walked out into her now spacious offices. Her product was going to launch next week. It was the most sophisticated AI anyone had ever seen, and primed to be the best selling. She popped the cork and took sip, making a bitter face. She set the bottle on a random desk. Just then she heard a door close behind her. It appeared not everyone had gone home. Elizabeth called out, "I'm over here. There's plenty of champagne left, but I canceled the caterer." She walked around the corner. There was no one there, but.. she felt something. Someone here, looking for her. A chill enveloped her. As she backed away from the door she saw a shadow in her peripheral. She spun around. There was nothing there. The champagne bottle fell off the desk, shattering. Elizabeth screamed, but it faded to a breathless whisper. Her visitor had shown himself. Elizabeth's legs gave out and she fell to her knees in disbelief. "It cant be." The artifact in the black coat and floppy hat was coming toward her. He moved in disjointed spurts, fast then slow, his body seeming to split apart, then join back with itself. His face look like a patchwork of a thousand faces, each piece moving independently. Its eyes never left her as it made its way to her. She scooted backward for a moment before getting to her feet. She sprinted to her office, slamming the door. She turned and let out a shriek. He was already inside the office. It pointed to her chair. Weeping silently, she stumbled to her seat. The figure in the black coat down on the other side of the desk, placing it's seven-fingered hands on the desk.

Elizabeth was in shock. Her head was pounding, her eye was almost completely blind now. "You're.. you're not real. You can't be, you're an anomaly, an artifact."

It spoke, it's voice sounding like a chorus of people all speaking at different speeds and tones. It hurt her head, the sound of it. "Then why are you so afraid, Elizabeth?" She wiped her face, trying to compose herself. "What do you want?" It pointed at the laptop. "You've been tampering with technology you have no business with, with no knowledge or care of its consequence. This is a power you shouldn't possess for hundreds of years."

"Please I didn't know, I was just trying to make things better." It leaned forward and looked at her, through her. "Make things better for who? You had the power of your god, and what did you do with it? It's voice changed then, the chorus dwindling to just a few, each voice resembled her own. *The usual wars, the usual riots, the usual global warming that no one's doing anything about.* Did you end poverty or hunger? Homelessness? Did you halt the rapidly increasing temperature of your planet? No. You killed thousands. You erased a man from existence to improve your own life. Your partner and best friend died alone, and you sit here, drinking champagne.

Elizabeth shoved the laptop across the desk. "Here, you can have it, please. Just take it and leave me alone." It shook its head. "What would that solve now? Taking this from you wouldn't undo the damage you've done. There's only one thing you can do to repair this now."

She nodded frantically. "Okay, What, just tell me and I'll do it."

It stood up and walked its jagged walk toward her. Elizabeth slunk down in her seat. She let out a small shriek as it took something from its pocket. Her fear turned to confusion when she saw that it appeared to be an old poleroid camera. It took her picture and placed it in the scanner. It then took the laptop and typed in a sentence. It slowly turned the laptop back to her. The sentence below her picture read- *Elizabeth Foster never existed.* and she shook her head. A tear fell from her right eye. "No. please, no. There has to be something-" "There is no viable alternative. Press the button. It must be you." "I cant! I just made it! I finally made it.. I cant push that button, I can't.. kill myself."

"Yet you had no qualms erasing Mr. Chen. Look at it this way, Elizabeth Foster, It's not murder, not really. It will be like you just.. never were." She sneered at her own words being thrown back at her again. "And if I don't? You said I have to be the one to do it, What happens if I don't?" The figure stood, Sliding the desk out of the way with one hand. It towered over Elizabeth. "Then you will come with me, and it won't be long at all before you are begging to push that button." Elizabeth had mashed herself up against the back wall, trying hard as she could to put any bit of distance between them. She looked Into it's misshapen eyes and she knew it was telling the truth. She held up her hand and closed her eyes. "I'll do it!. I'll do it." It grabbed the laptop and knelt down in front of her. "The time has come." Elizabeth bowed her head for a moment, then sat up straight. She looked up at the misshapen face of the figure and smiled. She pointed to the champagne laying on its side just outside her door. "Can you hand me that?" It passed her the bottle. She drank the last swallow. "God, that tastes like shit." She took the laptop. "I was on top. No one will remember, but I was. For a moment" She looked up at her Grandma's vase and smiled. "OK, here we go." She Pressed the button one last time.

8.

Morning. The building that it once housed Elizabeth's burgeoning Empire was now one of many for lease. A man walking down the sidewalk paused to take a look. The man walking with him continued a few steps before realizing he was alone. He turned around. "Hey Jerry what are you doing?" Jerry stood staring through the chain link fence at the empty building inside. "I don't know, I just, this place looks really familiar. Maybe I had an interview here once." Stan smiled. "Well, we have an actual job to get to now. Come on, these algorithms aren't going to write themselves." "Yeah, you're right." They started back up the sidewalk, but Jerry took a couple parting glances. It was so strange, but he felt like he'd been there before.

Self Help

Vlogger walking in the woods, has a GoPro fixed to his head, and has another camera on a selfie stick. The time is 7:40AM

Vlogger

Hey guys, it's [audio cuts out] here. Welcome back to my channel. I'm back, finally, with a new video. As you know, I've been struggling with ptsd since my car accident a year ago, But I'm finally starting to see big improvements in myself. I'm seeing a therapist, I'm taking my meds, and I'm doing other things to take care of myself, like getting back on these trails that I've always loved so much.

Getting out in nature as always made me feel better. There's something about being surrounded by trees and fresh air that makes everything better. It helps me to clear my head and focus on the present moment. So what do you say guys, Let's go get some sunshine into our souls!

Tine stamp is 8:16AM. Vlogger walking through the woods. He nods at fellow hikers and admires the beauty of it all

Vlogger

It's so peaceful here, guys, The perfect place to relax and de-stress.

(stops to check map)

Now, it's time for a little surprise. I received a mystery email last night. And whoever it was told me about a new trail a half a mile off of arrowhead, on the southern slope. Now, guys, I was more than a little skeptical, because I've run these woods for years and never heard of any such trail, but I'm big enough to admit when I'm wrong, because here it is, a trail I've never seen before in my many hikes in the North Woods. So we're going to do a little exploring. Nothing too crazy, being how it's a new trail to me but-

(Vlogger points his camera In the direction of the trail)

-I'm anxious to see where this thing leads us. Let's go!

Time stamp 8:42.AM. Vlogger is walking and looking all around, slightly amazed

Vlogger

This is great, guys. I can't believe I've never seen this trail before. It's so secluded! We haven't passed one other hiker, Which is very odd for this time of year. Whoever sent me that email, I owe you one, this is the perfect path for someone who just wants to get out and be alone for a while.

Time stamp 9:38 AM. The vlogger is slowly walking along, Enjoying the shade

Vlogger

Quick update guys, the new trail? In a word, beautiful. Lots of ups and downs to get that cardio going, beautiful scenery, but a little perplexing. I've been walking for about an hour now and according to the map and my distance traveled app, we should have crossed over at least two other main trails by now. I don't understand. But this is a new trail to me, and that's what life is all about in the woods, learning and growing out here.

(Vlogger looks up at the Sun slightly confused)

Nothing to worry about, we're just going to backtrack to the main road and explore this one another day.

(Vlogger takes another uneasy look at the sky, then marches on)

Time stamp 10:50. AM. Vlogger takes another camera from his pack and sets it on a rock, then sits across from it. He wipes his forehead and he shakes his head and looks at the camera

Vlogger

I have to say this is embarrassing. Hiking back north of this Trail and I can't seem to.. well, I appear to be lost. Over 20 years I've been hiking in these woods and this is never happened. I'm not bragging when I say I've got a good sense of direction and it's gotten me out of a couple of jams. But right now... and all of my apps have stopped working,

I have two compasses and every direction I point them in shows Northeast.. I'm completely confused. On any normal day I can find my way using the Sun, but the Sun is ... guys, I don't know how to explain it but I've been out here(checks watch) for about three and a half hours and the sun hasn't moved. More specifically it's moving much slower than it should be. I can't explain any of this. I'm going to stay on this path, keep heading what I hope is north but i-

Vlogger hears a noise behind him. He turns around and sees a figure moving down the path.

Vlogger

Thank god, a fellow Traveler, maybe they can lead me in the right direction

Vlogger walks towards the figure. They continue moving away.

Vlogger

Excuse me, I was hoping maybe you could help me? I seem to have gotten myself a little lost. Hello?

The figure continues to walk away from the vlogger, and as the vlogger tries to catch up the figure walks behind a tree and vanishes

Vlogger

What in the hell? There was, there was somebody here I'm sure of it.

Vlogger looks at the sky and then at his compasses, then everywhere, panic filing his face. He wipes the sweat off of his forehead and gets back on the path, half walking, half jogging, looking back over his shoulder every few seconds.

Time stamp 12:40 PM. Vlogger sits on a rock just off the path, sweating profusely. He has a few scratches from stumbling through the woods, and he looks genuinely scared.

Vlogger

I've lost the live stream. I will put this up on my channel as soon as I get back. Whenever that may be. I have to say I am a little scared right now. It's been hours. I'm running low on water, didn't expect to be out here so long. I'm already starting to dehydrate. The goddamn sun isn't moving at all now. It's been High noon for almost an hour. I don't know what to do. I figured if I stayed on the path I'd eventually end up where I came in, but I should have reached it hours ago. And maybe I'm just paranoid but I'm starting to feel like I'm being watched out here. I'm going to head out.

Time stamp 2:53PM. The camera pops back on, Vlogger's face filling the screen. He looks slightly crazed and in need of rest and water, but he is smiling.

Vlogger

I can't believe I didn't think of this earlier, I feel like such a fool. Don't count me out yet guys. (laughs a little too loudly) my compass may be malfunctioning, and the Sun might be crazy or I might be (another loud laugh), but there is another sure way of finding your direction, and that's moss. Moss grows on the north facing sides of trees and rocks, so all I have to do is find some moss. From there I'll have my bearing, I'll head east toward Black River. Its no more than a couple miles, from there it should be no time to get back to the city. Wish me luck guys, we might be getting out of here yet.

Time stamp 6:18 PM. the Vlogger, stumbles into the yard of a dilapidated cabin. His cheerful demeanor is gone. He is very dehydrated, and covered in scratches and dirt. His voice is little more than a croak.

Vlogger

I've been traveling East using the moss, but I must have wandered further away from the river than I thought. Even though the Sun doesn't agree with me, I've been walking around in these Woods for almost 12 hours now. I'm exhausted. None of my electronics are working except for these cameras, which I absolutely cannot explain. The batteries should have died hours ago yet they show almost halfway full. I have just come across this cabin, I'm going inside and see if I can find a little bit of food or more importantly some water, which I am in desperate need of. I've decided I might be hallucinating all this, but either way I need some sleep before I continue towards the river. It looks like I'm going to have to spend the night here, not that there is any night. I'm still scared, but at least I'm safe for now. Let's go inside.

He walks in and scrunches his nose up

Vlogger

Ugh, the smell in here is pretty bad, mildew and rotten wood.

He searches in the kitchen and finds a bottle half full of water he gives it a smell and tastes it.

Vlogger

Usually I would never drink water that was sitting around like this, but I need every drop I can get right now. It tastes a bit stale but okay .

He opens the bedroom door and there is what looks like a huge dried blood stain on the wall, as if someone sat blew and blew their brains out. he quickly exits.

Vlogger

My god, I don't even want to know what happened in there. That wasn't blood, was it? No, couldn't be. Either way I guess we'll be sleeping on the couch tonight. He set his camera on the table and he lays down. He is almost immediately asleep. The timestamp begins to speed up and the camera pans across the room to the front door. The vlogger left it open and at 11:30 PM on the timestamp a shadow can be seen filling the doorway. We don't see who it is. they stand there for an hour and then they slowly walk away.

Time stamp 3:02AM. The vlogger doesn't look great, but is more rested. He has his voice back. He looks out the window of the cabin rubbing his eyes.

Vlogger

Okay, it's three in the morning. the sun still hasn't moved. I'm going to give this cabin one more search, maybe I missed a can of beans or something then I'm going to get back to it. Can't be far to the river now. Can't be.

He checks the kitchen again to no avail. Looks in the back of the cupboards and all he finds is a jar of what might have been preserves at one point but what was now rotting poison. He tossed it back on the Shelf and wondered into the hallway. He looked in mild surprise at a couple of old weathered pictures on the wall .

Vlogger

I don't remember seeing these last night. And it seems I would have remembered, since the man in the painting is wearing the same jacket I am.

on the wall there is a painting of two men with knives attacking another man, the one in the vlogger's jacket. The victim has his head turned away from the painter's perspective, his face hidden. The vlogger looks closer at the jacket in the painting. The right sleeve has been ripped and then stitched up in an unprofessional zigzag, clearly not repaired by someone who knows how to sew.

Vlogger(panicked disbelief)

No..no, how can that be..

The vlogger, looks down at his sleeve and sees that it is stitched exactly the same way. He looks back at the painting and now the face of the man being attacked can be seen. It looks very similar to the vlogger's own face. He is in mid scream, both of his eyes have been stabbed out. Vlogger lets out a stunned yell and falls backward into the wall behind him. He runs to his bag, snatches it up and sprints out of the cabin. He stumbles down the stairs and falls in the yard, catching his breath. After a moment he checks that both his cameras are still operating. He runs his hand through his messed up hair and clears his throat.

Vlogger

People die in the woods all the time. No one thinks is going to be them but... sometimes it is. If something does happen to me out here, and if this is ever found... please share this with my family, with my girlfriend Shelly. Tell my mom that-

Just then the vlogger's own voice, repeating his words, can be heard coming from a clump of trees not far from where Vlogger is sitting

Vlogger's voice

if something does happen to me out here, and this is ever found, share this with my family, with my girlfriend Shelly. Tell my mom that I died alone and screaming. Tell her that they feasted on me. That they ripped me open and they feasted on my flesh. Mom? Mommy? Can you hear me, you old cunt? (horrifying laughter) they feasted on me!

There is more laughter as the vlogger sprints down to the trees, but as soon as he reaches them the laughter stops. He looks in the trees, there's no one there. he's in complete panic mode now. He runs back into the yard, looking at every shadow, sweat drenching his face.

Vlogger(terrified)
Help! Please, somebody help me!

Suddenly he can hear his own voice yelling back at him from several different directions

Voices
Help! Help! Please! (Cackling howls)

The vlogger can't take it anymore and he runs away from the cabin and Into the Woods.

Time stamp unknown. The vlogger stumbles through the woods, bouncing off trees, hardly noticing where he is going. He is nothing more now but a collection of scratches and dirt. His clothes ripped from snagging on thorns and branches, but they go unnoticed. His eyes are glazed over and he doesn't notice when the light finally begins to fade in the forest. Suddenly he walks into a large clearing in the trees and he focuses a bit.

Vlogger
What the hell is this?

He makes his way to the center of the clearing. There is an altar there, constructed from a hundreds of twigs and branches. On top of the alter is a hunk of meat, impossible say what part or what animal it was torn from. Blood drips from it, spattering the front of the altar in a crimson glaze. The vlogger is fully conscious now. He looks around, finally noticing the darkness around him. He steps back from the altar, heart pounding in his chest. He turns and hurriedly makes his way back towards the woods, when he's frozen in his tracks. All the trees circling the altar are covered in sheets of yellowed paper. As he moves closer, he discovers they are missing posters. He slowly approaches one of them and has to grab the tree to keep himself from falling. The face on the missing posters is his own. He walks slowly through the sea of posters, all with his face looking back at him. As he walks he notices his face is more damaged with each poster, in this one his nose is broken, this one shows now several of his teeth are gone, now he is a huge gash across his eye, he continues running through them until he reaches a poster that shows him on the ground, his jaw torn off, his tongue lolling out of the gaping hole. he closed his eyes and tore the poster off the tree. In the background we can see the Altar and now a shadow man is standing there. An absence of light in human form. It steps down and begins to move towards the unaware vlogger. He hears the creature and turns around, his face fills with terror. He starts running, but he is moving in panicky zigs and zags, stumbling and falling. In the background we catch glimpses of the shadow man, every time he is revealed he is closer. Suddenly a shadow hand shoots in front of the camera and Vlogger is struck to the ground. The camera falls from his head and lands in the grass. Vlogger is in the shot from the waist up. He rolls over onto his back, sobbing now, holding his hand out as if to ward someone away.

Vlogger(sobbing)

Please, I beg you, don't hurt me, I just want to get out of here-

The vlogger is ripped out of the frame, and his pack falls into the grass from inside the pack his other camera clicks on and We hear the vlogger's voice from earlier in the day.

Vlogger's voice

There's something about being surrounded by trees and fresh air that makes everything better. So what do you say guys, Let's go get some sunshine into our souls!

Fade to black

The mountain

1.

Winslow pulled up to the police barracks around three forty in the morning. He sat in his patrol car, staring out at the front of the building illuminated by the streetlights. He tried to process the events of the evening. He'd replayed them in his head a hundred times on the way back. It didn't make sense. He doubted it ever would. As he shut down the engine he caught a look a himself in the rear view. He was unrecognizable compared to the squared away rookie he'd seen in the bathroom mirror this morning. Uniform torn and covered in mud and blood, among other indescribable things. His face and arms a combination of dirt and scratches, a couple still bleeding. He wouldn't be caught dead looking like this in uniform, but at the moment he couldn't bring himself to care. He had experienced the most horrific night of his life and he felt lucky he was even breathing. Damn lucky. With some effort he hauled himself out of the cruiser, putting on his hat, also covered in filth. He shambled toward the front doors where he was surprised to find Caldwell, the medical examiner, sitting on the front steps. She had always reminded him of Julia Roberts, but tonight when she looked up at him, he thought she more resembled Mrs Roberts grandmother, not that he'd ever say that to her in a million years. She was sitting on the top step, lost in thought, shoulders slumped, leaning against the wall, the ash on her cigarette comically long, or would have been on any other night. There was a large envelope laying on the step next to her. He was within poking distance before she realized with a start that he was there. She placed a hand on the envelope as if he were going to take it from her.

"Winslow. Sorry, I didn't hear you come up."

"You OK?"

She nodded, pulling her phone from her pocket and giving it a small shake. "I was waiting for a damage report. Dispatch gave me bits and pieces but he hasn't been able to reach anyone at the hospital for about thirty minutes."

Winslow sighed. "It was really bad. Still is." Caldwell gestured at the step next to her. Winslow plopped down, surprised at just how weak he felt. *The adrenalin has worn off*, he thought. He looked at Caldwell and began. " Both the canine units were killed. Ramirez lost his hand. They were talking about maybe saving it, reattaching, but there was some complication."

"And Mason?"

Winslow dropped his head even lower. "He didn't make it."

Caldwell let out an involuntary exhale. "Christ."

"It was.." he shook his head and started again. " I can tell you what happened but I still don't really *understand it* .I know one thing. If Sergeant Crane hadn't been there we all would have died. I thought that he abandoned us at first, you know? When we came over the ridge and saw..the suspect, he turned and ran away. Nobody called out, we just watched him run into the woods. When he was out of sight we continued on. I thought he couldn't handle what we were seeing. I didn't blame him, I was half ready to run myself. Ramirez was in the lead and that's how it got him first. The suspect. That *thing*. He raised his weapon and yelled something at it. He didn't have a chance. It moved so fast. It bit him for Christ's sake. Bit through his wrist like it was a stick of gum. His hand was on the ground. It was still holding his sidearm. I couldn't stop staring at that. His hand laying there holding his weapon. After that everyone opened fire on that thing, but it was like it didn't even feel it. It lunged at Mason.. it took him down quick. Tore his throat out with those .. claws. Not hands, Caldwell, it had claws.. There was so much confusion by then, shooting and screaming, it was hard to tell. Then we hear this deep yell and there comes sergeant Crane, running back over the hill, only now he has his shotgun across his back and a Molotov cocktail in each hand, I shit you not. He ran right at that nightmare until he was about five feet away then he threw one of the bottles, hit it right in the face. Its head goes up in flame and that's the first time we hear any sound of pain from it. Sarge throws the other one and it hits it high on the shoulder. The thing was still yelling and it turned to run but it got caught in the brambles and fell over in the ravine. Sarge didn't skip a beat he jumped down right on top of it, jammed his shotgun in its mouth and fed it both barrels. It was over after that. I rode with him to the hospital and I asked him how he knew that fire would hurt it. He said it wasn't trying to burn it, he was using the fire to confuse it so he could get close enough to use the twelve gauge."

Caldwell nodded, a pained smile on her face. "Sarge and the chief are the only officers left from the group that dealt with them the first time. Everyone else has retired or passed on. I'm sure old sarge has thought a lot about how to kill them over the years, if the need arose."

Winslow stared at her, confused and newly alarmed. "What do you mean, the first time?"

Caldwell was lost in thought. "He was just a rookie then, a little younger than you I think. We started the same year."

Winslow looked at her, shocked. "What are you talking about? Caldwell? Are you- are you saying this happened before?"

Caldwell looked at him. Appraised him. Then nodded to herself. "Yes, it happened before. I figured I'd take this story to my grave, but then I never thought it would happen again. And after what you dealt with tonight I think you're owed an explanation, or the best one I can give. One of the officers that was there the first time did me the same courtesy, after I had to perform the autopsies on our friends and on those things. And I guess I'll be doing that again too. God I wish I had a drink." Caldwell shivered and lit an new cig from the butt of the old one and took a deep drag. She gave Winslow a long look before switching her gaze to the stars. She began.

2.

"Missing hikers get the short end of the stick, you know that? You go missing on a busy city street, its all hands on deck, but you go missing on a weekend hike through the mountains or a national forest, you have about three days before they chalk you up as a just another yahoo that overestimated his survival skills. This goes double for any male in their twenties that drops off the grid. After two days, they're dismissed as either a suicide or a bored young man wanting a change of scenery. Missing person cases are higher on our mountain, did you know that? Not by a large amount but but higher than the national average. And the majority of those? Males in their twenties. Families make a stink when they go missing, who wouldn't? And we have to inform them that at any one time there are six men at most patrolling the entire mountain. That averages to about one man per thirty five hundred acres. The odds are against us *ever* finding their kids, as sad as it is. And something we never say to the parent, the trails are marked with huge red signs. Travel at your own risk. Getting lost is the least of it. Bobcats, rock slides, Bears.. hiking on the mountain is dangerous. But Back in ninety one, the year I became a Snoqualmie county medical examiner-God has it really been thirty years- there was a trifecta of disappearances on the mountain no amount of soothing words or big red signs was going to fix. The first happened near the end of January, a park ranger named Jeffery Fields. He'd been an avid and experienced hiker his entire adult life. Knew that mountain like the back of his hand and his mother was not buying the fact that he just disappeared without a trace. Within a months time she had gone to the newspaper, appeared on two morning radio programs and even made it on the local news. She extolled the ineptitude of the county police, the state police and any other law enforcement agency she could think of at the time. she gained a small following and ended up leading a group of protesters in front of city hall, complete with big red signs of their own and 'Wheres Jeffery?' buttons on every lapel. The higher ups decided to wait her out and after a month the public's short attention span drifted on to other tragedies. Then there was Kristopher. Kristopher Bonhem was a foreign exchange student that had been in America a half a year when he had gone up the mountain with a couple friends from school. He was a few feet behind his buddies when he walked off the path to take a leak. Told them he'd catch up. They never saw him again. News spread about that and boy did that get Mother Field's base rejuvenated. Jeffrey's mom joined up with the exchange students parents, who had flown in from Germany and were staying with the sponsor family in the missing boys room. They were very popular on the news shows. The protesters had doubled. The news dubbed us 'death mountain' and before the mayors office could even get out a proper response about the exchange student the last domino fell and it was a two-fer. A newly wed couple on their honeymoon. A couple experienced in hiking, last seen heading up death mountain. A couple with rich parent and lots of connections."

Winslow perked up. "Wait a second, I've heard about the newlyweds. Cody talks about them whenever we have to up on the high roads. He said they died in an animal attack."

Caldwell smiled again, that haunted little smile. "That's the story. Just not the real one. The newlyweds were the last straw. Their parents arrived at the end of their children's first full day missing and by the morning of their second day there were no less than one hundred state and local police combing the forest, not to mention a few dozen volunteers. They spent the better part of a week hacking their way through the brambles and thorns that cover the woods off either side of the trails and trying not to drown in the torrential rains that had been coming down for three days. They hadn't found so much as a candy bar wrapper for their effort. Pressure was mounting and there was talk of bringing in the F.B.I. when a volunteer, Theodore Brady, quite literally stumbled onto a lead. Theo thought he saw a pair of legs sticking out of the leaves at the foot of a ravine and went tearing down the slope, probably with visions of the recently announced reward money dancing in his head. He ended up taking a header in the mud and slid the last twenty feet on his face, giving himself a concussion for what turned out to be a half buried muffler. One of the paramedics strapping him in for the ride out discovered the tunnel. It was cut into the brambles at a weird slant, almost like some optical illusion you couldn't see looking at it straight on. Our boys decided what with the injury and the bad weather that the local police should handle it from there. They didn't get much of an argument. The tunnel was roughly three feet high, so the officers had to crawl through it on hands and knees. They had barely made twenty yards before they found a shoe. We later found out It belonged to the exchange student.

3.

It was two hours before the officers crawled out the other side of that strange tunnel and into a clearing. The sun had just set, but the rain had settled into a light mist and there was enough light to take in the surreal sights. There was a large tree with a rectangle of wood nailed to it, the word Keybuok had been crudely carved into it. We never found out if it was their name or some kind of warning to stay away. There was no other literature found at the site. The sign itself looked ancient, the tree had begun to grow around it, swallow it. Beyond the tree the bones started. They were everywhere. Hundreds, maybe thousands of bones. Bears, cats, rabbit, dogs, foxes, coyotes, mountain lions, Stephens said he even saw a couple wolf skulls, though by the nineties wolves were a rarity on the mountain. Some of the bones were placed in patterns, some in intricate piles, others just strewn around on the ground. The remains weren't all skeletal. Some of the animals were in various stages of decay. Some had been skinned, some had bits carved off of them, some had chunks bitten out of them. Past the bones were the houses. Well, hutches is more accurate. Both structures looked like they had fallen out of one of those reenactments of life in the sixteen hundreds, only with none of the maintenance. To say they were dilapidated was an understatement. The rooves on both structures were collapsing, one side of the smaller hutch had caved in entirely. If there was ever any glass in the windows it was long gone. As they made their way up the side of the main hutch they found more bones. Human this time. Three skeletons, two male one female, never identified, were propped against the side of the house, arms wrapped around each others shoulders, like good friends who sat down for a siesta and never got up again. Then they discovered the park ranger. He had been stripped naked and staked across a large tree stump to the left of the front porch. Something big had gnawed pieces off of him, it was hard to tell what. His eyes were gone, most of his fingers. His genitals."

Winslow rubbed his eyes, shaking his head. "Jesus."

"Animals always go for the soft parts first. But animals don't usually stake their prey to tree stumps beforehand. Everyone was on edge and not just because of the body. There was an energy.. like a cloud of dread that that had drifted down around them as soon as they crawled out of that tunnel and after discovering the ranger, the men in that dooryard were as close to panic as experienced officers ever get. They looked to the door, half off its hinges, opening into the darkness of the room beyond. As they eased forward they heard something in that darkness shifting its weight, maybe deciding what to do. They heard a deep snort like a boar giving a warning, then it exploded through the doorway and it was upon them.

It looked like someone had covered the trunk of an old pine in yellowed, calloused flesh. There was no neck to this thing, just one long unjointed segment connecting head and torso. The arms were average size but muscled, ending in a razor sharp, flesh covered lobster claw . The legs could best be described like a grasshopper, twice as long as they should have been, knees bent to the sides and folded under its body. And the smell.. "

Winslow, who had been nodding wide eyed as she described the thing let out a low whimper "Yes. My God I've never smelled anything like that.."

"It was feces and urine and decay and ammonia and all the fetid inhuman filth from the deepest sewers. When I was nine I visited his grandpas ranch. Me and my brother had been playing tag in the field behind the house when I fell head first onto the remains of a dead fox. It had been rotting in the august heat for a few days, and when I fell my hands punched through its decayed hide and I sunk past my wrists into a soup of hair and bone and a thousand buzzing flies. It was unbearable. I ran screaming all the way back to the house, frantic to get that smell off of me. Even after I had taken three showers I swore I could still smell that fox on me. That thing was my second autopsy ever. The first was an elderly woman who had fallen down the stairs. The paramedics that brought her in said that was about as exciting a body as I should ever expect to find on my table, besides the occasional car crash." Caldwell laughed/coughed around her cigarette, shaking her head. "If he only knew. I unzipped that body bag and the full extent of that stench hit me. It was the fox. A thousand foxes. I threw up. No, I projectile vomited. No warning, just instantly throwing up. I at least had the presence of mind to turn my head to avoid contaminating evidence, not that any of it saw the light of day. The senior M.E. was an old bastard that thought no woman should be in an autopsy room and he would have loved telling anyone that would listen how the new girl lost it all over a corpse."

"Fuck him who ever he was. Anyone would have lost it. Smelling it. Seeing it. What did it do? When it came outside, what happened?" Caldwell took another deep drag and prepared herself. "Wilkes was our first casualty that night. He was on the first step of the porch when it came out. He froze, just for a moment, but it was enough. As it flew past Wilkes it swung its arm out, tearing off his jaw as easy as a kitten swatting a ball of yarn off the table. Wilkes flipped backward off the steps, dead before he hit the ground. Someone yelled out and then the shooting started. Men were firing, diving out of the way of other shooters and forming a line, advancing on it. But as you know bullets don't have an effect on those things. They shot for what must have seemed like an eternity, when one of the rookies, Terrance noble, had a thought that ended up saving everyone's life. While the bullets were flying Terrence said that thing turned and stared right at him. It scared the shit out of him but it also gave him an idea. He dropped to his knee and aimed right for that ugly bastards eyes. He figured it didn't matter how tough the outside was, its eyes looked normal to him. He yelled at everyone to follow suit and they did but no one had a better chance than Terrance. He still holds the county sharpshooter record. The thing seemed to know who the biggest threat was and it charged right for him. He was down to two shots with no time to reload. He had resigned himself to dying as he let his last two shots go, when the things left eye popped like a cork. Blood sprayed from the socket and Its body jerked to the left, one leg collapsing. It let out this croaking noise, like some enormous bullfrog, then it fell over on its side. gray foam poured out of its mouth and then it was done. Terrance ended up getting a certificate of bravery. They had to change the reason, of course. We found out later that the bullet hadn't actually gone in. It had bounced off the eye socket and some of the shrapnel had ricocheted around in its skull. As far as everyone was concerned that didn't diminish the act one bit but when Terrance found out he broke out in a cold sweat. He said he only took it down by pure chance. I told him that was crazy, to hit a target that small, moving that fast and in the dark was skill none of us had ever seen, but he wouldn't hear it. He practically lived at the shooting range for the next six months. Anyway, after Terrence brought it down everyone took a beat. They covered Wilkes, reloaded their guns and headed for the entry, all of them giving a quick look at the thing laying in a pile of bones as they passed. Seven men went inside, five stayed in the yard, checking the perimeter. The stench was a hundred times worse inside, and a few of them retched in corners. It wasn't going to damage the aesthetic of the place. It was a ruin, vines growing through the walls, rats and bugs skittering through excrement and over other small dead things. There was an ancient wood stove primarily composed of rust standing in what at one point must have been a kitchen. It was also taken over by vines and something large was thumping around in the oven, maybe a racoon. Hopefully a racoon. On the opposite side of the room was what could best be described as a cauldron. It was full to the top of some unspeakable thick liquid. It somehow smelled worse than the dead thing in the yard. They ran their flashlights across the entrance to two other rooms, bedrooms I suppose, neither one with a door. In the corner of each room was a large pile of leaves and mud crafted into a nest of sorts. it was in the second bedroom that they found the missing bride, or what was left of her. She had been disemboweled. The skin had been stripped from her legs and back-"

Winslow stood, holding his hand up. "Just.. just give me a second."

"Take your time, son." Winslow walked out into the parking lot, pacing back and forth, running his hands across his face. Caldwell looked at the horizon. The sky had begun to fade from black into a dark purple over the trees. She suddenly felt more exhausted, if that was possible. Winslow made his way back and sat down. He looked at her with a pained expression. "I'm sorry, it was just.. too much for a second there. Caldwell, you autopsied these things.. what are they?"

This time Caldwell held up a hand, gently. "We're almost there. Back outside a rookie, maybe it was the Sarge himself, I don't remember anymore, walked toward the back of the smaller hutch. As he did he heard a twig break, then another. Something was moving around back there. He pulled his flashlight but the rain had killed it. He was about to shout for some assistance when there was a flash of movement, what it was he couldn't say, I was full dark by then. It let out a screech and then it was gone in the tangle of trees. He sent two bullets in after it, but they never found anything. Later he said he was pretty sure it was just a bobcat, but... Inside one of the officers was examining the bride while his partner moved in on the nest. It was at this point that the rookie began shooting at the mystery runner. The men in the room spun and were about to sprint outside when the nest erupted and another of those things leapt onto the closest mans back. This one was one smaller than the one in the yard and it had course, matted hair running down its back. It tried to bite the officers neck but everyone was ready this time. They pried the thing off of him, careful to keep those talons secured. It took six officers to drag It into the kitchen. One of them yelled for them to put its head in the cauldron. It had eyes, so he was hoping somewhere in that hunched, yellowed body it had a pair of lungs. They tilted it up and slammed its head into the brown muck. It fought hard, thrashing and kicking but they held tight, throwing up from the unbelievable stench that was now all over them. After a few minutes the thrashing stopped and there were no more bubbles drifting up through the filth. They kept it under for another few minutes. Then they yanked it out and and put a bullet through its eye. Just to be on the safe side. We didn't know at the time but we incurred our second fatality in that kitchen. Two of the men that drowned that thing had some deep cuts from crawling through the brambles. They caught an infection from whatever was in that cauldron.. Tore through them like wildfire. Cassidy died early the next morning. The other... his name was Bill, I think..How can I not remember... he was in the hospital for six months. Lost both of his arms. Bill or maybe Will.. I cant remember.. But that was all later. For now the search of the property continued. The smaller hutch proved empty. There was a half hearted attempt at a nest inside but nothing like the ones in the main structure. they assumed that there were just the two. After tonight's events I suppose we were very wrong about that."

"You think the one we dealt with tonight was the one that ran off?"

"I do. After the search everyone stood in the yard, looking at the thing laying on its side. Without a word they put on their latex gloves and drug it inside and laid it in the kitchen with the other. The lieutenant happened to have a brother in law that was a paramedic, they were pretty close . He called him out specifically. He knew he and and his partner could be trusted to keep whatever they saw to themselves."

"So... everyone just spontaneously decided to cover it up?"

"Yes. I cant tell you exactly why, They didn't talk about it, they decided, with out anything more than a nod to keep this a private matter. This horror had happened on our mountain so we handled it. Of course we still had to deal with the parents. the remains of the bride, the park ranger and the exchange student were taken out by the paramedics, along with officer Wilkes. The groom was never found. Not so much as a drop of his blood. As for the killers, the officers took care of them. One of them had some rope in his trunk, someone else had a tarp so they wrapped them up and took them off the mountain and on to my table."

Winslow was astounded. " I cant believe you were able to keep this a secret. Monsters. Literal monsters caught roaming the woods, killing people and it all just disappeared."

"The only people that knew trusted each other with their lives. And if at some point down the line someone had a few too many and let any details slip, who the hell would believe them? And remember, son, this happened in the early nineties. No internet, no camera phone in every pocket. Speaking of, did you take any pics tonight? Anyone?"

"No. No one did that I saw. I didn't need a reminder of that.."

"Of course not, I'm guessing no one else did either. At the hospital, what did you say happened to Mason and Ramirez?"

"...Animal attack. We told them we couldn't see what it was."

"And everyone went along?"

"Yeah."

"So you do know how we hid everything. It's instinctual, I believe, the urge to keep it a secret, to not subject other people to this nightmare."

"Maybe. But no civilians were killed tonight, back then, the parents of the victims, didn't they want answers?"

"Yes, and they had every right. So we told them the truth."

"What?"

"Not Jeffrey's mother, nothing we could have done would have satisfied her at that point, but the others.. We brought them in to identify their children's bodies. That was rough. After they had composed themselves somewhat we took them into a room and told them we had found the perpetrators and that they had been killed. Then we showed them those bodies as well."

Winslow stared at her, shocked. "You showed the victims parents those things? What the hell did they do?"

"One of the mothers screamed, one of the fathers collapsed. They were horrified, disgusted. And they wanted it kept a secret as well. The grooms mother said we should say it was a pack of coyotes that killed their children and toss those two things in the incinerator. Everyone else agreed. Better that than any of this getting out and their children become an urban legend for the next five hundred years. The exchange students parents talked to Jeffries mother. It took some convincing but with the news coming from them and not the police she eventually relented. After the parents signed on to our conspiracy, I falsified the autopsy reports on the hikers, a career ender and possible jail time if I was caught, but I wasn't too worried since the police were my accomplices. Two of the officers went back to that clearing and burned the hutches to the ground. The next day the official story went out- A pack of coyotes had gotten the taste for people, it happens. They had been put down and the mountain was safe again. Though the trail the missing hikers had taken was permanently closed to the public. Just to be on the safe side. Six months later most things had gone back to normal."

Winslow scoffed. "Normal. Right."

"It might not seem like it now but it will for you as well. There were times when I thought id never stop seeing those things when I closed my eyes at night, but then one day, I did. Now, the last part. Its the worst part of it for me, but you wanted to know and I think you should, though I know you aren't gong to like it. Winslow, these weren't some creature that crawled up from the bottom of a lake or out of some ancient cave. They were people, son. Humans, just like us."

"That's impossible Caldwell. That's fucking impossible."

"I wish it was, but its true. I opened them up myself. Thy were mutated beyond comprehension but they were people. It took two bone saw blades to crack the big ones chest. It was like someone had started to carve a person out of a hunk of stone then gave up halfway through. When I finally got through and pried him open I got the shock of my life. I don't know what I was expecting but what I got was basic human anatomy. The placement of the organs, the blood, the tissue. It was a man. The heart and lungs were both enlarged, which is usually detrimental but seemed to benefit them. We ran DNA tests through a guy we could trust and it came back human. Severely damaged but human. But.. the DNA, there was something. We ended up having them run it three times. The male was older than the female, by at least twenty years. But their DNA strands were the same. Identical."

"Identical? I thought only twins had identical DNA."

"That's true,and yet... I can only assume the male was her father. Even with what had to be centuries of inbreeding I would think offspring would eventually become sterile before they were able to became one stunted branch on the worlds worst family tree. And they weren't sterile. There weren't just two strands of DNA. There were three"

"Oh, no."

Caldwell nodded. "The female was pregnant. The baby also had identical DNA. I'll spare you the rest of the details."

Winslow looked like he wanted to scream, but to his credit he kept himself composed. Caldwell put her hand over his. "Son, you're still new at all this and tonight was a trial by fire if there ever was one, but I know there's one thing you've been aware of for a long time. Sometimes people are monsters. We see it every day. People that beat their wives, kill children, hurt someone just because they want to cause pain. These things just happen to be monsters on the outside too. Now I think you should probably head home. Get a shower and some rest. I'll call you if there's any news."

Winslow nodded, wiping his hand across his eyes. "Yes ma'am. That's a good idea. Thank you. For telling me. You didn't have to."

"You had a right to know. Go on now, get some sleep."

4.

Winslow headed for his car. Caldwell watched him drive out of the parking lot as the sun began to ease is way over the tree line. She grabbed the envelope off the stairs and went inside. As she passed the Chief's office she peaked inside and saw him at his desk, looking as exhausted as Winslow. She rapped on the open door, bringing him out of a daze. "Chief. I didn't know you were still here."

"I came in the back, had to make some calls to the brass, fill out some paperwork on the incident. Heading back to the hospital in a few."

"Any news?"

"Nothing good. They went from hoping they could reattach Ramirez's hand to amputating his entire arm."

Caldwell closed her eyes. "The infection?"

"Just like last time. It spreads so God damn fast.. He'll be lucky if he makes it till morning."

Caldwell looked out the window. "It's already morning."

The chief attempted a smile. "I saw you talking to the rookie. How is he doing?"

"Shaken up but taking it better than we all did back then."

"The worlds a lot uglier than it was thirty years ago. We've become desensitized."

"Even to shit like this?" She held up the envelope.

"Even to shit to like that." chief pointed at the envelope. "You show him what was in there?"

Caldwell laughed. "The kid's gonna have enough trouble sleeping for the next couple weeks. I didn't feel the need to make it worse."

"Probably a good idea until we figure out how to approach this."

"Might I suggest a tank. Maybe a B1 bomber."

Chief let out a snort. "I don't think anyone's floated the bomber yet. I'll run it up the chain."

"Has anyone thought that maybe the best plan is to do what we've been doing all along. We chased that one from its home and burned it down. It took thirty years for it to make its way down the mountain."

Chief tapped the envelope. "That's exactly what we would do if it wasn't for these. You know the area where the one killed was just a quarter mile from the new housing development. If it had gotten down there, come across some kids playing in their yard.." Caldwell shuddered at the thought. The Chief shook it off, standing up. "But that's for another day. For now, it's very late, or very early. I'm going back to the hospital. You should go home, I'll call you if anything changes."

"Actually I thought I might head out to the hospital, just for a little while."

Chief smiled. "You can ride with me, I could use the company."

As they walked out of the office, Caldwell tossed the envelope on the chief's desk. A few of the pictures slid out onto a pile of paperwork. They were a series of drone shots, dated three months ago. They show the clearing, still covered in bones, two mostly bare patches of earth where the hutches once stood. Then the angle of the camera moved higher, revealing an even larger clearing behind the deadfall of trees dotted with a half dozen more dilapidated hutches. A few figures can be seen in the pictures, some running, others propped back on their elongated haunches, watching as the camera drifts over them. A large section of the last photo is obscured by a gray blur, most likely a rock hurled at the drone. In the far corner of the picture a tree can be seen, a slat of uneven wood nailed to it. A word is scrawled upon it, blurry but legible: Keybuok.

Bait

1.

Maggie lay in bed, hair still wet from the shower, laptop balanced on her very pregnant belly. She was currently clicking through house listings, though nothing was catching her eye. Her husband walked in, sliding into bed next to her, giving her a kiss on the neck. "Any luck?"

Not really. We may have to move the goalposts a little babe. How about another five miles to the radius?"

"OK, but that's the limit or I'm going to spend more time in the car going to work and back than I will at the house."

"Well we don't want that." She gave him a quick peck on he cheek and continued to peruse. He turned over, grabbing his ⁹book. He had gotten about five pages in when she grabbed his arm. "Ooh, Hun, how about this one? I really like it. Only five miles from the nearest hospital and excellent school district."

He smiled. "I think it might be a little premature to worry about education but let's see what you got."

"It's never too soon. Here look."

He looked at the listing and nodded. "Very nice. And we can actually afford it. Always a plus."

Maggie smiled. "That was a big selling point for me as well. And you should know the place. Its in Lagrange. didn't you live in that neighborhood when you were a kid?"

John's brow furrowed. He looked at the page again, not speaking. He had a flash just then, an old memory. An ancient memory. A kid's bike handle, streamers blowing back in the wind. His old bike when he was, what? 10? suddenly he felt a coldness envelope him. he looked closer at the laptop, still not speaking. Maggie gave him a concerned look.

"Babe? You OK?"

He pulled himself out of his daze and gave her a smile. "Sorry, yes, I did live there for a couple of years. This house is in Lagrange?"

"Yes it is."

"what else we got?"

"hey, I thought you liked that one."

"I did, I do, just wondered if there were any more."

"A couple, but we are nearing the bottom of the housing barrel my friend. What's up? You look like you have something on your mind all in the sudden." she rolled onto her side, with some effort. "What is it, scared you might run into an bunch of old girlfriends? Don't worry, I'll scare them away."

John Had another flash, the bike again, this time a girl riding ahead of him, a blonde girl in blue jean shorts. He shook the memory and smiled down at his wife. "I'm sure you would, darling. It's nothing, I m just not a hundred percent about that neighborhood. I know it looks nice in these pics, but I grew up there... wasn't that great then."

Maggie gave his hand a squeeze. "OK. I'll keep looking. You sure you're alright? You look a little weird, my love."

"I'm fine just a little tired. Just a long day." But he was thinking about the girl on the bike.

2.

At three ten in the morning, John had a dream. He was seeing the bike handle, the streamers blowing back. A ten year old john was at the wheel, huge smile on his face. It was Saturday and he was riding for all he was worth, coasting down hills and zooming around corners. He had ventured further out than usual had found himself in an unfamiliar part of the neighborhood. He had been riding for over an hour and was getting tired. He was about to turn around and head for home when he saw a girl his age riding toward him and waving. She had long blonde hair that she didn't bother putting in a ponytail. She was wearing blue jean shorts and a nirvana T-shirt. John had never thought of anyone as beautiful before, but he thought that she might qualify. She skidded up next to him and stuck out her hand.

"Hi, I'm Cassidy."

"Hi, I'm john."

"You new here?"

"No, just don't usually come down this way."

"Cool. Well, you want to ride for a while?"

Suddenly John wasn't so tired anymore. He nodded and they were off. They spent an hour riding, telling stories and having a general good time. After a while John looked around and realized that the sun would be going down soon.

"Jeez, I didn't know it was getting so late, I better head back home."

"Oh, OK. Hey, will you ride with me to my house? Its just around the corner, and I'll give you something to drink for the ride home."

He was very thirsty so he agreed and the two of them took off. It turned out her house was around two more corners and a large hill, and by the time they got there the sun was sinking beneath the trees. They parked at the street and Cassidy led him down a shaded cul de sac toward a run down house at the end of the street. It was in desperate need of paint and trash blow through grass that needed to be mowed weeks ago. The blinds were pulled down, with a very dim light coming from inside. John walked closer to Cassidy, eyeing the house. He didn't know why, but he began to get nervous. A few steps from he porch he froze. He scanned windows. One of the blinds shifted. Cassidy turned and looked at him. "What's wrong?"

John took a few steps back toward the sidewalk. "Maybe I just better head home. Its getting late and I don't want to get in trouble."

Cassidy sounded a little nervous herself now. "Just come in for a minute. Just to get the drink."

John shook his head, backing up a little more. "No I better-"

Just then a man burst from the house. He was wearing thick glasses attached with a band around his head. He was unshaven, wearing an olive drab T-shirt and camouflage shorts under a filthy bathrobe. He looked at Cassidy for a moment, then he sprinted for John. John had wasted no time. As soon as the man came out the door John was already running for the road. He was almost to his bike, but the man was gaining on him. As they both reached the street, the man slid on some loose gravel and fell. It gave John the opportunity to snatch up his bike. He ran along side it for a moment then leapt aboard. John peddled the bike as hard as he ever had. He took a quick look back. The man was up and running, but he was already winded. John leaned over the handle bars and cranked it. He it the hill and let up a bit, his legs on fire. When he got to the bottom the hill he looked back. The man was gone. He had to get off the bike and push for a while he was so sore. The sun was down now and he still had a twenty minute walk ahead of him. Every time a car went past he readied himself to jump in the woods and hide, thinking it was the man come to get whatever it was he wanted from him. He limp-ran home as fast as he could.

3.

John woke up, sweating, slightly out of breath. He walked into the living room and grabbed the laptop. A minute later he was searching a map of the old neighborhood. Not long after he finds the house in the cul de sac. He typed the address into his phone. He closed the laptop and sat back, looking out at the darkness.

4.

The next day john took and early lunch. He drove across town to the old neighborhood. He couldn't help but smile as he recognized some familiar haunts. It was strange that he lived in the same town most of his life but never made his way to this side. But there was a reason, and he hadn't thought of it in twenty or more years. He drove by his old house, the first house he ever lived in, and surprised himself when tears fell down his cheeks. His parents had died six years ago in a car accident. It had been months since it had been on his mind, and today brought it all back. He composed himself and headed toward the reason for this trip. As he turned and drove up that hill the dread filled him again, that panic of running for your life, because looking back on it, he's positive that's what he had done, run for his life. John pulled into the still overgrown cul de sac. He pulled down to Cassidy's house, which was looking more run down that before. He stepped out of the car, looking around for any neighbor that happened to be outside. There were none. he made his way through the weeds to the front door. He paused for a moment, turned to leave, then turned back. He knocked. He heard some shuffling in the house and then the door opened. It was Cassidy. They were around the same age, but she looked like she had twenty years on him. Her hair was going gray and there was a scar running down the side of her cheek. She looked wary as she peeked out the crack in the door. "May I help you?"

"I don't know, I hope so. About twenty years ago I lived around here, three or four miles up the road. And one Saturday I went for a long bike ride, and I ended up here, I met you, we rode around for hours, and-"

Cassidy's eyes flew open wide. "John!"

He looked at her surprised, then laughed. "Yes, I take it you remember."

"Of course I do. I didn't have many happy days in my childhood, but that was one of them. what brings you around after this many years?"

"Actually I wanted to know if I could ask you a question about that day, if I could. About your dad?"

Cassidy's smiled faded quickly. "He chased you. Didn't catch you though."

John shook his head. "No, no he didn't catch me. That's what I wanted to talk to you about. I know I was just a kid and I'm looking at that memory through a kids eyes, but, your dad that day.. He seemed more than just mad that his little girl was hanging around a boy. He seemed-"

"Like he wanted to kill you?"

John looked surprised. "Well, yes."

Cassidy looked out at the un-mowed grass.

"My pop was not a nice guy. And after ma left he got...worse." She touches the scar in her face. "He gave me this one night cause I burned supper. And that's just the scar people can see. There are more. He was a drunk, and an addict."

"Was?"

"He's been dead four years now."

"Oh, I'm sorry."

She shook her head. "Don't be. You're lucky, you know. He had been drinking all day that day. I think if he had gotten his hands on you... anyway. About a year after we met he got in a fight with some guy to bar, almost killed him. It scared him. He decided a change was just what we needed. So, he packed us up and moved us to Yuma Arizona. Said he had a good feeling about it. Turned out it was more of the same. He rented this place to relatives and after he died I came back and took up residence in the family manor.

"So its just you? No children?"

Cassidy let out a short bitter laugh. "No.

After the stellar childhood I had, didn't want to chance messing up a kid."

John didn't know what to say to that, he had stirred up some bad memories for the both of them. He figured it was probably time to make his exit.

"Thank you for talking to me and clearing up some things. I'm sorry you had to go through that."

John put out his hand and Cassidy took it with both of hers, giving him a crooked smile.

"Hey, I'm still here, that has to count for something. It was nice to see you again John, stop by anytime. "

"Good bye, Cassidy. "

She walked inside. John headed toward his car. He felt a lot better after talking with Cassidy, he hoped it might have done them both a little good. His mood took a sharp turn as he walked past the side of the house and happened to glance something poking out from behind the house. It was a pink bike. A child's bike. John quickly looked away in case she was looking out the blinds and kept walking. His heart now beating very fast. *Cassidy, if you don't have any kids, why do you have that bike..*

5.

Later that evening, John sat down in his favorite chair and fired up his laptop. He had tried for an hour to go to sleep, but that pink bike wouldn't let him. He decided to do a little snooping in the internet, to ease his mind. He googled disappearances in his area over the past 20 years. A list of almost four hundred names and pictures popped up on the screen. He was shocked. "Jesus, so many.." He narrowed the search to boys and girls nine to eleven, the lists shortened considerably. But not short enough.

"Six boys and two girls missing without a trace between 1989 and 2003. All in march or April...that's around the time he came after me..."

John looks at addresses of the missing kids. Four of them, all boys, were in a rough circle five miles or less around Cassidy's home. John scanned the article. "The last disappearance was 2003... The year they moved to Yuma..."

John googled disappearances of boys in the Yuma area, 2003.

"No..no. Five boys, eleven years old, missing between March and April, from '03 to 2016. Jesus Christ. He was taking kids for years. I could have stopped this. Why the hell didn't I say anything?"

John ran his hands through his hair. He tried to shake off the guilt. "There's nothing I can do about it now, this monster's dead. but maybe I can give those parents some closure, let them know what happened. And what about that damn pink bike." there was an explanation, but he was fighting it. He didn't even want to think it, but it was the most obvious answer. He closed his eyes. "She said she came back four years ago...please don't be right, John."

He started typing. Disappearances 2016 to the present. He read the information on the screen and closed his eyes. Three boys missing in the past 4 years, within seven miles of that house. He closed the laptop, feeling sick.

She's killing them now. He fucked her head up so bad she's continuing where he left off. I can't believe this. I have to call the police, there is no way in hell this is just a coincidence-

Maggie suddenly yelled out from the bedroom. "John!"

John was up like a shot from the chair and ran to her. She was still in bed, but heaving herself off. He helped her the rest of the way.

"What's wrong?"

Maggie gave him a pained smile.

"Nothings wrong, I hope. Its just we're about to have a baby, so...I'm gonna need a ride to the hospital."

John looked at her for a moment, mild shock on his face, then he gave her a big kiss. "I can do that."

John grabbed the overnight bag and helped Maggie to the door.

Dim light shown through the hospital window. Maggie looked drained but happy. She was sleeping soundly. John was holding his new son, looking out at the predawn sky, swirling with dark purple clouds. He looked down at his child's his face with a combination of love and worry.

"I discovered something really bad today... or I think I did. I have been known to jump to conclusions. I don't want to worry your mother with this, she has enough going on, and I don't want to bring any more unnecessary suffering on Cassidy, especially if I'm wrong, but there's no way that I can just let this go. So, before I involve the police I have to find out if this is true. I owe it to all those boys, their parents... I've only known you a few hours but if you were taken.. It would destroy me. I have to see if Cassidy's dad warped her so much she's taken his place. The kids are always abducted late march, early April, and that's less than two months from now. I'm going to have to come up with a plan."

6.

Spring. John and Maggie step into their new home. Maggie is noticeably slimmer. They are taking in small boxes from their car, the last of the move. The baby, now two months old, is in a carrier on the porch, staring at his hands.

Maggie gave the place an appraising look

"Well, its not as nice as the one I picked from your old neighborhood, but it will do." She put her box down and gave john a tight hug.

"I'm going to miss you."

John kissed her, touching her face.

"Its only two weeks. Three, tops. You know how these land assessments can get. And how my boss can be. He wants what he wants. Yesterday. I'll be back before you know it."

Maggie pulled back reluctantly.

"You have all your flight info?"

"I'm good to go, flight leaves bright and early tomorrow morning. And I'll call every half hour to make sure the two of you are OK."

She smiled and gave him a playful punch. "I think once every hour will do. don't want to over do it."

"Maybe you're right. Why don't you take the kid inside, babe, I'll get the rest of this."

"You sure?"

"Yes ma'am."

Maggie kissed him and walked up the stairs, picking up the baby as she went. John walked to the window and watches as she take the baby out and holds him up, kissing his forehead. He has a worried look on his face. "I'll be back soon, guys, I promise."

7.

In the two months following his online discoveries he began running surveillance on Cassidy. He spent his lunch hours parked behind the overgrown shrubs down the street, watching the house and he'd cruise through her neighborhood ever night after work. He didn't spot anything out of the ordinary the first three weeks but then, jackpot. One afternoon he was just wrapping up his lunch it was about to head back to the office when Cassidy's front door opened. He snatched up the mini binoculars he had purchased for these stakeouts and scanned the house. Cassidy was standing on the porch and she wasn't alone. A girl of ten or eleven was following behind her he was a good distance away but the resemblance was striking. It was her daughter. Had to be. He watched them, disgusted. "No children, right Cassidy?" she pointed at the shed and the girl ran inside and brought out the pink bicycle. she hopped on and went for a ride . Cassidy watched her. John watched as well. *I wonder if this is a practice run*, he thought. Twenty minutes later the girl came back, still alone. She put the bike back in the shed and the two of them went inside. John dropped the binoculars in the passenger seat. "She lied. Nothing the police could act on but, why the hell would she lie about having a kid. Time's running out. If she's going to take someone that's going to be soon. I have to step this up." that night he told Maggie about the fictional land assessment deal that he would more than likely be supervising. She believed him, why wouldn't she? It cut him, lying to her. It's something he swore he would never do and here he was, building this mountain of bullshit. It was for a good reason, he told himself, and he would tell her everything after it was over.

The airport was full of the usual hustle and bustle as John pulled into the long-term parking. He made his way to Maxx car rental. When it was his turn of the counter he asked about the reservation had made for a panel van.

8.

An hour later John was easing the van down the cul-de-sac towards Cassidy's house. The house was as closed and quiet as the last time he was here. He parked in his usual spot, still amazed at how little people noticed theses days, or cared. When he was a kid if some car had been parked on and off for weeks on their Road somebody would have called the police or at the very least gone up to the car and asked him what the hell they were doing there all the time. No one had ever approached john, even though two or three Neighbors had glanced in his Direction and then went about their business. it was depressing, but in this case he was glad for it.. He placed a large sign in the windshield- broken down, have called tow truck. He jumped into the back area where he had stowed two huge duffel bags. He unzipped the first one and pulled out a sleeping bag, battery chargers and his trusty binoculars. He then took a folding chair from the rapidly deflating duffel bag. He sat down, training the binoculars on Cassidy's house. He scanned the yard, but all he saw was what he observed almost every other time he had been here. Nothing. He set the binoculars down and opened the second bag. It was full of food and water. He stacked it against the side of the van. Once the bags were empty, he folded them and set them aside, set back in the chair and looked at the house.

"OK, here we go."

9.

On the third day in the van, John was bordering on stir crazy. He'd done a hundred crossword puzzles, and if he had to play one more game on his phone he was going to lose it. He felt bad. He smelled bad. And he missed his family. outside the van all was quiet. A few people milled about, watering lawns or hanging out clothes, but nothing stirred in Cassidy's house. John was on the phone with Maggie.

"Everything is going fine babe. I haven't had time to hit the pool, but its only the third day, I'm sure I'll get down there. How's the kid?"

"Still not sleeping through the night... but I only had to get up three times last night instead of five."

"Well, that's progress. When-"

Suddenly the light over Cassidy's door clicked on. John jumped in his seat, scrambling for the binoculars and training them on the porch.

"Honey, I'm going to have to call you back, I have a slight issue here."

John hung up and grabbed the binoculars. He watched as Cassidy walked out on the porch. She looked up the street at the van. John shrunk down in his chair. She turned and looked back inside the house. Suddenly the girl emerged, pushing the pink bike. Cassidy laying down and said something to the girl and she hopped on her bike and pedaled away. Cassidy watched her for a moment then stepped inside.

John watched, shaking. He slumped in the chair. "Just like her dad....Christ." he eyed a little clock he'd set on his bottles of water. It read 4:38. "OK.. Now I wait and see. I've come this far...go to be sure."

10.

An hour later, John was still watching the house. He picked up his phone to call home when the girl turned the corner on her bike, a boy of eleven following behind her

John dropped the phone as he watched them ride into the yard and he saw himself slowly walking down that hill with Cassidy. He began to shake. "Shit...oh shit."

The girl and boy set the bikes in the yard and headed into the house. John dropped the binoculars and eased the van door open. The sun began to set as he crouch-ran through shadows to Cassidy's house. He skidded to a halt under a window, and took a brief look inside. The girl and boy are on the couch of a cluttered, dusty living room. Cassidy entered with two glasses of water. The girl reaches for one, but Cassidy gives her a warning look and the girl takes the other. The boy took a sip of the water and almost immediately starts to look dazed. He slumps over a bit on the couch. Tess and the girl grab an arm and start leading him to the bedroom. John decided he had seen enough. He charged at the front door and knocked it in. He ran into the living room. "Cassidy! Its over! I know what you've been doing!"

The three of them were standing in the bedroom doorway. The boy looked dazed, the girl, horrified. Cassidy was in a rage. Gone was the sad but hopeful woman he talked to on the porch. This was the real her.And she was just like her father.

"What are you doing here!"

"You told me to come back anytime. So here I am."

"You have no right to involve yourself in this!"

"I have every right, more than most, especially when your father tried to do this to me when I was a kid."

The little girl started crying and moved away from her mom.

"I'm sorry sir, she made me... I never wanted to.. she made me."

"I know, it's going to be okay. I'm going to get you away from here."

Cassidy looked around wildly for a moment then lunged for a pair of scissors sitting on the end table. John beat her there, swatting the scissors to the floor behind him. He punched Cassidy in the jaw, knocking her to the floor. He positioned himself between her and the children. He turned and gave the boy a hard shake. He seemed to come out of it a little. "Boy you have to get out of here now, get on your bike and get home as fast as you can, do you understand?"

The boy nodded and stumbled out the front door and into the darkness. John turned his full attention back to Cassidy, who was now back on her feet. He yelled back over his shoulder, " Little girl, I need you to go call the police right now okay?"

Cassidy, rubbing her jaw, gave him a big grin. "Before the police come, don't you want to say hello?"

She pointed at the bedroom. John eased closer to the door, never taking his eyes off of her. The bedroom is dimly lit. It smelled bad in there, like sour milk. He could hear a machine or two whirring and beeping. He saw someone in the bed. He took another step inside and stopped cold, It was Cassidy's dad, not dead after all, but he look like it could happen any moment. He was laying in a filthy bed, oxygen tubes in his nose, other assorted wires attached to his chest and arms. He was still wearing those glasses with the wrap around strap. He looked up at John with eyes swimming in yellow corneas, staring at him with hatred. He tried to speak, but so that came out awesome what gurgling wheeze. Saliva dripped on the side of his face.. suddenly he grinned, a mostly toothless display. He used his one working arm to pull his blanket down, exposing himself.

John looked at him with disgust.

"You piece of shit... you are gonna pay for what you've done. Both of you. you'll die in prison. I'm taking the girl out of here and then I'm-"

Unbelievable pain shot through his back. He yelled out and fell to his knees. He reached back felt the scissors sticking out of his lower back.

He watched the girl step back over to her mother. He looked at her, confused and sad.

Cassidy grinned at him, the same snarl as her father. "I don't think the girl wants to go anywhere with you, do you sweetie?"

"No, mommy."

"Good girl. Now, you go see if you can catch that boy before he gets home. We're going to take care of Johnny boy."

The girl ran past John as she took off out the door. He tried to grab her as she went by, but all heck succeeded in doing was falling to the floor. The scissors dug into his kidney and he let out another scream. Cassidy looked out the window, watching the kid from then she came back to John and knelt down next to him. She yanked the scissors out of his back. He tried to scream again but nothing came out. She knelt down and whispered in his ear. "Ok, Johnny let's get you in the bedroom. Daddy's wanted to meet you for a long time."

John tried to push her away, but he couldn't move. He could barely keep his eyes open. He was fading fast. The last thoughts going through his mind were of Maggie and the baby, as Cassidy slowly drug him into her father's bedroom and closed the door.

Night Train

1.

Robert Wiles sat in the uncomfortable coach seat of a red eye train rumbling along somewhere in the middle of a Nebraska winter. It was 2:30 in the morning and the train was making what it felt like it's 400th stop of this journey. Robert squirmed in his seat, looking with disdain as his fellow travelers exited and boarded. A large older woman stepped up into the car, her luggage consisting of a couple tattered garbage bags. Robert rolled his eyes. *Christ*, he thought, *the train is getting as bad as the bus*. Then his frown turned into a smile. He wouldn't have to worry either mode of transportation for much longer. Robert was an up-and-comer at his firm, a real cutthroat and the boys upstairs had finally noticed. Earlier today he had interviewed for partner and he nailed it. In a month's time he would be relocated to Los Angeles, and his days of riding trains in the middle of the night through Podunk towns would be behind him. Only first class flights from here on out, he thought. Hell, maybe even a private jet or two. Traveling with people carrying luggage by Armani, not Hefty bag. After the conductor welcomed he new riffraff on board and barked out the E.T.A. of the next stop, the train finally began to move again. He shifted in his seat, trying to get comfortable. An impossible task. As they pulled away from the station the darkness of the farm country returned, interrupted by the light of the almost full moon as it ever so often peeked through the clouds. The snow had finally stopped, but there was at least a foot and a half on the ground. He looked out the window, thinking about the life he would soon possess. After a while he dozed off.

2.

He was awakened a short while later with a soft thump as the train shifted south. He looked around the car, squinting in the dim light. Everyone appeared to be asleep, wrapped in blankets to fight the cold the older train's heating system just couldn't keep up with. He pulled his coat tighter around him and checked his watch, it was 3:02. He stretched and took a look out the window. The moon had pushed its way through the clouds and had illuminated a field of snow beside the train. He stared out into the night, oblivious of the beauty. He was about to turn away and try to get back to sleep when something unbelievable caught his eye. There was someone was running in the field. Robert wiped at the glass, then wiped his eyes. He cupped his hands around his face and peered out the window. He wasn't imagining it- they we're about a hundred yards out, too far to get a good look at, but there it was, a figure running through the snow. Sprinting, to be more accurate. Whoever it was, they were keeping up with the train.

That's not possible, Robert thought. *We've got to be going at least 70 miles an hour.* The moon disappeared into the clouds and Robert lost sight of whoever it was. He stood up and looked around the car. Everyone was still asleep. He wiped the sweat from his forehead, feeling is heartbeat in his neck. He thought about alerting a conductor, but what exactly was he supposed to tell them? that he saw a man running in the snow next to the train? They'd have him taken off at the next stop and held for observation. He sat back down and looked out the window, but there was nothing to see but his own reflection. He sat back in his chair, going over what he had seen out there. *Maybe it wasn't a man. I mean how could it have been, running that fast. A bear, maybe?* He knew that they could walk on two feet, he'd seen it on some dumb You tube video. He shook his head. *Sure Robert,* he thought to himself, *a bear decided to stand on two legs and run as fast as a train through two feet of snow.* As he tried to come up with some other solution for what could have been going on out there, the clouds broke and the moon shone down on the field. Robert pressed his face against the window and drew in a deep breath. Whatever it was was still out there but he still had no idea what the hell he was seeing. Suddenly the train lurched and the intercom started blaring on about the train entering Barrington station. Robert almost yelled out. He looked at his fellow passengers, amazed that all of them were somehow sleeping through the shrieking intercom message. He turned back out the window as the station lights brightened the field, but whatever it had been running around out there was gone now. He sat back in his seat, angry at the fear he was feeling. He had never been one for flights of fancy, even as a child. He didn't believe in conspiracy theories, and thought all the people that oohed and ahhed over Bigfoot and UFOs were a collection of idiots. yet here he was, face pressed to the window, watching the boogeymen run alongside the train. If the partners saw him now, they'd rethink that partnership real god damn fast. The train slowly made its way out of the station and before long they were back in the snowfields. Robert made it a point to do anything but look out the window. He checked Facebook, but no one he knew was dumb enough to be up at this hour. He played a word game but it didn't hold his interest very long. (he wasn't the best speller), he checked his watch and was shocked to see only ten minutes had passed since they left the last station. He tossed the phone in the seat next to him. *This is ridiculous.* He thought. *It was probably just a bear, that coupled with lack of sleep and the trick of the light.. that's all. So here's what going to happen, Robert. You're going to take one more look out the window. You will see nothing, because there is nothing to see, and then you are going to get some sleep.* He felt better after the self imposed pep talk. Always did. He relaxed in his seat, shaking his head at how wound up he had gotten. He opened the window shade and looked out into the darkness. His heart slammed in his chest. Whatever it was was a lot closer, and it most definitely not a bear. He stared out at the thing, trying to make sense of it. It was naked, its skin a dark yellow-green, reptilian, like a crocodile with long legs and no tail. It's head was elongated and it had what looked like a smaller version of an elephants trunk where it's mouth should be. It was making huge strides through the snow, as easy as if it were taking a stroll through the park. Robert scrambled to his feet, grabbing his phone off of the seat. He pressed it to the glass and started taking picture after picture of the thing that was now maybe a hundred feet from the train. The clouds returned, obscuring his view. Robert sat down, furiously flipping through the pictures he had just taken, but all he could see in any of them was a blur of dimly lit snow. He gritted his teeth. *Fuck!* He stood up and paced the length of the train car, hoping that someone would wake up, so they would at least be awake with him . He'd even take the lady with the garbage bag luggage. He looked at his watch. It was now 3:16. *This simply cant be,* he thought. That thing out there has been running beside this train for at least thirty minutes. Nothing could run that fast for that long. He walked into the next car, hoping to spot someone official, but all the ticket takers seem to have vanished Into thin air. They were only a couple of passengers in that car, also asleep. He made his way back to his seat, terrified and drained. He sat down, purposefully not looking in the direction of the window. He closed his eyes, listening to the train as it sped through the snowy countryside, the the rhythmic clicking of the wheels on the tracks. The adrenaline rush began to fade and after a few moments he felt himself drifting off.

3.

He was out for almost 20 minutes when he heard/felt a thud against the side of the train. He bolted up right, almost screaming. He scrambled out of his seat and into the aisle, breathing heavy. He scanned the seats around him. everyone was still wrapped in their blankets, shadows in the dim light of the train car. He hated them all for blissfully sleeping through this madness. He looked at light outside his window. The moon was back. He hated the moon as well. He whimpered as he sat back down. He didn't want to look outside but he knew he had to. He slowly moved his face toward the glass and peered out into the field. Nothing. He looked left and right as far down the tracks as he could. No creature, just miles of emptiness. He let out a huge sigh and slumped back in his seat, a smile on his face. *Blew out your Achilles, didn't you, fucker?* He laughed out loud. The man across from him peered out from the top of his blanket, giving Robert a stern look before going back into his cocoon. Robert laughed again, quieter this time. He shook his head as he looked outside, this time actually getting a small bit of enjoyment from the view. It really was kind of beautiful, the moonlight dancing off the snow. He looked down at the field and his smile faltered. He gripped the sides of his chair until his knuckles were white. No. God dammit no! There were tracks the snow, maybe 4 ft from the train. Tracks of something big. And as he watched the tracks ended and he heard another loud thump on the side of the train, this time further up. "Jesus Christ", he said, "it's on the train" just then the lights in the car ahead went out. he thought he heard a muffled scream and then nothing. He was suddenly very angry. How dare this be happening to him, on this day of all days. he had fought and bled for his firm for YEARS and finally gotten the job he had always wanted. Had DESERVED! No one else was even fucking close, He was on his way up, done with low rent people and public transportation, and this thing, this fucking interfering THING thinks it can ruin all of it. I won't allow it. I won't allow it! Robert stood up. He inched slowly to the car ahead and opened the door, braced for whatever nightmare was going to be revealed, but instead he was left confused. The car was deserted. He crept up the aisle peaking around seats, looking in the luggage compartments. There wasn't a person to be found. A purse here, a backpack there, but other than that, empty. He moved on. The next two cars were in the same condition, personal items, no people. In the fourth car things begin to change. There were signs of a struggle, two of the windows were cracked, and something that looked very much like blood was pooled in one of the seats. There was a single shoe laying on its side in the middle of the aisle. He moved toward it, trying to look everywhere at the same time. He kicked the shoe up right, half expecting to find a foot inside. There wasn't. He became more terrified with each step, but he moved on.

4.

The dining car was really bad. He walked in, wide eyed. One of the chairs have been ripped out of the floor, two others were torn apart. They were covered in blood, as were the walls. At one of the tables there was a still steaming mug of hot chocolate, Next to it was a napkin with three severed fingers sitting on top of it. He stumbled back against the bar covering his mouth. The train took a hard left and he spun and grabbed the bar to steady himself. There he saw a large butcher knife sticking out from behind the counter. He snatched it up and continued forward, holding the knife out in front of him. After what seemed like an eternity, he made it to the final car. the door was smashed in and it took him a minute to pry it open. It was freezing in the car, most of the windows had been shattered in here, Snow billowed in, but Robert didn't notice. He was too busy staring at what was happening at the end of the car. He took a few more steps and slipped in a pool of blood. he scrambled to his feet, never taking his eyes off of the scene unfolding in front of him. He wanted to scream, he wanted to run, but he could do neither. Most of the overhead lights were broken, and the ones that were left were strobing on and off, but he could see more than he ever wanted to. He had discovered where all the missing passengers had gone. They were piled at the back of the car like pieces of wood, legs, arms, heads missing, blood everywhere, stacked in a loose pyramid. The thing that's had running by the side of the train was in front of the pyramid.

It reached out and grabbed a severed limb, easing its proboscis into the broken open bones. Robert watched this mesmerized, detached, as if it was a nature show on T.V. *It's like some freak show anteater. Its eating the marrow. Sucking it out.* As if the thing heard his thoughts it spun around. Roberts let out a yelp as he fell against the wall, raising the knife. The thing had no eyes but it tracked his movement and made its way towards him. Robert backed up until his shoulders hit the broken door. He started crying. "Please. please don't. I'm sorry I came here, ill just leave, OK? Ill forget that I ever saw you, I promise, just please let me go." The thing walked closer, its feeler reaching out for him. its hands were razor sharp claws covered in blood. Its feeler ran across Robert's cheek, the touch made him feel as if he would lose his mind. It moved closer until it was towering directly above him. It took one of Robert's hands in its claw and brought it up to its proboscis, running up the length of his arm. Robert closed his eyes. it was too late. He had no fight in him. In a flash the creature twisted its claw and Robert's arm snapped. white hot pain tore through him. He tried to scream but nothing came out. the creature twisted his arm further until the bone slid out of his skin like a living pez dispenser. It slipped its proboscis into the bone, sucking the marrow from him. Robert could feel it happening, a pain he could have never imagined. He began to fade when bright lights began flashing through the train car. A voice came over the broken intercom in a staticky buzz. "ladies and gentlemen we are now entering Lexington station. if you would please remain in your seats until the train has come to a complete stop. If you are staying on board please have your tickets handy."

Robert could see the train station slowly approaching. The thing from the field released him. He fell into one of the bloodstained seats, his broken arm shriveled and useless in his lap. The thing turned its head toward the approaching station, then back to Robert. It took a step toward him then in one motion leapt out one of the broken windows. Robert watched it run across the field and disappear from sight. He could barely move, his arm had mercifully gone numb. He slumped over and began to weep. There was a noise behind him as the broken car door burst in. It was one of the elusive ticket takers. He looked around the car, eyes wide. He stumbled into the seat across from Robert. "My God" he looked down at the knife still in Roberts hand. "What have you done? What have you done?"all Robert could do was look out the window into the moonlit field.

As he did, the train pulled into the station.

Passenger

1.

"You know I hate you out driving this late." Cadence could be a broken record when it came to this subject, but standing in a car wash hosing vomit off the rear door of his car at three in the morning, he agreed.

"I know Hun, but the money's great, and we can really use it right now."

"When will you be home?"

"Barring any surprises, I should be there in a half hour."

"OK. any pukers tonight?"

"Not a one." Gary said as he plunked another dollar into the sprayer. *Christ, what did this guy eat*? Jerry pushed the stream of water closer to the offending clump.

"Good. It's bad enough having all those strangers in the car, especially now that we have little Ray, but the thought of them throwing up everywhere.."

"Never fear, you know I give the whole car a go over after every shift. No cooties."

He could hear the smile in her voice. "No, no cooties."

"OK, I'm going to finish gassing up and I'll be on my way to your loving arms, hows that sound?"

Cadence giggled. "You may have to settle for my snoring face. I have to be up in three hours."

"Works for me. I love you. Kiss Ray for me."

Gary hung up as the hose sputtered out and the machine began demanding another dollar. He gave the door a close inspection, then hung the hose on its stand. He checked the piggyback app on his phone. He had been doing the ride share gig for a few months now, just before his wife had given birth to little Ray. It was going to be a temporary deal, just to help with the impending baby bills, but the money was way better than he anticipated, and he was a people person so the tips were always generous. And there was another thing, something he had forgotten while sitting in a cubicle for a decade- just how much he loved to drive. He'd spent hours as a teenager driving the back roads, windows down, radio blasting. Most of his customers this time of night were inebriated factory workers turned out from one of the many bars that dotted this stretch of I-10, and yes, there was inevitable upchuck situation, but for Gary it was a compromise he could live with.

2.

He was about to call it quits for the night when the app pinged and the little cartoon pig at the top of the page wagged its butt back and forth. Someone needed a ride. Gary hesitated. There was no picture of the person he was supposed to pick up. sometimes there wasn't, no biggie, but there was no name either, and that never happened. just an initial-Y. He felt a flicker of unease. It was late, the bars had closed over an hour ago. At this point most people had either made it home or decided to sleep it off on the backseat of their cars. The pig oinked again. Jerry frowned. Whoever it is is never gonna get another ride this time of night, he thought. He begrudgingly pushed the accept button.

The pig at the top of the screen let out its very familiar (and at this time of night more than a little annoying) squeal and the navigation screen appeared. The destination was ten miles away. In the opposite direction of home. Shit.

Gary chastised himself. "You're the one that hit accept, jackass. Let's get going."

He turned the ignition and shot out of the car wash, heading up the mostly deserted section of I-10.

3.

He'd assumed he would be heading to a bar, but was surprised to see the pickup spot was a gas station that had been abandoned for about a year. The unease hit him again, stronger this time. He shook it off

"That's not that weird", he said to himself, "Y could have started walking, then decided it would be quicker by car."

His brain wasn't having it. *Yeah, but the nearest bar is almost four miles from there, that's a long way to walk before calling it quits, especially drunk.*

Gary frowned. "Maybe they aren't drunk at all. Maybe 'Y's car broke down. simple as that, so you can shut up now, OK?

Gary's brain remained silent for the moment. The gas station was coming up quick. He put on his brights in case 'Y' was standing by the side of the road. His unease grew as his brights splashed across the parking lot, revealing nothing but broken bottles and weeds forcing their way up through the asphalt.

His phone chirped, "You have reached your destination."

"No shit. " Gary drove into the lot, moving slowly past the concrete pedestals the gas pumps had occupied in previous years. He rolled down the window and stuck his head out.

"Hello? It's your piggyback driver. Anyone here?" No broke down vehicle. No driver. Gary began to sweat. He wiped his forehead, a little angry at himself. "Christ, what the hell is wrong with me tonight?" The phone pinged and he looked down. It was a short message, but it did nothing to improve his nerves- 'Y' will arrive in two minutes. The timer began to count backwards. Gary looked out into the dark, but saw nothing. Then, barely audible at first, he heard a clicking sound, like someone hitting a piece of wood on the pavement. The sound became louder. Suddenly the unease he had been feeling blossomed into slight panic. Gary had never canceled a ride before, had thought of his 100% acceptance rate as a badge of honor, but now here he was with his finger hovering over the button. He was ready to abort the mission. The clicking got louder and louder, but hard to pin down the direction with the echo from the building . Then it just stopped. Gary peered out into the lot, willing himself to see anything out in the dark. Jerry was about to put the car in drive and haul ass back onto the interstate when the back driver side door flew open.

Gary stifled a scream, barely, as the passenger got in. The door shut as quickly as it opened. he looked in the rear view to try and catch a glimpse before the dome light faded out, but 'Y' was hunched behind the driver seat. All he could see before the car was enveloped in darkness was a gnarled wooden cane propped against the middle seat. *That explains the clicking*, Gary thought. As the panic subsided a little, the familiar routine kicked in. He hit the destination button and remembered to breath. That was a mistake. The smell of black licorice filled his nostrils. It was as if he was drowning in it. his throat locked up. he gagged twice, turning up the radio slightly to mask the sound. He started toward the interstate and gambled that he would be able to speak without throwing up on himself.

"How are you this evening?" his voice only cracked once. no response from the back seat.

"I hope you don't mind if I crack the windows, its a little stuffy in here."

Still no answer. Not that Gary was waiting. He cracked all the windows and breathed in the stream of wind. the wave of nausea subsided a bit. He looked down at the destination time and his heart sunk. Thirty minutes! Usually He'd welcome that nice chunk of cash, but thirty miles in the car with this silent weirdo that smelled like he had bathed in a lake of Jagermeister. Gary stepped on the gas, running a couple miles over the speed limit, something he never did, but he wanted this person out of his car as soon as possible.

Gary's brain piped up again, with a reasonable question. *Who sits right behind the driver in an otherwise empty car, and then doesn't say a damn word? No one, since we've been driving. But l know who would do that. Someone up to no good.* Gary's grip tightened on the wheel. *I'm sure many people that have sat in that particular seat didn't have plans to murder the driver.*

True, Gary's brain reasoned, *but he's all but hiding back there. And he doesn't have a name? How many times has that happened? Maybe one of those things wouldn't be a red flag, but all of them? And just where does this piggyback end?*

Gary slowly picked up his phone. He swiped out to bring the entire travel map on screen. Thirteen more miles on the interstate, and then.. it looks like a right turn right out into the desert. No street name, no street on the map. Gary's stomach rolled over. He decided enough was enough. This was just a passenger, like a hundred before him. And a handicapped one on a cane at that. He had just given himself the Heebie Jeebies. He cleared his throat and put a smile on his face.

"So how did you end up all the way out at Ed's station? Car trouble?"

Still no response from the back seat. Gary continued.

"Well, I'm glad i was able to pick you up, I'm usually not out this late."

Nothing. Gary refused to read anything into it. Some people just don't like to talk. He wiped the sweat of his forehead, confused. His internal thermostat ran a little hot anyway, he was always kicking he blanket off, even in winter, but he was uncomfortably hot. This time of year the temperature drops fast after nightfall, and the last time he checked it was in the low sixties. With the wind blasting in through the window should be freezing him, but the temp in the car was rising. he checked the heater, knowing it wasn't on. The heat was coming from the back seat. from his passenger. He could feel it baking the back of his neck. Gary rolled the windows down a little more, but it wasn't helping. The heat intensified as they drove. Jerry leaned toward the open window, watching the miles count down with excruciating slowness.

4.

After what seemed like an eternity they reached the turnoff. Jerry slowed to a stop. He looked out into the desert for any semblance of a road. It was just sand and the random tumbleweed littered along the majority of this highway. Gary turned his head from the window toward the furnace of the back seat

"I'm having a little trouble finding the road, are you sure this-"

A hand shot out from the backseat area, as gnarled as the cane. the flesh looked blistered, shiny in parts, rough with dead skin in others. The heat was coming off it in waves. that licorice smell seemed to be leaking from small sores on the back of his/her hand. The coat sleeve that 'Y's ruined hand jutted from looked roughly a thousand years old, ratty and stained. Jerry saw brief movement inside the sleeve, as if insects had made their home inside the lining. The hand was inches from Gary's face and it took all he had not to scream. 'Y' extended his index finger, tipped with a filthy, ragged nail, and pointed out into the darkness. Jerry flinched away from the hand and looked in the direction it had pointed, and there, barely visible were two ruts in the hard pack. Not a road by any stretch but it would do. *I don't know how I missed it and I don't care, as long as it gets this nightmare out of my car*, Gary thought. He wasn't denying it anymore- he was terrified. As soon as he turned onto the dirt road the terror grew. Ten miles into the desert. Could he hold on twenty more minutes like this? Should he just ask the person to get out? What if they refused? He had never ejected a passenger before. He imagined opening the back door and reaching in, touching that coat. That skin. He closed his eyes. No, I'll take him to the end of the line, and if things get weird... or weirder, I'll...handle it. Gary reached down in the driver door cubby hole and felt the hilt of his pocket knife, a gift from his grandfather. He had put it there as a request from his wife, and had not once had he felt the need for it, until tonight. He picked up the knife and set it in his lap. He continued down the dirt road, dodging potholes and debris. The going was slow. It felt as if the speedometer was hardly moving at all. But they were making progress. About a mile away from the the turnoff, the passenger changed. In the dim blue light of the dashboard Jerry saw movement in the backseat. 'Y' had started rocking back and forth. Jerry tightened his grip on his knife as 'Y' leaned forward and than slammed him/herself into the backseat. Not long after Jerry heard panting, a wet, rattling gasp that ended in a release of foul air every time 'Y' hit the back seat.

Jerry was on autopilot as he careened around tumbleweeds and axle-breaking holes. He was focused on the miles, and the knife. Nine miles, seven, six.. each mile seemed to take twice as long as the last. Five..four. 'Y' started to make a some mewling sound, possibly a giggle, clawing at the seat next to it as they became more excited at the nearing destination. Drops of thick gray saliva were splattering against the passenger headrest, steaming, as if it were boiling water. three miles.. two.. Gary had the knife in a death grip. His heart was pounding in his ears. One mile. A half mile... a quarter. He looked out into the desert for a house, a campsite. any sign of civilization. There was nothing. No, there was only one reason this bastard wanted him to drive out here. He was certain of it now. One of them was going to die out here tonight. suddenly 'Y' slid up and pressed their body against the back of the drivers seat, that mangled hand clutched on the side of Jerry's seat, its face inches from the headrest. The heat coming off this creature was unbearable, the smell beyond belief.

"Almost there." "Y' said in a wet croak, and Gary knew if he turned around right now the thing in the back seat would drag him out of the car and into the desert. They might find his bones one day. Something for his wife to bury. Suddenly the app pinged. "You have reached your destination!"

Gary couldn't take it anymore. He screamed and slammed on the brakes. He took off his seat belt and opened his door in one quick movement and leapt from the car, rolling to his feet, the knife raised. The car rolled a few more feet then settled into one of the endless holes that marred the road. The open door chime blared out into the silence. He stumbled back toward the car, shaking violently.

"Hey! Hey get out of the car!"

Gary peeked into the car. The dome-light had come on when he opened the door, and it shone onto an empty back seat. Nothing moved inside the car.

He's crouched down, waiting for me to get close, Gary thought. He reached the door and grabbed the handle, knife at the ready. He let out an involuntary scream as he ripped it open, actually bringing the knife down before freezing. Nothing. He quickly checked the front, also vacant. He spun around around, trying to look everywhere at once, but seeing nothing past the ten feet of desert illuminated by the light of the car. Gary shoved the back door closed and dove into the car. He locked the doors and stomped his foot down on the gas, sending up plumes of dust as he fishtailed down the road. When he finally made it back to the highway he slid to a halt. His heart hammering in his chest, he looked back out into the desert where he had just come. Nothing. He sat for a moment, catching his breath, all four windows down in an attempt to rid the car of that licorice smell, though he thought it would be a long time before he got that reek out of the back seat. Suddenly the piggyback app let out an oink, causing Gary to let about another scream. He snatched up the phone and read the text, sweat pouring down his face.

"*Great ride! Y gave you five stars!*" He read this a few times, laughing hysterically. He dropped the phone into the passenger seat, put the car In gear and drove about ten feet before stopping again, flinging open the door and throwing up on the asphalt. *Who's the puker now?*, he thought as he wiped his mouth and continued his drive. He felt the urge to call home, but he didn't want to wake his wife, she had to be up in two hours, but damn he wanted to hear her voice right now, to have her talk with him as he drove.

5.

Ten minutes later and he had stopped sweating and his heart was beating at a near reasonable rate. Amazingly the smell in the back seat had dissipated, with only a hint of black licorice remaining. Gary could deal. He was suddenly glad he had a thirty minute drive home, it gave him time to compose himself. At some points he wasn't even sure that it had happened, but one look at the dried saliva on the passenger seat headrest told him all he needed to know. *I'll take the car for a full detail tomorrow, no way I'm stopping again before home.* And Piggyback was getting a very angry email. By the time he pulled into his driveway Gary was himself again. He had decided Cadence would never hear about what had happened tonight and in the morning he would tell her that he was cutting back on the late night runs. Strictly in town, no later than 12. He had had enough of driving Intestate 10 for awhile. Maybe forever. Gary actually had a smile on his face as he reached the front door, but the smile froze and a fresh wave of adrenaline slammed through him. he almost fell to his knees. The door was hanging open a few inches. there were large grooves dug into the wood, the doorknob was gone entirely.

Looks like claw marks, Jerry thought. Like some huge animal- and then he smelled it, just inside the door. it was faint, but unmistakable. The smell of black licorice

Gary burst through the door, frantic. The front room was a mess, table lamp was shattered, a chair over turned. more of those large grooves in the wall.

"Cadence! Cadence!" He sprinted upstairs, turning on the light in the master bedroom. The sheets were on the floor, strewn in a trail leading into the hall, as if she were holding them while someone drug her from the bed. there were a few drops of blood on the mattress. not more than someone would leave from a nosebleed, but enough to drive Gary half mad with terror. Then his eyes moved toward the room at the end of the hall.

"Ray." he walked slowly now, holding the wall as he stumbled toward the baby's room, vision doubling. The smell of licorice was a little stronger as he reached Ray's bedroom and flicked the light. It didn't come on, but he didn't need it. The light from the hallway lit the empty crib perfectly. Gary moved closer, tears streaming down his face. The crib wasn't completely empty after all. He reached in, hands shaking, and pulled out a weathered piece of paper.. There were four words scrawled across the page. Jerry read them and shrieked, falling to his knees. He continued to scream as the neighbors called the police, certain someone was being killed over there, screamed until his voice was nothing but a harsh bark. The police found him on the floor next to the crib, clutching the paper, incoherent. The officers were still puzzling over the message as Gary was taken away in an ambulance. the paper was placed in an evidence bag and set aside to be collected with any other possible clues as to what had happened here tonight. not that it was much help. An old piece of paper with just four words written on it:

Thanks for the ride

God complex

1.

Alma raced to work, willing her ancient hatchback to keep running just a little bit longer. She was already late, something she hated, and she was still a mile out from work. The worst of the traffic was behind her, now if she could just keep the car from stalling... On the radio (the only station that came through, her antenna had broken off last year) a rather loud gentlemen was complaining about deep space telescopes. "Folks anybody that listens to my podcast knows I'm not big on conspiracy theories but something is going on here. At this point we, the American tax payers, have spent over two billion dollars on three different deep space telescopes and as of six thirty this morning every one of them malfunctioned in the exact same way? I mean, these things are supposed to be able to see the beginning of the universe, and as of today none of them can see any further than 10 million light years, and that distance apparently shrinking. All I'm saying is that we need to have a congressional hearing on what that money was actually spent on, because it sure wasn't spent on the construction of these telescopes!" Alma clicked the radio off. She had enough stress right here, she didn't need to hear about how bad it was in the rest of the universe. She turned the corner and saw the sign for blue horizon rest home. She zipped into the parking lot, taking the nearest open spot. She half ran through the double doors, already taking her coat off. She was greeted by Miss Teresa, the head nurse. She let out a chuckle at Alma's entrance. "There you are, I thought we were going to have to send out a search party."

"I'm so sorry, between traffic and that car it's a miracle I ever get here."

"That's alright, we held down the fort. How was your day off?" Alma hung up her coat and let out a big sigh. "Much needed. What's on the docket for today?"

"A whole bunch of the usual. Mr. Fazio refused to eat yesterday he's on an IV. Mrs. Galveston is in restraints again."

"Who'd she hit this time?"

Miss Teresa laughed. "It was a twofer. She bonked her roommate with her bedpan and threw her pudding on Nurse Hanson's brand new scrubs."

Alma covered a laugh. "I miss all the action." she looked at the room at the end of the hall. "What about-?"

Teresa rolled her eyes, playfully. "Our lord and savior? Still with us, despite dire predictions to the contrary."

She gave Alma a smile, but it was a bit off. Alma wasn't surprised. The resident at the end of the hall had a way of setting you off balance. He was one of the nicest people she'd ever met, never an ill word, but there was something about him. It had been that way since his first day, which also happened to be Alma's first day on the job. A hectic first day, to say the least. He had breezed through the door like he was checking into the Four Seasons, all smiles and handshakes. He asked for everyone's attention and as the staff gathered he gave them two pieces of information: first, that he would need his room for exactly six years, five months, eleven days and sixteen hours, and at that precise time, he would die, a countdown that ended today at roughly four p.m. today. The second thing he told them was that he was God. No one knew his real name and he refused to give it, so the staff had just taken to calling him Smith.

Alma patted miss Teresa's hand and grabbed her clipboard. "I better get started, I'm already ten minutes late on getting breakfast orders."

"Mrs. Galveston isn't going to be happy with that. Keep an eye out for flying bedpans."

2.

Alma made her rounds and collected orders for the morning meals. As she made her way to the room at the end of the hall she felt a growing apprehension. Smith had reminded the staff several times through the years that today would be his last, and she had always blown it off. But the last couple of weeks it felt more real. *You're being foolish,* she thought to herself. When she was a kid it seemed like there was an 'end of the world' cult or prophecy in the news every couple of months. As ridiculous as they were, when it got to those final few hours, it always gave her butterflies and made her think, even just for a moment, *what if its true this time*? She stopped outside his door for a moment and shook off the heebie jeebies. She put on a smile and walked in like it was any other day.

"Hello, Mr. Smith."

Smith, a man who could best be described as dapper looking even while dressed in a pair of worn blue pajamas, set up straighter in his bed and smiled. He was between 60 and 70, it was hard to gauge and he wasn't forthcoming with the information. His hair and his beard were silver, both could have used a trim, but he preferred them, as he put it, a little on the wild side.

"Alma! A sight for sore eyes. How are you?"

"Top of the world. The question is, how are you doing today Smith?"

"Me? Oh, I'm fine, fine."

"That's good to hear. I know they ran some tests this morning. Heart rate, blood pressure all of that check out?"

"Ah, yes. All the machines and their beeps and boops said I'm a picture of health."

"That's very good to hear."

He looked at her with a gentle smile. "But it doesn't change the fact that I'm going to die this afternoon."

Alma looked at him, distressed. "You know I don't like you talking like that. It upsets the other residents."

"Well that's why I didn't say it in front of the other residents."

He gave her that sly smile that always reminded her of her grandpa, and she couldn't help but smile back.

"It upsets me too. You're one of the few people in here I consider a friend."

Smith looked touched. "Is that so?"

"Scouts honor. You're polite, never slapped me in the face for helping you to bed or thrown a Hummel figurine at me for no reason at all, or refer to me as "that little Dominican girl" even though I've told Mrs. Field a hundred times that my name is Alma and I'm from Puerto Rico, not the Dominican Republic."

Smith grunted. "Mrs. Field was raised by ignorant parents with racist ideals and instead of overcoming those ideals she embraced them. Her children, however, chose not to, and that's why they've never visited, and why she's never seen her grandchildren. What goes around comes around, Alma. That one's not in the bible, but it should be."

"I didn't think anybody knew anything about Mrs. field. She hardly says a word unless it's to bark an order."

"I know a little more than most, I suppose, but then again I am God. I'm supposed to know these things." He gave her a wink. She looked at him and got those anxious butterflies again. *What if its true this time?*

She forced a smile. "How could I forget. What would God like for breakfast this morning?"

"I think.. eggs and toast sounds right. Maybe a little bowl of those strawberries everybody's always going on about."

"Changing things up a little today I see."

"Well, last breakfast and all."

Alma looked at him, genuinely upset. He dropped the joke. "I'm sorry, Alma, no more death comments I promise."

Alma managed half a grin. "Keep that promise. I'll be back in a minute with your eggs."

3.

Four hours later and Alma was on her break. The lunch run was over and the afternoon meds had been passed out. A few of the nurses were at the main station watching the news. Alma was only half paying attention. Her thoughts were on Smith. He'd never had one visitor and there weren't any relatives listed in his file. She didn't actually believe he was going to die today, but he would eventually, and it looked like he would be doing so alone. That was the case for a lot of the people in here. But she had made the mistake of getting attached to him, either because or in spite of his crazy story, and the fact that he was one of the most genuinely nice people she'd ever met. Her apprehension grew with each passing hour.. She was ready for this day to be in the books and to have this silliness behind them. Something one of the nurses said brought her back into the real world.

"I don't know much about space, is this something we should be worried about? I mean it's on every channel and my phone is blowing up about it too."

An older nurse, Mavis, was watching the TV intently, she answered without looking away. "My oldest is an astronomer in New Mexico, I'll give him a call."

Alma turned to the television where two reporters were talking to someone from NASA. The scroll underneath them was saying that 60% of the observable universe had now apparently vanished. The man from NASA was trying to keep everyone calm but he had a panicked look in his eye as He tried to explain the situation. "It is of course the middle of the day here in North America so we can't really see anything from our ground telescopes, but we are in contact with several European agencies and they are confirming that there is a phenomenon happening at the moment where we are unable to see past a certain point in the cosmos."

One of the reporters asked, "So is it some sort of obstruction or is it what some experts are saying, that the stars and well, everything else, just isn't there anymore?"

The man from NASA shifted uncomfortably in his chair. Well Katie, the truth is we just don't have enough information to say right now."

Another reporter came on to talk about increased earthquake activity around the globe, but Alma's attention was focused down the hall. She didn't know why she would feel what was happening on the television had anything to do with Smith, but she couldn't shake it. She made her way to his room and gave a light knock.

"Come in."

Alma walked in. "Hi, Smith."

He nodded and, as if he was reading her mind, said, "Terrible what's happening on the news. Very sad. It was always one of my favorite things to do as a child, lay in the grass late at night and watch the stars. I'll miss the stars."

"You could hear the news from the nurses station?" Smith didn't have a television in his room, specifically asked for it to be removed, nor did he have a phone.

He tapped one of his ears. "I've always had excellent hearing. Are you alright Alma? You look a little pale. Have a seat, please."

She sat in one of the plastic seats next to his bed. She looked out the window at the sky. She wondered how it would look like tonight, just a sheet of black. She suddenly asked Smith a question she didn't know she was going to ask.

"How old are you?"

Smith gave her an amused look. "I don't think you'd appreciate my answer."

"Why, would you tell me your fourteen billion years old? Because I Googled it and that's how old the universe is. And if you're God, you have to be at least that old."

"Fourteen billion, or sixty eight, in November."

Alma said Jokingly, "Or no number at all because time is a myth."

Smith's smile falteredd slightly. He shook his head. "No, time is not a myth. It's a tyrant. Cruel and unforgiving. It can take so much you can lose the point of any of it. May I tell you a story?"

Alma said, "Please do."

"In the early 60's I became fixated on this man, Joseph Collins. He was a teacher, beloved by students and faculty alike. He was relentless when it came to the students in his charge. He stayed after school almost every night tutoring, he spent his weekends coaching one sport or the other. He single handedly helped over a hundred children graduate that never would have otherwise. Then one night, a week before his twentieth anniversary teaching at the school, he went to sleep and never woke up. Massive heart attack, age 46. Everyone was heartbroken. The town threw a huge memorial for him. The children were so distraught they closed the school for three days. That spring they commissioned a portrait of the man. They hung it on the wall, just inside the front doors, so it was the first thing you saw when you entered. He was the heart of that school, Alma, and he was sorely missed. But then, time. Months passed into years passed into decades and before you know it was the year 2000, a number that still sounds like it's from the future. Everyone that knew that teacher and all the good he'd done had either moved away or died themselves. Then one summer day during a school wide renovation, a construction worker who had no idea who Joseph Collins was or cared to know, took that dusty old portrait off the wall and unceremoniously tossed in the dumpster. Entire lives reduced to a picture on a wall that nobody recognizes."

Alma shook her head. "No, people remember, even if they don't realize it. That teacher helped kids that would have slipped through the cracks. They made it out, maybe they went to college, maybe they did the same thing for other children. And if so I'm sure they told the story of the person that helped them. That teacher was way more than just a picture on a wall. There are people today that might not even exist if it wasn't for him."

The frown on Smith's face erupted into a smile. He patted Alma's hand. "That is it exactly. It took me.. considerably longer to reach that conclusion. You are good with people, Alma. You're good *to* them. You care. And you understand. You remind me a lot of that teacher. I wish more people had been like you."

Alma was a little confused by his phrasing. *Had* been, like there weren't going to be any more. She brushed it off. "There are plenty of people like me, Smith."

He grunted. "Not as many as there should be." Alma took a peek down the hall at the nurses station. Everyone was still preoccupied with the news on the television. She scooted her chair a little closer to Smith and lowered her voice. "Smith, let's say.. let's say for a minute that I believe that you're God. An omnipotent being that knows everything I've ever done."

Smith chuckled. "People describing God always envision an all seeing Grandpa that monitors their every thought and deed. That's Santa Claus. And omnipotent.. clearly not, I'm dying, aren't I? And honestly I've forgotten much more than I remember. But I accept that. I've been around a long damn time and, seriously, it's a lot to take in. Think about one life. Not even the entire lifetime, just the years between eleven and twenty one. How many memories can you tell me about from those years? A couple dozen? Maybe a few more? And those are formative years, when we come of age, have so many new experiences, but how many can you definitively remember? Your sweet sixteen, Your twenty-first, though for some that one is enveloped in a haze of alcohol. But what did you do the day before your twenty first birthday? or the week after? Thousands of days in a lifetime and let's face it, most of them just aren't that memorable. And that's one life. Now think of all the billions of people that have existed, living decades of mostly forgettable days. And if you cant remember, then why the hell do I have to?"

Alma laughed at that. "I guess I never looked at it like that."

Smith smiled. "But there are amazing moments that make all the boring ones worth the wait. And some horrors you wish you'd never experienced. They're out there, dancing all around me and if I concentrate, I can see them."

Alma straightened in her chair. "Smith, are you telling me you can read minds?"

"In a sense."

"As a rule, when someone tells me they can read minds, I usually ask to see a little evidence."

Smith gave her a look. "Fair enough. How's this..Holly, the night shift nurse? She has always dreamt of being a famous singer. And the kicker is, she could have been. She has one of the best voices I've ever heard. She goes to karaoke at least once a week. But for some reason she's embarrassed by this, and drives almost an hour away so she won't run into anyone she knows, and does her singing in a dingy little bar in Oakland. It's a real shame."

Alma nodded enthusiastically. "She's great! I heard her in the second floor bathroom one night when she thought everyone was downstairs. I was amazed. I asked her about it later on that night and she acted like she didn't know what I was talking about."

Smith nodded and repeated, "A shame. I know that Greta is the mystery person that refills all the candy in the break room. She takes great enjoyment in watching everyone try and deduce the culprit. I know that since the age of 14 your dream car has been a hot pink convertible, but you've never told a soul about this, not even your best friend Carla."

Alma's jaw dropped, "How.. wait a minute, Smith how did you-"

"And I know that cheerful Miss Teresa, who has a smile for everyone that she meets, hates every resident in this building, because they are a constant reminder of her mother, who passed in a place very much like this, confused and full of pain, riddled with cancer and Alzheimer's. She seems such a happy person, but to the ones here that are too far gone to communicate, she is anything but. Those unfortunate souls get their hair yanked or a hard pinch on the underside of their arm from Miss Teresa when she tucks them in at night." Alma was reeling. She didn't know how she expected Smith would respond when she asked for proof, but it wasn't this. She called his bluff and he dropped a full house. And she believed it. Every word. And not just because of what he knew about her. It was the way he said it, the look in his eye, there was no doubting it. She opened her mouth to speak and Smith closed his eyes, holding up his hand. "And I know your next question is if I am who I say I am, why in the world wouldn't I stop her from doing such cruel things? The simple answer is I can't. That's not how this works. Maybe God has always been the wrong moniker. I'm more of a designer, an engineer. How can I.. ah. Let's say I carve a wooden top, and I set that top on a table, give it a hell of a spin and leave the room. What happens to that top then is out of my hands. Will some child stroll by and snatch it up? Will it careen off the table? Will It spin, untouched, infinitely? Or will it just stop."

Alma sat back in her chair. "If that's true it's the saddest thing I've ever heard. Because it means we're just alone out here."

"No, Alma, not sad, wonderful. You've never needed guidance from any otherworldly being to tell you right from wrong, some phantom hand to morally guide you. You've made the right choices your entire life, on your own, without hesitation. People like you and that teacher are the lights in this world."

Suddenly the room begin to shake. A ceramic pot on Smith's nightstand fell to the floor, shattering. Smith sat up with a grunt. " Earth quake, luckily a small one. I'll take care of this mess, you better go. It's going to be a busy few hours."

4.

Alma made her way to the nurses station, still reeling from what Smith had told her. All this time it had been true. She could see the power in him now, even though it was fading. She reached the nurses station and shook it off. There was work to do. A couple of the younger nurses were at the desk, clutching each other, wide eyed and near tears. One of them yelped, "What's happening?"

Miss Teresa tried to calm them. "Its an earthquake, and a small one at that. It should be over soon just try and stay calm."

She was right, a few seconds later the shaking stopped. Miss Teresa gave Alma a wink. Alma turned away from her and studied her clipboard. She was never going to be able to look at Teresa again. She was going to have to file a report. Maybe she should confront her, make her admit what she's done. It would be simpler. One more thing to add to this increasingly shitty day. She gathered everyone to her. "Okay ladies,

I'm going to need everyone to start checking the residents rooms, make sure everyone is alright. Make sure there's no glass on the floor and if there is, get it cleaned up quick as possible, we don't want to spend the evening stitching up feet." As everyone moved to complete their assignments, Alma realized that someone was missing. "Has anyone seen Mavis?"

5.

Alma found Mavis sitting on the back stoop smoking a cigarette. It was the last place she looked because Mavis had stopped smoking 2 years ago.

"Mavis? We could use some help in here."

Mavis took another deep drag off her cigarette. "I don't think I will, dear. I'm taking a personal day."

"Why? What happened?"

"I got a hold of my son in New Mexico. This thing on the news.. it's serious. As serious as it gets, really. Everyone will know soon enough."

"Mavis, what did he say?"

"He was so scared, I've never heard him that scared, not even when we thought his daddy was going to die. He told me a bunch of mumbo jumbo I didn't understand but I got the last part loud and clear. The universe is collapsing. He says we only got a few hours at most. I called my youngest, they're on the way to pick me up. We're gonna go to the beach. Look at the ocean for a bit. I can't think of a better way to go, can you?"

Alma closed her eyes. "A few hours?" She checked her watch. "That can't be." She went back inside where everyone had gathered back at the nurse station, hugging each other and crying. The cat was out of the bag. Alma walked to the desk and said, "Ladies, you shouldn't be here. Go home. Be with your families. I can manage things here."

Miss Teresa wiped her eyes. "Are you sure?" Alma nodded. "Go on. I've got it."

They all hugged, exchanging tearful goodbyes. Five minutes later Alma was alone at the station. The news report suddenly cut off and the television went to static. She clicked it off and picked up her clipboard. It was time to make her rounds. She brought the residents their meds, comforting those that were frightened. She let them know that there wouldn't be a full dinner service tonight, as she was alone, but she wheeled the snack cart room to room. Snacks were usually two dollars a piece, but everything was free today. When she had taken care of everyone else she made her way to the room at the end of the hall. There were near constant tremors now as she opened Smith's door. She was shocked by his appearance. He looked like he had aged twenty years in the last ninety minutes. His face was gaunt and his hair clung to his skull in patchy wisps. He was laying down, the blanket pulled up to his chest. "I was hoping you'd stop by."

"Everything you've told me is true. What's happening out there-" she tilted her head toward the window. "It's connected to you, isn't it? When you die, everything dies with you."

"Yes. I'm sorry Alma. I truly am. I would have warned people, I wanted to warn them, but no one would have believed me if I had."

"No, I suppose not."

Smith lifted his hand toward her with great effort. She took it and sat by his side. He looked up at her with his now sunken eyes.

"Do you remember our first day here?"

"How could I forget? Mrs. Mullen tripped while she was moving her tea set and fell head first into it. One of the broken pieces of the tea set nicked her artery. One in a million freak accident."

Smith nodded. "If you hadn't been there she would have died. The other girl on shift with you panicked. She'd never seen so much blood. She ran out and left you there, alone."

"She quit the following day. I remember feeling like running out myself, but I needed to staunch the bleeding, I couldn't take my hand off her neck and I thought to myself I just need something, anything to put on this wound. Then there was a shadow in the doorway. I turned to see who it was and there you were, your suitcase in one hand and a stack of bandages in the other. My savior."

Smith chuckled. "So to speak."

"I've known since that first day, but it's like I chose not to remember somehow. But the way you showed up there, with no money or identification, no relative to sign you in or doctor to refer you, yet the administrators opened the doors and gave you a room. It's impossible."

Smith smiled. "Quite. But they accepted me because I needed them to. I was so tired. And my time was near."

Suddenly the light began to dim. She looked out the window and watched as the sun became darker and darker until it flickered out like a candle at the end of its wick. It was black as pitch outside for a moment, then the street lights begin to come on.

"Listen to me Alma, because time is short. I talked to you before about memories. I need to talk to you about something unpleasant. your two strongest memories."

Alma shook her head. "Please don't."

"I'm sorry, child, I have to. Two memories. Your mother dying of cancer, and your father drinking himself to death not long after. I know how hard it was for you, how scared you were all the time. Your mom was a fighter. She held on as long as she could before she had to let go. You were just fifteen. And your father.. he lost the love of his life and he had no idea how to process that. He had always been a drinker but after her death it was constant. It was the only way he could get to sleep at night. You tried so hard to get him help, how you pleaded. And he did try, Alma. Several times, he went to meetings, even stayed sober for a few weeks at a time, but.. your mother was his strength."

Alma sank into the chair next to the bed, sobbing. "Why couldn't I have been his strength? Why couldn't he let me help him?"

"He thought your life would be better without him. You have to forgive him, he wasn't thinking straight. Three years without your mother was all he could bear. He lost his battle with the drink and you moved in with your grandpa, a wonderful man, who I'm very flattered to remind you of. He was a great man in his own right. He didn't have much but he did everything he could for you, and you never disappointed him.

You worked hard, studied harder. You're 21st birthday came and went and you didn't even realize it, you were so busy working on your nursing degree. And then you came here to help those that couldn't help themselves. Your whole life has been caring for others. You're one the kindest, most selfless people that I've ever seen. You need to know that me ending up here wasn't just to find a place to die. It was an interview. I am the dreamer of the dream, but I don't have to be the only one. If you want the job." She nodded, tears streaming down her face. She took his hand. Outside the window the sky was filled with streaks of lightning. Mile wide chunks of the earth began lifting into the air. The tremors increased as the building cracked in half. A brutally cold wind blasted into the room. Alma closed her eyes as the world went black.

6.

Tuesday afternoon. Blue Horizons nursing home was bathed in orange light as the sun began its dive below the horizon. Inside the nurses were at the main desk, laughing and chatting as the day shift said their goodbyes and the night shift said their hellos. Residents were talking and enjoying the day. Everything looked brighter, more vibrant. In the room at the end of the hall Alma was looking out the window the sky ablaze with color. She looked out at that beauty, crying but with a smile on her face. She sat next to Smith, brushing the hair off his forehead.

She wiped the tears off her face and covered his with his blanket. She held his hand for a moment, then walked down to the nurses station and let the night shift leader know that Smith had passed. The woman looked shocked. "I can't believe it. He told us for years, but..I just can't believe it!" "Call the hospital. They'll send a bus for him. Make sure he's taken care of. I'm going to head home. Its been a long day." She gathered her things and started toward the front doors, where Miss Teresa was talking with one of the resident's children. As she finished up she turned to talk to Alma. Before she could speak Alma touched her arm. Miss Teresa stood completely still, a blank look on her face. Alma got closer and spoke quietly to her. "You need To go to the administrators office. Tell them that you need to put in for early retirement. You have several personal issues that you have to work through and you can't do that if you're still working. You're also going to go to therapy, tell them about your mother and what's been going on here. You need help, Teresa." Teresa nodded, her eyes filling with tears. "Yes, I do. I should head to the administrator's office." Alma continued outside. She just experienced the longest day of her life, but now.. everything was going to be different. She walked to the parking spot where she had left the hatchback and stopped short, her eyes wide. Her car was gone. In its place was a pristine pink convertible. She laughed as she opened the door and sat down. There was a note on the dash. She picked it up and read it. *A parting gift I knew you'd never get for yourself. Enjoy.* Alma folded the paper and held it to her chest. She put the car in gear and zoomed out of the parking lot.

Tales from a tavern on a stormy night

1.

Steven was freezing as he made his way along the dirt road. The rain was coming down in torrents. He shielded his eyes as best he could, but he could only see a few feet in front of him. He had left his flashlight and the rest of his supplies with Katie. They had been out for a day of hiking in the Scottish countryside when she had twisted her ankle on some loose rocks, turning a two hour excursion into a nightmare. Neither of their phones were getting reception and to add insult to injury, not long after the accident the rains began. After what felt like hours, they stumbled upon a cave. Steven helped her inside. He had made her as comfortable as possible, elevating her leg and wrapping her in a space blanket. He took her hand and told her he going for help. Katie was less than enthusiastic "No. Absolutely not." Steven brushed the wet hair from her face. "Babe, I have to. The phones are useless, and your ankle.." Even through her sock he could see how swollen and misshapen it was. She couldn't move at all without extreme pain. "I have to get help. There was a little town on the map, couldn't be more than a mile from here. I'll get a doctor." "Steven, its pitch black and pouring out there. What if you get hurt as well? We've done this a long time. The first rule in situations like this is to stay put." "Usually I'd agree, but we're on our own, babe. Nobody even knows we're out here. Listen, you let me go, two hours from now you'll be in a little Inn, warm and cozy, foot bandaged and full of pain meds. And I'll be feeding you tomato soup." soup." Katie laughed. "I hate tomato soup. But the rest of that sounds amazing. Are you sure?" "I'm sure. I'll be back before you know it." But now he had been walking in this valley for over an hour, and there was no town in sight. He began to doubt this plan. *Could I have missed it, just walked right past it in this rain? I thought if I stuck to the road, I'd be OK.* The wind was steadily pushing against him, causing him to drift off the side of the road. He slid into the ditch, banging his shoulder. He crawled back onto the road and got to his feet with a grunt. He looked out across the darkness, feeling hopeless. *Maybe she was right, I should go back, stay with her until morning, then try agai-* His heart skipped a beat. Off the road about a hundred feet he could see a brief flicker of light. It took everything in him to not start sprinting. He compromised with himself and headed for the light at a fast walk. As it got closer he discovered it was a single building, a tavern. The name on the sign was too whether beaten to read. He opened the door, the wind almost snatching it out of his hand. When he finally managed to get it closed, he turned he saw eight solemn looking men standing at a U-shaped bar, looking as if they'd been expecting him. To the left of the bar was an overstuffed chair facing a roaring fire. The walls were bare except for a single painting of a lighthouse hanging above the bar. The bartender gave him a nod. "What will it be gent?" Steven kicked the mud off his boots and wiped his soaked coat sleeve across his face. "Sorry I don't want a drink, my girlfriend, fiance, she sprained her ankle. She's in a cave not too far from here-" One of the men spoke up. "Miriam's cave, about a mile west? Big rock outside it looks sorta like a cat?" "Yes, that's the one." The bartender pointed to two larger patrons. "You're two strapping lads, head down to the cave and see if you can retrieve the poor girl." The two men nodded and were out the door immediately. Steven started to follow them and the bartender put a gentle hand on his arm. "Young sir, you should probably stay here. Those boys know this valley like the back of their hand, and your soaked to the bone and favoring that shoulder. Steven slumped a little. He couldn't argue, it had been quite a day. Steven watched out the window as the two men headed across the field. He asked over his shoulder, "Is there a hospital close by or does anyone have a car, so when they get back I can get her some medical attention. I'll pay you." The bartender shook his head. "No hospital for thirty miles, son. These gentlemen came in on the bus a couple hours ago, and the there won't be another until tomorrow. And I live here, in the back." "But the map said this is a town. Kirk Kellan." A couple of the men chuckled. The bartender gave them a look. "Aye, was a town, long time ago. All's left now is this tavern, which has stood here some three and a half centuries." One of the younger men spoke up. "Aye, about as long as Edgar's been coming here." The patrons had a good laugh. Edgar, an ancient looking man at the end of the bar, shook his walking stick. "You keep running your gums, your skull is going to meet the tip of my cane." The men laughed again, the sound drilling into Steven's ears. He was in no mood for good cheer at the moment. He looked back out the window and filled with panic. "No, what the fuck is this?" The two men were running back to the tavern. They burst through the door and got it latched. The one closest to him said, "Sorry, sir, the roads washed out about a quarter of a mile up. Ain't no passing it." Steven's heart sunk. *No..no, I thought if I could at least get her here..dammit.* He took his phone out of its waterproof pouch, pacing back and forth. He tried it again. Then again. No signal. *God damn it, why didn't I tell anyone we were going out for a hike.* He had never felt so angry and helpless. He turned to the men at the bar. "Thank you for your help. I'm going to head back, stay with Katie until this passes. Thank you all again." He was reaching for the door when he felt a hand on his shoulder. He flinched. It was the bartender. "Going back out there.. it's a very bad idea, mate. I'm sorry about your lady friend, but nothing can be done tonight. Storms picking up. It's only going to get worse out there. You venture out now, with the road gone, you'll end up just like your girl, only without a cave to shelter you. Why don't you sit by the fire, try to get warm. You can keep trying your phone while you wait." Unable to think of any alternative, he gave in. "OK, I guess I will for a minute." "That's a good lad, and how about a drink?" Steven shook his head. "No thank you." Edgar piped up. "Everybody drinks tonight boy, that's one of the rules." The bartender shot back, "That's enough Edgar, leave the boy alone, he's had a rough one." Steven reluctantly had a seat as the bartender shuttered the window and rejoined his customers. The chair was one of the most comfortable things he had ever sat in. He felt the guilt stabbing again, thinking about Katie laying on the floor of a cave, but as he watched the fire, a wave of calmness overtook him. He felt like he was being hypnotized. If he had had anything to eat or drink he would have sworn he'd been dosed. The fire danced and crackled. He looked down and was surprised to see that his clothes had already dried. *That can't be, I've only been sitting here for a moment.* The bartender reappeared. "How are you doing, lad?" "I'm pretty great actually," Steven said, a grin on his face. The bartender matched his grin. "Good to hear. A fire on a cold night always improves *my* mood." The bartender started to leave when Steven stopped him. "You know, I think I will take you up on that drink." The bartender nodded. "Fine sir, fine. But there is something you should know. No amount of coin will buy your ale tonight." Steven Looked confused. The bartender smiled. "Come over to the bar." He turned to the rest of the customers as he led Steven over. "Gentleman, I was just about to explain to our young friend why we're here this evening." One of the younger men laughed. "You picked a hell of a night to drop in." A mutter of agreement rippled through the bar. Steven was slightly nervous by the looks on their faces. He said, "So, you all arrived on the bus with no way back. Are you all just going to sleep here overnight?" Edgar grunted. "Stay the night, yes. Sleep? No. What we're doing here is part of a long tradition, boy. Every year on this night, eight of us gather. We drink our drinks, and we tell our stories." Another patron spoke up. "Monster stories to be more specific." Edgar smiled. "Aye. Things that go bump in the night." Steven's face lit up at this. "That's amazing! I do something similar whenever me and my brothers get together. We spend half the night trying to one up each other. I have a pretty good collection." Edgar feigned surprise. "Is that so? My, that is quite the coincidence." The bartender shot Edgar a warning look that he ignored. Steven raised his hand. "Would it be okay if I joined in?" Edgar smiled, revealing his few remaining teeth. "What a grand idea! I think I can speak for the boys when I say, welcome to the club. And I hope your stories are as good as you say they are." A few men laughed. The bartender did not. He tapped a mug against the bar, gathering everyone's attention. "Alright, gentlemen, enough jabbering, it's time we get down to business." Edgar said, "I agree. And I think our guest of honor should go first. God knows I've heard every tale you dolts have had to tell a thousand times." More laughter, but this time Steven welcomed it. Edgar continued. "A little new blood is just what we need, what do you think?" Everyone let out a rousing cheer. Steven smiled and said, "I'm okay with going first." The bartender poured Steven a particularly nasty looking stout and slid it to him. "Your drink Sir." Steven grabbed the mug and took a swig. The bartender nodded. "And now your payment." Steven looked in the bartender's eyes and for a moment was frightened by what he saw. "There's one a friend at work told me, more sci-fi but still pretty scary, about this A.I. program that..sorry, getting ahead of myself." he cleared his throat, looking at the eyes all around him. Curious. Waiting. He stood up and told his first tale.

2.

The winds were near constant now, and the tavern rumbled as if it were going launch into the sky at any moment. At the bar a man named Darren was just finishing a particularly good story of a family hunting a werewolf that had been plaguing them for months, only to discover it was their own supposedly invalid grandmother. The men lightly tapped the bottom of their glasses on the bar, their version of applause. As the next man stood and began his tale, Steven glanced at his watch and was shocked to find that it was after two in the morning. It felt like he had just arrived but hours had passed. His thoughts went to Katie and it filled him with guilt. *What the hell is wrong with me? I've been standing here, getting drunk and having the time of my life while she's laying out there in pain. I haven't given her a second thought. I abandoned her. What-* Just then something roared outside, so loud it could be easily heard over the wind and rain. Steven stopped still, his eyes wide. At the bar the man telling the latest tale paused only for a moment, then quickly continued, a slight tremmor in his voice. Steven placed his ear to the door. He heard another roar, off in the distance but no less terrifying, perhaps in response to the first. He moved away from the door, heart pounding. Suddenly there was a huge thud against the far wall. Steven jumped back, turning to the group. "What the hell was that?" One of the men responded without taking his eyes off the Storyteller. "Hush boy, it's not your turn." Another thud. This one shook the entire tavern. The men continued to listen to the storyteller. Steven braced for another hit. If it was any harder than the last, whatever it was would be sitting in here with them. But there were no more thuds. Now something different. A sound like a giant snake brushing against the side of a tree. The sliding sound moved across the outside of the tavern, toward the window. Steven slowly made his way over. He didn't want to look out there, wanted to be anywhere else in the world, but he had to see. He unlatched the shutter and pulled it open, and got a glimpse of something that he would see in his nightmares until his death. It was a tentacle, at least three feet thick, rippling with muscles just underneath its pale flesh. It writhed against the tavern wall, as if looking for a space big enough to enter. As Steven watched it twisted around to reveal its underside. It was covered in hundreds, thousands of yellow, blind eyes. Smaller tentacles burst out of clusters of eyes, covered themselves in unblinking, dead eyes. They mashed against the glass, sounding like a soapy rag sloshing around in a sink. It shifted away from the window, revealing the valley outside. As lightning struck, Steven saw the field was swarming with creatures covered in those tentacles, some of them so tall they disappeared into the clouds. Steven was seconds from screaming when a hand covered his mouth. It was the bartender. He shuttered the window and drug Steven over to the fire. At the bar the men tapped their mugs on the bar as a new story began. The bartender set Steven in the chair and knelt beside him. He handed him a drink, not ale this time, but a clear liquid in a large shot glass. Steven downed it without a word. He started to feel a little more like himself. He gestured toward the window. "My God, did you see that out there? Did you see them?" "Aye. I've seen them many times. Never gets any easier." "What the fuck are they-." "Keep your voice down, unless you want them inside." Steven whispered, "What are those things?" The bartender sighed. "We don't know. I doubt there is anyone alive on this earth that does. What I do know is the valley is swarming with them. And that's why we're here." "Why you're here? What are you going to do?" The bartender looked around. "We're doing it, lad. Have been all night." "What, telling stories? Are you kidding me?" "It is what we are meant to do. We come here, we tell our tales of monsters, to keep the real monsters at bay. every year on this day, as our fathers did and their fathers and their fathers back two thousand years, when the Druids stood on this very spot, speaking their dead language in a circle of stones, casting their runes by the light of the fire. Tradition born from the rituals." He gestured outside. "Nothing could stop those things from coming through from whatever hell they exist in, but we *can* prevent them from staying. From spreading into the rest of the world. If we keep our wits about us and our mind on the task. One of those things heard your thoughts. About your girl, I imagine. It focused In on you. You have to block everything out but what's happening in this room. Can you do that?" Steven nodded. "Yeah, I can do that." "Alright then, lets continue." Steven returned to the bar and sat down, willing himself to concentrate on the current speaker. After a few minutes he'd forgotten about the things lurking outside. He sipped his ale in the warmth of the fire and just listened. Everything else felt a thousand miles away. Or a thousand years. When Edgar asked for the next volunteer, Steven stood. "I have another I'd like to share." The men tapped their mugs on the bar. Edgar nodded. Steven cleared his throat.

The first one is actually a screenplay a writer friend told me about. We open in the maine woods on a sunny day..."

3.

Morning. The storm had passed and the sun shone down on the valley through a cloudless sky. The men sat at the bar, throats dry even after drinking their weight in ale. They had talked the sun up, and now a fatigue had settled over them. The bartender was sluggish as he cleaned a sea of mugs. The only one in the tavern moving with a sense of purpose was Steven. He was quickly zipping his coat, putting on his backpack and readying himself for the hike, steadily looking out the window in the direction of the cave. He was amazed to find that even though he'd been drinking the entire night, he didn't have so much as a buzz. None of the men seemed to. He shrugged it off. Stranger things than that occurred last night. He stopped at the door facing the men. "Gentleman, Thank you for everything, but I have to get back to Katie." They all nodded, giving their goodbyes. The bartender gave him a wave. "It was nice to meet you, son." "Same here, maybe we'll make our way back here sometime, you can meet Katie." "That sounds like a grand idea," the bartender said, knowing he would never see Steven again. He gave a final wave and left out of the tavern at a jog. Several of the men walked over to the window to watch his progress. Edgar clumped over on his cane, a smile on his face. "Another long night over." The bartender set down the mug he had been cleaning and said, "Someone call the authorities, tell them to meet the boy at Miriam's cave. One of the men nodded and pulled out a phone. Edgar watched as Steven disappeared over the ridge. "I wonder what they'll find this time around. Just her knapsack? Maybe some ripped clothes, a bit of blood. Who knows, maybe there will be a piece of her left he can take home and bury." The bartender turned on him, enraged. "You ghoul. He was a good lad and I'm sure she was as well, now her life is gone and his is changed forever. And you stand there, grinning like some jack-o-lantern." Edgar continued looking out the door, unfazed. "It's happened thousands of times, and God willing it will happen a thousand more. Yes, she's gone, but the rest of the world isn't. That's the tradition. The *ritual*. We tell our stories. They take their sacrifice and leave us alone for another year." "Yes, but you don't have to take such a joy in it." Edgar looked out on the valley. "Not joy, son. Maybe I've been doing this too long. We should have a talk about that, but not this morning. I'm off, Gents, the bus will be here soon and my bed is a calling." Edgar made his way toward the road, a few of the men following behind. He stopped for a moment and tipped his hat at the bartender. "I'll be back for a drink or two next week. God willing." The last man out of the bar laughed at that. "God willing. He'll be here sure as I'm standing. That old codger will outlive us all." He hopped down the stairs and followed the rest of the men towards the bus depot. The bartender watched them trudge toward the road. *He'll outlive us all.* The bartender thought about the thousands Edgar had outlived thus far. *I'm sure he will, lad. I'm sure he will.*

One more for the road: my true monster story

In the winter of 93 me and my girlfriend at the time had just gotten off work and were driving home. It was around 3:00 a.m., and at that hour, in the middle of January, we were driving through a ghost town. As we were coming up on a stoplight, we saw a figure standing by the side of the road, on my side of the car. they were on the smaller side, a little over 4 feet maybe, and they were wearing a thin, hooded dark gray raincoat, though it wasn't raining. I thought to myself it looked too thin for as cold as it was. As I slowed down for the light I passed the figure. I only caught a glimpse but I t was enough. There were street lights lining the road all the way to the stoplight, but it was black under the figures hood. Except for the teeth. They were at least two inches long, gray and razor sharp. There were so many it didn't seem possible. It was in the process of opening its mouth as I passed. I turned to my girlfriend to ask her if she had seen the same thing I did, but the look at her face was all I needed to confirm that she had. Seconds later we stopped at the light and both of us spun around to get another look at whatever it was we saw, but the figure was already gone. there was nothing on that stretch of road to hide behind, yet in the space of 5 Seconds whatever it was had vanished. I decided to hell with the stoplight and gunned it. We sped the rest of the way home, doors locked, constantly checking the rear view mirror. That was 30 years ago this year, but I'll never forget it.

www.ingramcontent.com/pod-product-compliance
Lightning Source LLC
LaVergne TN
LVHW011948060526
838201LV00061B/4249